"I WAS MESMERIZED . . . REFRESHINGLY UNIQUE . . . NO DOUBT ABOUT IT, JOVE HAS A NEW STAR ON ITS HANDS!"
—**Katherine Sutcliffe**, bestselling author of *Once A Hero*

"EXQUISITELY POLISHED . . . I LAPPED IT UP AND WISHED FOR MORE!"
—**LaVyrle Spencer**, bestselling author of *Family Blessings*

"A WONDERFUL, ROMANTIC TALE full of complex, intriguing characters. Judy Cuevas is a terrific writer who has a great gift for creating a sense of time and place. I savored [this] rich and many-layered story. . . . *Black Silk* is delightful, unpredictable, and very special."
—**Amanda Quick**, bestselling author of *Mistress*

"**★★★★** . . . ALL THE SUBTLE NUANCES OF *DANGEROUS LIAISONS*. . . . Ms. Cuevas [writes] with a fine hand and a keen wit. . . . This is a book for very special readers on a quest for the out-of-the-ordinary diversion."
—*Romantic Times*

"THE BOOK IS RICH in description, abounds with interesting characters, and possesses an intriguing plot. Cuevas has written an ambitious first novel where love triumphs over all."
—*Ft. Lauderdale Sun Sentinel*

Titles by Judy Cuevas

BLACK SILK
BLISS

Bliss

Judy Cuevas

JOVE BOOKS, NEW YORK

BLISS

A Jove Book / published by arrangement with
the author

PRINTING HISTORY
Jove edition / April 1995

ISBN: 0-515-11587-8

A JOVE BOOK®
Jove Books are published by The Berkley Publishing Group,
200 Madison Avenue, New York, New York 10016.
JOVE and the "J" design are trademarks
belonging to Jove Publications, Inc.

PRINTED IN THE UNITED STATES OF AMERICA

10 9 8 7 6 5 4 3 2 1

No themes are so human as those that reflect for us, out of the confusion of life, the close connexion of bliss and bale. . . .

—HENRY JAMES,
"Preface" to *What Maisie Knew*, 1897

Contents

Prologue

I would do just about anything if it would get me to Paris.
—from the diary of Miss Sue-Hannah Van Evan,
    March 18, 1903

MRS. BESOM HAD expected Miss Seven-Minutes-of-Heaven to match the magnitude of her notoriety. Or at least to look as salacious as her mean nickname implied. Instead, Miss Sue-Hannah Van Evan was tiny and demure.

"No references?" Mrs. Besom asked. Of course, Miss Van Evan would have none, but she wanted the girl to understand that notice was being taken of the fact.

"No, ma'am."

"Have you never worked before?"

"Only here and there. Errands."

Mrs. Besom knew this vagueness for what it was—a lie by omission. She sat back, tapping her pen on the edge of the writing table while she eyed the girl. Miss Van Evan's hands seemed to fidget for a moment in her lap.

The room, the front sitting room of Amelia Besom's suite at the Royal Palm Hotel, was splotchy with shadows and splashes of sun. Late-afternoon sunlight dappled the edges of heavy draperies to spill over a dark mahogany writing table, a lowboy, and onto velvet-cut carpeting. A few moments ago Mrs. Besom had pulled the chain on the

1

electric lamp at her elbow, though not so much for the small glow it now provided as for lighting up the colors of its hand-painted, silk-fringed shade; it was a work of art. The lamp, the room, the Royal Palm Hotel of Miami were all accoutrements of a smart and expensive holiday, the sort favored by New York high society—and especially favored by Amelia Besom, whose life's creed could have been summed up as "Live as smartly and richly as possible."

Miss Van Evan sat in a chair directly in front of the writing table, the sunlight brightly spotlighting her skirts, skirts the deep saturated purple of sloe plums. This color was the predominant note in the girl's presence: folds of dark, dark purple in a halo of sunlight. Sun shone at her feet up along her skirts to her knees, to become by her lap a waving pattern of palm fronds—there was a tall palm tree just outside the window to Mrs. Besom's back. Thanks to this and a deeply brimmed hat, any more personal impression of the girl was lost to a conspiracy of shadows and indirect light.

Amelia Besom contradicted the girl. "My dear young woman, I understand that you *have* worked at a steady job before and that you were let go because of inappropriate conduct." When the girl did not explain or expound upon this, Mrs. Besom leaned forward, pointing her pen at the young woman. "There is hardly a soul in Miami, even a visitor such as myself, who doesn't know the gist of your sad little story, Miss Van Evan. You were a live-in, a kind of servant to a family who winters here in Miami—and who recently dismissed you without notice, recompense, or letters of reference. Is this true?"

"Yes, ma'am."

"Then I am giving you this opportunity to elucidate the particulars of your dismissal."

The girl merely sat there straight-backed until her silence, as it stretched out, began to feel ambiguous: resigned one moment, a woman waiting for the ax to fall; intransigent the next, a child caught by the scruff of the neck yet still stubbornly unwilling to give details, name names.

The older woman prompted, "Well, do you intend to explain this matter or not?"

"No, ma'am, I don't."

Mrs. Besom was taken aback.

The girl tempered some of her bluntness by adding, "It wasn't for anything dishonest, if that's what you're thinking. Or for anything that had to do with my job there actually." The girl took a breath then let it out with a rush of words. "I can do sums and balance ledgers. I'm a good typist, and I can take shorthand, the Pitman system, which is more difficult to learn but more accurate than the Lewis. And, as you can see"—she indicated two papers she had brought—"I graduated first in my class." A diploma and a certificate of award assigned Miss Van Evan the dubious honor of being the top student at St. Mary's School for Young Ladies, a small local girls' school. "Also, on my own," the girl continued, "I am learning Reed's French phonography for English-speaking phonographers. I understand you are going to France."

"I am." Mrs. Besom contemplated this windy, earnest response as she glanced down at the certificates. St. Mary's had provided its best student a most banal "finish": Sewing, Latin, French, Sums, Spelling, Typing, and Shorthand. Nonetheless, the top was a good place to begin if one were to rise above a commonplace education. "I take it you would like to go to France?"

"I would be happy to."

The older woman arched one brow. "Is that why you seek this employ? To get away?"

"No. I would enjoy the travel."

"Is that the only reason?"

"It is the main reason."

"You don't need the money?"

"I do, but, begging your pardon, I think I could get other work."

Amelia Besom smiled slightly. "So you consider employment as my secretary-companion a choice position?"

The girl's hand, small as a child's, came out of the

shadows to smooth her skirts—the hand was gloved in black, crocheted cotton lisle. There was another second of almost offensive hesitation before she assented with a nod.

Mrs. Besom drew herself up from her chair. She was an imposing woman, a good seven or eight inches taller than the young woman in front of her. And a good sixty pounds heavier. At age sixty-eight Amelia Besom considered herself to be a substantial and handsome woman. She never felt compelled to apologize for her height, her weight, her age, or for that matter anything else. She stared directly at the young woman in front of her.

The girl's training, though modest, spoke of a pleasant innate intelligence; her speech and manners were attractive. She seemed forthright, her demeanor hardly that of someone who had large sins to hide. Better still, the scarlet shadings that had overtaken Miss Van Evan's good name—as reprehensible as they were—might make it possible to hire a capable, presentable young woman at a lower-than-usual salary. Amelia Besom smiled to herself. She was not above saving a dollar. While saving a soul, of course.

"No references then," she repeated. She wanted to drive the point home before she launched into expenses and salary.

For an instant the girl was appropriately at a loss to have this fact brought forth again. Then she spoke up in a voice that was soft but surprisingly firm. "No, I don't have any. But I am well qualified and exactly what I seem—healthy, willing, and wanting this job, ma'am."

"Don't call me 'ma'am.'"

"Yes, ma—um—"

"'Madam.' The dignified word is *madam*."

"Yes, madam."

"And stand up and move into the light. I want to look at you, if that's all I'm expected to go on in order to decide whether to employ you or not."

The girl stood, a diminutive creature with a full bosom and full hips. Still Mrs. Besom could not see her face.

"Take off your hat."

She did so, and Mrs. Besom was further surprised.

There was little mistaking why this young woman might engender more than her share of gossip. Standing there in her purple dress and black lisle gloves, she was as contradictory—and provocative—a creature as Mrs. Besom had ever seen. Mrs. Besom motioned, and the girl came a step nearer.

Miss Van Evan's hair was red, a shining, rich, near—cardinal red streaked with copper. This hair was thick and heavy and seemed to defy gravity. Tied in a loose Gibson knot, with a strand here and there coming down, one waited for the rest of it to unfold under its own weight. This bright, copious halo framed a round, little face with a pointed chin, a bow mouth, and a smattering of freckles over a dainty nose. Her features were as perfect as a doll's, their petite regularity lending her visage a kind of glossy, trivial prettiness that was contradicted sharply by one strikingly anomalous feature: her eyes. These were large, wide, and dark. Set against very fair skin, the girl's eyes seemed to burn with intensity, giving her face—whether she deserved it or not—the look of depth and character. Even as she stared down inanely at fingers making a mess of the ribbons of her hat, Miss Van Evan's face had the look of deep, passionate concentration—an intensity one saw on the faces of visionaries and temperance leaders. Though temperance, in anything, was apparently not one of Miss Van Evan's passions: The hat she was mangling was an impossible congeries of ribbons and flowers and feathers, her dress an incredible froufrou of pleats and cheap lace over the bosom.

"Well, you are certainly ornamental."

"Ornamental?"

"Attractive. I don't like having anything unattractive around me. I am a rich woman and can afford to have every aspect of my life lend to its refinement and intelligence. Your attractiveness is one of your advantages."

"Thank you, madam."

"Your disadvantages, of course, go beyond the mere fact

of no references. I believe the reason for your last dismissal had something to do with flirtations and young men. A rather messy involvement that saw you saddled with a cruel nickname—we won't mention it, but we both know it."

At this, Miss Seven-Minutes-of-Heaven looked directly up, her eyes performing their neat little trick, an intense, perfervid regard. But she didn't protest.

"I simply won't have such behavior," Mrs. Besom continued. "I have my standards." She paused to allow this to sink in. "If I hire you—and I am thinking of it—you would have to behave with the strictest sense of propriety. That means there would simply be no, and I mean *no,* cavorting with the opposite sex at any time or under any circumstance." She scowled suddenly, asking, "You're not a suffragette, are you? Or one of those New Women who believe in free union between the sexes and whatnot, like that Sarah Grand?"

"Who?" The girl looked genuinely blank.

"Good." Mrs. Besom was particularly pleased by this vein of ignorance. Modern girls could be such a bother with their uppity, newfangled notions. "Then it's settled. I am willing to allow you to enter my employ on a trial basis. You may start tomorrow morning, at which time we shall begin to prepare for my trip abroad at the end of the month. Meanwhile, you must understand: If you give me any cause to be sorry I have associated myself with you, I shall dismiss you on the spot, no matter where we are, no matter how stranded that might leave you. Is that clear?" One simply had to be firm in these matters.

"Yes, ma'am—I mean 'madam.'" The girl followed this with, "Do we go from here straight to France, then?"

Mrs. Besom was taken aback to be questioned herself. She answered, "No, we go first to New York."

"Then to France?"

"No. To England."

"Where in England?"

The older woman blinked. "I don't see that this is a relevant discussion."

"It's not relevant to know where I'm going?" This observation was offered with quiet and humble bewilderment.

Amelia Besom felt like an old fool for a second. She answered abruptly, "Hampshire, the countryside. Whenever I go to Europe, I go there first. I always gather and ship a container of antiques to New York from Southampton. Then we go across the channel to France. I will be appraising some items for an estate in Normandy then appraising an exhibit for an insurance company in Paris."

"This is most satisfactory."

How very big of her, Mrs. Besom thought.

"And at what salary?"

"Pardon?"

"At what salary do you propose my employment to begin?"

The older woman frowned. "We shall discuss this tomorrow, when we discuss your duties in detail."

"I would prefer to discuss this today. I have been out of work a month and have debts I must settle. I need to know how much money I will have."

Mrs. Besom could hardly object to this. She thought for a moment before saying, "Well then, I imagine ten dollars a month should suffice."

"Ten dollars?" The girl frowned. "One of the girls from St. Mary's in Palm Beach gets eighteen dollars a month plus room, board, and all travel expenses."

"I'm sorry, my dear, but you mistake me if you think I'll haggle over money. It is most unladylike. Of course, your room and board and all travel expenses shall be covered. As to pocket money, however, ten dollars is perfectly adequate."

The cheeky girl looked her straight in the eye. "To my mind it isn't."

Mrs. Besom stared, astounded that such a sweet face could hide such defiance. "Then you shall have to seek employment elsewhere."

Miss Van Evan stood there a moment, then turned in a

flurry of purple skirts, placing her feathered, flowered hat back onto her cherry-glow head. At the center of the room, however, she faced around once more. "Mrs. Besom," she said, "I mean no disrespect, but since we are talking of what others say: You have a reputation yourself."

Mrs. Besom bristled.

"You are said to be"—the girl hesitated—"difficult."

"Difficult? Who says this?"

"The help here at the hotel." She paused again, for effect perhaps. "You have been advertising for a companion for seven and one-half weeks, and so far as I know, I am the only applicant for the position. In ten minutes I can be downstairs getting a job as a bedder in this hotel, but I don't fancy making beds all day. And you don't fancy leaving for Europe at the end of the month alone." She took a breath. "I'll take twelve dollars a month," she said, "but not a cent less."

Amelia Besom smiled slightly. "How old are you, girl?"

"Twenty-four."

"I am almost three times that. I own two antique stores in New York and buy and trade for a dozen museums. I have furnished five houses exceptionally, have outlived three husbands, and traveled four continents. I will not be bamboozled by a presumptuous young chit whose last employer was so distraught with her that she has been thrown out—"

"Twelve dollars."

"Ten."

"You could afford twelve, and you are not likely to find anyone else willing to take this position at twice that."

"Eleven."

"Done."

Amelia Besom smiled slightly. "Fine." She placed her palms on the writing table as she contemplated the girl. "So be here tomorrow at seven in the morning, when we will begin on my correspondence. In the afternoon we shall visit my travel agent, then see my seamstress—who can also make you a new dress. That one is ghastly." She glanced up the girl's purple skirts, past the cheap lace of the fussy bosom to the brim of the young woman's hat that sat a foot deep in faux flowers. "In fact, we'll get you a new wardrobe. For which you may repay me at a rate of four dollars a month that I shall deduct from your wages." Mrs. Besom's smile bloomed. "That will leave you with seven dollars a month pocket money. You can manage on that?"

The girl opened her mouth as if to object, then apparently thought better of it. "Yes." She laughed, a light, breathy sound. "I can manage." She stepped forward again, offering her gloved hand, like an equal. "Good-bye."

Mrs. Besom stared at the small extended hand, at its childlike pinkness peeking through the crocheted pattern of black, hard-twisted threads. There were breaks in the lisle, she noticed, for which the girl had compensated by drawing in the missing lines directly onto her hand with black ink. More for lack of any other response occurring to her, Mrs. Besom put her own hand into this strange bit of enterprise. For an instant she felt her large, knobby fingers wrapped in something small and remarkable—the warm, textured grasp of seeming confidence and good wishes.

Once more, Amelia Besom was all but dumbstruck. She could find nothing to say beyond, "Yes, good-bye."

Two weeks later Hannah Van Evan wrote:

March 31, 1903
Well, I think I have come to these pages angry every single night this week, but this takes the cake. We leave tomorrow for New York, and today all the clothes we ordered from the seamstress arrived. I seem to have purchased, through credit with my employer, a single evening dress with short sleeves and a modestly décolleté neckline. Other than that, however, every inch of me will be covered and tied up in clothing, from my earlobes to my feet. All my new blouses (white to a one) have collars so high it takes boning to keep them standing. Their lace, at the very top of my throat, gets caught in the loops of my

*earrings (which are "very vulgar and piratical any-
way"—the ear loops must go, so Mrs. Besom tells me).
And gloves. My Lord, I have no idea how I shall write or
carry or do anything with my fingers perpetually uphol-
stered in white cotton. Mrs. Besom has "very generously" bought me five pairs of such gloves (when I
bristled at paying for what I did not like or see use for) at
her own expense.*

*She has also bought me a "health corset" that "my
mother should have had the good sense to have gotten me
long ago." It itches like the blazes and makes me arch my
back; my bottom sticks out, as this is the only way to walk
and still be comfortable. Mrs. B swears that this undergarment is what all the proper young ladies wear in
Europe, but I swear I have seen dozens of fancy ladies
here in Miami and not a one looks as afflicted as I feel in
it. ("Showgirls," Mrs. B states flatly, "every one of these
gloveless, loose-looking creatures are showgirls or par-
venue heiresses.") I suppose I shall have to trust her. She
says it won't itch nearly so badly when we are in cooler
weather.*

*The only really delightful thing is a petticoat I have
bought. It's made of forest green taffeta layered under
and over mounds of dark purple tulle, every hem of it
edged in black satin piping. It reminds me of the cancan
skirts that Edward Stanton showed me once on a poster
he brought back from Paris. I adore it. I'd better: The
darned thing cost me eight dollars, of which Mrs. B, in
this instance, did not offer to pay one red cent—ho! In
fact, she hates it and tried to stop me from buying it. I
don't know why, since it is the lightest, foamiest concoction imaginable: pure, ethereal loveliness. Well, never
mind what she thinks. If I can go into debt for a trunkful
of tedious, uncomfortable costumes, I can jolly well have
a "gaudy, bespangled unmentionable" (her words) to
wear underneath where no one can see it anyway.*

*She worries, I know, that my eye for beautiful petti-
coats has something to do with my "trouble with young*

*gentlemen" here in Miami. And of course I wouldn't
know anything about such petticoats if it weren't for
Edward Stanton and his friends.*

Hannah lifted her pen. Oh, what a mess she was leaving
behind in Miami. Good riddance.

She daydreamed the rest.

None of the gentlemen she knew in Miami, including
Edward, were really the right sort for her. But what was the
right sort?

A poet, she thought. No, no, a revolutionary. No, a
deposed prince who had sacrificed his own glory for the
sake of his homeland. He would live in a castle—no,
something simpler, a cottage in the countryside, where
Hannah would live with him. They would be madly in love.
This prince, of course, would be rich as a king, so they could
go anywhere they wanted: sail the Caribbean, or take his
private railway car to Vienna, where they would waltz in the
New Year. Or they could sit in the plush dark together and
watch a lavish, heart-wrenching story sung on the stage of
the Paris opera.

Ah, Paris. Hannah went to sleep imagining this city.
Edward and his friends had painted quite a picture of it:
wide boulevards blooming with tulips in April, dancing with
lights and music every evening in the summer. She was
going to see Paris at its finest, the city of gaiety and laughter
and champagne, all a lady could drink, a place where a
person could live life to the fullest—and not find herself
destitute, accused, and ashamed in the aftermath.

The Ether Drinker

A dog that dies in Paris
is more interesting than
a world that collapses elsewhere.

—Villemessant, French journalist

Chapter 1

London, April 3, 1903
Mrs. B had a terrible row with her shipper,
which has resulted in her deciding not to gather
old things in the south of England as usual. "It's
all picked over anyway," she claims. "One has
to hunt a week to find anything worth having."
Thus, we are "holidaying" in London until the
end of the month when we cross the channel to
France, "where there is a better class of busi-
ness." To keep ourselves busy, I think we have
seen every monument, cathedral, and tomb in
Baedeker's guidebook. I will be so glad when
Mrs. B has something to do with herself again
besides broaden my "narrow, provincial expe-
riences."
—from the diary of Miss Sue-Hannah Van Evan

Across the channel in Paris, Sébastien de Saint Vallier rang the front bell of a large home in the faubourg Saint-Germain. The air was chilly, the doorstep on which he stood dark. He kept his gloved hands deep in his pockets. Then a wedge of light opened before him, and a maid admitted him into a large, well-lit foyer.

He made a sarcastic face as he entered. *"Le grand sculpteur est là?"* His brother, Nardi, the "great sculptor"

15

whose whereabouts he was inquiring after, seldom did anything more artistic these days than carve angels on tombstones.

"*Oui, m'sieur. Là-dedans.*" The maid rolled her eyes and pointed toward a noisy hallway. Sébastien handed her his hat and gloves, then turned so she could take his coat as he slipped one arm out of it.

Somewhere down the hallway, great crashing discords of notes jangled the air, as if someone were pounding the keyboard of a piano with his fist. Sébastien could hear a kind of soliloquy—it sounded like Nardi's voice—rising over this. Sébastien headed toward the sound as he slid his other arm free, the maid catching his coat then his scarf as she followed after him.

Running to keep up, she began to chatter. *He came here about an hour ago, as lit up as a street lamp, picked a fight with the butler, leveled him, then threw up into the piano. Three gentlemen tried to make him leave, but he threatened them with your father's name then with financial ruin.* . . . Sébastien didn't particularly need these details; they were all variations on old ones.

As they rounded the salon doorway the maid held her hand out. "*Et voilà.*"

And there he was. Nardi, one knee on the piano bench, the other banging around on the keyboard, his buttocks in the air, his head bent into the string box of a six-and-a-half-foot grand piano.

Ah, yes, Sébastien thought. The flower and pride of the de Saint Vallier family, the youngest, the prize and the prodigy. And the only family member capable of fighting a musical instrument—and losing: Nardi's elbow hit the piano's prop stick, and the lid dropped abruptly.

Sébastien leaped to catch it. "*Oo là là, balourd! Tu est le plus grand idiot du siècle.*"

Several others rushed forward with Sébastien, the group of them gaining hold of the lid only after it had given Nardi a hearty thwack on his coccyx. The man in the piano barely complained. The area reeked of stomach bile minted with camphor and another milder but equally strange and chemical odor, perhaps chloral. Whatever the intoxicant tonight, it had put him in a state of bliss that precluded apparently feeling the pressure of a piano lid dropping onto him. Inside the piano, the sloggy echo of his voice bounced off the instrument's soundboard. *"Je vous prie, mademoiselle, de votre très grande patience. Je ne me suis qu'introduit un petit peu . . . pas exprès. . . ."* He was apologizing to the piano in bawdy terms for having accidentally inserted himself into her.

The rest of the room, fifty or so people, were pulled back toward the far wall. They stood there, feathered and jeweled, spruced and dapper; morbidly quiet. Out the corner of his eye, Sébastien recognized a few of these people, acquaintances, clients, he had almost avoided seeing tonight. Sébastien was a lawyer of some note in Paris. He had been invited to this gathering but begged off, feeling he had little in common socially with either the host of this affair, Georges Du Gard, or his guests: For one thing, they were all the sort who would tolerate a belligerent inebriate making an ass of himself at their expense, for no better reason than he had once had brief fame as a sculptor and had enjoyed, all his life, the privileges associated with Old France aristocracy.

"Bernard." Sébastien used his brother's full first name. Nardi, thirty-two years old, had yet to outgrow the diminutive of his childhood.

Nardi hit his head on the piano lid as he straightened. His face turned toward Sébastien, his eyes preternaturally alert, brilliant and glassy as if he were running a fever. Nardi's face was handsome, classically French: long, with a straight, thin nose, the jaw and chiseled cheekbones of Roman conquerors. At the temple and under the sockets of the eyes, this beautiful face was beaded with the sweat of a man who had ingested a stimulating amount of camphor—and confronting the heavy, sweet odor now directly, Sébastien knew it: ether. Whereas other people might breathe its fumes during surgery, Nardi preferred to drink its liquor as entertainment.

"Having a fine old time tonight, aren't you, Nardi?" Sébastien moved readily into English, especially in situations that called for tact, diplomacy, and as much privacy as one could muster in the presence of fifty awestruck people. He spoke the language regularly during the business day, the jurisprudence of finance having made him fluent.

Nardi's English, on the other hand, was about as heavily accented as any French tongue could make it. "And what woo'd you know about 'aveeng a fine ol' time, *mon vieux,* ol' 'Bastien?"

"Not so much as you, that's certain. Come on. *Je suis venu te chercher. Allons-y.*" Sébastien steered his brother off the bench and onto his feet. Nardi was not stable; even through his clothes he felt cold and clammy. To their host, still standing nonplussed, holding the piano lid, Sébastien offered regrets and apologies. *"Je suis désolé, monsieur. . . ."* He promised to send a piano tuner in the morning to repair the damage, for which, *bien sûr,* Nardi would pay.

Du Gard smiled faintly, let the piano lid close, and held out his hands in the first gesture of forgiveness. *"C'est pas grave.* Not serious—"

Nardi came alive. "Ah, we are *all* goeeng to speak Eengleesh. The language of money. My brother's language—"

Sébastien grabbed him by the back of the coat and turned him, shoving and walking him toward the door. Nardi more or less stumbled along in front of him, complaining about his rough treatment, then about the queasiness in his stomach, then his rheumatism—the bane of anyone who worked with damp clay on any sort of continuing basis— then, when Sébastien gave him a particularly hard push, about possible injury to his hands.

"Salaud! You are going to break something. *Lâche-moi."* He tried to twist away, but only lost his balance and landed on one knee. He pulled his hands in protectively—his reflexes even sober were not those of a normal man. Nardi

would never use his hands to break a fall; he would sooner land on his head. He knelt there on one knee a moment, as if dazed, without a shred of dignity, hunched over, his hands tucked into his armpits.

A dozen years ago Nardi had broken a finger. This finger, the smallest of his left hand, was more susceptible to the rheumatism, which at times made him hold the finger out stiffly. It was a strangely elegant gesture. Years ago Sébastien could remember the odd, dexterous grace it had lent Nardi's hands: one long, slender finger raised out from the rest, as his thumb scooped an eye socket from a mound of clay or squeezed out the bridge of a nose. Nardi had once been able to make raw clay breathe with life, the stiff finger no handicap, held out with the same stylish delicacy with which a swell might balance the handle of a china teacup.

These days, however, the rheumatic finger was put to other uses: Sébastien lugged his brother to his feet, his arm up and over his own shoulder—"Easy"—then got for his trouble, right in his face, Nardi's little finger held straight up, his three good fingers folded over with a cock of his wrist: an obscene hand gesture.

"Lâche-moi," Nardi muttered again.

"I'm not about to leave you be, so stop being such a cretin."

"Tu m'emmerdes."

"Oh, lovely. Is this the sort of social chatter you have been entertaining everyone with tonight?"

The truth was, however, if Nardi had wanted to, he could have caused much more trouble than merely issuing forth a few obscenities. Sébastien counted himself grateful that he was getting more cooperation than had the butler or the other men who had tried to put Nardi out before this.

Bernard de Saint Vallier was a large man; an inch and a bit over six feet tall (more than two inches taller than Sébastien), broadly straight-shouldered, long-armed, long-legged. Just the weight of his solid trunk and lanky limbs would have been enough to make any progress impossible by his merely floundering around in resistance. He didn't.

He went along, staggering against Sébastien, then against Du Gard, who took it upon himself to shoulder the other half of Nardi's weight. In this manner, like three drunken chums, they made their way down the hallway, Nardi's unsteadiness driving them into a doorjamb then a table full of objets d'art before they came into the rosy light of the foyer.

By the front door, the maid was holding Nardi's overcoat. Putting it on him was a feat. Besides his being limply unconcerned with what was being done to him, the coat itself was handfuls and handfuls more of cream-colored alpaca than was necessary for either warmth or practical maneuvering. It was a fancy piece, about as stylishly unobtrusive as the Eiffel Tower—no doubt one of Nardi's questionable "gifts" from any of a half-dozen women who were known to give him such things; "patronesses," he called them.

Outside, under the stars of a crisp spring night, the maid, Du Gard, and Sébastien loaded their grumbling, alpaca-wrapped burden into Sébastien's carriage. Then Sébastien climbed in and reached through the open doorway to offer Du Gard his hand. Du Gard took it, professing to be terribly grateful. He thanked Sébastien for coming so quickly; he denied there had been any trouble at all. *It was nothing, really. . . . Just see that your brother is put to bed safely and well taken care of. . . . Such a shame . . . Such a nice young man, so much polish, so knowledgeable in matters of art and music, so fine of manners . . .*

And Nardi truly was, Sébastien thought, which was the great, sickening pity of it all. He was a prince among men. When he wasn't high as a kite or filling up pianos with the contents of his stomach.

They jostled along in silence for a time, Sébastien thinking that Nardi had passed out. Through the open carriage windows, the air off the Seine, as they crossed over the Pont Neuf, was particularly cool and brisk. Sébastien pulled up his scarf and the collar of his overcoat, eventually settling with his arms folded to stare at the man in the seat opposite him. A succession of street lamps was throwing light into the carriage, flashes that passed over Nardi like light through a stroboscope. The same fixed image flickered over and over in the dark: a once handsome gentleman gracelessly sprawled, self-anesthetized. Then the carriage descended the bridge into the tree-lined street, and there was only the vehicle's own side lamp outside the window, a small glow swinging back and forth.

As they turned down onto the rue de Rivoli, Sébastien was surprised to hear Nardi speak. "I thought we were through with this." He didn't raise his head; nothing, no movement in the dimness. He looked dead.

"With what?"

"Your chasing after me and hauling me home."

Sébastien snorted, then left a space of silence before he said, "Monsieur Du Gard has come to me to consult on the law. He's a client, did you know that?"

Nardi gave a faint laugh of seemingly genuine surprise. "No, I didn't." He laughed again, less ingenuously this time. "Well, well. Sorry." He added, "Maybe you should give me a list so I don't throw up on the wrong people."

"You sound amazingly alert."

"Ahhh—" His voice descended in tone, as with a deep sigh. "You should see me when the stuff first hits. I'm positively brilliant."

"Then it must be afterward that you turn into a heaving, raving ass." Sébastien looked out the window, too angry to say more. After a few moments he turned back to add sharply, "In your own stupendously ridiculous and drunken state, you staggered halfway across Paris just to make sport of Georges Du Gard. Why? Why bother yourself?"

"I wasn't making sport of him." Long shadows cut over Nardi's face as the side lamp swung wildly round a turn, these swaths of light providing just enough illumination to point out that Nardi needed a shave. He had needed one for at least two days. He'd needed a haircut for months. His hair lay limply on the shoulders of the extravagant coat.

Sébastien wanted to hit him. Sébastien leaned forward.

"*Imbécile,* then what were you doing there—" He stopped.

From the alpaca coat's inside pocket, Nardi had taken out a small silver flask. He tilted it back, drinking, then wiped his mouth with the back of his hand. He repocketed the flask and laid his head back again, relaxing against the seat so well that his head began to rock with the same jostling rhythm as the carriage.

Sébastien stared at him, at the bobbing head seemingly unattached atop the absurdly expensive mound of alpaca. Irritably Sébastien realized that he himself, who made more money than anyone in the family, could not have bought that coat without at least considering its cost for a moment. In the dim, moving light, Nardi's face looked dark against the white fleecy fabric. He looked tan. Or else jaundiced. His hair, normally brown, was streaked with brassy gold, presumably the result of a sojourn in sunny Italy. Nardi had spent the fall in Milan, the winter in Naples, working at casting facilities—making bronze sculptures out of other people's piece molds, out of other people's art.

Sébastien felt an uneasiness descend on him. He repeated his question, really wanting an answer. "Nardi, why were you at Du Gard's house tonight?"

Nardi lifted his head and looked at him vaguely. "What?" He seemed lucid a moment longer, then he closed his eyes and lay back, relaxing in a disconcerting manner. His whole body went limp; his head lolled to one side.

Sébastien leaned forward and nudged him, sitting there poised until he realized he was waiting for a response from a man who was not going to give him one. The whole carriage now smelled exactly like Nardi, of ether and camphor and God knew what else. The sweet, sickening smell of hospitals and mortuaries. Sébastien found himself watching for the rise and fall of his brother's chest.

It was there: slow, shallow breaths. Nardi's hands were folded neatly in his lap, his legs out, his body swaying gently to the movement of the carriage. Sébastien watched as the light, cast by the creaking, swinging lamp outside, cut back and forth across his brother's expressionless face, his uninhabited posture. Then Sébastien had to look away. For the rest of the trip he stared out the window, letting himself be dazed by the lantern. But he was nonetheless aware of Nardi's inertness across from him, the vacant motion of his body rocking along, as unfettered and unbothered by life as if it were already on its way to the cemetery.

Claire, Sébastien's sister, had waited for them in the downstairs lobby so they wouldn't have to wake the concierge of the building. As she let Sébastien in she peered over his shoulder. "Shall I help you?" she asked. She remained on tiptoe for a moment, trying to see past him out into the dark. Claire was in her nightclothes.

She was five years younger than Sébastien, thirty-three, and lived with their parents in their two-story apartment on the Place des Vosges. Sébastien had sent word an hour ago that he would be bringing Nardi here. He had no idea where his brother lived and tonight didn't trust Nardi with anything so particular as streets and house numbers.

"No. Let the butler and footman do it," Sébastien told his sister as he walked past her. He had left the two servants to wrestle Nardi out of the carriage.

The lobby was dimly lit. Sébastien could barely see the steps as he went up to the first landing. The door to the apartment was open. He went in, setting his hat and gloves on the table in the foyer. This room and the apartment beyond through shadowy doorways glimmered with the faint glow of gas jets turned low for the night. Sébastien reached over to the lamp on the wall, turning its valve, and the vestibule brightened into a wide radius of light.

The room in which he stood was actually more than the usual notion of "vestibule," being a rather graciously large greeting room. It was also, like the rest of his parents' home, better furnished than one would expect. Sébastien's parents lived in Le Marais, an upper-middle-class neighborhood in Paris to which a bit of regal history was attached—their building had been the pet project of a king, Henri IV's palacial dream before his assassination cut that dream short.

With graceful colonnades outside and spacious rooms inside, these apartments were generally sought-after residences. It was nonetheless uncommon to walk into one of them onto eighty-year-old Persian carpets and to set one's hat on the red marble tabletop of an authentic Louis Quinze—this one being especially authentic in that it had once actually belonged to Louis himself.

The shuffle of feet behind Sébastien alerted him to move out of the way. Claire held the apartment door open, and the butler backed in, the footman following after him, Nardi in the middle. Or at least it seemed to be Nardi. He was slung between the two men in his own voluminous coat like the carcass of a beast being hauled in a sack.

"Ah, Nardi." Claire tsked. She peeked over the edge of Nardi's coat as they all filed in. "What have you done?" she murmured. She always especially loved Nardi's exploits, since they invariably made her little one—marrying (then not living with) the coachman's son—look so much less egregious. To Sébastien, she said, "He looks awful!"

"He looks unconscious," Madame de Saint Vallier said from above. She stood in the balconied walkway that overlooked the entry room from the second floor. She, too, was in her nightshift, though she wore over it a long silk dressing gown. She turned and disappeared into the stair-well.

Justine de Saint Vallier was the mother of four children, two of them standing there, a third hoisted in his coat. Sébastien was the oldest, then came Louise, not present; Louise seldom even visited though she only lived in the *seizième* across town. Claire was the second-youngest, Nardi the youngest of the lot. Their father, Sébastien imagined, would be upstairs asleep; his wife took care of the messier episodes of family life, anything that might intrude into his existence in a way that was other than regally harmonious.

Madame de Saint Vallier appeared in the stair alcove, descending slowly into the large vestibule. She was an attractive, slightly heavy woman in her early sixties who carried herself with a deceptively soft mien. Sébastien knew his mother's rather maternal appearance hid a sharp tongue and a ready bitterness, though she was very circumspect about when and how she used these. She was a shrewd woman who possessed the genuine self-assurance that came from being the bulwark of her family, a family of renown and enormous social importance. Motherhood in this context was a role she relished.

"In the *grand salon*," she said, pointing the way for the servants. "Lay him on the sofa. We'll have a look at him there and decide what to do with him."

Sébastien followed the little caravan through the entry room, his mother turning up gas jets as she went, the apartment brightening. The others went into the *grand salon,* but Sébastien stopped at the doorway. "I have to go," he said.

He stood there looking in on another room furnished by time, privilege, and providence. There was a mahogany drawer chest, its mounts chased and gilt in bronze. It was a hundred and twenty years old, a Riesener, a gift to the family from the master cabinetmaker. Across the room there was a long sofa, once their grandmother's, recently re-covered in stiff, green moiré. It was stuffed with down. Nardi's limp body sank into its cushions as they lowered him onto it.

Sébastien called again from the doorway, "I can't stay—"

His mother spoke over her shoulder. "You can't leave until I've spoken to you. Where did you find him?"

"I didn't exactly find him. I was summoned." He hesitated. "Georges Du Gard called me when Nardi showed up at his house about an hour ago."

She glanced at him. "Du Gard? The Georges Du Gard who just bought the Château d'Aubrignon?"

Sébastien was startled to find his mother in possession of this knowledge. He hesitated before he said, "Yes."

The servants stepped back, giving Sébastien's mother her first true opportunity to look at her younger son, now splayed out on the sofa. "Well," she said after a moment.

"He doesn't look so bad, actually. He looks better than when I last saw him. He's been in the sun. He has some color."

Sébastien pulled a sarcastic face. "Probably from liver failure—jaundice." He paused before saying, "All the way here I had the keenest fear that he was going to die on me, that he was dead already."

His mother looked around at him. "Don't say that." To the servants she said, "That will be all. You can go back to bed."

Sébastien pressed himself sideways to let the men by him. His mother followed them to the doorway, watching until they were beyond earshot, then asked quietly, "What was it tonight? Ether?"

"And camphor, I think. Though in the carriage he brought out what may have been something else. Whatever, it put him out like a light."

They both stared at Nardi on the couch. He lay in the exact, slightly awkward position in which he'd been set down, narcose. Claire was unwrapping him like a package, loosening his narrow black tie, taking the top studs out of his hard shirtfront, opening his collar. She may as well have been trying to make the fringed lamp beside him comfortable.

There beside Sébastien his mother spoke, returning to a topic he had hoped they'd left behind. "Georges Du Gard bought the château in Aubrignon, and you didn't even say it was happening." Sébastien had only known himself for the first time last week. He had been consulted by Du Gard on a matter of noncontractual liability holding up the transaction.

"The sale only just went through this afternoon. I can't imagine how you found out so—"

"Never mind how I found out. You knew and didn't tell me."

Sébastien understood by the little pinch in her voice that this offense ranked equally with being dragged home unconscious.

"I was going to tell you—" He tried to pretend for another moment that Du Gard's purchase of the château was

nothing more than a routine piece of business. Then he
glanced down. "All right, I should have mentioned it. But I
didn't want to get into it with you and Pater." All the
children, even as adults, used the Latin form of address with
their parents. "I want you to know now, though—I don't
consider offering my services in the interests of the château's sale any sort of betrayal, not of you or Pater, or of
anyone in any more abstract or historical sense, either. I
would have been happy to argue the case, if it had come to
that. Moreover, I get along well with Du Gard, who all but
reveres my abilities and background." Sébastien gave up
another piece of information that might not meet with much
enthusiasm. "I'm hoping he will name me the manager of
the estate."

This startled a laugh out of his mother. "The manager?"

"The financial administrator, actually. He will need
someone to handle the whole, from buildings to properties
to extrinsic capital assets."

Again she laughed, as she had when he was small and
come in excited over a frog or new playmate, something that
mattered to him which she deemed of no consequence.
"Don't you at least find this a little ironic?" she asked.

"Not at all."

"The estate agent? For a château our family owned for
four centuries?" A little ruthlessly she added, "It's the job of
a lackey, Sébastien, not for one of France's most respected
legal orators. And Du Gard is such a—" She was not
hunting for the right word so much as leaving a dramatic
pause. "Such an arriviste." This was a word an old-line
duchess could use without coyness or reluctance.

Sébastien's father was the nominal Duc d'Aubrignon, a
title disinherited by revolution then confused by a series of
empires, reinstated monarchies, and republics. The truth
was, however, people still kept track of such things and paid
homage to remembered honors. It was well-known that
Sébastien's father was "in line," that is, he was the seventh
or eleventh or twelfth in line to the defunct French throne,
depending on which monarchy, empire, or republic one was

following. The de Saint Valliers could freely use the word "arriviste," having "arrived" so far back they could lay claim to descending through Charlemagne.

"As I said," Sébastien disputed, "I would be the financial administrator, not the estate agent. The properties have at present three estate agents, who would be under the person who takes the overall position." Then he could hardly believe his own voice as he heard himself say, "I would have every prerogative, as if the estate belonged to me."

Justine de Saint Vallier's brows raised a fraction of an inch. She looked at him for several long seconds, as the full realization dawned on him: He wished he *did* own it; he wished he *could* please her.

The château had never belonged precisely to his mother and father. It had belonged to his uncle, though in Sébastien's youth their family had visited it often. They had spent holidays and summers there, along with other uncles, aunts, cousins, grandparents; the place could have housed an army. It had been almost a dozen years now, however, since his uncle had lost it and, along with it, the better part of the family's fortune. Since that time Sébastien could not remember a day when his family didn't bemoan their economic fall from grace—or covet that old castle on the Seine as if it were their lost chance into heaven.

Over on the sofa, Nardi stirred slightly. Justine de Saint Vallier turned toward them, then seemed to think Claire had things in hand. She cut straight back into the subject of the new owner of the Château d'Aubrignon, saying, "Monsieur Du Gard exhibits his wealth." The crime, of course, was more that he exhibited it outside her notions of decorum. She found him flashy.

"He's not so bad, really," Sébastien responded, trying to be generous. "And his wealth will be good for the estate." He couldn't resist adding, however, "Though you're right about his taste. It's boorish. He wanted to cover the walls of the large entrance hall with gold velvet. When he saw all the blood drain from my face over this, he quickly suggested mirrors—"

"You were there?"

"Yes. I've been there twice. It's a mess. A fortune and a lifetime may never make it right again. But Du Gard wants to, and he has both these prerequisites." Sébastien continued, "I also had to dissuade him from the notion of architecturally straightening out the main staircase 'so it doesn't take half the morning to get down it.' And he wanted to sell all the furniture and paintings 'to make room for something comfortable and modern.' There is nothing I can do to stop him from putting in plumbing on at least the ground floor. But I've given him a long lecture on history, elegance, and glory. Which I think he took to heart.

"He let me recommend a woman, an American museum agent, to come and appraise the contents. She can get a good price in New York for some of the lesser things. And she'll list the dollar and franc values of everything. Du Gard understands worth when it can be assigned a numeric value and placed in the context of money. He'll quickly come to see what merits keeping—and displaying." Sébastien shook his head. "Though God knows he may put fan palms in the cuspidors then set them out in the ballroom. I half want to become the administrator just so I can defend the poor old place."

His mother stared blankly at him. She seemed lost to him for several moments, her thoughts miles—more than a decade—away. Then she came back to earth abruptly. "Well," she said, fixing a smile on her face. She looked joylessly up at him. "Never mind. Thank you for fetching your brother." Her gaze dropped to focus on his tie pin. "Give my regards to Marguerite," she said. Marguerite was Sébastien's wife, with whom he no longer lived, though everyone in the family pretended this was quite normal, even he: He made connubial visits. "And the children." Sébastien and his wife had five of them.

"Certainly." He leaned down, about to plant two cursory kisses onto his mother's cheeks, when Nardi's groggy voice called to him.

"Sébastien, you were talking of the château in Aubrignon?"

Over on the sofa, Nardi had raised his arm and laid it over his eyes. Claire was still fussing over him, stroking his hair.

"What, Nardi? I have to go."

"The château. I think it is ours again."

"You misheard. I am only trying to become its administrator."

"No. The reason I was at Du Gard's tonight . . ." He left the thought unfinished to lift his arms in front of him. He stared at his hands. They had a pronounced tremor, a shake so regular it was as if he lay on the *couchette* of a train rattling along to somewhere, nowhere. He gave an impotent laugh. "Not good for much," he said.

"Shhh," Claire crooned. She took his hands in hers, crossed and folded them, then pressed them to her.

Nardi let her, looking over her shoulder at his brother and mother. "But I think I can stagger down the aisle to an altar."

"What?" Sébastien turned more fully.

"Du Gard has a daughter."

In an instant this brought Sébastien to the foot of the sofa. He looked down the length of it into his brother's rheumy, vacuous eyes. "What in God's name are you saying?" he asked.

It took several moments for Nardi to form those words into a coherent question. He wet his lips once, closed his eyes, then said, "I went to Du Gard's tonight to suggest marriage between myself and his daughter, a kind of exchange, a name for a castle."

"What." It wasn't a question, just a blunt expression of incredulity. Sébastien couldn't seem to stop saying the word. "What," he repeated.

Nardi shrugged. "Why not? In one fell swoop it will net us the château and the money to run it." He shrugged again, murmuring, "Why not?"

"Why not? Why not! I will tell you why not. The offer itself is insulting. Du Gard is not that stupid." Sébastien added, before he could think not to, "And we're not that desperate. The man's a bumptious, cigar-smoking philistine. His whole family are philistines." He came round the sofa, pushing Claire out of the way and grabbing Nardi by the shirtfront. "And you are an idiot!" he said. "No man with half an once of pride would let his daughter come within fifty feet of you."

"Except a philistine with a hunger for salon gatherings." Nardi spoke right into his face, unfazed by the hold his brother had of his shirt. He lay there in the sling of fabric, so relaxed he was limp, and went on. "Who longs for mention in the Paris society columns. I may be a sot, but I wear the de Saint Vallier name"—Nardi held out his hands with a mock courtliness that just hung there six inches off the sofa—"proudly," he added, then belched. He put his palm over his mouth, as if surprised by this. "Oh, pardon."

It was a joke. Sébastien had taught him to burp at will years ago; now he would like to throttle the juvenile dimwit.

Sébastien let go, dropping Nardi back into the down-pillow cushions. "What an imbecile!"

Nardi said, "He was interested, Sébastien. He listened."

"And threw you out."

Nardi shrugged. "And threw me out. But he'll think about it, I'm sure of it."

Sébastien turned his back. Their mother was standing there with her arms folded, frowning at Nardi. Sébastien rolled his eyes at her. "How can anyone be so asinine?" he asked. "Of all the shallow, seedy, prostituting—" Words weren't good enough. He could have cheerfully killed his brother for adding yet one more cataclysmic embarrassment which amounted to another hurdle between himself and the management of the old family château. "The only consolation," he said, "after I somehow apologize to Monsieur Du Gard for the offense of such an unwholesome offer, is that the man is generally magnanimous. And he's much more shrewd and ambitious than Nardi has given him credit for. He'll never rise to this."

For one eerie moment, however, Sébastien could imagine Georges Du Gard considering the idea, and that was even more frightening. Sébastien could envision himself locked into a lifelong nightmare of having to soothe Du Gard while having to play nursemaid to his soggy-witted brother. He would get all the responsibility, while the two of them happily and respectively blackened the house with cigar smoke and emitted belches so chemical they could have been used for anesthesia. The whole notion was offensive— though the concept behind it was something of a revelation. Sébastien stood there awestruck. Imagine. At one stroke, the château and the money to run it. Only an ether addict would have thought of such an impossible thing, or attempted to gain it by such a crude method. Nonetheless, Sébastien knew that he and his entire family—mother, father, wife, sisters, their husbands, children—would have given all their eyeteeth in a sack if only such an end were possible.

"Du Gard will take to the idea," Nardi insisted. "I'm going to marry the girl, make her wonderfully happy for a month or two—and pregnant—then throw myself in the river. How does that sound?"

"Couldn't you start with the river?"

Nardi laughed, then began feeling around in his coat, which lay under him. This time as he retrieved the flask Sébastien grabbed it.

"You stupid bugger," Sébastien said. "Drown yourself in something else tonight."

Nardi slowly pulled himself up. And up and up until he had risen to his feet to stand in an ugly, rather menacing posture in front of Sébastien. "Give that back to me or I'll plaster you onto the floor."

"You'll hurt your hands."

He laughed. "I'll use the lamp. Or an umbrella. Or Pater's walking stick—there's sure to be one those around here."

"Sit down, Nardi," Justine de Saint Vallier said. She interposed herself between the two brothers. "We don't threaten people in this house. Sit down and behave." She took the flask from Sébastien into her own keeping. "Thank you, darling," she told him. "You go home now. We'll take care of him. Call in the morning. I'm sure he'll be fine by then." Turning toward Nardi, she held out the flask. "Bernard, you're going to have one last sip of whatever this is that you like so well. Then we're going to pour the rest down the sink in the kitchen. Go on, take it."

Like an animal wary of bait, Nardi reached slowly. Then once he had the flask he sat, cocky again, with a *plompf* into the cushions of the sofa. Sébastien watched him uncork the thing, upend it, and drain it dry. They had to call the butler and footman again to get him up the stairs to his bedroom.

Chapter 2

> When mixed with twice its volume of rectified
> spirits, [ether] is administered internally as a
> remedy for nervous headache, flatulence, hic-
> cough, hysteria, spasmodic vomiting and asthma.
> —Encyclopaedia Britannica, ninth edition (1898)

NARDI CAME TO consciousness slowly, like rising up from
the bottom of the ocean. Light and coalescing images
floated over him, brightening. Then a reality of sorts, almost
too vivid after the murk, came into focus: the details of a
bedroom. It was morning. Or daylight, at least. He didn't
recognize where he was for another moment while he
racked his brain. What the Christ had he been doing last
night, and where had he been doing it? His mouth tasted
tinny, as if he'd been eating soft solder. Then a curtain blew
out directly over his face, from behind and over his head.
White lace, light as voile, crocheted by his sister Claire. *"Ah
là là,"* he groaned, and rolled over onto his stomach.

His cheek lay on a cool sheet that was rigidly flat, pressed
to the smoothness of paper by the platen of an ironing
machine. Where he lay his head smelled so familiarly of
soap and sunshine he shuddered: sheets washed in lilac then
dried on a rooftop in the bright sun. They held, as always,
the faint hint of yeast that saturated the air every morning
and afternoon, coming from the bakery on the street behind

his parents' home. Nardi hadn't smelled this particular scent
in a year and a half, and it was both the best and most
painful odor he could imagine; it was certainly the cleanest
smell he'd awakened to in a fortnight. *"Ah là là,"* he
crooned more quietly, like a lullaby. He pressed his eyes
into his forearm and whispered, *"Sacrebleu."* Oh Lord, oh
Lord, how had he gotten here? And how could he get out
without anyone seeing him?

Too late. Out in the hallway his mother tapped on the
bedroom door. "Nardi?" She continued to tap. This must
have been what had awakened him. "Nardi? Are you alive
in there?"

"Yes," he called back.

"Come down. We are waiting for you. Monsieur Du Gard
arrived half an hour ago."

Du Gard? He tried to piece together why this name was
familiar. Then, oh God, it all came back to him. Or parts of
it anyway.

Her muffled voice continued beyond the door. "Nardi, do
you hear me? It is one o'clock in the afternoon. Bring
yourself down. We all want to talk to you, Monsieur Du
Gard included."

We? Nardi wondered. All who? Nardi wasn't sure if he
was pleased or alarmed by the mandate in these words.

He pulled himself out of the bed, rubbed his face, his
eyes, then looked around for his flask. It wasn't in the
dressing room or by the washstand; he couldn't even find
his coat. He couldn't remember if there was anything in the
flask anyway or, if so, which liquor it might happen to be.
He gave up. He was wearing only his shirt and his socks.
He had no idea where his clothes were, no idea how he'd
come to be sleeping in this room dressed as he was. Typical.
He couldn't account for whole weeks of this past winter.

In the dressing room, he found clothes. They looked to be
Sébastien's, intentionally laid out for him. He washed
himself and put them on, having to roll up the shirtsleeves
to hide their insufficient length. There was also a razor with
which he shaved. Then he stuck his head under the tap for

good measure. Afterward he took the elastic off a sachet hanging in the armoire and used it to hold his hair back. *Voilà.* A neat, semiclean future son-in-law. He didn't look so bad, he thought, if one discounted the grey beneath his eyes and the hollows of his cheeks. He looked a little carved out, perhaps, though he preferred to think of this in decorative terms: He looked channeled and fluted, more finely detailed than he used to be—certainly worth acquiring.

Nardi had never doubted that Georges Du Gard would come after him. He had known it within the first minutes of arriving at the man's house, after Du Gard had begun to reprove him soundly. There were rules to be laid down, face to be saved. Then there had been the summoning of his brother, the apologetic waiting among the guests, the solicitous exit. None of this would have been necessary merely to rid oneself of a drunken nuisance. Nardi smiled to himself. He was about to make everyone very happy with him. His family would have access to the château again, as they once had. They could spend holidays there, perhaps even whole summers—all the while enjoying the prospect of future de Saint Valliers inheriting the place. (He hoped he could make some. He was rather out of practice. If he couldn't, though, he thought it perfectly acceptable that his wife make de Saint Valliers with someone else. He would very generously claim any children he brought home to him.) Meanwhile Du Gard could enjoy the idea of having given his only daughter and heir the one thing he couldn't bequeath her, a profoundly aristocratic heritage. Nardi himself would have the pleasure of getting and staying as mindlessly drunk as he wanted. And since providing all this happiness for himself and others was worthwhile, he could stop worrying that he would never do another worthwhile thing in his life. Ah, to be drunk without the guilt. Pure bliss. He might even like it so well he could swim through the rest of his life; no more gloomy ruminations of doing himself in.

The moment he got to the foot of the stairs, Nardi knew something was not right. His father's favorite walking stick was in the umbrella stand, indicating he was present when normally he was at his club this time of day. Through the front window Nardi could see his sister Louise's carriage parked across the street. Sébastien's was parked beside it, blocking a lane of traffic. The real unsettling element, however, was a black automobile parked right below the window, a chauffeur leaning indolently against a fender. There were other motorcars in Paris, though not many and none so large and fancy as this one, its driver all but liveried in his deep-brimmed hat and shiny black leggings. The sight was as inconspicuous as a brass band, trumpeting the wealth that made it a spectacle. It bore witness to the flash and style of Georges Du Gard.

At the parlor door Nardi heard, "The garden's a tangle. The domes are peeling. The outbuildings all need to be reroofed. But it's still the same solid beauty underneath. As to Nardi, we'll reroof him, too."

Claire's voice chimed in. "He's not a building."

More somberly someone added, "You can't make a person change. You can't make Nardi be what he is not."

Hear, hear, Nardi thought. He tapped on the parlor door then entered, smiling.

"Ah, Bernard, there you are." His mother was always the most gracious.

Nardi's father nodded. He stood behind his wife's chair, a tall *Gaulois,* white-haired and stooped from age. Sébastien scowled from across the room where he sat, his legs crossed, his arms folded and pushing the seams of his tailored suit coat. Sébastien had the physique of a Viking, a robust build Nardi had always thought more appropriate to, say, a stevedore than a lawyer.

Du Gard came forward, trim and natty, dressed by an English tailor and smoking a cigar rolled in Cuba. He didn't offer Nardi his hand as he had the night before, but embraced him, kissing both cheeks and saying, "I have just discussed with your family the fine offer you made last night, and we are all simply jubilant." He spoke confidently, with the forceful, decisive joy of a businessman who knew what he wanted and how to get it at good value. "I have come to discuss your marriage to my daughter."

Nardi sat down in a settee beside his sister Louise. She was there with her husband, Étienne; their children were notably absent. Claire sat in the chair by the fireplace. There were also two men in brown suits and bowler hats standing to the side by the front window; Nardi didn't know them and assumed they were more of Du Gard's lawyers or accountants. He hadn't expected quite everyone to be so involved in this decision, though he had expected at least tangentially to please the lot of them. Nardi stared as Du Gard began pacing.

"It is so good." Du Gard was beaming. "So perfect for everyone."

Sébastien took over. "What Monsieur Du Gard is saying is that we have all agreed there might be mutually beneficial terms on which the Du Gards and de Saint Valliers might be joined through matrimony between yourself and Monsieur Du Gard's daughter." He paused. "He has offered as dowry the Château d'Aubrignon."

This was the first shock. Nardi had imagined he might one day inherit it, or his children would, and that this alone would make everyone ecstatic. These people were not ecstatic, he realized. They were stunned. Stunned and somehow determined: conspirative.

"That sounds wonderful," Nardi agreed. He folded his arms, waiting.

"The dowry," Sébastien continued, "will also include a sizable sum to help renovate the château as well as a free hand on my part in reorganizing its finances, resources, and lands so as to make it run at a profit."

"Congratulations." Nardi couldn't help a growing sense of unease. He hadn't expected to bring his family quite this much good fortune. "You ought to be very happy." Sébastien ought to be bloody delirious. This was what he had wanted last night but was afraid he wouldn't get.

"We are *all* happy," Sébastien said, Nardi's father nodded, as if on cue. His mother, the girls, and Étienne all looked at him. Claire, he noticed, had been crying. "In addition," Sébastien added, "we are all to be given a portion of the estate."

"Is that so?" More amazing and more amazing. "Exactly what are you to be given? Land? What?"

"Claire wants land. Papa wants the backwoods for hunting. Louise wants the paintings in the grand hall. She needs the money. Different for each of us, I would say." As if an afterthought, Sébastien added, "But you get the bulk, the château itself, most of its contents—"

"I get its tangle and loose shingles and gold domes with the leaf peeling off?"

"It will all be repaired."

"A fortune and a lifetime couldn't repair it. You said so last night."

A little peeved: "Well, a fortune will be applied to it, and you have a lifetime, Bernard."

"Ah." He laughed. "And you expect me to redo the gesso and buff up the marble." He was joking.

Sébastien thought a moment. "Actually that's not a bad idea. After you get back, of course."

"Get back? Get back from where?"

The room grew silent. Only Du Gard kept smiling, that self-assured smile of a man who had just bought and paid for the Taj Mahal and was extremely happy with his purchase.

"Switzerland."

Nardi shifted in his chair. "Switzerland?"

"There is a clinic there. For dipsomaniacs, really—"

Du Gard interrupted. "Yes, but I sent a few telegrams early this morning. They will take you." He raised a finger and smiled, as if to answer any foolish reservations. "It is expensive, of course, but let me assure you I believe you are worth it. I won't regret one sou of the money."

Nardi looked again at the two strangers by the window. They were tall, brawny men, their blunt purpose no longer hidden by their brown suits and bowlers.

"And if I refuse to go?" he asked.

Sébastien glanced at the two men. "You have to go. We have all agreed. We have in fact just signed and witnessed the papers that commit you."

Nardi stood. His leg hit the edge of the settee, pushing it crooked. "I don't think so."

"Sit down, Nardi," Sébastien said, a man in command of the situation.

His tone irked Nardi, who leaped over a tea table and around Claire, to seize Sébastien by his stuffy starched shirt. He yanked him to his feet. But that was all the satisfaction he got before the two bowler-hatted men grabbed him. He lashed out at one of them, swung an elbow, but they quickly contained him, like handlers at the zoo who could bring down the giraffe or camel by just grabbing, pulling, or kicking the right place. Nardi felt his arm twisted, then his hand—they had his hand. They pushed him onto his knees by it, with him yelling bloody murder. Claire called out. Nardi's father had to take hold of her arm to prevent her from interfering.

Sébastien threw her a withering glare as he straightened himself, then looked down at Nardi. "You are going to Switzerland, where you are going to become as sober as the pope," he said. "When you return you will be clean of every trace of ether, camphor, chloral, every drug or drink, including alcohol, you have ever laid a hand on. And there are more conditions. When you return you will live in Aubrignon at the château, where we can watch you till the wedding. By the time you are back we will have had an apartment there made up." He added conciliatorily, "And a studio if you like. You can have all the clay, plaster, or marble—"

"I have a studio—"

"Shut up. You can have all the artistic supplies you wish, all the clothes, food, soap, toiletries, though we have been advised not to allow you a razor. But you positively will not be allowed one drop of anything harmful. You will be guarded if necessary—"

With a kind of ludicrous somberness, Du Gard added,

"There is no point to your ruining your life." He seemed the only person in the room with even a hint of charity on his face. "You could be an exemplary husband." He frowned, saying more seriously, "You will be, in fact." He paused, then added very quietly, "You have underestimated me if you think I will have an ether drinker for a son-in-law."

The two thugs in bowlers lifted Nardi onto his feet, wrenching his hands behind him. They were trying to lock his arms into a contraption of straps and canvas.

"Don't." He tried to jerk free as the men bound his arms to him. He promised cooperation: "All right," he said, "I'll stop. Don't do this. It's unnecessary. I can stop on my own."

No one listened.

He attempted to evoke pity: "For goodness' sake," he pleaded. He looked his family in their faces, one by one: Claire, Sébastien, Louise, his mother, his father.

His plea met only guilty, greedy silence.

He let his anger burst forth: "Damn you all!" he shouted as he stood there trussed up like a goose at Christmas. "The first time you turn your backs, I will have a pint of ether down my gullet with another pint in my pocket! I can play this game blindfolded—and straitjacketed—because, you see, getting ether may be the only thing I do well, but, by God, I do it with practiced, predictable proficiency!"

Chapter 3

Beware of all enterprises that require new clothes.

—H. D. Thoreau, *Walden*

THE WHEELS OF the little one-horse calèche whirred along, flinging bits of dirt and gravel into the air. The driver from his dicky box in front kept up a steady click of his tongue, the pony clopping along briskly. Hannah had to brace herself into her seat, one gloved hand gripping the armrest, the other holding down a straw hat to her head. As she breezed along thus in the open carriage, under the trees, in and out of filtered sun, her progress itself dazzled her eyes. The air—French air at last!—smelled crisp and green. Her spirits were high, as exuberant and pell-mell as the ride.

Mrs. Besom, on the other hand, seemed somewhere else entirely. She jostled there beside Hannah, her back braced stiffly upright against the carriage seat, her hands in her lap, sedate and poised by sheer will alone. Her hat was tied securely to her head, its bobbinet veil masking her face to end in a crisp gossamer bow at the side of her neck. The veil also served additionally to muffle Mrs. Besom's words. Through it and over the road noise she was attempting a discourse, as near as Hannah could make out, on fifteenth-century French architecture. Every so often Hannah caught a word on the fly; she could make out little else over the

clatter of wheels, the bounce of springs, and the lovely
sound of whistling air.

They rolled along, lickety-split, over a forested clifftop,
following a road that paralleled the Seine River. Now and
then, where the banks spread wide, Hannah could see the
waters far below. The Seine was a dark, milky jade, not at
all like the blue Bay of Biscayne back home. Hallelujah! she
thought. She was all but in Paris! If she followed this river,
it would flow right by the Eiffel Tower! Hannah felt she
knew what it was like to be borne along in a speeding
chariot toward heaven.

Heaven would be delayed slightly, however. The carriage
turned inland and plunged into the thick of the forest,
heading toward a château just off the channel coast. Instead
of going directly to Paris as Hannah might have liked, she
and Mrs. Besom were staying the weekend at this castle, the
Château d'Aubrignon. As they plunged now into the dusk-
like denseness of trees, the temperature immediately dropped.
The atmosphere grew darker, more cut off from sunlight.
Hannah's eyes had to adjust, as did also, apparently, the
driver's. The carriage slowed down considerably. The
peaceful noise of travel gave way to conversation.

". . . Monsieur Blois?" Mrs. Besom was asking Hannah
a question.

"I'm sorry. What about Monsieur Blois?" she responded.
"I couldn't hear all that you were saying." Monsieur Blois
was the curator of a museum in Paris where Amelia Besom
was to have done an appraisal on Monday.

Presently Mrs. Besom braced her gloved hand, flat-
palmed, on the seat bench, tapping an impatient finger. "The
telegram to Monsieur Blois, you remembered to send it,
didn't you?"

"Yes, madam."

Hannah had reported on this matter already. Mrs. Besom
had scheduled the appraisal of this château in among a
number of other commitments she already had in Paris. This
had made for a tight schedule with her imagining that she
and Hannah would go back and forth between the little town

in Normandy and the French capital, catching their sleep on the train. Even the amazing Mrs. Besom, however, had realized two days ago how exhausting this would be. It had become Hannah's job to open up space between the woman's various appointments.

Hannah assured her again. "I did exactly as you said. I wired the museum two days ago that we would be delayed. They said next Tuesday would be fine. Yesterday morning I sent another telegram confirming the new appointment— Tuesday at two o'clock in the afternoon at Monsieur Blois's office on rue de Lafayette—"

"No, no, yesterday morning you telegrammed Monsieur de Saint Vallier." Monsieur de Saint Vallier was the man they were presently on their way to see at the château.

"I sent both wires yesterday," Hannah explained, "one to Monsieur Blois confirming the new arrangements in Paris and one to Monsieur de Saint Vallier telling him that we would be arriving today on the noon ferry from Southampton." Monsieur de Saint Vallier's driver, presently carrying them along in Monsieur de Saint Vallier's carriage, had met their boat just half an hour ago.

"Yes. Well then. Good." Mrs. Besom nodded. "Very good." Her tone sounded reassured yet somehow unsettled. She never seemed to know quite what to make of Hannah's general efficiency. If anything, she cast a suspicious eye on it, the way someone does who has bought cheaply what appears to be of impossibly high quality.

After a moment Mrs. Besom made one of her swift, unprologued leaps in conversational logic. "Did you work for a very good family In Miami?" she asked.

Hannah looked at her, blinked, then answered, "Yes."

The woman may as well have asked, *How can you be so thorough and competent? From what dire circumstances could such a capable yet pitifully paid creature as yourself have come from? I don't understand this at all.*

Hannah did not expand on the woman's understanding.

Mrs. Besom had skirted this issue before, and as before found all maneuvering fruitless. She had yet to ask directly

about Hannah's last employ, there being a tacit agreement
between the women she couldn't: Since Mrs. Besom was
not paying for names and references, it seemed Hannah's
privilege not to give them.

After perhaps a minute Mrs. Besom said, as if it were a
rational part of the same conversation, "You have on that
petticoat."

"Pardon?" Hannah turned in the carriage seat, having to
scoot back and brace herself better over the pitted roadbed.

"The one that rustles when you walk. I have hesitated to
mention this," Amelia Besom said, "since it may hurt your
feelings, but I think you should know. In chic circles, it is
considered most vulgar to call noisy attention to the fact that
one is wearing an undergarment."

"I see." Yes, vulgar little thing that she was. The petticoat
had become a bone of contention between the two women,
the focus of what was coming to be a battle of wills. Mrs.
Besom had criticized Hannah's underskirts as "gaudy,"
"tasteless," and "unstylish." They were now becoming
immoral as well. Amelia Besom had obviously not thought
of this line of attack before or, hurt feelings or no hurt
feelings, she would have used it. The woman was not a
sensitive soul.

She told Hannah, "I think one shouldn't wear something
that might stimulate comment—or, God forbid, the imagination—of the cruder sex." When Hannah just looked at her
dumbly, she explained, "The males of our species."

"Gentlemen?"

"They are not all gentlemen."

"I see."

"Just as females are not all ladies."

Hannah couldn't help but say, "I think when we get to
Paris such an underskirt will be fine."

To this, however, the older woman let out a yelping
snicker. "Yes, if you're going to dance on the tabletops at
the Moulin Rouge."

Hannah felt herself color slightly. The poster that Edward
Stanton had showed her, in which a woman had on a

petticoat very much like her own, had been from a place of exactly this name, though Hannah was not sure entirely what the Moulin Rouge was. A place to dance, she thought, which seemed entirely proper to her. Yet, she knew somehow she was missing something. . . .

Mrs. Besom looked off, turning the back of her head to Hannah. Hannah stared into the spot where her face had been, at the back and crown of her hat. It was some hat. Its veil was made of dotted silk bobbinet that lay in voluminous, diaphanous, charcoal gray folds over greenish gray felt. The crown of the hat was banded in dark, moss green faille, the brim mounded with silk, salmon pink roses. This morning, when Hannah had taken the hat out of its box, its feel, the lightness and softness of it, had been astounding. It was made of the best felt, sheared beaver, the thick, silky undercoat of a winter animal, as light as down. Hannah stared at the back of the brim where the flowers lay against the faille band—the band was pleated, part of the myriad muted details beneath the dotted tulle, the dots themselves actually tiny octagons of hard-spun silk.

Hannah admired the hat. Just as, oddly—perversely, she thought at times—she admired the woman who wore it. There was not one speck, one hint, one moment in Mrs. Besom of anything even remotely vulgar. Amelia Besom, grande dame and daughter of New York society, gave new meaning to the word "class."

Hannah bunched a fistful of her own skirts a moment. She wasn't certain a noisy petticoat could make someone vulgar, any more than she was sure that a wonderful hat could make a person admirably refined. Still, she wondered, could Edward Stanton and his friends have been just a little more, well, banal than she'd imagined? Or worse, did the fact that she liked her own petticoat, the shush and swoosh of it, make her vulgar somewhere at her core? Hannah felt her throat clutch for a second as her new self—this new person of taste, intelligence, and perfect composure who wanted to promenade down the boulevards of Paris—seemed to waver, becoming nothing more than her old self dressed up

in new clothes. She feared she was somehow irreversibly
common, vulgar; second-rate. She would have worried
further, but her focus was demanded elsewhere as Mrs.
Besom spoke to her.

"Stop squirming."

"What?"

"I don't know how you can fidget so, even in a moving
carriage."

Hannah realized one of her hands restlessly clutched and
unclutched her dress, while her other clung to the lip of the
carriage door. "Yes, madam," she answered. She tried to
relax into the swaying movement of the calèche.

Mrs. Besom launched into the next topic. "The château is
of course likely to be less glorious than Monsieur de Saint
Vallier says— Are you paying attention, Miss Van Evan?"

"Yes, madam."

"As I was saying, the French are given to exaggeration.
The truth is, France has hundreds of old castles, all filled
with mounds of old gilt furniture, walls of weavings and
paintings, most imitative of masterworks without ever
measuring up to them—except in the way that age, equally
and democratically, has brought decrepitude to all of them.
Merely being old, you realize, hardly makes something
wonderful. . . ."

Yes, indeed. Hannah's mood became subdued as the
woman rattled on.

The road turned again, narrowing, the boughs of trees
folding into each other overhead till the roadway became a
kind of tunnel and the leaves above became a deep, vaulted
ceiling. It was at the end of this, in an open square of
sunlight, that Hannah caught her first glimpse of the
Château d'Aubrignon.

It appeared in the opening of the trees, a composition of
rose-colored bricks interspersed with quoined geometric
patterns of white eggstone, the whole perspective peering
from behind a bramble garden that rose in front of the
building. Hannah's preoccupied glance became full interest.
As the carriage proceeded, the brick walls rose upward

into three stories of high French windows topped off by a steep mansard roof. Then this was revealed to be only a front building when a skyline opened up to what appeared to be hundreds of chimneys. There, ahead of her in the widening aperture, Hannah watched the amazing place expand, bend, turn. At every corner was a tower, a turret, its conic rooftop worked in patterns of slate and topped off with a finial. And there were many bends and corners. The place went on and on in several directions, intersecting with itself over and over like a game of dominoes.

The carriage clopped out of the avenue of trees, then turned, trotting along the length of the facade. There was a chapel off to the side, spires, stained-glass windows. It was like a small cathedral. Behind this, the backlands of the old château were built on a series of terracing perspectives that looked down on the river, the back of the château proper crowned by a huge and ceremonious cupola, its oval dome made of what looked like peeling, bubbling gold. The whole was at once majestic and ramshackle. Everywhere, Hannah realized, the place was run-down, overrun.

As they rode closer to the main building she could see that many of its tall windows were missing panes; the roof was missing tiles. Meanwhile the carriage bumped over potholed cobblestones, along parterred shrubbery beds gone wild, the fountains and reflecting pools gone to wheat, the weeds and brambles so high as to cover the shoulders of eroding statues.

The carriage passed by huge, heavy front doors—one appeared to be off its hinge—and continued around under an arch into the interior of the maze. There, finally, in a small, high-walled courtyard, the vehicle stopped. Hannah stood up immediately in the carriage, amazed. Here was a completely different style of architecture. Hannah looked up at three half-timbered stories to a thatched roof. The courtyard itself was small, its straight-wall perimeter at least fifty feet high, these stone walls lending an echo to the serene silence of arrival.

The shifting of the horse's hooves, the driver's feet on the gravel, the creaking springs as he helped Mrs. Besom down, and, from above, the song from an unfamiliar bird— Hannah listened to these sounds as they reverberated off the walls. She located the bird. It sat way up in an opening on the far wall, in what appeared to have been a lookout along an old sentry walk.

"Vikings," Mrs. Besom said from the ground as she looked up at Hannah.

"Pardon?"

Hannah's voice, and Mrs. Besom's, chattered and ricocheted in the tiny canyon of the courtyard.

"The Vikings settled Normandy," Mrs. Besom said. "You are looking at an architecture borrowed from carpenters and shipbuilders, a way of building that pirates designed. A little barbaric, isn't it?"

Barbaric? If so, Hannah didn't mind. She liked the duality, the surprise of country rustic being obverse face to classical baroque.

This pleasant moment dissolved into sudden fluster, however, as Hannah descended the carriage. Vikings indeed. The high stone walls multiplied the rustle of one small, stiff petticoat into an echo that rose like Valkyries ascending with their clamoring souls into the skies of Valhalla.

Inside, the driver murmured something in French about fetching their host. He indicated an office in one direction as he tapped off into another, into the nether reaches of what was a monstrous place. Hannah and Mrs. Besom were left at the doorway to a huge kitchen, as large as the main dining room of the Royal Palm Hotel in Miami.

It smelled dank. The walls—dear goodness, the walls!— were at least six feet of solid stone. Hannah followed Mrs. Besom into the long kitchen that appeared to be in the midst of an orderly cleaning. There was no one about, but pots and pans sat on the floor. Ladders overhead indicated a twenty-foot iron pot rack, hanging catawampus, was being remounted to the ceiling. Someone had half swept out a large fireplace; a chimney brush stood canted against the mantel.

In addition to this fireplace, there was another one that fed an oven—three separate cooking fireplaces in all, plus a wood-burning stove.

The mammoth kitchen led into a commensurately large scullery with a wall of sinks and drain boards under a window that opened through to the kitchen. Beyond this was a huge wet laundry. With all this space given over to service, Hannah could hardly wait to see the rest of the place.

Edward should see this, she thought. Or Sara Bartlett, the girl Edward Stanton would probably eventually marry. Silly thoughts to remember, she knew, but she couldn't help it. Edward and his friends were her reference points for anything even remotely like this castle. They had all enjoyed impressing her with their talk of their travels in Europe.

"Hannah? Are you coming?"

"Yes, madam." Hannah had to run to catch up with Mrs. Besom.

In the wet laundry there were a dozen deep washtubs, each with an ornate brass tap—a pheasant, a swan, a peacock. Brass birds would have opened the tap valves to water, had there been water. The sinks were dry as dust. Several were off their brackets at the wall, their plumbing broken.

"The place is a disaster, isn't it?" Hannah commented. No one in Miami had ever mentioned to her that a huge old wonder of a castle could also be a huge old mess. It didn't seem quite real, as if this place were some preposterously enormous stage set.

"Yes, a nightmare," Mrs. Besom said from behind. "Though there are a few nice things to be salvaged. I could sell the set of brass plumbing birds for a tidy bit. Not museum quality, of course, but antique and sure to please someone in Newport or the Berkshires building their little dream bungalow. And Monsieur de Saint Vallier mentioned paintings, several Monets he doesn't care for. Not worth so much as the work of a dead painter, mind you, but still the estate is probably worth a day or two's inventory."

Off the wet laundry the women found what they had been looking for: a bright, airy room had been made over into an office. It was small, perhaps once a backdoor mud vestibule. But in contradiction to the rest of what the ladies had walked through, it seemed to be in good repair. Its windows were open, every pane in place and clean. Simple, fresh curtains fluttered inward on a breeze, lightly folding round a lamp on a desk, where a fountain pen lay in the binding groove of an open ledger book.

Through French doors that gave out onto a terrace, Hannah caught sight of a man coming up the slope, his head then shoulders rising into view as he plodded, his arms full, up an embankment of overgrown grass and snarled bushes.

Mrs. Besom, beside Hannah, smiled. "Monsieur de Saint Vallier," she said.

The man who entered the little room was broad-shouldered and barrel-chested, a slightly burly man with intense, preoccupied eyes in a deep-jawed face. He had a thick, dark moustache, which like his clothes lent him a formal air, more conservative than stylish. Had his face held a hint of humor, he would have been a handsome man. As it was, he looked severe, sharp-edged, a man one wouldn't want to cross.

He came in, maneuvering two large trays and making apologies. "Oh, I say—I'm so terribly sorry for this less than gracious welcome." His English was startlingly good. He sounded exactly like all the Englishmen Hannah had just left across the channel. "Everyone has gone home for lunch," he explained, "and won't be back for another hour."

Not quite everyone, it seemed: The two trays he set down contained the remains of two lunches, presumably his and someone else's.

He came forward to greet Amelia Besom. *"Chère madame,"* he said, taking her hand and kissing her fingertips. It was one of those silly, Continental gestures that Hannah had always found artificial, though this man seemed somehow to carry it off with aplomb.

Mrs. Besom made introductions, then got right down to business. "Where are those Monets you wrote about?"

He smiled, pleased. "This way." And they were off, with Hannah trailing behind them.

Monsieur de Saint Vallier and Mrs. Besom both walked with purposeful, long-legged strides, so that Hannah found herself having to trot to keep up—her damned underskirt making a ruckus as she did.

As they made their way toward an upstairs *petit salon,* each new vista made Hannah stifle laments of "Oh" and "Oh, no." In a library it seemed that someone had actually taken an ax to the furniture. In another room the draperies were riddled with moth holes and drooping on their supports where weight and time were pulling them from the wall. In a ballroom cherubs flew over huge, dusty chandeliers in ceiling firmaments turned green by the gas jets. Age, insects, misuse, and vandals. The havoc of these was mind-boggling.

Yet the grandeur of such ghostly beauty beneath the disrepair was eerie. Light flooded each room despite the dinginess of the glass in the long, paned windows. Hannah marveled at the orchestra balcony of the ballroom. It sloped slightly, like a ship just beginning to capsize, yet what remained intact floated *sans souci* above the dance floor, light and airy, its scrolling balusters delicately detailed in gold. Hannah found the scope of both—the beauty and the devastation—almost impossible to absorb.

Mrs. Besom, on the other hand, not only could absorb it, she could envision dismantling it, selling it, boxing it, and shipping it across an ocean.

"Would you be interested in lifting up the *boiserie*?" she said as she tapped on a wall panel. "I know a man in Paris who can get these up perfectly, and this is authentic Louis Quinze paneling, if I am not mistaken. It would net you a pretty penny."

Monsieur de Saint Vallier laughed and waved his hand. "No, no, we are not touching the walls except to repair or clean them."

"A fireplace here or there then, perhaps?" she continued. "They usually break down fairly easily into three pieces, and I know of half a dozen people in the States who would pay to add such details to their homes."

"No, no, madame, I do not wish to sell anything integral to the château or its character." Monsieur de Saint Vallier was firm but polite. "I don't even wish to sell some of the more easily removed fixtures. I am trying to renovate the structure, not destroy it." When Mrs. Besom responded with a peevish snort, he added, "Don't worry, *chère madame*. I told you the place is rich as a king's larder, and I will pay you well simply to help me assess its contents. You can sell some things. The Monets we are about to see. A few other items. Two hand-painted folding screens, Louis Quinze chinoiserie—I am very curious to know what you think of them."

The Monets were in a room that had been converted over into storage. They sat on the floor facing the light, three in all, each one leaning against a large wooden crate. Before Monsieur de Saint Vallier could say anything about them, however, a voice from somewhere in the rooms behind them interrupted. Someone was calling him from the direction in which they had come.

"Par ici," he called back. *"Dans le petit salon."*

After another exchange of soundings, a very large man in a bowler hat came through the far doorway. He spoke English with a heavy accent. German or Dutch; he was not French.

"I go down to relieve Hans. I left Werner at the café over a strudel and cream. He will be here shortly."

"Very good. Tell Hans and Stefan to come see me before they go to lunch."

"Ja. I will do this." The man went out through the room then a moment later could be seen outside disappearing down the terrace steps—steps that ran across the entire back of this wing.

Mrs. Besom asked the question in Hannah's mind. "Who

was that?" The man was not a workman, though he was burly.

The Frenchman waved his hand nonchalantly. "A guard."

"Does the château have trouble, then, with thieves and vandals?" Hannah asked.

"Oh, no." He seemed surprised by this question. "Aubrignon is a quiet, country village. We have no trouble. And the estate is so remote that even the local villagers seldom stray here." He looked over Hannah's head. "Have you looked at the paintings?"

"Yes. They're wonderful," Mrs. Besom said from behind Hannah.

Then Monsieur de Saint Vallier was flustered. "No, no." He went around Hannah, toward the pictures and Mrs. Besom. "These are not the Monets."

A little huffily she said, "I can see that."

She was stooped over a painting, her pince-nez lifted to her eyes as she carefully examined it, then glanced up at him, making a tight little smile. "If I didn't know better, monsieur, I would think you had hauled me all the way here to show me a few baubles while hiding treasure up your sleeve, treasure you are not even sure you wish to show me, let alone sell. You have a Rembrandt sitting over there."

The man laughed, partly embarrassed, partly delighted to be found out. "Yes, it's wonderful, isn't it? But it is the only one here, so far as I know, and we do not wish to part with it." He smiled most charmingly. "And I assure you, madame, that I intend for you to see—and price—everything. And for you to sell at least several dozen pieces. You will not be disappointed."

They looked at the Monets, three small pictures with so much light captured in their paints that sun seemed to shine on them even among the shadows of crates in an over-stacked storage room. Hannah could barely take her eyes off them, while the other two people talked strictly of what they were worth, whether they were auctionable or only fit for private offering.

Rembrandts, Monets. Hannah's ears buzzed with the

names, her eyes glued to the canvases. These three small oil
paintings were extraordinarily beautiful and obviously of
local landscape—one even featured the Château d'Aubrignon in an upper corner. The estate looked to be the size of
half of Dade County back home. *I wish they could see this,*
she thought, again remembering Edward Stanton and his
friends. *It's not at all like they said.* She reconsidered. *Or at
least not at all like I imagined. Reality is so much more
grand*—she looked around her—*and so much more awful.*

Beside her, Mrs. Besom and Monsieur de Saint Vallier
came to a decision. Private offering: the Monets were
judged not to be major enough works to bring the necessary
bidding at the big auction houses in London, Paris, and New
York. This done, Monsieur de Saint Vallier dropped the
protective covers back over the pictures.

He led the ladies around to some boxes and crates in a
corner, "only a few of many that I have not had time so
much as to open." Depending on the nature of their
contents, he said, he might or might not be willing to sell
what was in them. The ladies were invited to look through
these, if they would like to, during the course of the
weekend.

Monsieur de Saint Vallier began to outline his hospitality.
"I have had two rooms made up for you upstairs. The baker
brings fresh bread in the morning. One of the daily women
makes coffee," Monsieur de Saint Vallier said. "For lunch
and dinner, I have added your names to the list for meals to
be brought in. There is a good chef at La Normande, a local
inn. He works for us, helping with the restoration design of
the kitchen, while also cooking the main meals and sending
them over. . . ."

Hannah lost track of the details as she found a good view,
through a smudged window, out over the back estate. Below
the terrace, a long-running, faintly geometric bramble garden stretched out into lost perspectives and ruined sight
lines. It encompassed a canal and what would have fed the
reflection pools and defunct fountains, the sum of which
foretold of failed hydraulics on a grand scale. Nonetheless,

it was lovely, green, and inviting. Spreading out from this center of civilized decay lay weeds and grass gone wild and thickets that ended down a slope in trees. Off to one side were a few outbuildings. In the other direction the trees tightened into copses then a woods. Below this, at the horizon, one could see a bend in the Seine River, a glimmer of water, a glimpse of cliffs and clifftop pastures running up to the edges of orchards and farms in the distance. A domain as pretty as a Monet painting, only as large—and explorable—as all outdoors.

Hannah stared at the Seine in the far distance. "It looks beautiful." Below, she caught sight of an overgrown path that seemed to skirt the worst of the brambles. "Would I be allowed to wander the grounds?" she asked. Then she caught a glimpse of color, a trace of reddish russet showing through the dense green of trees where the path plunged into the thick of the woods. The terra-cotta of a simple rooftop, a thin wisp of smoke rising from its chimney. "See? Where that cottage is. I could walk along—"

"You can't walk there."

She looked over her shoulder at the Frenchman, at this blunt answer.

His face was stoic, his mouth pulled taut. "I'm sorry." He put a smile on his face, as if having to will a pleasant expression back into his features. Then he raised his eyes to include Mrs. Besom. "You cannot go near that cottage." He tempered the peremptory tone of his remark with, "Though I have no objections to your walking elsewhere."

"What's down there?" Mrs. Besom asked. She came up behind Hannah now, curious too, looking out the window.

Monsieur de Saint Vallier hesitated before he answered. "The old gamekeeper's cottage. My brother lives there." Somewhat severely he pronounced, "He must not be disturbed." The silence that followed was imbued with the sort of embarrassment reserved for misfits: the dim-witted, the disfigured, the family idiot. There was something wrong with his brother.

Hannah was sorry she'd asked.

Mrs. Besom responded similarly. "Of course. It's not a problem. We won't disturb him."

It took several moments for Monsieur de Saint Vallier to smile again, to regain his proud, expectant mood. Then he said, "I think you will find this old place a jewel—more a treasure chest than you can even imagine at this moment." With a broad gesture he indicated the room and, by extension, the whole complex, rambling, unpredictable set of buildings. "Mesdames, I hope you will agree by tomorrow that you stand in the midst of a most amazing—and profitable—project, so that in the morning we can discuss your schedule or commissions and fees." He bowed slightly, then his courtly retreat was interrupted.

Outside on the terrace, a floor below, a man's voice called up to him. "Monsieur de Saint Vallier!"

The Frenchman went swiftly over to open the window. He called down, "I'm here. What do you need?" With an edge in his voice he added, "Did you leave him alone down there with only Emil?"

"*Ja,* for a moment only. Can you come down immediately? Emil wants you to—" From below, the man perceived Hannah as she opened an adjacent window. He censored himself. "To see something."

Hannah looked down at him. This man, like the one before him, was huge. His coat didn't properly accommodate his shoulders, pulling in a way that said he was more muscular than any tailor could imagine. He was dressed all in brown, with a dark brown moustache, a walrus dressed in a bowler and frock coat.

De Saint Vallier didn't hesitate. "Excuse me," he said, turning to the women. "Until dinner, then." With no further words, he walked out, his footsteps tapping down the stairs.

The ladies watched through the open window as he appeared on the terrace, then, along with the new man, disappeared into the weeds and wild grass that sloped toward the river.

Hannah turned and looked around the room again. "Well," she said, "this is quite some place, isn't it?"

Mrs. Besom did not seem to share her good humor. "Crafty old devil," she muttered.

Hannah looked at the woman. Mrs. Besom had folded her arms across her chest, letting her disgruntlement now show in all its peevish glory. "He's not going to let me have a thing that is really valuable. I could kick him."

After a few moments of bristling silence she turned again to survey the roomful of crates and boxes. "His uncle did this, you know. I'll bet that Rembrandt is only the tip of the iceberg. The statue in the far crate is about three hundred years old, an Italian piece. His uncle was a real collector, now that I remember, though I had no idea of the extent. . . ." She let a few seconds tick by, then continued. "I sold him a pair of Foo dogs myself once. Years ago, of course. Huge things. Jade, exquisite. He had quite an eye, old Pascal de Saint Vallier. Though he was a lunatic—the uncle, that is. As dotty as a hatter."

Mrs. Besom shrugged then walked over and peered under the cover of the small Dutch painting that was being withheld from her. She sighed. "It would be a coup just to handle such a sale." In disgust, she dropped the oilcloth. "Not that it matters. Sébastien has long wanted to rebuild this stupid old castle, and rumor has it he has at last found the money. It seems his family is about to marry into a fortune."

Hannah's eyes lifted from the crates. She could understand why someone might want to bring this place back, if it were possible. This room, like the others, beneath the rubble possessed an unearthly beauty that one hated to think of as past and gone. The magnificence of it would be worth resurrecting.

She gave a humorless laugh. "Well, I don't know much about fortunes, but it seems this huge old place might exhaust one or two in the repair of it."

This remark was met with silence—as Hannah followed a watermark on the wall backward and up from whence it had come, until she was staring up at a patch of gesso thirty feet overhead. Plaster that had once been a raised, molded pattern on the ceiling had been softened by a leak from above. Water stained a wide area. It had made a nine-foot-square patch swell, buckle, peel, then mildew. One touch, if one could have reached thirty feet, and it would no doubt have fallen in a powder, as delicate as ash on a burnt cigar.

Hannah looked back to Mrs. Besom. "Are you all right?" she asked. It all really was such a sad sight, the antithesis of all Mrs. Besom appreciated.

Blinking, the woman broke her silence with a sound that might have been called an ecstatic sigh. As her eyes met Hannah's Hannah was surprised by the glow on her face. Mrs. Besom's expression was radiant, almost epiphanous: the beatific look of Bernadette having just seen Our Lady in the caves at Lourdes.

"Oh, Miss Van Evan," she said, her voice low with rapture. Her rheumy eyes sparkled. "You are absolutely right. Poor, dear Sébastien. I don't think he has looked all the hard, cold facts in the face yet. This place is a disaster. Worse than a disaster." In whispered reverence she spoke her words of revelation. "This place would take a *dozen* fortunes to restore it. *No one* has this kind of money."

Unless of course he possessed a few Rembrandts to sell.

Chapter 4

Miami, December 28, 1902
The young Mr. Stanton has come home from
college. He does not mean to go back. Today (I
think to spite his parents with whom he is
arguing) he took me out sailing. As we floated
along he talked and talked, about everything,
about life; I listened raptly.

I like young men who don't say "ain't" and
"she done it" and can talk about something
besides the night cutworms came from nowhere
to eat up a crop of tomatoes. I like men who are
as sleek and neat as sailboats, whose buckles
and shoestrings are as shiny and unfrayed as
new fittings, their clothes as white as new sails,
who say things that glide along my mind as
smooth and pretty as Edward's daddy's boat
cutting across the water—after we got out a
ways from the shore, he said I should call him
Edward, which was surprisingly easy to do,
especially after he kissed me.
—from the diary of Miss Sue-Hannah Van Evan

HANNAH SAT IN a dusty, spiderwebbed parlor-salon, label-
ing pieces and writing entries down in a notebook as Amelia
Besom, beside her, dictated. *Item eleven, one three-masted*

sailing ship, three feet tall, made of crystal; Baccarat. About twenty years old, if memory serves properly. Valuable, but not preciously so. Write to Monsieur Belmont in Paris asking how many were made and if the mold still exists. Item twelve . . . In this manner Mrs. Besom and she were randomly going through crates and pasteboard boxes in a room that was otherwise empty, except for a few pieces of furniture with sheets thrown over them.

Hannah tagged and listed objects as Mrs. Besom pronounced on their value. Sitting now in the midst of open boxes, sealed boxes, tagged items, and discards, the women worked together quietly, a sense of mild excitement alive in the little spirals of dust that rose up around them from their activity. In addition to the crystal ship, they had brought forth from the boxes around them an even dozen of salable items, including a small porcelain vase, Ming dynasty. The vase now sat out and away from the rest on a make-do shelf made of wood planks set across two sawhorses. Hannah glanced up at the vase now and then, at the delicacy of hand-painted aquatic birds sitting so incongruously on the crude timber. The birds were minutely painted, elegant, perfect, with a hint of sly humor; so interesting to behold that Hannah's heart had caught in her throat as she had watched Mrs. Besom unwrap the vase then turn it slowly around in her fingertips. Hannah had known before her employer had pronounced: "A treasure, Miss Van Evan. We have found our own precious object, the sale of which I hope we shall be allowed to arrange this time." The vase was marked in the notebook as being about five hundred years old, in perfect condition, museum quality, value unknown, "though the auction floor should begin upward from a hundred thousand francs." This calculated to about nineteen thousand dollars.

For one small vase. Hannah was mesmerized.

This discovery had been two boxes ago. Since then, Hannah had found herself humming once or twice as she wrote down entries. ("Miss Van Evan, is that you making that mumbly noise? Will you please be quiet?") Now she was quiet, but the pleasure she felt in being part of this enterprise was irrepressible. Across from her, Mrs. Besom had grown pensive. The unboxing of the last few wonders, especially the Ming vase, seemed to have changed her attitude. Such beauty—brought forth as if by magic from a growing mound of junk so worthless that Monsieur de Saint Vallier was going to have to pay someone to haul it off the premises—held out immeasurable promise. Hannah and Mrs. Besom had slowed their progress, each new crate, new box, filled now with, if nothing else, rapt expectation.

"This is a bit like an Easter egg hunt, isn't it?" Hannah murmured, then instantly regretted voicing this silly thought. It was such a simplistic comparison. It spoke of how spare her life had been thus far, that Easter egg hunting was the closest thing she had experienced to the reward and expectancy of this substantial, high-priced undertaking.

But Mrs. Besom glanced over the top of the small crate she was working on and smiled. "Yes, an Easter egg hunt," she agreed. "Exactly. The same anxieties. Lifting, looking, while possibly overlooking. Then finding and marveling." Her smile was benign, the look of a woman thoroughly absorbed and enjoying herself. "Going through old estates like this always makes me feel like a child. How I suffer—from fear I will miss something someone else will find tomorrow—and how I relish going through them anyway."

Hannah was surprised to hear her comparison treated so seriously and generating such a sincere response. She basked for a moment in the simple communion of shared emotion, agreement.

With her forearm Mrs. Besom pushed hair from her eyes. Strands had come down in places through the course of the afternoon. She had a cobweb on her elbow. She grinned at Hannah and pointed.

"Look at you," Mrs. Besom said. "Where you've leaned to cut the tops of the boxes, you've made the sleeves of your jacket white with"—she made a face—"mildew or something."

Hannah lifted her elbow up to look at the back of her sleeve.

Mrs. Besom laughed out loud at this gesture. "Now you're getting it in your hair."

Hannah stared over the top of her elbow at the woman sitting across from her on the floor. Hannah had never heard her laugh. Not in more than four weeks of working for her. The laughter was dry, deep in the woman's chest, rickety, as if coming from someplace rusty.

Hannah wiped at the dust in her hair, her hand coming away with something in it that was tacky and gritty. Where she looked, the dark sleeve of her jacket had the powdery-gray print of her forearm. Hannah laughed, too. "One would think I were important for all this dirt. Like the fly that sits on the chariot axle: 'My, what a dust I do raise!'"

Mrs. Besom laughed again her abrupt, ragged laughter, looking at Hannah in wonder. "Why, Miss Van Evan, that's Carlyle you're paraphrasing."

"Is it?" Edward Stanton had studied the writings of Thomas Carlyle at Harvard.

"Yes, mixed with Aesop, I think, from 'On Boswell's *Life of Johnson.*'" Her laughter ended, however, a moment later. She frowned slightly, an expression akin to the one she'd worn earlier in the carriage: wary appreciation of a dollar prize purchased for a penny.

Hannah grew silent, picking up her tablet again, and turned to a fresh page, though there was nothing to write down.

Mrs. Besom slid a new box around in front of herself and began once more to forage. As she bent over the box she asked, "How did you end up in Miami, Miss Van Evan?"

"I was born there."

"Of parents who insisted on such accomplishments as the reading of British scholars?"

Hannah didn't know whether to be wary or flattered by this interest. "My father was a pharmacist."

"Where is this pharmacist?" Mrs. Besom moved and

shuffled things around in the box, pulling out a handful of books. She thumbed through these. "Do you have a mother?"

"Both dead."

"I'm sorry." Of the books she said, "These are badly foxed." She tossed them into a crate of rejects, then paused to look at Hannah. "So how do you know about Carlyle?"

Hannah's pen touched her notebook in the margin of the new page. "Friends." She made a doodle.

"Friends?" Mrs. Besom repeated dubiously. She braced her forearms on the box corners and studied Hannah. "You know, Miss Van Evan, you are most mysterious. You speak only vaguely about your past—not that I blame you, from what little I know of it. But you realize, my dear, all these hedges and silence only pique a person's curiosity."

Hannah wondered if the woman were right, if her own evasions were making the simple facts into more than they were. "If you're interested," she tried to say nonchalantly, "in Miami I kept house for the Stantons. Mr. Stanton is the U.S.—"

Mrs. Besom frowned and sat up straighter. "I am perfectly well informed as to whom Mr. and Mrs. Felix Stanton are."

She took her arms off the box edge, glancing at Hannah, a momentary glare of indecipherable ill humor. Then she scooted herself around, stood onto her knees, and bent all the way over into the box in front of her. She rummaged through this, making things clank at the bottom as if there were nothing but broken pottery. "So," came her voice from within the muffling pasteboard, "Felix and Mildred Stanton, these are the people you worked for?"

Hannah stared at Mrs. Besom's bottom raised there in the air like an upended kettle drum. It didn't take a genius to realize that the candor the woman had encouraged—wanted, fished for, and dallied about having for four weeks—was now being greeted with something less than enthusiasm. "Yes, madam."

"I'm surprised that you have never traveled abroad, then."

"I took care of their home in Miami year-round. Myself and an elderly couple who, when the Stantons were there, served as their cook and coachman. I wasn't part of the staff that traveled with them."

"Mm, yes, of course. Well." The woman came up, red-faced. Her hands held nothing, her tight, forced little smile everything. "Isn't that nice."

No, it wasn't nice. Clearly. Not to Mrs. Besom. She tossed pieces of something into the closest junk crate, something broken tossed a shard at a time. *Clank. Clank. Clank, clank.* While in glances over her shoulder, over this busyness, her eyes worried over Hannah—a glimpsing, piecemeal scrutiny that seemed based in puzzlement. The woman knew the Stantons. Or of them. Of course she would, Hannah realized. The Stantons were well-known people, famously respected and of Amelia Besom's social stratum. Mrs. Besom's darting looks and genial words reflected the conflict of someone asking herself why *she* should be happy with a girl that an admirable first family of the nation had rejected outright.

Mrs. Besom stopped to look at Hannah squarely. "Why were you dismissed?" The question had taken on new importance. The woman would not be outdone, outmaneuvered— outfired—by possibly more knowledgeable, more clever competitors.

Hannah understood she must lay out at least a part of her sordid little story. "The Stantons let me go," she began, "because I caused a problem." She fiddled with her pen, drawing doodling circles. "You see—" How did one present this in a good light? "Two young men one evening— Well, they ended up tearing into each other over me while tearing up the Stantons' front lawn and shrubbery in the bargain."

Amelia Besom sat back onto her calves, her small, glaucous eyes wide open. "You mean to tell me they fired you because two ill-bred young scoundrels—"

"Actually they fired me because one of those 'ill-bred young scoundrels' was their son, Edward. He wanted me to marry him."

Mrs. Besom looked dumbfounded. "Edward Stanton asked you to marry him?"

Hannah was afraid for a moment that the woman didn't believe her. "Yes, ma'am—I mean, madam."

"Well." Mrs. Besom seemed at a loss for words. She said finally, "That at least explains why Mr. and Mrs. Stanton were so put out with you."

Did it? Oh, good. Hannah was relieved; she needn't say more.

Mrs. Besom continued, "They would have more ambitious plans for their son than his marrying . . . well, the housekeeper."

Yes, it sounded so simple when put this way: true love run amok in the bog of class distinctions and highbrow snobbery.

Except, of course, Edward Stanton had not been true love.

Mrs. Besom's expression bent into a little smile. She tilted her head, as if seeing Hannah for the first time. "So they prevented you from marrying their son and fired you without references for good measure. How ghastly."

Hannah felt a little uncomfortable. "I—ah, I prevented myself from marrying him."

Even more astounded, the woman said, "You told him no?"

Hannah laughed self-consciously. "Oh, I definitely said no. A dozen times. He was very persistent."

Mrs. Besom sat there, so obviously struck with wonder that Hannah could not help but glow a little. She had been struck with wonder herself. That someone like Edward would ask her to be his wife. That he would pursue her so hotly, in front of all his friends, despite his parents' protests. Hannah had liked this so well, in fact, she had allowed herself to think she could indulge a little, that she could talk to him, walk with him, go with him dancing, sailing, could eat with him at a restaurant, could visit an art gallery with him, without putting her job in jeopardy. It had seemed so harmless in the beginning.

Mrs. Besom was puzzled. "So they fired you because you *wouldn't* marry him?"

"They fired me for a host of reasons. Because Edward wouldn't listen. Because everything got so complicated. Because, in tearing up the garden, the other young man broke Edward's arm. And because Edward remained throughout all of this so staggeringly dense." Hannah shook her head, remembering. "At one point his parents said they would cut him off without a penny if he married me, and he said, 'So what? It's not as if Hannah would need a housekeeper.' It was so incredibly insensitive; it really set them off. It set me off, too. I think he meant it to sound loyal and brave and maybe even romantic. But all I could think was, 'Well, how cheap. He wants to move out and prove he doesn't need Papa's money, so he's going to marry someone who'll make his bed for free.' After that I went with Michael O'Hare to a dance at the Royal Poinciana in Palm Beach. Michael was Edward's best friend and a bit of a blowhard. I knew Edward would find out I'd gone. Only Edward found out a bit too soon. He was waiting for us. When Michael brought me home, Edward punched him in the nose."

"Oh, dear. How awful for you."

Hannah looked around at Mrs. Besom, amazed. She should not have rambled so, yet here she was, after telling her albeit somewhat refined and edited version, staring oh-so-unexpectedly into the face of someone—the most unlikely of someones—who seemed to be on her side. Mrs. Besom's expression wanted to believe the best of Hannah and the situation, and this view of Hannah, as a kind of heroine of the ordeal in Miami, was one that Hannah herself, she realized, was desperately trying to see.

"And how awful for the Stantons, of course," Mrs. Besom added.

There followed a strange minute, in which her sympathy faded in and out. It was vacillation, Hannah thought, that Mrs. Besom—they both—should have bridged into a new place, a rapport.

Yet they didn't.

Hannah sat there puzzled, wondering what she was doing wrong, then she realized: Amelia Besom had responded outside the social context, listening and speaking to Hannah as an equal, from the parallel of human experience. This had put her on unfamiliar ground.

The woman reached for what she knew solidly. "I can't fault the Stantons for dismissing you, of course." She drew herself up, as if she could wrap herself in the mantle of her fierce propriety. She had refound her allegiance, her place. And Hannah's. "It was the appropriate thing to do, from what you've told me. I might have done the same." She tried to soften this with, "It was nothing personal, you see."

"No, nothing personal." Hannah felt foolish for having said so much, idiotic for the instant of closeness she'd assumed.

"I might have handled it a bit—" Mrs. Besom left this open.

Hannah filled in for her, "Better."

The woman frowned, too cagey to agree with such flagrant patronizing—and too full of herself to dispute it. She said, "You simply couldn't stay there. Under the circumstances."

Which was true. "Of course," Hannah said.

Still Mrs. Besom wasn't comfortable. She frowned at Hannah a moment longer, the way someone might at a backward child, someone she didn't know what to do with or how to respond to. Her unbroken, puzzled stare made Hannah feel . . . wrong, bizarre. Someone hopelessly out of step. Awkward. Impossible to place. The pharmacist's daughter with too much backdoor acquired knowledge, who with this—a sharp mind, a pretty face, and fancy ambitions— had mustered for herself in Miami all the social éclat of Hester Prynne.

Before the woman could say anything more, Hannah asked her, "Are you hungry?"

It was getting late. The room was aglow with predusk brightness, the low sun shining in.

Mrs. Besom blinked. "Why, ah—well, maybe yes."

Hannah was already coming to her feet. "I'll go down, then, and ask about dinner."

Hannah found the servants' stairs that went across the western length of the building and down into the wet laundry. At the landing, however, she stopped. The tall landing window gave onto a different view of the distant rooftop by the woods, the cottage that sheltered Monsieur de Saint Vallier's backward brother. Actually, from this angle she couldn't see the full rooftop, just the whole of its chimney emitting a steady breath of smoke. Hannah stood up on her tiptoes, moving her head from side to side, then ducked down to see if this angle did anything; she peered curiously now with no one to stop her. Poor soul, she thought. Out there alone, an outcast, no one but guards and a brother whom he embarrassed. He was probably monstrous to look at. Crippled, disabled. Maybe crazy to boot.

Then the sound of English turned her around and brought her down the last set of stairs. The door to Monsieur de Saint Vallier's office stood open, the low evening sun shining in directly, making the room golden. She stopped in the empty, unlit laundry room, able to see straight into the office and—unusual after a day spent in random contact with French workmen and cleaning women—able to understand every word.

"I am terribly sorry this is necessary. But of course you understand." Monsieur de Saint Vallier was apologizing to a small, neat man in a black frock coat who was being relieved of a black leather bag.

Monsieur de Saint Vallier set this onto his cluttered desk. "We go through everything," he assured the man as he opened the bag. "No matter who comes to see him. We simply cannot afford to be complacent. The baker took him bread last week, with twenty francs in his pocket." Monsieur de Saint Vallier shook his head as he lifted a biaural stethoscope. He turned the instrument over in his hand, then put it back into the bag. "People feel sorry for him," he continued. "For his downcast looks and doleful eyes. The

imbecile. Anyway, twenty francs was train fare and then
some. We couldn't find him for three days."

"*Ach nein,*" the man responded. "How very dangerous.
And what a fool the baker was, *ja*?" He spoke with a
German accent. "I only wish we could have kept him at the
institute. But he became simply more than we had the means
to handle, you understand?"

Monsieur de Saint Vallier's glance said he didn't understand, but he apparently wasn't willing to argue. Instead he
began a kind of running commentary of the satchel's
contents as he continued to unpack it. "No interesting
chemicals," he said, taking out a brown bottle of something
and setting it on the desk. "No telling what he will drink."
He brought out a scalpel—the visitor appeared to be a
doctor. "And of course nothing sharp. He gets very depressed. As well as getting a little abusive. He slammed
Emil's hand in the door today when they were arguing over
whether or not he could walk down by the river—no
walking by the river, of course, since he mentioned he might
throw himself into it—"

At that moment Monsieur de Saint Vallier looked past the
doctor through the doorway to see Hannah standing in
the shadows. He didn't take his eyes off her as he closed the
bag. "All right," he said to the man. "Hans is outside. He
will take you." The doctor picked up the bag and walked out
of Hannah's line of vision. She heard the door to the terrace
open then close.

"Yes, Miss Van Evan?" Monsieur de Saint Vallier was not
happy to see her. "What may I do for you? I'm very busy."

To disarm him, however, Hannah only needed to come
forward, her eyes itemizing: The desktop was strewn with
bottles, scalpels, a bleeding cup, a coil of rubber tubing, the
doctor's wallet, a leather card case, as well as a breathing
cup with a funnel attachment, the apparatus for administer-
ing ether.

It looked as though someone had emptied the cabinets of
her father's pharmacy right here onto the surface of Monsieur de Saint Vallier's desk.

He began to shake his head, as if he could minimize or deny these things that lay out plainly between them.

Hannah wouldn't let him. "What's wrong with your brother?" she asked.

"Nothing." He tried to wave it off.

She didn't move. "Why does he need a doctor?"

"Don't worry," he said. He chose to interpret her question to mean she was concerned for her own health. "It's not some deadly disease. In fact, he's not sick at all. Not really. He just has—" He made a face, a quick shrug combined with a snort. It was the sarcastic gesture, the guttural sound that distanced a person from something ugly. "He just has some oddities that require a doctor to closely watch his health. In fact, he's quite healthy." As if to explain the multiple and growing contradictions, he said, "He has a . . . condition."

"A condition," she repeated.

The card case on the table contained the doctor's business cards. Dr. Wilhelm Friedenmeyer of *Der Institut* of something or other. The card was in German. The address was *Zürich*, Switzerland. The family lunatic was apparently here fresh from an institution, where he had been thrown out, if she understood correctly, because they couldn't contain him. Hannah imagined the man down by the woods. Not just disfigured, but wild, half-witted. A grotesquery, restrained, bled, anesthetized, pondered over—and trying as best he could to catch a train out of here. She shivered.

"It's not what you think," Monsieur de Saint Vallier assured her.

She didn't believe him.

More emphatically, he said, "Well, it's a private matter. You must not go down there."

"I wouldn't."

"Good. Now, why are you here? And where is Mrs. Besom?"

She didn't blink. There was something about this man she didn't like, she decided. "Upstairs," she said. "I was sent to arrange for dinner."

* * *

Dinner would be another hour. Hannah went back upstairs to report this, then, sitting down again beside Mrs. Besom, picked up her notebook. Hannah had no sooner settled in, however, than Mrs. Besom stood up stiffly, saying she needed to stretch. She strolled about the room for a minute, then wandered into the next.

She and Hannah had walked through the room next door earlier but decided not to work in it, since workmen had then been in the process of bracing its ceiling with four-by-fours. A structural column had collapsed, taking part of the ceiling and an archway with it. When Hannah first heard Mrs. Besom calling—"Hannah! Oh, my Lord, Hannah! Oh, myGodmyGod . . ."—Hannah thought something might have fallen on the woman.

Hannah scrambled to her feet and rushed into the room, only to discover Mrs. Besom standing safely—dancing, in fact—before a painting that hung on the wall among a line of others, all of them unprotected.

"Hannah!" Mrs. Besom exclaimed again. "Look!"

Hannah. The woman was using her first name. Hannah didn't know what to say for a moment.

"It's a Goya!" Mrs. Besom exclaimed. "No, it's not just a Goya! Look!"

Hannah looked at a rather unprepossessing painting unscathed by the ruin around it except for having crescents of dust in the corners and an overall layer of soot. This whole end of the room, she realized, was covered with the black grime and charred markings of an old fire.

The best Hannah could say for the painting was that it was lucky. It didn't appear to be very old, only dirty. It was in surprisingly decent condition, the colors beneath the dust and dirt being pleasant, rich. Golden reds, greens, and browns. It was an elaborate scene of a party traveling with a caravan of elephants. The people in it were straining, their faces realistic, individual.

Meanwhile Mrs. Besom was beside herself. She continued excitedly, "Look, oh, look!"

Hannah did, but couldn't understand the woman's high agitation. Still, she felt her own blood quicken in response to Mrs. Besom, who had actually begun to tremble.

The woman took hold of Hannah's arm, grabbing for something stable. Her hand was clamplike, full of strength and cold as ice. Her face was flushed. Mrs. Besom wavered on her feet as she made an erratic gesture, again indicating the painting. "Look!"

"Yes, the signature does look like it belongs to Goya. And he is certainly one of the better-known Spanish painters." Hannah tried to calm her. "But this is nowhere near the Rembrandt surely. And the Monets—"

"Oh, you and Sébastien can sit on the Monets! If I want a Monet, I'll run over to Giverny and ask Claude to paint me one. *This* is *The Lost Hannibal*!"

"The what?" Hannah frowned into the painting again, looking now, trying to read from it why Mrs. Besom's— indeed her own—heart was picking up speed as from a kind of compression, like steam in a train engine.

"*The Lost Hannibal*! One of the last works of Francisco de Goya. People knew it existed but never knew where it had run off to. It has been lost to the art world for eighty years!"

"Eighty years," Hannah repeated. She began to smile, then when she looked at Mrs. Besom, couldn't help but smile wider. The woman was so happy.

Mrs. Besom laughed a full, joyous laugh that rattled its way out from someplace deep in her chest. "It is an incredible discovery. I can't tell you how wonderful!"

Hannah laughed, too. "Really?" She looked at the painting. Another find. A rarity. She laughed again.

"Yes, a truly spectacular find, and I have found it! Isn't it fantastic?"

"Yes, oh, yes!" Hannah felt light-headed looking at the painting, laughing, looking at Mrs. Besom. Another miracle! Something wonderful, extraordinary! She helped Mrs. Besom imagine out loud what all the world would say to this.

"Well, congratulations!" Hannah told her.

"Muños at the Prado in Madrid will be beside himself with jealousy."

"And your name will be in all the papers."

Joy spread into Amelia Besom's face. "Well, yes," she admitted, "it might be." She laughed. She hooted.

Then she took hold of Hannah and, as graceful as an ostrich, waltzed her out into the center of the room. One large woman, one short one—two mismatched birds, a tall ostrich dancing with a redpoll finch made dove-breasted in a health corset.

"Just look at this place! What an incredibly gorgeous disaster!" Mrs. Besom clomped Hannah around a hundred and eighty degrees, Hannah laughing. "He *has* to allow me to sell this or the Rembrandt or something. And there's more, Hannah. I'm sure of it!" She leaned back—Hannah embraced her to keep her from falling—and swung them around. "Look at all this glorious decay and destruction! This place is a gold mine!"

With no further preamble, Mrs. Besom threw her arms around her new little secretary and clasped her to her bosom. For a moment Hannah was engulfed by the mass of the woman's body, by the scent of lilac powder mingling with the charry-damp smells of spiders, dust, mildew, and soot. The bosoms of the two women—Mrs. Besom's low, sagging one and Hannah's copious, high one—met and held them apart a little but didn't prevent a full, gleeful hug.

Hannah felt the exact moment when Mrs. Besom realized what she had done. Her body stiffened. She took her arms away. "Well. How silly of me." She stepped back and brushed the front of her dress as if she had gotten something on it.

Hannah was left with her arms out, empty, her emotions hanging. The pleasure of finding the picture, seeing it, crowing over it, the shared thrill of momentous discovery seemed to have been cut out from under her. Not that this was completely unpredictable or unexplainable: If showing Hannah a little sympathy an hour ago had unsettled Mrs.

Besom, having hugged the girl had completely unraveled her.

The woman didn't know where to look, how to find her former dignity. After a moment she threw a frown at Hannah. "How did you know Goya was Spanish?" she asked.

"Pardon me?" Hannah was angry to have been taken in twice. Angry and wary.

Amelia Besom took a step back. The room grew silent, little tourbillions of dust settling in the wakes of the women's skirts, in the fading beams of sunlight.

Mrs. Besom asked again, "How did you know Goya was Spanish?"

Hannah blinked. "Isn't he?"

"Yes, but in my experience most pharmacists' daughters don't know he is. Is this more information gleaned in the employ of the famous Mr. and Mrs. Stanton? Or just a little something you picked up at that silly St. Something-or-other's School for Young Ladies?"

"St. Mary's. And neither. Some friends of mine took me to an exhibit in Palm Beach."

"More mysterious friends?" This time the way she said it was not kind or curious.

Irritated, Hannah lifted her chin. "Sara Bartlett and Michael O'Hare and, of course, Edward Stanton. Do you know these other names, too?"

"I know *of* them. They are all the children of rich society families who visit Miami."

"Just so."

"What were *you* doing with them?"

Hannah was tired of this. "Enjoying myself." A bit too defiantly she added, "Seeing an art exhibit, then dancing and buying a hat." And drinking champagne until she could barely stand up.

The look on Mrs. Besom's face said she was not deceived by Hannah's omission. Hannah felt her face color. She turned away, looking about the room rather than show the embarrassment that had risen, uncalled for, into her cheeks.

She felt as if the old woman could somehow see back three months into time—into the dark carriage in which she and Edward had returned home alone together to Miami.

Mrs. Besom spoke quietly, as if with genuine lament. "I don't know, Miss Van Evan," she said. "I truly don't know—"

Hannah looked back at her. "Mrs. Besom. You are happy with my work, work you are getting for eleven dollars a month—and work for which I would have been paid thirty a month in Palm Beach, if I had had what you seem to want me to have—the blessed credibility of an unblemished past." Hannah took a breath. *Don't be nervy,* she told herself. *Don't be pushy. You are on the wrong side of the ocean in a place where you don't even speak the language.* But she continued. "I can't help that I seem to know a bit more than you bargained for. I would *like* to be knowledgeable. I would *like* to be refined and cultured. I worked hard at St. Mary's trying to gain that, then found, as you yourself seem to have known already, that a local girls' school was not the place to acquire this.

"So, yes, I was delighted to find that Edward Stanton liked me. He took me places I couldn't go by myself—and not just literally. In my mind. He made me aware of new things. He talked about Europe, Europeans." She was saying too much, but she couldn't stop now. "Stupid things that made me curious or made me laugh. How wide and beautiful the boulevards of Paris were. How the French ate with their forks in the wrong hands." Hannah took another breath, on a roll now. "He introduced me to his friends. They had all been to places so far beyond Miami, places with castles and tapestries—"

"That is quite enough, Miss Van Evan."

Hannah stopped, swallowed.

Mrs. Besom stood rigid. "Yes, I can see clearly how you have thus far come by your knowledge of Europe. And I can just imagine what 'silly things' Mr. Stanton liked best to show you. From here on, I would prefer that you refrain from any further reference to what you learned from 'friends' in Miami, since I cannot be exactly certain of the extent or nature of said 'knowledge.' " She lent the word an edge of biblical wickedness.

"Mr. Stanton was perfectly nice—"

"The young Mr. Stanton is a nincompoop. Sara Bartlett is a spoiled brat and a floozy. And Michael O'Hare is the son of a furniture manufacturer, for goodness' sake. Don't talk to me of these young people or any other of your 'cultured' companions in Miami."

"Edward and Michael are refined gentlemen who—"

"Who know nothing. My dear Miss Van Evan, you are impressed with money, which any poor vulgar soul can get if he only works for it. Or, worse, inherits it. Edward Stanton, Michael O'Hare, and most of their peers so far as I have met, are bored, purposeless young people, who live off their families, without the first notion of independent thinking or an original thought in their heads. And you deceive yourself if you believe you were anything but pleasant holiday entertainment. How very wonderful for them to have had such a beautiful and rapt audience for all their perfectly mediocre little tourist experiences. Castles and tapestries, indeed. I imagine they all waxed poetic over such things as the Eiffel Tower—"

Hannah felt her eyes heat as a flush spread over her face.

Mrs. Besom gave a snort of impatience. "You were salve to their egos, my dear. Edward Stanton failed out of Harvard this last term."

"He told me—"

"I'm surprised he was that honest. But not surprised he felt more comfortable telling it to a pharmacist's daughter. You provided ego balm, and God knows what else, for what was no better than secondhand recountings of second-rate experiences. From the mouth of a young man whose idea of self-worth and interesting information combine in the profound cultural insight that the French hold their forks differently from Americans."

Mrs. Besom lifted a finger toward Hannah, continuing, "You may think you have sold yourself cheaply to me, but let me tell you: What you are getting at my side is far and

away more authentically first-class knowledge of the world
than you would ever get from some callow young tourist.
Moreover, I will be more direct about what I expect from
you in return, without harboring unspoken designs on your
person."

"I beg your par—"

"Don't you beg my anything. Unless you can state flatly
that Edward Stanton's interest in you was purely intellectual."

"As a matter of fact—"

Amelia Besom let out an exasperated rush of air through
her lips.

Hannah was left speechless, breathless: dignity-less. She
would have replied if she could only have thought of a
substantial defense. Of course Edward's interest had been
more than intellectual. And Hannah was not certain she
would have wanted it otherwise. His interest had been
sexual, social, *and* intellectual. He had liked her; she was
sure of it. She was equally sure, however, that his offer of
marriage—as happy as she had been to have it and thus turn
it down—had had something more to do with her open
blouse, his hands trembling at his belt buckle, and her own
reluctance to allow him to open his pants than with his
desire to make her his lifelong companion.

The real humiliation was that this snobbish, self-righteous
woman should hit so nearly the mark of Hannah's own
suspicions, speaking them and thus destroying by this the
last vestiges of all she had: nice, if edited, memories; pretty,
patched-together fantasies.

Mrs. Besom cleared her throat, then said, "I'm going
down to tell Monsieur de Saint Vallier about the Goya. Are
you coming with me?"

"No."

At the door Mrs. Besom turned. "May I say, Miss Van
Evan—and I promise to let this be the last of it and am
grateful that you have finally been so forthcoming—but
may I just say that when two young, um, gentlemen scrap in
the middle of the night like young tomcats, people assume

it is over a female in heat." She let this sink in. "You would do best not to allow yourself to become the object of hot-blooded young gentlemen."

Hannah just stared, fury heating the backs of her eyes till her vision itself seemed to waver.

Amelia Besom watched her standing there stewing, then added, "And something else: I know you think I am coming to depend upon you, and of course in a way I am. But I do not want you to think that I become . . . attached to people. To employees, I mean. It is most unbusinesslike, and, besides, we are not of the same . . . background. I appreciate your skills and amiability, but I will not allow myself to become fond of you. I like you, of course. But it simply wouldn't do to form a friendship with you."

She let this register for a minute, then continued. "In the meantime I am going down to tell Monsieur de Saint Vallier that I want to devote myself to this project. Tomorrow I want you to go to the nearest telegraph office, from where you will reroute our trunks and luggage, then wire Monsieur Blois in Paris. Cancel whatever can be canceled. Delay what can be delayed. I want to start work here immediately and devote as much time as possible to it." She paused. "I assume you want to continue with me?"

They were not going to Paris, Hannah thought. No Paris. But what else could she say? "Yes," she answered.

Mrs. Besom smiled a smug, knowing smile. "Good. I'll see you at dinner."

The moment the woman left, Hannah broke for the servants' stairway, taking the length of the building in seconds. Her feet tapped down the metal runs, rotating her through the stairwell, then at the ground floor she darted out of the laundry room, through the servants' hall, and into the dark formal rooms that lined the west side of the building. She ran along the terrace doors, trying one then another until she found one that gave. Hardly realizing how she'd gotten here, she stumbled out onto the terrace, where the cool air of evening hit her full in the face.

She kept going, down the steps. It was almost dark. The sun was below the horizon. Crickets were chirping as Hannah hiked up her dress. She stepped high and moved fast through the weedy, knee-high back grasses. She didn't understand what she was doing, only understanding that the breeze felt good, like cold water, and that taking this into her lungs was better than sobbing and crying.

The grass gave way to thickets. Hannah darted around shoulder-high brambles, scooted between copses of trees. She didn't know where she was going, though she saw the twinkle of light in the distance and knew what it was: not a rooftop anymore, not a chimney, but glimmers of window light through the trees, shining from the cottage at the edge of the woods.

There was no reason to go there and good reason to stay away. But she continued, running faster till there was a catch in her chest. She thought again of the poor idiot at the cottage. Poor, dribbling, bumbling fool. A freak, a monster—

Down a steep embankment, she slipped—her feet were not familiar with terrain as steep as this. She landed squarely on her bottom, but bounded up again, propelled if anything by the fall, going pell-mell.

She was going there; she knew it. Because it was forbidden. Because she was curious. Because she was in a state of outrage. Because she felt witless and moronic herself. She ran like a child running to view the circus's most grotesque creature: She wanted to see someone, anyone, more backward than she. Hannah wanted to see someone so stupid and horrible that a family would hide him. The family idiot or hunchback. Quasimodo. "Let him be horrible," she murmured to the night.

Her vision blurred; her eyes filled with tears as she ran. All her own hopes for herself seemed to run together, silly, impossible, pretentious, ruined like aquarelles run with water. Something in her, a part of her spirit, bayed and howled over the ugliness of what she'd been told, over the truth in it. In the hollow of her soul, this something cried out, inchoate, unexpressed, lost before it had begun; still-born. *Quasimodo*. She tore down a gentle slope, through some wet bushes, this refrain twisting and permutating in her aching mind to become *Quasi modo geniti infantes* . . . Rote words, learned as a child in catechism, repeated mindlessly now as a soothing litany: the Latin from her Sunday prayer book, the introit antiphon for the Sunday. *As just born children, turn thyself, reach, long for what is good, for the pure spiritual milk, that by it you may grow to salvation and live peacefully,* not hunched over, bent. Quasimodo. Let him be horrible, let him be horrible, let him be frightening, I want to feel anything but what I am feeling . . . so horrible, so alone, like a single ray of intelligence beating inside the body, the face of a hopeless, irredeemable freak. . . .

Chapter 5

*What often saves us from abandoning ourselves
to a single vice is the fact that we have several.*
—La Rouchefoucauld, *Maxims*, Number 195

NARDI SAT BACKWARD astride a chair in the front room,
every lamp lit, the fireplace bright with fire, every window
open. He liked lots of light. He liked the crackling of a big
fire in the hearth, even though the weather was really a bit
warm for it; he'd opened the windows to cool the house
down. He especially liked the idea of using up wood and oil
and gas and costing everyone money. The waste sent
Sébastien, who watched every sou as if it were his own, into
fits of apoplexy. Nardi found the whole luminous arrangement of this evening very satisfying.

He sat at the far end in the shadows of the long room,
away from the fire and facing the chair back while working
on the chair post's finial knob with a dinner spoon. His
fingers around the handle, his thumb applying pressure at
the bowl, he was carving a crude (what could one expect,
given the tool?) but rather nice gargoyle into a Biedermeier
chair he found a little austere. Overhead, the ceiling fixture
swayed gently on the evening breeze, swinging interesting
parabolas of light over his activity. Intent, slightly hunched
to the chair, eye to eye with its knob post, he was so

absorbed that at first he dismissed the noise outside as an
animal in the woods.

When it came again, he glanced out the far window.
Nothing. Dark. But it was a fairly large animal, and it was
close. He bent over the chair knob, only to become slowly
aware that the hair on the back of his neck had begun to
stand on end. The noise, having crept to just outside the
window, had quieted into eerie silence. He looked up again
and found himself staring across the room into the face of
stranger, its chin on the windowsill.

"Qu'est-ce que—" He came up out of the chair, unstrad-
dling it in his startlement. *"Pour l'amour du ciel—"*

The face dropped out of sight for a moment, then popped
back: a woman looking as dumbfounded as he, as if the
house and window had been suddenly shoved in front of her.
Then this face tottered and tilted in the window frame, as if
from an earthquake outside, slipping from view. He heard a
scrape and thud as he crossed the room. At the window he
had to lean out into the dark to find her, but there she was,
a toppled voyeur scrambling in the shadows on the ground
five feet below him—the house sat high. She'd moved a
rock, apparently half climbing into the overgrown hedge
and hanging on to the flower box.

"Nom de Dieu, madame—" Only she wasn't a madame.
Flustered, tiny, a little frenzy of knees and elbows as she
tried to get to her feet, she was the size of a large child.
"Calmez-vous, mam'zelle. Vous vous êtes fait du mal?"
Some curious country local, he thought. The people in these
parts sneaked around like this. They were sly, superstitious,
and ignorant as gourds.

Then he heard, "Oh, damn it," break like a sob from the
girl's throat as she stood up onto her knees. She tugged,
shaking the bush beneath the window like the Furies in her
efforts to scramble away—her dress was caught in the
hedge.

He bent over to unhook it, and she nearly leaped from her
skin in trying to stay clear of him, pathetic noises coming
from her larynx—too much gasping to get out a healthy

scream—like a beast at the instant of slaughter. Nardi raised
himself back into an upright position, holding out his palms.

"Easy," he said. "If you are all right, you survived the
worst already. I won't hurt you." A little irritated, he added,
"It is you who are skulking around in the dark, no?"

She stopped dead—his English having stopped more
than a few people dead, he pronounced it so badly. From on
her knees below the window, caught on the bushes, she
stared up at him.

He shifted to let light by and thus to better see her. But
she was so close to the wall and low on the ground that the
light from behind him only cut out and across the topmost
portion of her head—she had red hair, the color of an Irish
setter. Her face was no more than pale shadows in the light's
penumbra. He knew it only as upturned attention fixed upon
him.

"Who are you?" he asked.

She didn't speak, but only stared up at him now as if he,
not the hedge, had immobilized her.

He looked to the left through the casement panes, peering
up the embankment. "From where have you come?"

Still she didn't speak, though she put her knuckle in her
mouth, either from fear or because she had scraped it. She
sat there mute on her knees, sucking on the back of her
finger, gawking at him.

He glanced again around the window jamb, more wondering to himself than to anyone else: "How did you get by
them?"

She took her finger out of her mouth. "By whom?" she
said. Her voice was small and disproportionately frightened.

He lost patience. *"Écoutez, mam'zelle,"* he said. Listen
here. "We no longer shoot people for trespassing in these
woods—" Then the reason as to how a trespasser might
have gotten down here occurred to him. *"Ah là là,"* he
groaned. He turned, calling over his shoulder, "Werner!
Have you fallen asleep again?" The idiot. The crazy Swiss
was going to get everyone in trouble. Nardi glanced back to
the girl, again raising his hands cautiously. "I am going to

bend over and unhook your dress, yes? I can see where it's caught. You understand me?"

She nodded.

He called once more behind him, "Werner! Wake up!" Then, bending forward, he tried to chat up a sense of normalcy. He explained, "He has found a girl in the village." In the dark, hanging upside down, Nardi made a kind of shrug, as if to say, What could one do? "He spends the day with her then he falls asleep here." He unhooked the girl's skirt then had to push it over twiggy branches. Her hand darted out and grabbed it. Nardi lifted himself up again, turning toward the front porch and calling, "Werner, *Dummkopf, jemand ist hier.*"

Nardi turned back into the dark, expecting the strange little intruder to have fled, but his eyes found her readily again. She'd stepped back into the shadows of trees. She remained there, still staring up at him.

When she finally spoke a whole sentence, her voice was filled with astoundment. As if it were news, she said, "You're not ugly."

He hardly knew how to respond. "Thank you." It wasn't the nicest thing anyone had ever said to him, but she certainly seemed sincere about it.

"Ja?" a voice said from behind him. Nardi looked around to Werner and explained briefly in German: *Sébastien is going to have your hide, and I am going to have to find someone else to play cards with, someone who might actually beat me*—That is, Nardi explained this in a kind of German with a lot of hand signals. Werner's English was bad, his French worse. For communication he and Nardi relied on a pointing, gesticulating German that Nardi had picked up in Bavaria. When Nardi pointed emphatically out the window, however, what he was saying apparently became clear outside below as well, because the little stymied, staring object of his communication came alive, objecting violently.

"No. Oh no. No, no—" the girl said. "You can't—" She bolted.

With dismay— *"Ach, du lieber!"* —Werner shot out just as quickly in the other direction. For a moment Nardi stood in the middle of blind, well-lit ignorance, a lot of snapping branches and tramping outside, voices, protests, scuffling, the sound of Emil running up from his little rest spot by the river.

When Nardi stepped outside onto the porch, he could hear them bringing her around, the sound of *oof*s, kicking, and pleading. "Oh no. Don't tell them. Don't say I came here. I'll lose my job. I wasn't supposed to come down here."

Emil and Werner more or less dragged the girl around the side of the house, her heels kicking in the dirt, then pulled her up into the light of the front porch.

Nardi told them to let her go.

They put her on her feet at the bottom of the front steps and moved back an arm's length. She shook herself a little, brushed, straightened herself. She was wearing a high-collared, narrow-sleeved outfit, all of it gray and tailored in such a manner as to suck everything in then push it out, making her into a kind of severe-looking, small-waisted, puff-breasted wood pigeon. She was older than he'd thought, more than twenty, though probably not thirty.

He watched her, standing himself slightly huddled, his hands in his pockets, his arms close to his body. It was cool outside, and his shirt was only a light, open-weave linen. The air went through it.

"Who is she?" he asked, again in German.

Werner and Emil seemed to think she had arrived this afternoon, in the company of an older woman, both guests for the weekend up at the château.

"What? Is Sébastien renting it out as a hotel now?"

They didn't know Sébastien's reasons. Who did? The sanctimonious bunghole was incomprehensible.

In English he asked the girl directly, "You are staying at the château?"

She jerked in startlement, but her gaze didn't break from him. He found himself the focus of the same fixed look that had stared up at him from the shadows on the other side of the house. In the light now, this unblinking interest felt slightly rude and most discomfiting.

"What?" he said finally. He looked down at himself. "Have I spilled something?" Had he left his trousers open?

She answered his original question. "Yes, I'm staying there." Her eyes sluiced toward the bright room behind him, as if it were a cage at the zoo and he belonged in it. "Can I go now?" she murmured.

"Why do you stay at the château?"

"I'm helping to inventory it. Look, I was curious—" She held out her hands in supplication. "I came down here to see Monsieur de Saint Vallier's half-witted brother—"

Nardi blinked at her. *"Pardon?"*

"I shouldn't have, I know. Monsieur de Saint Vallier warned me it was dangerous—"

This startled a laugh from him. "I am half-witted *and* dangerous?"

The girl's jaw snapped shut. After a moment she asked, "You are his brother?"

"This is what my parents tell me."

She looked at the guards, then at him again. "Why are you down here?"

He snorted, a laugh withheld, then became philosophical. He shrugged. "Why is anyone anywhere?"

"You slammed Emil's hand in the door," she accused.

He frowned. "It was an accident—"

"You took the baker's money."

"The baker?" He didn't understand, then of course—but how the hell? He pulled a face and defended. "My friend Pierre is the local *boulanger*. He brings me bread. Or he *brought* me bread—he has not been here since he lent me money." He scratched a finger in the growth of beard at his jaw, wondering where the hell she'd gotten all this information for having been here only half a day. At the sight of him scratching, however, her frown deepened. He added preemptively, "And the barber was a"—he couldn't find the word—*"un petit con*—how you say?—a jackass. I was only joking him."

She blinked at this, while his jackass assessment of the barber drew vigorous support from Werner and Emil; they both nodded. "*Ja, ist* true," Emil said. "He was being jackass. Skinny-necked jackass. Afraid of foreigners. Nardi only cut a small piece of his hair, and the razor never touched his neck—Nardi never even said it would. He said only in German, 'Let's scare him.'" The two guards shook their heads, helpless against such misunderstandings.

The girl seemed capable only of blinking and gaping, now at all three of them. Then she smoothed her skirt at her hips, hips that were round and full yet nicely compact. She was pretty, it occurred to Nardi. If one discounted a puffiness about her eyes—he and his two nursemaids must have really scared her—and the fact that she sniffled then wiped her nose with the back of her hand.

"Well," she said, "that's all very interesting. Now, if you don't mind, I'll just go quietly back up to the château." She looked up at him, at his face this time. He found himself suddenly in communication with large, dark eyes filled with pleading. Her eyes were extraordinary, at once doeish, brimming with diffident request, yet lionhearted: willing to take on all three of them if they stood in her way now. "I would appreciate it greatly," she said, "if you wouldn't say I was down here."

Nardi shrugged, then nodded. "It would look bad for Werner and Emil that you arrived down here anyway. We will all pretend this did not happen." The idea was greeted with a round of approval. He came down the porch steps. "Come. I will take you back."

She shied away. "What? Well, I hardly think—"

"Don't be silly. You should not have come down here alone at night. There are wolves in the woods. And *belettes*—I don't know how you call them in English, but if you encounter them suddenly, they bite." He made no further motion to touch her or go near her, but rather walked past her. He stopped when she didn't follow, motioning with his head. "Come."

She didn't trust him. "And what are you going to do? Hit the wolf on its nose with your fist to protect me?"

"No, I am going to walk with you. And where I go, Werner and Emil follow about ten feet behind—they both have guns."

This didn't reassure her. "Why do they have guns?"

He gave her a peevish look. "To protect me from the wolves and *belettes*." He made another faint shrug. He was tired. "Besides, everyone has guns around here." He looked back at the other men. "Except me, of course. Country Frenchmen imagine themselves great hunters. *Venez*." Come.

She followed tentatively for the first forty or fifty yards, staying back a good distance from him. Finally he stopped and turned around. "Do you want me to go back?" he asked. He explained, "Neither Werner nor Emil can accompany you alone. They can't be seen up near the château again separately. Sébastien thinks that togetherness will prevent hands from catching in doors. Do you want to return by yourself?"

The girl said nothing but remained back in the dark, stopped, quiet. In front of him there was some light from the château, but it was faint, a small glow on the night horizon that said a lamp or two might be lit on the ground floor, a level invisible at present due to multiple embankments, the rise of terraced land. Mostly the château was a dark, hulking shadow against the sky, crags and bends among the trees overhead lit only by a few stars, a sliver of moon. More than ten feet back Nardi could hear Emil, his wheeze and step, midway between himself and the girl. Then something off to the side in the woods made a snap, a dry branch, that became a flap of wings and a loud hoot; an owl, a large one out hunting.

"I'm coming," the girl called. A few moments later she materialized as a clear silhouette, her step measured and determined as it fell in beside his. She asked, "You come and go as you please? With these men following you? You seem on friendly terms with them."

"*Oui*. I suppose that I am."

"Then what makes you stay here?"

Nardi looked at her, a shadow bobbing along at the level of his shoulder. She was much shorter than he, having trouble keeping up. He slowed his pace. "Two reasons. First, no money to go elsewhere, with no one willing to allow me to earn any, borrow any, or for that matter keep a sou, centime, or radish I might find on the street. It's a little game we play here, keeping Nardi poverty-stricken—"

"Nardi?"

"Forgive me. Bernard de Saint Vallier. Nardi to my friends."

She introduced herself simply as, "Hannah." A name with an English aspirated "H," which put it in the category of things difficult to say.

"*Enchanté, mam'zelle.* It is *mam'zelle?*"

"Yes. And you said 'two reasons.'"

"Ah. The other, well . . . Here is as good a place as any, no?" Again he shrugged. "Why not?"

Bluntly she asked, "What's wrong with you? Why would your brother want you here?" He watched the dark outline of her head shake in bewilderment. "I really don't understand this."

He frowned down at the dark movements of his own feet tramping along, hesitated, then said, "I have been . . . sick. I am better now, but my family worries. They think I could have a relapse."

"Could you?"

"Possibly." He corrected this more honestly to, "Probably."

"What's wrong with you?" she asked again.

This time he lied outright. "I have . . . a disease. Not contagious," he added quickly. "I do not know how one calls it in English."

"What is it in French?"

He said the first run of syllables that came to mind. "*L'astuce mensongère.*" Deceitful cunning. He trusted she wouldn't know the words.

She didn't. She accepted this. At least he thought she did.

She was quiet then said, "What do you think? Do you need all this—special attention?"

"No." Then he changed his mind. "Maybe, yes. Unfortunately."

"And would they want you walking people, probably half a mile, back to the château? Should you be doing this?"

He laughed. "Absolutely. I am bored to death down there." He followed this quickly with what seemed like brilliant inspiration. "Will you come down again? Tomorrow? Werner, Emil, the others will look the other way if I say so. The only one you have to get by is Sébastien, but apparently you can do that."

"I, ah, I don't know."

"Do you play cards?"

"No."

"Do you want to learn?"

She laughed. "No."

"Will you come anyway?"

They were ascending the last embankment into the once cultivated garden space, the formal reaches of the castle. He stopped.

"Maybe," she answered.

"Will you bring me something?"

She turned to look at him. But he put himself in the umbrage of branches, letting the few stars, the dim light now from the château shine on her. He was struck once more by her face. It was genuinely pretty. She had a long, graceful neck as well as hair, he suspected, that by daylight would be quite stunning. Beauty, he thought. If he still involved himself with such things, she would attract him. Presently, however, he looked at her neutrally, as if seeing fine stone, as if knowing the veins of good marble.

He watched her pretty face ask a little nervously, "What would you want me to bring you?"

"Cake."

She laughed. "Cake?"

"Pâtisserie aubrinoise. It's a kind of local bakery item

with sweet cheese and apples. The doctor forbids it, I think out of sheer perversity. I love it. Will you bring me some?"

"Maybe."

"And a razor."

This alarmed her. "I don't think so."

He slouched against a tree, irritated. "Well, it is not as if I am an ax murderer asking you to bring me an ax. Emil," he called over his shoulder, "would I hurt anyone if I had a razor?"

"*Nein*. No," came back the response, like an echo from an unseen source. "You would shave your ugly face with it. Bring him a razor." The voice added, "That barber was a *Dummkopf*-imbecile."

"Why doesn't Emil bring you a razor?"

Nardi shrugged. "If Sébastien found out, well—"

"If Sébastien found out *I* did it—"

"You don't work for Sébastien. He could not do anything."

She didn't seem so sure of this. "Well, maybe," she said again. Then she laughed. "In any event, thank you for walking me up here."

Yes, what a nice man he was, Nardi thought. Harmless, innocent, put-upon. "Oh, and some ether," he added to the list, "to tighten the skin and sooth the irritation of shaving."

"Ether?" she said. Her alarm was tangible, a declension of voice, an acceleration of breathing.

He weathered the moment, knowing he had exposed her worst suspicions again, like little bugs on their backs, wiggling, their pale, clicking little segmented bellies up. He laughed. "Yes. It is cheap. It evaporates quickly. I quite prefer it. But never mind, if you don't want to." He continued, patiently flipping her reservations over one at a time so they could skitter away. "Though it is wonderful for after a shave. Really. And I would only want a little, not enough to hurt anyone"—he laughed again—"or put them under so I could slit their throats." He held his hands out in the dark, as if letting her openly look at him. "I am not sound exactly, but I am not violent."

She stood there, her forehead creased in the dim starlight, her eyes squinting, as if she were trying to see better whom she was talking to. "Ether?" she repeated.

"Ether," he said. "And come tomorrow——"

"I don't think so," she answered.

He felt himself slump.

She added, "I'm not even sure I could get away."

No, of course. He sighed in the dark, resignation coming up out of his chest from the very depths of him.

In apparent response to this, she said, "Though I would like to. I'll come if I can." She added, "But I don't guarantee I'll bring you anything. If I come at all, it may be very much on the spur of the moment, when I can get away and when Monsieur de Saint Vallier isn't looking."

Chapter 6

EARLY THE NEXT morning, as she passed through the scullery, Hannah recognized the soft glow of a desk lamp coming from Monsieur de Saint Vallier's office. She stopped, looked in. This early in the day, the room sat in the long, westerly shadows of taller buildings; it was cool and dim. Monsieur de Saint Vallier stood inside this office, bent over his desk, his chair pushed back and away. In this slightly awkward position, he wrote by the light of the desk lamp.

Hannah spoke from the doorway. "I'm going into the village to send some telegrams. Do you need anything?"

Monsieur de Saint Vallier didn't look up, his concentration following his fingertip down a column of figures in a ledger book. "No, thank you."

Hannah remained in the doorway.

After a few moments he raised his head. "Yes? Is there something further?"

Still bent over the desk, he shifted his weight to an elbow, a man too busy to stand and talk, too busy to sit and work, poised as if he might drop his pen at a moment's notice, called away elsewhere.

When Hannah just stood there, he frowned and asked again, "Yes?"

Tentatively she said, "I wanted to ask you a question." He waited. "A kind of gentleman's question."

"Go on."

"Well, my brother runs a pharmacy, you see, in Miami, and if it's true, well, it could be valuable information to him. He could package it, be the first to sell it. It's cheap, you see, much cheaper than—"

"What *are* you talking about, mademoiselle?" he asked.

Hannah realized she was rambling. She gathered her courage. "Is it true," she asked, "that gentlemen in Europe sometimes use ether on their faces after shaving, to take the sting out?"

He made a pull of his mouth. "Now, if we did that, we would have gentlemen passing out every morning all over the place." He shook his head then smiled politely; silly foreigner. "No, Miss Van Evan, that is not true. Where did you ever hear such a crazy notion?"

"Nowhere. Thank you."

"Certainly."

Hannah turned, straightening her hat and buttoning her gloves. Well, she thought, at least she would not be a complete dupe. Ether, indeed. And razors. That man down there *did* intend to put someone to sleep. (Then possibly slit a throat?) She shuddered. He didn't even deserve cake; the devil take him.

Realization hit Sébastien a moment later. He moved around his desk quickly, following the sound of the girl's steps through the scullery then the kitchen, behind her not twenty feet in the entry corridor and gaining. At every moment he intended to call out her name, stop and confront her. But after sixty seconds of ardent pursuit he found himself standing in the courtyard, his pen still in his hand, watching her disappear in his own carriage.

He raised a hand no one saw, an attempt to hail the driver, but nothing came out his mouth, save a guttural sputter.

The little chippy—hardly more than a shop girl, a secretary, for God's sake—had gone against his authority, violated his hospitality, and trespassed against his goodwill. She'd been down there, the cheeky, offhand little thing!

Sébastien's indignation bloomed into a quiet, seething fury. He simply would not have such a presumptuous creature under his roof—that is, under Du Gard's roof, whom he would be protecting by getting rid of her. No telling what kind of bollocks she would make of the order he had established, the snooping, interfering, disrespectful, little— By God, he'd see her fired. He'd see her ruined, run over, and left for dead on the road of commerce. She would never work again. Not here, not anywhere, on or off the Continent.

Sébastien tromped back into the château, marching straight up the main staircase to Amelia Besom's room. There, he knocked. Then knocked again. And again. No one answered. He went down to the salon where the women had begun yesterday. Mrs. Besom was not there either, or in any of the adjoining rooms. He stopped a workman (who hadn't seen her), then went into the kitchen and asked a cleaning girl (who had, but not since she had taken the woman her breakfast).

Sébastien was stymied. He knew Amelia Besom was in this château somewhere, but the place was so damned large. She would crop up, he assured himself. She must be exploring elsewhere—with more respectful restraint, he hoped, than her young protégée. And the moment he saw Amelia Besom, he promised himself, he would make it perfectly clear that any further "exploring," any further work on this project, was contingent upon getting rid of the overcurious young chit who simply didn't know her place.

Sébastien left word with the workman, the cleaning woman, and several more people that whoever next saw the older American woman was to send her to his office directly.

In the little village of Aubrignon-sur-Seine, Hannah had sent instructions that, with luck, would reverse the direction of her own and Mrs. Besom's luggage. The luck she hoped for had to do with the fact that she had sent these instructions by French telegraph in French that had taken her till three in the morning to concoct out of a dictionary and a passing acquaintance with French grammar. (Weeks ago, when Hannah had first begun to correspond with Paris, Mrs. Besom had told her simply to write to everyone in English. The French would figure it out, she said; they all spoke English anyway. Hannah had discovered, however, that, aside from Monsieur de Saint Vallier and his brother, the French spoke, wrote, and read . . . well, pretty exclusively French. The burden had turned out to be hers to make herself understood, or else be sloughed off, misinterpreted, or ignored.) Similarly, she canceled the house in Paris, the small staff, a grocery delivery, and theater tickets, then began the rescheduling of business appointments. This altering of appointments required an exchange; she had to reply to the responses, once she'd figured out what the responses said.

To this end, Hannah sat presently at a weathered table in the shade of a copse of trees behind and down from the château, her legs curled up under her on a bench. She paged through her open dictionary, making her way, one word at a time, through seven inscrutable telegrams from Paris—she was not even sure which party one or two of the responses were from. Only halfway through the first, she'd already circled two words she couldn't find in the dictionary. They were either unusual words, business words perhaps, abbreviations used for telegraph communication, or irregular verb conjugations; God only knew, because Hannah herself could only guess. Beneath this telegram lay the others like a stack of sly puzzles: a few French words easy to decipher, a few (it always seemed to be the crucial ones) impenetrable, the whole task beginning to look monumental if not impossible.

Hannah sighed, thinking perhaps that she should go up to the château and ask Monsieur de Saint Vallier.

Oh, yes sirree, he was in just a jolly mood to help her. As she had come in the door from Aubrignon he had irritably demanded to know just where Amelia Besom was, as if Hannah had hidden her somewhere. When Hannah didn't know the woman's whereabouts, Monsieur de Saint Vallier stalked off in a horrible humor. And, even in his best mood, Hannah suspected, Monsieur de Saint Vallier would only view her as a bothersome fly in the ointment of his exceedingly busy existence. No, she couldn't ask him.

Mrs. Besom's French was worthless, beyond *s'il vous plaît* and *merci*. Besides, after the brouhaha yesterday evening between herself and her employer, Hannah was keen to show herself to be enormously competent, indispensable. She wanted to prove to the woman, and herself perhaps, that there was more to Hannah Van Evan than the foolishness that had on occasion overtaken her when it came to money, status, and fancy young men.

Trying to do just that, Hannah labored over her telegram for a while longer, checking and rechecking while growing more frustrated by the moment. Then the wind happened to lift the edges of her writing paper up, making a flutter that drew her attention; the paper was kept from blowing away by the weight of the contents of a paper sack.

The sack had once held *pâtisserie aubrinoise*. In Aubrignon she had found the pastry that Nardi de Saint Vallier had asked for to be everywhere. Hannah had bought some, telling herself she might send it to him as a formal thank-you and good-bye to a man who at least had not caused her trouble over her spying on him. She was put off by this ether business of his, but she had to admit he had been good-natured, and thankfully mum, about her embarrassing shenanigan.

On the way home from Aubrignon this morning, however, the pastry, hot and fresh in her lap, had smelled too interesting for her not to have just a little peek—then a little pinch off the side just to taste. *Pâtisserie aubrinoise* was light and buttery, a thick spiral of sweet bread with a dollop of creamy-tart cheese glazed into a custard around a topping of sticky-sweet apples. Hannah had taken another pinch, then another, until she had eaten the whole thing. In the sack now was something else, something she'd consolidated into the bag that she'd bought for herself earlier at the village produce market.

Hannah suddenly sat up very straight. Why, the present contents of this sack could make an even better gift for the man down at the cottage! This gift was healthier, not forbidden by his doctors so far as she knew. Besides, last night Nardi de Saint Vallier had even made passing mention of what the bag held at this very moment. He might actually want it, like it!

Hannah snatched up the bag, this sudden inspiration costing her a quick, slapping chase over the tabletop as she tried to stop writing paper from flying all over the place. Catching this, she tucked loose sheets helter-skelter into her notebook, then gathered up the rest of her things in her arms. Of course there was someone who spoke both English and French! What effort she could save! This Nardi fellow had invited her to come again. He didn't seem busy. He could help. And this ether business, well, she wasn't taking him any, was she? It would all be perfectly safe—while cutting hours off all the work of these telegrams! What an immensely practical plan!

Chapter 7

BY DAYLIGHT, THE cottage was a nosy woman's delight: fantastical, as likely to be sitting on a French river slope as, say, the gingerbread house out of "Hansel and Gretel." The building was a two-story structure made to resemble a chalet in Bavaria, complete with carved wood at the eaves and beams, lichen on its rooftop, the whole surrounded by rhododendron and mountain laurel.

It was rather funny really, a little alpine joke on the Norman countryside—a joke that became a conundrum: Behind the porch's rustic wood railing, like a fixture in his chair by the front door, sat a member of the Legion of the Brown Bowler: Hans, Werner, Fritz, whomever—Hannah had no idea which. Nor any clear explanation of his presence or purpose: a guard who guarded nothing—he made no attempt to delay her or turn her around as she descended into the clearing.

Whatever the man's duties, they seemed to include serving as herald. He stood and called, "Nardi!" His bowler head swiveled around, directing his glance behind him toward the interior of the house. "Nardi!"

From within the house came a petulant reply. *"J'arrive, j'arrive. Une minute!"*

It took another call of the Frenchman's name then several seconds more to get tangible results. She stopped at the base of the steps just as footfalls inside came across a wood floor.

Then he walked out of the dimness of the house and onto the porch to stand above her, looking about a league taller than she'd remembered, wearing nothing more than trousers and a sleeveless undervest. In his hand he held an open razor.

His face was wet. It had the sheen of perfect, tactile smoothness, a man fresh-shaven. A man with his throat cut: Down his neck, from beneath the wet, polished plane of his chin, a bright drop of blood ran, cherry red. It trickled toward the base of his throat. Distractedly he touched two fingers to this, looked at the blood on his hand, then wiped his fingers on the towel round his neck. He glanced at the edge of the white towel, at the smear of red, then ignored the whole business.

His eyes fixed on Hannah. "Ah," he said. He left a pause, the amount of space needed to search one's memory for an unrecalled name. Apparently drawing a blank, he came up with a new identify for her: "It is the girl who rinses her eyes with me."

"P-pardon?" Hannah managed to stammer out.

One corner of his mouth lifted. "It must not translate," he said. "It is an expression—who looks through windows. *La voyeuse.*"

A voyeur. Good heavens, yes. Hannah felt like a voyeur as she gawked: He was handsome. Razor-sharp handsome. Bloody handsome, as it were. Monstrously handsome, to put it in terms of her fears last night. And try as she might, she could not remember this sun-bright fact from her backlit, shadowed previous impressions of him. His suspenders dangled down the sides of his trousers—beautiful, tailored, expensive trousers made of soft wool the color of chamois. His sleeveless undervest scooped deep down his chest. Gold hair, as if shaved from an ingot, curled just above this U between ridges of muscle. His neck, delicately bloodied, broadened at the back into sinew and wide shoulders. Then there was his face, all planes and hollows— his cheekbones so high they encroached on his eyes, his brow so deep it put these eyes in cavernous shadows, his nose so long and thin and straight, the bone of the bridge bowed out in the middle then narrowed again for a considerable span before it fanned out into sharp, elongated nostrils.

He was the sort of man who should have been jaunty, a little cocky for all these blessings of nature, winking and smiling. Like Edward Stanton. But this man only stood there looking cordially puzzled as to why she was here and what might be expected of him: uncertain but agreeable, imperturbably gallant in his undershirt.

Down his throat, another sliding red droplet materialized. He touched the crevice under his chin again, where beard met neck, then kept his hand there. "I have to get some cold water," he said. "Would you like to come in?"

Yes, she'd like to come in, Hannah thought. And, no, she wasn't going to. Why hadn't she seen or remembered how fine looking he was? Or had she? Was she out for trouble again? She never seemed to know what hit her until she was bowling along in a carriage with the young Mr. Stanton all over her. Or in a dark hallway off a hotel restaurant wiggling up against Michael O'Hare. Or on a beach with Aubrey Winfield. Or on a sailboat with James Lee Vandermeer. The truth was, in Miami she had been a certifiable sap for holiday manners and Ivy League style. And where was she now? In France, on the threshold of the private dwelling of another handsome gentleman, rich enough to afford trousers tailored in a princely fabric, idle enough to be on some sort of endless holiday, and polite enough to seem genteel standing there bleeding.

He disappeared back into the house. Hannah stood dumbly at the base of the steps a moment, then followed him up onto the porch as far as the doorway. She let herself peer into the cottage, fairly burning with interest to see if the inside of it was as strange as she remembered.

It was indeed and more so. The ground floor was all one room: at one end, a sitting room with a sofa, chair, tea tables, reading lamps, all arranged before the hearth of a fireplace. At the other end, the room became a kind of workshop: shelves with objects on them covered over in canvas, a huge mixing trough of some sort on the floor, a mystifyingly low and large traylike platform beside it. Between these two unlikely halves of a whole room stood an even more illogical fixture: a long, metal-topped counter with a sink. Nardi de Saint Vallier was bent over this, flushing his neck with water.

He stood up and toweled his face. "Are you coming in or not?" he asked.

Hannah remained where she was, staring in. There were cloth bags of something stacked uniformly in a far corner. Something white and powdery had sifted out of them, dusting the general area as if in flour. She could read upside down the labels of several which said, *"plâtre de moulage."* Plaster of some sort—whatever *moulage* meant.

"What is this place?" she asked.

The Frenchman looked about himself, as if the question held no interest for him, though he would out of courtesy find an answer for her. "It looks to me like a sculptor's studio," he said.

"Really? Do you think so?"

"Yes."

"A sculptor's studio. How wonderful!" The great sculptor Rodin had a studio in Paris. Enthusiastically Hannah asked further, "And that? What is that?" She pointed to the large traylike platform on the floor at the end of the counter.

It was a substantial-looking apparatus made out of thick, unfinished planks rounded out to a kind of flat wheel, a giant tray about four feet in diameter sitting low to the floor.

He glanced over the counter's corner edge to where she pointed, then took the step needed to give the contraption a kick with his foot. It moved. It rotated freely, rumbling with large ball bearings. Hannah stood mesmerized in the doorway, watching the thing turn smoothly, though with a slight gyrating wobble. It was big enough to ride on.

He explained, "It is a chassis."

"What's it for?"

"For blocks of stone, marble, whatever. The sculptor, he turns the piece on it toward the best light as he works."

Hannah threw a glance at him, at this strangely specific information delivered out the mouth of a man with a very French accent. *Too-ord ze bes' lite az 'e oo-airks.* She let her eyes pass freely again over the dry, unused work area, over all the mysterious shapes, objects neatly covered in canvas, bags and boxes unopened. The platform slowed to an audibly distinct clack and shift of the bearings. "Have you been here long?" she asked.

"Two weeks or so. Are you going to stand in the doorway forever?" he said. . . . *een ze door-oo-ay foray-vair?*

Hannah stepped forward a few inches and leaned back on the doorjamb. "Who lived here before you?"

He shrugged. "A gamekeeper, I think. A long time ago."

"Do you suppose he was a sculptor?"

"Oo?" Who, he meant.

"The gamekeeper."

He laughed, a brief, quiet burst. "No. My brother imagines that I am. He brought all this in."

Hannah contemplated this information. "Are you?" she asked.

He looked around again briefly then shook his head. "No, my brother is a dreamer." *My brawzer eez a dreamair.*

She watched this Frenchman close the razor's blade into a mother-of-pearl handle then clank it into a monogrammed silver shaving mug. He picked up a shirt—linen with pleats—slipped it on, then began to button its placket. Like his trousers, his shirt was generously and beautifully tailored.

Hannah dropped her gaze to the silver cup. "I see someone brought you what you needed for shaving," she said.

After a brief, vacant moment he said, "Oh. Yes, Sébastien brought down a box of my things that he retrieved from my apartment in Paris."

"Paris?" The word fairly cooed out. Hannah straightened. "You live in Paris?" she asked, trying to keep the awe from her voice, a perfectly useless endeavor. She heard herself say, "I came down to ask you a favor"—she stepped forward into the room—"and give you this." She brought forth her paper sack from where it had been nestled between her dictionary and bosom.

He had been halfway through the maneuver of shouldering up silk suspenders, but stopped dead. The suspenders fell. He stared for a moment at her small package, then smiled, instantly lit with interest. He came round the counter, full of charm and fully present in a way he simply had not been to this point.

"Merci beaucoup, mam'zelle." He said something more that Hannah didn't understand, though it sounded elaborately polite and mellifluously beautiful. French on his tongue was gorgeous. Like the surprising, indecipherable harmonies of a fugue or the surface, without meaning, of particularly rhythmic poetry. His French was nothing like anything she had heard in the village. It was nothing like anything Hannah had heard anywhere. And it was accompanied by something even more powerful: His hand cupped her elbow, and he drew her forward. He pulled her into the room and lifted the sack from her fingers, alive and responsive in the most intriguing way that made something at the base of Hannah's breastbone quiver.

She watched him glance toward the door, then drop the sack into the sink, beneath the line of view of anyone outside. He was hiding it. As if cleaning up the sink, he opened the bag, looked in, then looked up at her.

"Radishes," he said. His voice was flat with disappointment.

His eyes scanned her briefly, discreetly, to settle among the papers and dictionary pressed against her bosom. He was searching, she realized, to see if she'd brought him anything else.

"You asked for them," she said.

"Did I?"

"Yes. Last night, you said no one here would let you keep a sou, centime, or radish. You seemed to want one—so now you have . . . I don't know, there must be twenty or thirty there."

"Thirty radishes," he repeated. He stared at her.

It did seem sort of stupid—and of course it was: He hadn't asked for radishes literally. It had been a figure of speech. Hannah wished suddenly she'd brought the cake. She half wished she'd brought the damned ether. Radishes. How idiotic. "Well, I know of course you weren't really longing for radishes—" She giggled nervously. "But, you see, there was this woman in town who had a whole flat of these, and they looked so pretty, like bouquets of flowers—"

He lifted the bag from the sink, as if to smell it. As if smelling to verify something impossible. Radishes didn't smell like flowers, of course. Hannah was appalled at herself.

Radishes smelled like spicy turnips. Why not bring him turnips? They were larger. Why not pumpkins, for that matter? Why had she bought these? "They're not a bit like the ones at home," she babbled, "which are red, like my hair." She indicated her head, a place of confusion and colorful, baffling circuitousness. "French radishes seem to be pink, more subtle, more lovely, and tied up so prettily." No, please, no, she told herself. Please tell me I am not rattling on about my hair being like radishes that grow too red and smell like turnips. Oh, please, oh, please, not in front of this elegant, well-dressed Parisian. "And they're very crisp and tangy, don't you think? I like to eat them—"

As a matter of fact, she loved radishes, though she was sure by the look on his face that he didn't.

Hannah felt so unsettled, so inept. She paced round the counter, a movement that made her noisy petticoat sing like a chorus. "Well," she said, turning again toward him, "you don't have to eat them if you don't like them."

"No, I like them." He said this deadpan. "They are fine. *Merci beaucoup.*"

Dear heaven, he was being generous. Hannah just stood at her end of the counter, fidgeting.

"Excuse," a voice said from the doorway. "May I see?" It was the man from the porch, wearing an officious face beneath his brown bowler. He wanted to examine the bag that Hannah had just handed over.

The Frenchman gave it up to him with no objection, no remonstrance, not the first hint of agitation.

The guard reached into the bag and pulled out the cluster of vegetables. He seemed more perplexed than anyone. *"Radieschenz?"* he said. He frowned, as if some trick had been played on him. As if he'd wanted something else, something more interesting, to be in the sack, which somehow had transmogrified into these. He pulled out Hannah's stupid radishes—no longer theoretical—into full view.

Hannah shifted on her feet. The bowler-hatted man examined the bouquet from every angle, then spread the individual radishes apart and poked his fingers in between them. Then he looked into the bag again, saying something to the Frenchman in German.

Who promptly snatched the radishes away. He answered, "Yes, they are pretty. And, no, they are mine. Get her to bring you your own." He looked at Hannah. "Thank you," he said, this time in English. He smiled, scrupulously polite. Generous. Kind. Noble. A man who didn't want her to feel bad.

The guard wandered out the door again, as Nardi de Saint Vallier set his "present" on the counter. He leaned on the sink edge and looked at Hannah, politely inquisitive: Now what? He waited for her to say, perfectly motionless, remote again.

Hannah couldn't say anything. She clutched her telegrams to her, the silence stretching out as she twitched and shuffled and straightened the waist of her jacket, each moment a new and fruitless attempt to ready herself for the next when she planned to be still. She would be dignified in a second or two, as passive as stone, she promised herself—a promise no sooner made than, as if allergic to it, her nose itched. She scratched her nose, a wretchedly inelegant necessity, while the man across from her stood watching from the aloof posture of someone who had never itched in his life. He was so incredibly tranquil.

Standing there in his drooping suspenders, so nonchalant,

so handsome, so posh, he seemed to be all she had ever wanted to become: stylishly at ease, so upper-class as to be bored with the whole concept of class, so sophisticated that things couldn't touch him. How coolly detached, so dégagé, *détaché*—

Détaché, however, was not exactly how Nardi felt. *Défoncé* was more like it. Knocked in the head. Dazed, with little pluses in his eyes like a cartoon. On another planet. He had slept only fitfully last night, and the night before, and the night before that. For three weeks now his mind had operated in the glare of sobriety, if it operated at all. Usually by evening he was more himself, capable of mischief, mayhem, and being a general nuisance; but by day he was *détaché, dégagé, défoncé—débranché*, in fact: as disconnected from what was going on around him as an electric lamp with its wire unplugged.

As for the girl in front of him, she was every bit as headlong and overly excitable as he remembered from last night, though she was much more colorful. Daylight made the red of her hair glossy. Her cheeks showed a high flush against skin that was as flawless and fair as, well, Normandy radishes. She was prettier than memory. Too pretty: one of those wasp-waisted, pigeon-breasted, apple-cheeked little fantasies out of a soap advertisement or from the top of a biscuit tin.

And she was much too trusting in appearances—anyone who wasted time gaping and smiling at him had to be. She wasn't very discerning. He tried to place this foreign girl in a context. She was not from New York or London, two cities he knew. She was not from any big city. And it was this small-town credulity that he fixed upon, intending to capitalize on her naïveté to the extent that it would yield him ether or something close to it.

She walked round the counter, her hips swinging, her finger running along the counter edge, then she stopped before the ball-bearinged platform. "What did you call this again?" she asked.

"A chassis."

She tapped it with her foot, but of course it didn't budge a centimeter. Its resistance surprised her. She looked up.

Nardi reached with his toe to press the lever ring beneath the platform, then gave the thing a kick. It spun freely. "It has a brake," he told her. "So it does not move when you don't want it to. It is underneath. You can touch it from anywhere along the circumference."

She reached her own small toe beneath the edge of the platform to confirm this, setting then releasing the brake. Then she tapped the platform solidly with her foot. It spun wildly, clattering and wobbling, making her laugh from surprise, pleasure, a silly giggle she tried to contain then gave up; it came out. More or less bubbling with it, she asked, "Will it hold me?" She set her papers and books down on the counter.

Nardi frowned. "Yes." He didn't know what to make of her—she was going to get onto the chassis. "But it is as slippery as mud with the brake off. It will throw you—"

But she had already stepped gingerly onto the moving apparatus, saying, "Can you balance me?" as she offered her hand to him.

He was able to briefly. She took his support for granted, gripping his arm as she wobbled. She caught a shriek back with an indrawn breath, sweetly thrilled. For an instant she spun like the piece of fluff she was, a feather compared to a block of marble. Then she lost her balance, leaving him more or less to catch her.

Nardi found his hands momentarily full of arms, elbows, the wriggling torso of an active and rather energetic young woman who was round and small and surprisingly limber. She came off the platform, depending on his stability while also squirming free of him, slightly embarrassed, greatly delighted, and totally breathless. What a strange little creature. She clearly liked the chassis as a toy par excellence. While she thought of him as stalwart and solid— Nardi wanted to burst out laughing.

She straightened herself, trying to assume a dignity she would never possess by picking up her papers and book and carefully organizing them back together again. She said, "I, ah—I'm beating around the bush a little—"

He had no idea what bush-beating meant, unless it had something to do with the hedges last night.

She continued, "I mean, I, ah, came down here to, um, ask you actually a kind of favor—"

Favors Nardi understood. He smiled broadly. Yes, do tell, *ma petite étourdie,* my little dizzy darling, because I think we can exchange favors. He said, "Yes? What can I do for you?"

An earnest gratitude filled her face as she looked up at him. She thumbed the loose assemblage of papers sticking out of her book—it was a French-English dictionary. "I received seven telegrams this morning," she said. "I wrote nine yesterday, all in French. You would think I would be getting good at this, but it's such a labor. I was up most of the night. I'm not even certain I said all the right things. And now the answers are beginning to come back—" She took a breath then continued, "You see, I know the grammar, or some of it anyway, but my vocabulary is short and some of the words"—she shook her head regretfully—"they're not in my dictionary." She slid the pile of telegrams from the book and held them out, as if they were evidence of something. "And this is all business and terribly important." She left a pause, one meant for him to rush into with offers of assistance.

Nardi could only look at her blankly. *Merde et contre-merde,* but the girl babbled. Her head was as full of pigeons as an empty attic.

"Can you help me?" she asked.

He knit his brow.

She added, "Are you busy?"

He laughed outright. He had to recover himself to inquire, "You are asking me to translate French to English?"

"And English to French. I have to write answers."

"My brother is better at this. Have you asked him?"

"No." There was an awkward moment, which she eventually filled with some of her nervous laughter. "I am simply overwhelmed. If you could help, I would so much appreciate it."

Toutes les couilles en salade! Nardi frowned deeply. What a thing to ask of him. To finagle the only thing he wanted—ether—he must deal with what he despised— words! The telegrams she'd revealed were long ones and numerous, pages and pages of dry, elliptical, telegraphed French. If translating then responding to so many of these damned things were not beyond the scope of his ability, it was certainly beyond the scope of his patience.

There was nothing for it, however. He answered, "All right." He only hoped that his reluctance was not as clear to her as the sound of it in his voice to his own ears.

Apparently it wasn't. "All right?" she repeated. "You will?" Her mouth opened broadly into a smile. What a smile she had. Pretty, healthy. White, nearly straight teeth. Her pleasure was so wholesome as to make him feel a degenerate. "Oh, this is wonderful!" she continued. "This is so fine."

"I'm not good at it." His offer felt suddenly hasty. Even for the sake of ether, he hated to put himself in the position of her counting on him; he was so good at disappointing everyone and anyone.

"No, no. You are so kind." She hurried over to a table by the window.

"I'll try. That's all I'm promising." He followed, taking an extra chair with him and falling into it across from her.

She remained standing as she arrayed her things out onto the table, saying, "You will be great help, I'm sure of it." She neatened her telegrams into a stack, opened a little zip pouch from which she produced pens, ink, pencils, and a small sharpener, into which she stuck a pencil. She stood there twirling away, with little shavings falling all over everything as she exclaimed, "This is going to be splendid. We will be done lickety-split. How grand that you are willing to help—" She kept smiling, beaming at him.

Nardi just sat there uncomfortably, watching her be impressed—of all the damned foolish things—with him.

While she kept chatting away about how noble and kind he was. She was boundlessly grateful. Her energy exhausted him. Finally he stopped her by interrupting. He said, "Oh, do shut up and sit down."

She did. She plonked into the chair, her mouth shut tight, her large eyes fixing on him with a wretched stare. For a moment he thought she was going to cry. Tears, whimpers, sobs, the whole watery display of feminine hurt feelings. Then she straightened her shoulders and did something more amazing: She bent over her telegrams, opened her dictionary, and became utterly still.

She did this not because he'd said to, but because her dictionary and papers—her work in front of her—absorbed her energy as surely as if it were the earth and she were the sun. She settled over the task of translation with a focus that contradicted everything else about her. For a moment she was an impossible enigma to Nardi, not simple at all.

"Here," she said. He watched her turn the paper around so he could see. She leaned toward him as she shoved the sharpened pencil into her bright red chignon. With her finger she pointed down at the page in front of him. "Right here is where I start to have trouble. Can you just read it to me from the start? I'll take notes."

He looked at her for a moment longer, then, sighing, did what she asked. He took the paper and read, *"Attention, euh, Mademoiselle Van Evan. Des troncs arrivent, euh, Aubrignon par train mercr—no, mardi quinze heures trente. Prière envoyer, euh, une grande voiture puisqu'ils—"*

"Excuse me."

"Oui?" He corrected, "Yes?"

"I was hoping you would read it to me in English."

She didn't seem to notice his difficulty with reading, even in French. He admitted, "I don't know what all the words mean in English."

She stared at him a moment, disbelieving, then burst out giggling.

"This is funny?" he asked.

"I am funny. Nothing is ever as easy as I dream it will

be." Her laughter went deep, right into her belly. Part nervous release, part delight; it was self-mockery. Hannah Van Evan laughed and sighed both, while shaking her head. "Can you help anyway?"

"I suppose."

"Oh, good." She couldn't stop giggling. She sat back and pressed the knuckles of one hand to her mouth while with the other hand, she contained the tremors of her generous, round breasts.

Watching her, Nardi felt the urge to laugh, too, but resisted it. He sat there straight-faced—as her laughter moved across the table to insinuate itself around him, whether he liked it or not, making his skin prickle, as if something warm and alive brushed up against him. A soft, small creature sniffing and mousing around him, not close enough to touch him but close enough to walk the hair at his arms, at his neck, up his spine, backward against the way it normally lay, against its natural, customary position.

Chapter 8

WHEN THEY CAME to a word the Frenchman didn't know in English, or didn't know precisely, Hannah would look it up, resorting when necessary to a cognate that he supplied. They would then discuss the possible meanings until they lit upon something that seemed to make sense to him in both languages. Nardi de Saint Vallier's English was really rather fluent, though his accent was ghastly. His accent was so thick, he sounded to Hannah more like a bad stage actor, say, from Kansas City, trying to put on a French accent rather than the real thing. *Ze peeple een Paree oo-ont za'tyu send a—eu—'ow yoo say?—uh confermasseeon.* Only a real Frenchman would have dared sound so awful.

He was also rather short of patience. When she reached for the dictionary for only the third time, he said, "What does it matter? That's close enough what it says." *Zat's closs eenuf oo-ot eet sez.*

Hannah could only stare at him, blink, then explain: "I want to do this well," she said. She wanted every word, every nuance. She didn't want to make a mistake. She was going to become wonderful at making these sorts of arrangements here and anywhere else. If she had to learn French to do it, she would. If she had to wheedle and prod the French out of someone else's brain for the time being, she would do that.

"Why?" he asked.

"Because it's important."

"To whom?"

She drew her mouth up into a peevish line. "Have you got something else vital to do?"

"No." He laughed. "Do you know you are relentless about these silly telegrams? Half an hour ago, you were so sweet. I would not have expected this of you."

Hannah liked the idea of having surprised him. She enjoyed telling him, "They're not silly, I'm not sweet, and what does the next sentence say?"

She coaxed him through the routine. She looked up every unknown or ambiguous word; they discussed all the possible meanings, the variations, and, when appropriate, the conjugations. He complied, but he complained—"You're boring me"—and whined—"*Dieu sans pitié*, not again"— then lied—"That's what it means, I'm sure. Are we done?"

"We'll never get through at this rate." She threw down her pen. "Do you not want to do this?"

He seemed surprised by the question. "No, I will do it."

Hannah sighed. She was sure he meant well—and equally sure he was going to continue to be difficult.

As if her sigh signaled a recess—a child let out to play—he smiled and leaned backward, tipping away from the mess on the table while balancing on the rear legs of his chair. He announced cheerfully, "I was terrible at school." He smiled wryly at her, right into her eyes. "Sébastien was brilliant," he said. "You ask the wrong person to do this. He could read any one of your telegrams to you, without stumbles, then improvise a reply as fast as you could write it down. Why do you not ask him to help you?"

"He's busy." She hesitated then added more honestly, "And I don't think he likes me very much."

Nardi de Saint Vallier raised his brow, a show of wicked delight. "Well," he said, "you and I have in common more than I imagined. Congratulations." As if proving he remembered her name, he added, "'Anna."

Hannah didn't know whether to correct him or not. She said finally, "It's Hannah, with an *H*."

"That's what I said." He laughed. This time he breathed the name out, manufacturing the initial *H* from an elaborate French sigh. "Hhh-annah," he said.

Hannah smiled, embarrassed by this meticulous rendering of her name and also charmed by it.

She managed to direct him back to the business at hand for another few sentences, almost another complete telegram. At this point, however, he leaned forward and stole a yellow telegraph sheet off her pile along with her pencil. He turned the page over and began to doodle something on the back.

He drew a few lines, looked up at her, then drew a few more. He held the pencil oddly, at a kind of precious angle, one finger raised out. After perhaps thirty seconds, he slid the paper around and across the table for her to see it.

Hannah stared down, bewildered. There on the paper, distinctly, was her own face.

"I'm an artist," he said. He paused, as if waiting for her to say he wasn't. Then he said he wasn't himself: "I draw these for the tourists on the Pont Neuf."

The picture was an extraordinary likeness. The hair, the eyes, her small, plump mouth. Hannah marveled at the drawing. "This is wonderful." The more she looked at it, the more she knew it was true. He had either lucked into a few extremely felicitous lines or else he was remarkably good. "It is spectacular," she amended.

"No, it's not. You're much prettier than that."

Hannah looked down, trying to see the drawing, the telegrams, pens, pencils, anything, anything at all through the haze of the horrible satisfaction she felt. He thought her pretty.

Hallelujah.

Oh, dear God.

With this man's help she had taken care of almost two telegrams in less than half an hour. This seemed fast to her, miraculous. While he sat there smiling at her, drawing pictures on the back of her work, making indecipherable, inappropriate, deeply pleasing comments.

"Well. Yes," she said. Hannah straightened her skirt then touched her hair, surprised to find a pencil there. She pulled it out. "Shall we finish?"

He reached across the table and covered the telegrams with his hand. "Let us take a pause."

A pause? Hannah looked at him, at his handsome face brought closer as he leaned into his stretched arm. His eyes were thick-lashed, heavy-lidded, dramatic—of that light, indeterminate color between gray and gold; black pupils stood out vividly. Hannah could only stare at these eyes, mildly horrified by their attractiveness and the idea of pausing for any length of time across from them.

The Frenchman, however, only laughed again and murmured, "*Mon Dieu,* this is not a seduction. I was only saying you are pretty. I like beauty. I like to look at it. Who doesn't?"

Hannah was not reassured. In her experience, which she considered vast, gentlemen who were about to make unseemly advances frequently began by decrying loudly they weren't. For all those who had tried, not a single gentleman had ever begun his seduction of Hannah Van Evan by saying, "Excuse me, miss, but I am going to do away with your clothes and composure and what remains of your reputation." They had all denied it to a one.

When she only sat there rigid, Nardi de Saint Vallier touched her hand. *"Calmez-vous."*

She took her hand back. Hannah knew herself: She was a round, pretty little thing with a bad streak and a good heart. She meant well. She tried hard. But the bad streak was very bad; black, in fact. She liked a stranger. She adored handsome, rich men. And she *wanted* this one to look at her, to see how pretty she was. While a part of her was appalled by his attention, another part of her was jumping for joy—and it was this jumping, joyous part of her that always tended to make her into a fool.

She started to get up.

He put his arms around her pile of telegrams and scooped the slew of them across the table into his lap, as he clicked his tongue in mild reprimand. "Don't make such a *tralala*," he said. Under the table with his foot, he pushed her chair out, an invitation to sit down again. When she didn't, he explained, as if to a three-year-old, "Mam'zelle. You are fair and lovely—I have noticed. *Mignonne comme tout.* But I am sorry to say that I am immune."

Immune? She frowned, then stammered, "I don't know. I think—you see—" Oh, dear God, this had so little to do with him and so much to do with her: "I've been, um, like this before," she confessed. "In fact, I always seem to get into situations like this where young men make horrible, fumbling messes of things—"

"Well, I'm not young and I wouldn't."

She felt humiliated. "Well, no, of course, you wouldn't." He was much too refined, too noble and gentlemanly—

"More to the point, I can't." When she only looked at him blankly, he said, "You know—" He rotated a hand that tried to wave in a leap of understanding, as if she could fill in the rest. "Women don't— Not anymore anyway." He shrugged. "I don't know. They just don't."

"I'm sorry," she said. *That he couldn't make a horrible, fumbling mess of things?* She corrected, "I mean, I'm glad." *That he was somehow incapacitated?* "Good heavens, I think I'll sit down." She returned her bottom to the seat, sliding into it gratefully. She wasn't sure what he was trying to tell her, except that she did not attract him. Which was a relief.

Then she felt a prickle of irritation: It was also mildly insulting.

She looked around, feeling restless, annoyed, disoriented, until her gaze settled into focus across the room, on the stack of cloth sacks in the corner—dry plaster-of-something-or-other, *moulage.* "What's *moulage*?" she asked.

He looked in that direction. "Ah. You call that plaster of paris."

Hannah frowned. "What do you do down here?"

"What do you mean?"

"If you're not a sculptor, what do you do here? Being as

you are," she said a little meanly, "so far from tourists and the Pont Neuf."

"Nothing," he answered.

"Nothing?" She looked at him, a grown, healthy-looking man who did nothing. "All day?"

He smiled crookedly. "And all night."

Hannah had never been able to understand this, for "nothing" had also been what Edward and all his friends had ultimately enjoyed doing most. Of course, she had known them while they were all on vacation, but, so far as she could tell, none of them had had any particular hopes or dreams or aspirations for their lives. Hannah imagined this, her fondest dream—having so much money she could do anything—then tried to imagine, with all the choices this would put before her, choosing to do nothing at all.

She frowned at Nardi. "Well, it's not good for you to be useless."

"Useless?" He raised his brow and cocked his head at her.

"Oh, dear," she said. "That was gauche." Hannah put her hand over her mouth. "And mean. I'm sorry. I say things like that. I get too full of myself. I only meant that you should do something. It's not good for a person to be idle."

"I thought I *was* doing something. I thought I was doing your telegrams for you."

"Oh, yes." She took a breath, looked around, blinked. Where were her telegrams? She realized: on his lap. "Um—can I have them back?" She held out her hands.

He looked at her blankly. "Have what?" *'Av oo-at?* His voice was all vowels; it was luxuriously deep. Hannah tried to ignore how ridiculously much she liked the rasp and rhythm of his speech.

"My telegrams," she said again. After a hesitation, he put them onto the table and pushed them across to her. "Can we continue?" she asked.

He rolled his eyes. "*Oui.* No point yet in throwing my useless self over the bluff into the river. Not when I have such an important task"—he threw a wan smile at her— "and someone so lovely as you with whom to do it."

Hannah twisted up her mouth. This simply had to stop. "I thought you were 'immune,'" she said irritably.

"I have eyes."

"It's not your eyes I'm worried about. You don't know me well enough to speak so familiarly."

"A man has to know a woman to notice she's pretty?"

"To comment about it, yes."

He pursed his lips, frowned, then mumbled something in French, something about *les Américaines*, but seemed duly chastised.

She offered him a telegram. "Do you want to do this or not?"

He raised the telegram, putting it between them. She couldn't see his face. He read from the sheet thusly: "My dear Mam'zelle Hannah-with-an-H. Stop. You are most sensitive to what in France is merely politeness. Stop. I was only making conversation. Stop. I am bored with your telegrams; would you like to go for a walk? Stop. If I promise not to make unwholesome comments about your being nice to look at, that is. Stop. *Fini*." He stood up.

Hannah sat back. "That's not what the telegram says."

"Ouais," he said—congratulations—"you get a prize."

He walked over to the counter, only glancing back at her. "Are you coming?" he asked.

"I can't go for a walk." With a sigh Hannah gave up on having his help. She stood, straightening her papers and putting them into the dictionary. "I have to figure out what these say then answer them." Quickly she added, "But you don't. Really." She intended to make it easy for him courteously *not* to help.

When she faced him again, he was leaning back against the counter, his arms folded. He stood there frowning at her, then picked up the empty bag in which she'd brought the radishes. He held it to his face wistfully and smelled it, audibly drawing breath through his nose. "You know," he said, "for a moment when you first handed this to me, this bag smelled exactly like *pâtisserie aubrinoise*." He sighed and looked at her. "Have you tried it yet? It's very good."

She blinked. "I, ah—yes, I've tried it."

He smiled. "And ether? Have you found any place where they sell ether?"

"Um—" She shook her head no.

Nardi watched her swallow. He watched her large, guileless eyes stare at him. Really, he thought, this was all terribly unfair. A woman this unfamiliar with artifice and manipulation simply didn't expect it could be so direct.

He smiled at her. She blushed and dropped her head. Her blush was wonderful, an infusion of crimson pink into pale, creamy-smooth cheeks. She had a baby's complexion.

She had a baby's longing to trust: He saw her staring down at her fingers, blinking, frowning, trying to be friendly, trying to be careful. "Ah—I—" she began. She finally got it out: "In town I noticed the barber also does dental work. . . ."

Nardi continued to smile. How sweet. She already had a source.

Then she fixed him with a look of wide, inquisitive trust, a look that said there had to be some reasonable explanation for such a nice man to ask for ether. And something sank in his chest. Should Sébastien find this little foreign yokel entangled in his smugglings and sneakings and consumings of contraband, his brother would throw her off the estate by the scruff of her neck. She would lose her underpaying, overdemanding, overprecious little job in one blow, a blow she wouldn't even see coming.

He snapped off a radish from the bunch at his elbow, rolling it in his fingers as he pondered this disturbing attack of conscience. In the end, the radish distracted him. It was gritty—unwashed—but solid, a nice round shape with a rather delicate root tail. He brushed his thumb over the surface. The curve, the taper were the sorts of things his fingers liked.

A radish. Nardi frowned at it a moment, as if he had never seen one before, then looked up asking, as suavely as possible, "Do you like radishes, *ma mignonne*?" He picked up the whole bundle, fairly sure that she liked them. He was going to feed them to her, little globelike root by delicate root, chat her up nicely, then send her off to fetch him ether with a sweet pat on her backside.

"No, thank you," she said. "I brought them for you."

To whatever purpose, he couldn't imagine. *Sacredieu.* He felt another odd stirring of guilt.

"Here. Let me." She dropped her papers and book on the table, then a moment later startled him by taking the radishes from him.

She began to rinse them under the sink tap, then—*snap, snap, snap*—she began to decapitate the blessed things. For a moment he was terribly worried that she intended to feed *him* the radishes. Thirty of them would give him a terrible stomachache; never mind that he didn't like them.

She cleaned them into the sink then asked, "Do you have a knife?"

"No."

She picked up and opened the razor. She looked a perfect danger to herself as she worked on the radishes with the instrument.

"My father used to grow radishes," she said as she sliced. "Red ones." She laughed. "And what the bugs didn't eat, I would." She turned, holding out to him a handful of radish rosettes. She'd turned the radishes into flowers. "Want one?"

Nardi shook his head. "Not hungry."

She took a bite of a fat radish herself, crunched for a minute as she set the rest down. She smiled and said, "Eating them makes my mouth tangy all day. I used to keep them in my pockets, bring one out now and then, crunch it, chew it, sometimes just suck on a bit of one." After a moment she added, "We didn't have much money." She leaned a hip against the counter and looked at him. "But we had other things. Radishes. Carrots from my father's garden. Tomatoes." She shook her head in fond dismay. "He also tried to grow opium poppies, peyote, and belladonna. My father was a pharmacist—actually he was more of a quack.

But he grew delicious radishes and could cut them into flowers." She laughed shyly.

Nardi himself would have preferred the opium, peyote, and belladonna, but he just leaned back and listened to her.

"They were always a treat," she continued. "So fresh tasting. And piquant." On impulse—or maybe she was making herself hungry—she picked up another radish. She held it thoughtfully for a moment, then took a bite, then another, as if rationing it out, trying to make this one last longer so as not to eat into his supply.

Nardi picked up several and handed them to her.

She didn't know what this meant for a moment; that he didn't want them or that he wanted to share with her. So Nardi popped one into his own mouth, and she grinned. The two of them stood there, chomping away.

Nardi's radish was mustard-hot. He had to hide the fact that it made his eyes water. The aftertaste wasn't bad though—a biting, clean flavor as bracing to the taste buds as a drink of cold rain. Nonetheless, he wouldn't want another one. Meanwhile the girl before him popped two more radishes into her mouth and chomped away noisily. Nardi found himself staring at her mouth. It was puckered slightly to contain, as politely as possible, her mouthful of crunching vegetable; her tongue had to be on fire. How could she like that? he wondered.

He continued to stare at this mobile, munching mouth. Her lips were small but full at the crests, well formed; a perfect, chiseled little bow. Then her eyes raised to him, and he found his regard forced downward in self-consciousness.

"I can finish them by myself." It took a moment for him to realize: She meant the telegrams. "You've already been of great assistance—"

"No, I'll help finish," he said. Though he couldn't imagine why in the world he should say this and mean it, he did. Maybe it would make him feel better; if he helped her now, he could use her later with a less troubled conscience.

It took a moment to convince her he was sincere, but in

the end she followed him over to the table and sat down again. She sheepishly handed him a telegram. Poor little bundle, she really wanted help so badly.

And he gave it as best he could. Five more miserable telegrams. It was nothing short of torture. It took more than two hours, doing them her way with unbearable care. Words and more words. They reminded him of how stupid he was—he frequently had to back up or stop on a word because he'd transposed its letters, reading it as a different word or seeing it as nonsense. She didn't seem to understand he didn't read well; he read French so much better than she did, he supposed. So he battled words for her, like a knight might battle a dragon. Many dragons. Dragons that reversed themselves half the time in his brain. Dragons that reminded him of how clever Sébastien was with them; and how, with them, Sébastien could talk Nardi into doing what he didn't want to or into feeling bad because he did as he wished. Words. Nardi hated them in a very real sense beyond dragons, in the way a soldier hates the random, flying cannonballs of the enemy. In fact, he would have preferred cannonballs. They were round. A man could feel them. They had weight. Words were like trying to hold and form air.

Eventually Nardi heard her say, "There. Done. Thank you. Now, if you don't mind, I'll just sit here and neat everything up myself."

Ah, yes; something sighed with release inside him. With a sense of deliverance, he sat back and watched the woman before him.

She produced blank telegram forms. Onto these, in a perfect, neat hand, she began to copy over the rough-draft responses that he and she had worked out. He watched her bend to this task, her head bowed in scrupulous concentration, the crown of her head leaning forward into a shaft of sun coming through the window. As the sun cut across the top of her head, it washed her flaming hair a pure cochineal red, as if it came out of a tube of paint—Titian himself would have shied away from so bright a color. Van Gogh

would have, for that matter. Her hair, thick and rolled round
the back of her head, was so rich red in the light it seemed
prismed, shot through with separations of saturated color,
ruby, claret, magenta, plum, purple, hyacinth, heliotrope,
cardinal.

Yes, she was pretty, he thought. It wasn't all caddish
twaddle to tell her she was. With her doll's face and large
eyes and petite-plump little bow of a mouth, she was very
pretty—she just wasn't his sort. Nardi liked tall, elegant
women, sophisticated and subtle women, French women;
the women of Paris. This girl was petite, round, and bright
on the eyes. As lush and colorful as a tropical butterfly. And
about as erratic.

When she finished, she stood with a leap of energy,
saying, "Well. That's it. Every last one." She was so
refulgently pleased with herself he had to look away from
the light of her smile. "And there is still time to take them
all back to the telegraph office today. I am so grateful.
Thank you again."

He didn't respond but rather stood and walked over to the
sofa where he knew he had left his coat. "I'll walk you up
to the château," he said.

"No, no." She laughed a silly, nervous laugh, then said,
"Don't trouble yourself. I can find my own way back." She
was suddenly eager to leave.

"I don't mind."

They met at the doorway, with Nardi lifting his coat,
sliding his arms into it.

She reached out, touching the fabric, as her face became
a canvas of openmouthed awe. "My goodness, this is
lovely," she murmured. "What's it made of?"

He looked down at himself. "I don't know the word in
English. A kind of—" He settled on, "Sheep. With a long
neck, from South America." He said the French word.
"Alpaga?"

She understood. "Oh, yes," she said. "Alpaca. It's luscious." She held out a fold of it. "There's so much of it. And
the color, hmm, yes, like buttery cream." Of the coat, she

said, "Incredible." Then she looked up at him, her eyes warm with sincerity. "*You* are incredible. You were so very kind to have taken the trouble to help me today"—she laughed—"when you could have been out walking around in this." She paused, then said, "Thank you."

Nardi nodded, frowned. "Don't forget your telegrams," he said finally.

They went into the trees with Hans and Stefan following behind at a distance. Nardi took them all up through the woods so no one from the château would see her with him. Matted leaves tramped underfoot. Sunlight filtered through the dense branches overhead, making a chiaroscuro that played over her, fluttering. These bright, leaping patterns suited her.

He heard her take a deep breath. "Hmm, fog," she said. "How nice. It smells good, like rain."

He didn't contradict her, though he thought the air smelled more like rotting leaves and that fog in Normandy was hardly remarkable.

She walked, her head swiveling to take in the panorama of trees, paths, the picturesque little cottage disappearing behind them. They walked just a few feet in from the clearing. He could see across it, to outbuildings, pasture land, black-and-white cows in the field.

She stopped. "The light!" she exclaimed. "Look!" It was the usual overcast day, the sun trying with its usual intensity to burn off a thin fog that had risen off the Seine. "It's like the Impressionist paintings!" she said. "Luminous. As if everything stood in a mist of light, as if the sun reflected off particles of fog! Oh my." She laughed. She brought her hand to her heart. "Oh me, oh my." She bounced in her step once before she caught herself back and tried to walk normally.

As if she could. She walked along beside him, as calm as a bouncing ball, a rubber ball who loved Normandy. *Sacredieu.*

After a few steps she leaned toward him and breathed a confidence in his ear. "I get too excited."

"Mmm," he said.

"I bound all over the place, while my petticoat makes an indecent hubbub around me."

"Mmm."

"Do you think so?"

"Think what?"

"That my petticoat is too noisy?"

"I hadn't paid it any attention."

She grinned, suddenly delighted, then skipped ahead of him.

What a piece of work she was. Could anyone's life be like this? Every moment so earnest and heartfelt? Her hopes were so overwrought and expectant, the poor little creature seemed doomed to disappointment.

Ahead of him three feet, she turned around to walk backward, watching him with her moon eyes, so obviously impressed with him, it made him uncomfortable.

"How lucky you are," she said. "To live here. And have so much." She smiled like the sweet, idiotic, little country bumpkin she was, then in wonder said, "Radishes, la-di-da. You could have a cartload, couldn't you?" Her eyes glanced down his coat. "There is nothing you couldn't ask for, nothing you couldn't have here, is there?"

Well, as a matter fact, there was—and he had asked her for it, but she hadn't brought it. Which was an excellent entry. He was going to mention this, watch her face, use her awestruck mood to get what he wanted from her. Since she was so blessed simpleminded and doomed to disappointment anyway . . . Besides, he remembered now, she'd called him useless. He wasn't useless. Or no more so than the cows in the field. Like them, he was being husbanded, fed and scratched, driven into the barn, driven out again. . . .

His mind said this, but he walked on in silence, the decision settling over him: *Leave her alone and get rid of her quickly, before you change your mind.* It would cost her too much if Sébastien found out. Nardi walked along, avoiding her wide, admiring eyes, knowing he held the chance in his hand. He let it go with only a mild self-rebuke for doing so: Congratulations, he told himself. You have now become the noble ass she has tried to make of you all day.

It was at this wonderfully selfless moment—the first he could remember having in a very long time—that he heard her say, "Your brother tells me that gentlemen, neither here nor anywhere, use ether after shaving."

"Pardon?" Nardi looked at her, annoyed, alarmed. She had spoken to Sébastien about ether?

She fell in step again beside him, asking, "What do you want it for?"

He made a sniff of disdain, of surprise to find himself suddenly speaking of this subject in such a different context. "Why, to asphyxiate women, of course," he said, "so I can have my way with them." Trite, silly. But this seemed to be the limit of her imagination. He wanted to kick her. He wanted to protect her. The silly goose. Why would any sane person ask such information of Sébastien?

She frowned. "Are you angry? Have I caused you trouble somehow?"

Nardi was so bewildered he could only answer honestly: "No," he said, "you have not caused me a speck of trouble."

Though she had certainly made a mess of things for herself.

With sudden desperation, he wanted to be rid of her. He stopped. "It's just through those trees, over the next rise," he told her. "You'd better go the rest of the way yourself so no one sees me."

She halted and turned. "All right," she said. She smiled up at him, virtually beaming gratitude, awe, worshipful respect. "And thank you again. You were grand to do what you did for me today." She lightly lifted her armload of books and telegrams, as if tipping them in homage like a hat.

"It was nothing," he said flatly.

She laughed. "You hated it."

He raised his brow and stared at her, or at the top of her glossy, near-carmine red crown; she'd shyly bowed her head. Had his aversion been that obvious? Had he been that transparent?

"And you did it anyway," she added.

Yes, champion that he was. *Because,* ma mignonne, *I was going to use my generous posture to leverage ether out of you.* But never mind. The nit. Telling Sébastien. Really. This was too much. How could anyone save a creature who rushed this brainlessly toward destruction? He gave her a forbearing look, a roll of his eyes.

She said it again: "You're grand."

And despite himself, for a moment he was. Not in his old way of grand, for all the world to see, but sincerely grand in one young woman's eyes.

Then she did the most extraordinary thing. She suddenly leaned forward and clutched his shoulder. She pressed her small, bosomy body against his forearm, then Mademoiselle Hannah-with-an-H raised up onto the tips of her toes, lifted her creamy face, and brought her soft, chiseled, pucker-bow mouth to his cheek. She kissed him, landing the kiss on skin still tender for having not known a razor, till today, for almost a week.

By this, the poor creature embarrassed herself. She leveled out onto the ground again, breathless, a little unsteady, blushing furiously. Then she flustered out a croak of apology, turned, and ran off like some schoolyard miscreant who had just thrown a rock through the rectory window.

Nardi stood there holding his cheek, as if a rock had indeed hit it, feeling as sharp and edgy as shattered glass.

He had at one time been used to people making a to-do over him. It had seemed normal that they do so, hugely, grandly. He had been a favorite, a prince, the toast of Paris—though a man who now only drew sketches for tourists was certainly not anymore. The amazing thing was that still sometimes people fussed over him, like this silly girl. Even after his fall from grace, there had been the occasional woman, a fellow, a chum. They had feted him, befriended him, given him tokens, and praised his art.

They had pretended he was someone.

Oh, he didn't doubt it, they liked him. He had some sterling qualities. (He was a wonderful liar, which made for good stories. He was a sharp at cards, which made him fun to beat when they could. And of course he could drink ether, in quantities that would have anesthetized a battalion of legionnaires, and still remain standing. He was always a good drinking companion; he had a hollow leg.) But in all his years, he could never remember liking himself better than he had for his youthful renown, his public success at age twenty. The honor he had brought on himself and his family then had lain sweet in his soul. Nardi had loved his celebrity; he missed it still, like an old dear friend passed on. For years he had tried to recapture it, finding it elusively in the arms of women or in the shoulder-to-shoulder company of drunken boonfellows, attracted to each because he or she saw him in the poetical glow of his past reputation, the Great Artist Fallen on Bad Times, then abandoning each when he or she began to know him well enough to see him as a man—a poverty-stricken man with his nerves frayed, in need of something cheaper and stronger than liquor.

Ah, Celebrity, my old darling, he thought. Nardi sighed. For he knew: He had taken up with Intoxication and Notoriety, old bastard girls that they were, strictly for the sake of their being half sisters to the one whom he loved who had left him behind.

Chapter 9

This part of the dream that has been wrested from forgetfulness is always the most important part.

—Sigmund Freud,
The Interpretation of Dreams, 1901

NARDI AWAKENED WITH a start, his body gulping air, leaping in spasm, like a fish breaking the surface of water. The desperation of his unconscious mind brought him to life that suddenly and flopped him on the shore of reality in the dead of night. He lay there in the dark trying to catch his breath, feeling his heart pump. The sheet beneath him was damp. His body was covered in a fine sweat. While his mind scrambled to piece around the slippery dream, trying to gain a footing in consciousness.

The dream dominated for several seconds. A woman's skin. So smooth and pliant in his hands, like glycerin mixed with silt or raw porcelain, only resilient—his kneading fingers making indentions in her buttocks, in warm flesh that pushed back. While his hips slid against her and he penetrated flesh of such exquisite heat and texture . . . in and out . . . long, liquid strokes—

His penis was thick and hard, the tip faintly weeping. It throbbed. Nardi swallowed, then expelled air and put his forearm over his eyes. He waited for the feeling to subside.

It didn't, not quickly, at least. The dream kept washing up over him. A mouth, open, the fragrant-sweet taste of a woman. Roses. She tasted the way white noisette roses smelled. Kissing her was like eating these, his tongue slathering up the delicate savor of round, blushing, radish-sized flowers; as, lower, he penetrated and repenetrated something divinely beyond flowers or radishes or anything else, something strictly female, of the animal kingdom, his species—

"Ah, bon Dieu." Nardi threw his legs over the edge of the bed and sat up. *"Très bien, mon vieux,"* he congratulated himself sarcastically: from impotence to priapism in one twenty-four-hour period.

He rubbed his face then held his head at this new development. He looked up across the moonlit room at the clock. Ten minutes till four in the morning. Another little shock. He'd actually been asleep. For almost four hours. On his own. With no chemical inducement. *"Ah, chapeau!"* he celebrated, again with more irony than enthusiasm. He had not slept more than half an hour at a time since they had taken away the ether. Then suddenly he is out cold for four hours and—what does he do?—he almost brings himself off in the sheets like an adolescent.

Ah, ether, he thought. How easily this would all disappear with just a little to breathe or swallow. Oh, the light-headed calm. The little spin it put on such bodily complications. No sweat, no thunder in his chest—as he got up from the bed he looked down, amazed by his own heaviness—and no ridiculous, persistent, overladen erections. With ether, he had known only the utter darkness of sound sleep, a sleep that suppressed dreams, bringing only the occasional chilling nightmare.

From the open window, the breeze blew. He felt his skin pucker in a run of gooseflesh from his neck down his back. Gooseflesh. Though less lately, he had had a lot of this. Normal. They had given him medical journals to read, case histories. What happens to people when they stop using this or that chemical, yet only two specific articles on ether— and the answer here was, Nothing. A little "horripilation"—

gooseflesh. Nothing more. Except of course, you were suddenly cold sober.

Radish-sized flowers, the noisettes . . . Suddenly remembering the American girl and her radishes-into-roses, Nardi laughed. All that round, lovely flesh, his dream was of her, poor little Hannah-with-an-H. If she only knew she were even faintly linked with such a bizarre dream . . . How embarrassing.

He looked out the window, the window she had stood under the night before from where she had watched him out there alone in the dark. The breeze blew over him again, and he closed his eyes and thought, No, how interesting.

Chapter 10

*Bernard de Saint Vallier, who astounded us four
seasons ago with his youthful genius has astounded us this season merely with his youth:
The only thing fresh about his* Rising Venus *and
the other fifteen stone corpses of his exhibit at
the Bisque National Gallery this week is the
incredible candor—like that of a child unwilling to flush its own bowel movement—with
which these stinking, mushy redigestions of
great work are offered for viewing.*
    —excerpt from a review by Amelia Hortensia
    Besom, Supplement to the *Times,*
    London, 19 September 1895

"AH, MADAME BESOM, there you are." Sébastien pulled his
mouth into a smile as Amelia Besom walked into his office.
At last. He came around his desk. "I have been wanting to
talk to you all day."

"Yes. Three or four people have said so in the last few
minutes. I was out at that rather grand chapel. Do you know
which of the things there belong to you and which belong to
the church?"

Sébastien's smile faltered a moment as he stifled offense.
"We are not going to sell anything from the chapel," he said.
He couldn't help adding, "My parents were married there."

137

He turned a chair around so it faced his desk. "Here. Please. Sit down."

The woman did, and Sébastien went around the desk and sat facing her, picking up his pen. He tapped the cap of it on the desk, turned the pen once, then slid his fingers down to tap its end. He smiled again, a grim smile of duty—a look Amelia Besom would know and understand in an instant.

"What's wrong?" she asked.

"Well, to tell you the truth, there has been an unfortunate incident involving your companion, Mademoiselle Van Evan—"

Nardi came up to the back door of Sébastien's office, while behind him Emil sat down on the terrace-wall coping. Nardi had talked the man into waiting there while he himself went inside to speak to Sébastien privately. Similarly, Werner would meet them back on the terrace. He had gone into the château to forage in the kitchen for any strudel left over from yesterday.

It felt a little strange standing here in the quiet. Nardi had been on this terrace only twice in recent memory. He had been marched across it three weeks ago on his way to the cottage, after having been thrown out of the Swiss clinic. He had been shoved across it again a week ago, having been retrieved from his self-awarded excursion into Paris. Other than that, Nardi had not stood on these flagstones since he was ten years old.

Presently the door panes jangled as he knocked. He unbuttoned his greatcoat. It was warmer here just this little bit up from the water.

From within the office Sébastien's voice called, *"Entrez."*

Nardi delayed. He could hear the chatter of birds from the old wych-elms that still paralleled the terrace. To stand here in their shade, without someone shoving at him, felt pleasant, familiar. He breathed in vague, remembered feelings, when life was secure and simple, then turned the doorknob.

As he entered, Sébastien stood in surprise, even pleasure. "Why, Nardi—" His pleasure quickly mixed with suspicion. "What are you doing here?"

The office was as Nardi remembered it, cool and damp as a tomb. Its stone walls and western exposure meant it never warmed up till the day was over. Nardi snugged his coat around him, the chill of the room requiring that he leave it on.

Then, as he turned to sit onto the edge of the desk, he discovered an even better reason to shudder: Sitting in the chair before his brother's desk was a huge, death-eating bird of prey posing as a human being—a woman Nardi had not seen in many years (a century would have been too short a span): the old vulture Amelia Besom.

Nardi nodded at her, the most he could get out of himself in the way of cordiality. This old bird had more or less presided over the carrion feast of one of the worst of his exhibits eight years ago. Amelia Besom had written an extremely unkind review, one that was not only articulately negative, but also scathingly funny. Her precious review had circulated widely in the English-speaking world, then had been translated into French, printed in full in *Le Monde* and quoted in a dozen other French publications. Nardi might have forgiven her for seeing so clearly where and how his art was failing or for being so facile and clever with words, but to combine these required a third aspect of character for which he could never forgive her: a purely mean, gloating spirit. Nardi detested the woman.

He turned where he sat on the desk, pulling his thigh up to rest on the edge, letting his foot dangle. He folded his arms and fixed his eyes on Sébastien—who wouldn't look at him.

After a few moments of uncomfortable silence, the American woman cleared her throat. "Well, my dear Sébastien," she said, "you did imply that your brother at the cottage was deranged, but I just didn't put two and two together. Of course. How many lunatic brothers can any one man have?" She made a pasty smile. "Bernard. How nice to see you again." She raised a smug brow. "How is your work going?"

"Wonderfully," Nardi said. "Though I have not made anything so satisfying since the statue I made of you at Fouquet's." Shortly after the vulture's egregious review, Nardi, at the salon of a mutual friend, had dumped a bucket of plaster onto her from over a stair railing. It had oozed over her remarkably well, making of her a marvelous, stammering work of art.

To Sébastien, Nardi said, "I want to talk to you."

"By all means." Sébastien glanced across his desk at the woman seated before him. "Give Madame Besom and me five minutes. If you'll wait in the——"

"No." He'd be damned if he'd be shunted aside in favor of the old bird, old trout, old scaly, beady-eyed dragon. Nardi took a breath then looked over his shoulder in order to present Besom with a full display of teeth, half snarl, half-unctuous smile. "If you please, madame, I would like very much to speak alone to my brother."

The creature was about to object, but Sébastien came around the desk, holding up a conciliatory hand. "Please, *chère madame,* you know how difficult he can be." Nardi glared as his brother continued. "And he has never come to see me before like this. It may be something truly important. Please, make yourself at home here. I will step outside and talk to him. I shouldn't be more than a moment."

With this, Sébastien tried to move Nardi toward the door through which he'd come. Nardi shrugged away as he launched himself off the desk and walked pointedly in the opposite direction. Sébastien was forced to follow him into the wet laundry.

They nearly tripped over a woman on her hands and knees scrubbing. Two workmen were yanking on pipes at the end of the room, removing a sink from a wall. Nardi found the most private place he could, at the far end of the row of sinks, and asked pointedly, "Why is she here?"

"Besom?"

Nardi pulled an impatient face. He leaned back on the last sink, shoving his fists into the pockets of his coat.

Sébastien raised a nonchalant hand. "She is pricing the estate."

Nardi expelled his derision through his lips, a burst of vibrated air.

"She's the best."

"She doesn't know art."

"She knows something better than art. She knows fair market value."

At the far end of the room, a pipe clanked onto the floor. Dirt and debris fell in a patter. The men working on the sink let out grunts of triumph—this to the accompaniment of the woman with her wet scrub brush scratching, rubbing vigorously on stone. She was trying to take a bad stain off the brick flooring.

"Ah, c'est joli," Nardi said. How nice. He made a sour face. "Beauty made into a simple consensus, a dollar a vote." A little testily he asked, "Is she making the listings in U.S. currency?"

"No. French francs."

"But everything is itemized in English?"

"This is the only language she speaks." It was also the language to which they had reverted, as a form of privacy with three other people in the room. "Am I to take it that if she did what she does in French, it would be all right?"

Nardi stared at his brother. He never liked to take Sébastien on in direct verbal combat; he inevitably lost. "The girl," he asked finally. "She works for the dragon?"

"What girl?"

"Hannah-with-an-H."

Sébastien frowned. "You mean Mademoiselle Van Evan?"

"Small, red-haired. A bosom like a balcony and buttocks"—he held out cupped palms, fingers spread wide— "like the *Venus Callipygos*." The hand gesture was not so much because he imagined grabbing the young woman's hindquarters (although come to think of it, this was not an unpleasant thought) so much as for Sébastien's benefit:

Sébastien was sexually shy and apt to be thrown by such graphic images.

Sébastien blinked and looked down. "Yes, I suppose we are speaking of the same young person."

Nardi laughed. "Yes, 'young person,'" he repeated, delighted to hear his brother neuter the girl's gender entirely. Sexuality was one of the few areas in which Nardi presumed himself to be, even in relative impotence, better off than his brother. Sébastien was the sort of gentleman to be uneasy with anything blatantly carnal; Nardi, on the other hand, had been known to sketch pornography on napkins in order to pay for his dinner.

"This girl, this Mam'zelle Van Evan," Nardi announced, "came down to see me."

"I am aware of this."

"She also told me that she asked you about ether."

Sébastien stiffened, indignant. "She's been down there again?"

"Pardon?"

"For her to have told you she asked me this, you have spoken to her since."

"Ah." Nardi nodded somberly. His brother's face was tight, his bottom lip pinched outward; a look gratifyingly irate. Nardi grinned at his shoes and flapped the edges of his coat with his hands in its pockets. "Yes," he admitted. "She slips by you easily, I think."

Sébastien snorted. "Not for long. I intend to rout her out like a pack of dogs on a field dove."

"Which is why I am here. I have come to ask you not to."

Sébastien raised his brow.

Nardi continued. "Sébastien, it is perfectly fine if she wants to visit. It does not bother me. She is very sweet, really. And her job with *la mère* Besom—only God knows why—means everything to her. Besides, I am a little lonely. I wouldn't mind if she came down now and then—"

"And brought you a little ether while she was at it."

Nardi smiled foolishly. "All right, I regret this. I did ask her to bring me some. I shouldn't have. But asking for ether was my sin, not hers. She didn't bring any. You should be encouraged that she asked you about it."

"Well, I'm not." Sébastien folded his arms. "She was contemplating bringing it. And we both know that what you lack in drive and talent these days you make up for in—" He was looking for an unoffensive name to call it, then found: "charm." Sébastien's eyes fought a little battle— down once, up, down again—trying to look at, without admiring, Nardi's coat. He pulled a disapproving face. "No one is more adept at getting gifts from women." He paused for a second, still without meeting Nardi's eyes, then said, "The issue here is what's good for you."

"What is good for you, you mean."

Sébastien arched one brow partly in challenge, partly in supercilious, self-righteous injury. "I know you don't give me credit for this, Nardi," he said, "but I am genuinely concerned for you."

"Concerned I won't survive till the wedding."

"Concerned you won't survive beyond Mademoiselle Van Evan's next visit, or the one after that—beyond the one where she finally brings you ether or chloral or morphine or God knows what."

"I have never indulged in morphine." Not regularly at least.

Sébastien made a mock-helpless laugh, a burst of condescending humor. "Though you have probably indulged in ten vices I simply don't know the names of."

Nardi sighed, accepting this insult. "All right. I deserve a measure of distrust. And I will take my medicine, so to speak. I will allow myself to be thrust into a country cottage with four gorillas, my friends not permitted in, no visitors save a doctor who seems to take somewhat malicious pleasure in poking at me ever since I burned down half his clinic. I will even suffer you to hire that vulture, Amelia Besom, who sliced me up a decade ago with every sharp word and judgment available. But this young American girl, she is happy and innocent. Let her be."

Sébastien glared at him. "This 'happy American girl' has

trespassed unforgivably. She is about to be fired, Nardi, and there is nothing you can do about it."

"If you cannot leave her alone because it is right to do so, then leave her alone because I insist. I want her to stay. I want her to be allowed to come see me if she wants to."

Sébastien contemplated him a moment, then said, "Nardi, I'm in charge here, and I'm going to do what's best for you."

"What is best for me is not to have this girl on my conscience. I am sorry that I involved her. Now, don't bother her. Leave her alone."

His brother only shook his head no.

Nardi stared at him. Then he said, "If you cause her trouble, I will leave."

Sébastien laughed.

"You know I will, Sébastien."

He laughed again. "You have no money, no way—"

"It doesn't matter. I will just walk away. The only reason you found me last time was because I didn't mind if you did. The only reason you hold me now is because I stay." He shrugged. "Sébastien, your big advantage is: I don't care."

"And you care about seeing her?"

"Not terribly." Again Nardi shrugged. "Probably I'm just bored." In anticipation of further objections from his very proper brother, he added, "Don't worry. Emil and Werner, Hans and Stephen, the 'fellows' are always around. I am not likely to do her any harm, one way or another."

The two men stared at one another.

Nardi contemplated his larger, older brother, a sibling who had always attempted to dominate, to bully him. For the most part, Nardi had let him. Sébastien had always been so clever and capable anyway, it had just seemed natural. Sébastien, however, had never seemed particularly grateful to have such respect. When Nardi just gave in, it seemed to sap the fun from it. When he didn't, it meant kicking, biting, bruises, broken bones, an unyielding fight to the death. Nardi seldom fought Sébastien, but when he did he had always been willing to risk more, which in a strange way always made him the winner. Worse, it galled Sébastien that

Nardi should be the one to choose, deciding what would and would not be an issue.

Middle age, however, seemed to be making Sébastien more savvy. He took a page from Nardi's book, shrugging. "All right, it doesn't matter," he said. "She can stay. She can sleep down there, so far as I'm concerned. You can plug her day and night—"

"I don't want to plug her, thank you." In truth, Nardi didn't think he could. The erection had subsided. He had thought about her since; it hadn't come again. Sexual performance seemed dubious or, at best, unpredictable. "I just want to talk to her, if she chooses to visit me."

"Oh, of course." Sébastien contemplated him a moment, then asked, "How is it going?"

"What?"

"The ether."

"I haven't had any, if that is what you're asking."

"Why not?"

He shrugged. "Too difficult. The one apothecary here in the village won't sell it to me. Nor will the local barber, surgeon, or animal doctor."

Sébastien snorted. "And I felt so foolish—so suspicious—for bribing them."

Nardi smiled ruefully back, at this game they'd both pursued without any spoken initiation. Again he shrugged. "Or maybe I am just not wild for fire."

His wing of the institute in Switzerland had gone up in smoke when an electrical spark had hit a few teaspoons of ether he had finagled from a nurse—*mais sacré bon Dieu,* one would have expected a nurse to better understand its dangers: She had sneaked it to him in the bottom of a lamp, apparently splashing it all over the wires in which there must have been a short. When an orderly turned it on later, the lamp, curtains, and walls exploded. The place burned for two hours.

The truth was, beyond minor difficulties and the one bad fright of his room igniting spontaneously, Nardi didn't know why he hadn't bothered to find what he had found with ease and efficiency for years. He didn't imagine he would stay off ether forever, this dry spell being somewhat less than voluntary. But he had discovered one thing: sober, he was better able to harass, and enjoy harassing, Sébastien.

"You won't prevent her coming, then?" Nardi asked his brother.

"I won't. But her employer won't like it."

"Don't tell Besom."

"I don't plan to. But the woman may ask."

"Lie."

"Pardon me?" asked fastidious Sébastien.

As if speaking to an idiot, Nardi told him, "Make something up, *espèce de connard*. Use your imagination. If Besom asks, make up something feasible that puts the girl somewhere else—somewhere that hides the fact that she might spend her free time as she wants to, without asking permission. Or tell the old cow skin that it is none of her affair."

Sébastien looked at him. "My, my. All this concern for an innocent young woman. Toward whom you have only the most noble intentions."

Nardi stared at the wall, at a crack that needed plaster. "I like her." These words didn't sound very convincing, not even to himself. He turned his face to look at Sébastien fully and spoke what he knew to be the truth. "And I like contradicting you. I like demonstrating now and then that you can't control me—except with my consent and blessing."

Sébastien sighed. "Fine. Mademoiselle Van Evan has free run of the place—and my best lies to her employer should she feel compelled to run in your direction."

Nardi felt relieved. And good; it felt really good to hear this. Never mind that he had saved little Hannah-with-an-H; he had saved himself from being a worthless, conscienceless—worse than useless—human being. There should have been trumpets, it felt so nice. But there was only the sound of murmuring plumbers and the soft shush of a scrub brush on brick; the scrubwoman had moved closer. On her hands and knees, she continued to work at the large stain on the floor, the edge of which ran under Nardi's feet.

"Thank you," he said.

Sébastien snorted. "Thank you nothing. I know better than to thwart you once you have taken a notion into your head. You would rather run yourself straight into a wall than let go of it."

Nardi smiled. "Yes. I like to think of it as my own brand of backward, wall-banging strength of character."

His brother harrumphed. "Well, I just wish you would apply all this strength of character in a different direction. It might make you into a man again."

Nardi scowled into his brother's back as Sébastien returned to his office. Mind your own business, he thought. As he sat there, perched on the edge of the sink, his hands in his pockets, a little flicker of rage began to glow. He drew his arms in toward his body so that his coat enveloped him completely, right down to the turn-ups of his trousers. He felt himself sink into this, encompassed by the coat, wrapped from neck to ankle in a deep, rekindled, luxurious anger.

He didn't want to be a man again, thank you very much; piss on Sébastien, Nardi thought. The interfering, smug know-it-all.

I am more comfortable drunk. No one expects anything of me. The second he was sober, the second he tried to do anything even a little right, immediately Sébastien started speaking in such far-reaching terms as "being a man again," whatever that meant. Why am I doing this? Nardi asked himself. Why stay sober, when sober was so damned . . . blindingly bright? Being sober was like living in daylight all the time; no shade, no night, no rest. And there was nothing for him to do by daylight. Useless, useless; this word echoed a moment. There was nothing really here for him. He wasn't going to sculpt again, and nothing else was worth doing. . . .

Nardi was on a roll now. How dare Sébastien, he thought. How dare he bring that old stoop-shouldered, skinny-necked—vulturine—art "expert" into this place and sit

her down right in front of him. The old she-monkey, old
trout, old dragon . . . Old Besom had always been a rich
source—a regular zoological garden—of hateful, spuming
epithets—

Something tapped his shoe. Nardi looked down. The
scrubwoman sat back onto her heels right there beside him.
She had tapped his shoe with her scrub brush.

"*Excusez-moi,*" she said. Her hair was streaked with
gray, though she appeared hardly older than Nardi. She
smiled, somewhat coyly this time, and repeated, "*Excusez-
moi, monsieur.*"

Damn them all anyway, Nardi thought. He smiled back,
glanced around. The plumbers were absorbed in their own
problems. Werner could be heard just beyond in the kitchen,
talking to someone. Nardi smiled more warmly at the
woman then squatted, bringing himself eye to eye with her
as he rested his arm leisurely across his knee.

With a casual finger, he pointed to the stain, asking,
"*Saviez-vous, mam'zelle* . . ." Did you know, miss, that
there exists something extremely effective for such stains
and as easy to get as walking over to the icehouse or
stopping in at the photographer's on rue Dupoil?

Chapter 11

NARDI CAME OUT onto the shady terrace again, where he fell in step with Emil and Werner, who were waiting for him. He got only as far as the steps, however, when a voice called from behind him. "Nardi!"

He turned, and there, fifty feet down the flagstones, was none other than Mademoiselle Hannah-with-an-H herself coming out a far French door.

She was scrubbed and pressed, as neat as a kerchief pulled at four pins, obviously dressed to go somewhere, somewhere remarkably unexciting: She wore an austere gray tailor-made buttoned high and tight, the stayed collar of a white blouse barely showing, white gloves, all topped off by a gray felt fedora with a black hat feather. In this dull-colored, straitlaced outfit, she bounded toward him, bouncing on the balls of her feet, beaming.

Nardi returned her smile as best he could. Except for the hat, nested at an almost rakish angle atop her ruby-red head, she looked like something out of the reign of Queen Victoria. No, she looked like Amelia Besom had dressed her, which was probably the case. He tried to be polite. "What a lovely hat," he said. Its feather, split and curled, fluttered in the breeze.

Her smile brightened further. "Is it?" She touched her hat briefly. "Thank you," she said. "Though I'd rather prefer more feathers, pleats, and netting, if only I could afford such things." She laughed, shrugging, then said, "I'm going into town again. The telegraph operator is saving some telegrams for me that came in last night from Paris."

He nodded. He found himself staring into her level gaze. This young woman's eyes were simply amazing. They were so large and open as to show a rim of clear white under each dark iris, her lashes so thick and long as to outline the roundness of her eyes in smudges of color—the rich coppery umbers of autumn. These warm, dark eyes smiled at him, direct and beautiful and . . . something else. For a second they seemed almost intelligent. No, Nardi decided, they were just foolishly self-confident. Poor little radish.

She looked down. With a gloved hand she smoothed her perfectly ironed skirt. As if to explain her presence out here, she said, "I am looking for my employer. She is about—" She raised her hand to demonstrate someone taller than herself.

Nardi cut her off. *"Oui.* She is inside with my brother." He nodded curtly toward the office door across the terrace, then found the stair rail as he backed up into it. He meant to turn and lope down the stairs at this point, to drift peacefully back to the cottage where nothing further would be expected of him. But politeness held him.

The babbling girl continued to talk. "Oh good," she said. She rattled on about having to double-check something or other with old Besom before leaving, then took his frown to mean he was bored with her busy, double-checking life and changed the subject. "Do you notice anything?" she asked. She held out her arms and stepped back.

He looked at her full-length.

She shied a moment, as if she hadn't quite invited such direct scrutiny, then a kind of resolve took hold. She stood up very straight and opened her arms wide to let him stare at what she'd asked him to stare at: her. "Well?" she asked.

Nardi stepped down backward, which put one foot on the step below and left one foot on the terrace, his knee bent; a man divided. He wanted to leave; he wanted to study her. The sight before him became a whole vista: a young woman

standing on a shady, sun-spotted terrace, a majestic old
ramshackle château behind. It was all humdrum, he was
sure. Nothing extraordinary here. He'd seen, and ignored,
the back of this château a thousand times in his life. He'd
looked at a thousand women, many of them prettier, and
often wearing considerably less, than this one. So he
glanced up and down Mademoiselle Hannah dutifully,
unexpectantly. And as he did so the girl's smile grew shyly
wider, prettier. She stood there with her arms out.

Nardi blinked, frowned. *Ventre Dieu, non,* he thought, it
was nothing; he was looking at nothing save generous
bosom and buttocks all buttoned and corseted and uphol-
stered in gray. Then his eye, the eye of a sculptor, caught a
line, a nuance, and he knew himself to be looking at
something that simply had not been here before. . . . He
straightened, focused his attention. It had to do with the
contour of her body, the curve of her hips. These were
somehow more . . . fluid.

He couldn't put his finger on it. He shook his head,
smiling mutely, and held out his hands: Tell me.

She laughed. "I'm more sedate."

He let himself look again, eyes down, eyes up the full
length of her. She turned around once for him slowly. Even
as she came to a standstill to face him again, she was a little
flurry of movement: a sway of hips, a settle of shoulders, an
indrawn breath that raised her bosom. The glossy black
feather in her hat band ruffled in a light gust then bobbed
again from the movement of her head. She suppressed a
self-conscious sound, a strangled giggle. Nardi could only
stand there, his smile becoming more tentative by the
moment. He liked looking at her, but—dull clothes or no
clothes—well, this girl was as sedate as the bells on a
bowling sleigh; she was as sedate as the bubbles that sent
the cork from champagne.

"Well?" she asked again.

He shrugged, trying to understand what she wanted him
to say so he could say it and be done. Inspecting her so
carefully, inch by inch, was beginning to make him uncom-

fortable, like the too-vivid memory of a dream he shouldn't have dreamed.

Nardi glanced toward Emil and Werner for help. They had stopped in the grass at the base of the stairs, where they waited patiently, with mild curiosity, for what the ether-drinking Parisian might do with the persistent attention of this naive little foreigner.

"The noise!" she exclaimed. She laughed deeply, producing a rich, deep-belly burble of mirth as free as a child's uninhibited laughter. The sound made Nardi's spine tingle. It made him want to put his ear to the bare belly that made it, to feel the vibration against his cheek as he rested his face against a smooth, warm abdomen.

When he remained speechless, she said, "My petticoat, you dunce! I took it off." She laughed again. "Now I am the quietest lady on the street." She turned, a pirouette of pure self-delight.

Nardi felt a wide smile begin to pull on his own mouth, his wary mood becoming a casualty to her silly, contagious good spirits. "Yes," he said. "You look quite nice."

"I *sound* nice," she corrected, laughing again.

"*C'est ça,*" he agreed. "No petticoat is an improvement." No jacket would be another improvement. No skirt, no blouse, no drawers—

Nardi's smile faltered, for he suddenly understood something, as if a layer of petticoats had dropped away from a mind swaddled in stupidity: This girl's charms were elsewhere than in the immediately obvious.

Wholesome she was. Wholesome and pretty and bright on the eyes. But her cuteness was a kind of distraction. It was so pronounced and colorful that it overstamped all initial impressions, masking the direction whence her true and stronger appeal came: Hannah Van Evan was voluptuous. Like everything else about her, her sexuality was direct and exuberant. She bubbled over with it. It had to do with her luxuriant bosom, the hourglass cinch of her waist, the wide, pendulous swing of her hips; with her energy and laughter and unwithholding manner.

"Well, I'm off," said the divine Mademoiselle Hannah. On the move again, she swung past Nardi, then turned suddenly right at his elbow. She leaned her hands onto the capstone of the stair post, raising up onto her toes. "The cake," she whispered at his ear—the little darling was now going to speak in secrets—"the pastry you wanted, shall I get you some while I'm in town?"

"It is Sunday."

"Oh. So no one sells cake?"

He blinked. "Actually a café behind the post office sells it after mass."

"Wonderful. So shall I bring you some?" She leaned a little closer, her nose not six inches from his.

Nardi nodded yes. He glanced down at Emil and Werner. They had come a bit closer, up to the very edge of the steps.

The girl beside Nardi rocked back down onto the soles of her feet and spoke softly. "Good. I'd like to." Then she smiled and asked, "Why is it your brother won't buy it for you?"

"Sébastien is being *difficile* . . . eh, difficult, *c'est tout.*" Nardi looked at her. She smelled of some grassy-fresh eau de toilette. He liked the smell of it. He leaned his elbow onto the capstone, his forearm lying within an inch of her fingers. He liked, too, the hushed-voice control he suddenly had over his own destiny, or at least over his own diet. He said *sotto voce,* "Sébastien and the doctor say I can't have cake till I am eating 'the good food.'" He shrugged, smiling, being—knowingly—a little charming. "It's childish, I suppose, but all they bring me is chicken and rabbit, and I hate both."

She laughed. "What do you like?"

He had to think. He could barely remember. He had once liked *le veau* though he could not remember the word for this in English. "Unborn calf," he said.

She grimaced. "You mean veal?"

"*Ah, oui,* veal. And duckling with orange glaze. And Camembert cheese, eggs, fruit. Celery." He pulled a face, shaking his head. "Not radishes, I am sorry."

"I know." She listened to the sound of her soft, sweet

laughter muffled there in the space between them. "Then I shall bring you cake this time."

"Thank you."

"And ether?"

Nardi stiffened and straightened. *"Qu'est-ce que vous dites?"*

She repeated, "Do you still want ether?"

"No—*euh*—*oui*—yes. No! Don't trouble yourself." How had they gotten onto this again?

"It's no trouble. You've helped me, taking my side on faith. I should return the favor."

"No, *vraiment,* I, *euh*—" He was without words, bewildered, guilty, needy. Of course he wanted ether. But the scrubwoman had just promised to bring him some. By dinner, in fact. He'd been very persuasive. He shook his head no, then yes, then no again. He could always use *more* ether.

"Well, do you or don't you?" the lovely Mademoiselle Hannah asked. "If I can find the barber I saw yesterday, I think I can buy you some. Does he go to mass on a Sunday?"

Nearly everyone in Aubrignon went to mass on a Sunday. There was nothing much else to do here. The barber would probably even be at the café afterward, when she went to buy the cake. Nardi was so nonplussed by this conspiracy of circumstances that he couldn't form a coherent response to her question.

"Well, never mind," she said. "I can probably find him. What do you do with the ether, by the way?"

Something. Say something. "I—*euh*—" he began. Nardi's brain formed some reasonable lies in French that rather irrationally translated into English out loud as, "I drink it." What an astounding thing to tell her—the truth.

But she didn't grasp it. She giggled. "Why, that would make you drunk! Or unconscious!" She laughed outright. "Or it would kill you!" She put her hand to her mouth. "You are really very funny," she said. Hannah Van Evan thought drinking ether was nothing short of hilarious.

Nardi laughed, too, feeling giddy himself. *Sacredieu,* she was making him as brainless as she was. Trying to recover, he said, "*Ah, bon,* a good joke. Cake would be nice. No ether." He caught himself. "Unless you can bring me gallons and gallons of it." One had to have standards. If he was going to ruin this girl's life, he didn't want it to be for nothing.

Her laughter quieted as her wide, doey eyes settled on him. "Gallons?" she repeated.

Nardi laughed self-consciously. "Well, a lot. If you bring any. You know what I mean."

"I'm not sure I do." She continued to smile, faintly, pleasantly, as she regarded him with an oddly contemplative look. Her gaze felt preternaturally intense, fully and surprisingly cognizant in a way that made Nardi thoroughly uncomfortable. After a moment she said, "Some people do drink ether, don't they?" She paused. "I mean, I never knew anyone in Miami who did, but my father mentioned once a whole town in Ireland where everyone drank it as a means around their temperance pledges."

"Draperstown," Nardi supplied. He knew of the town. "In Londonderry fifty years ago. Hardly anyone drinks it now."

She didn't blink but held his eyes.

A disturbing prospect occurred to him: This sweet, curvaceous young thing might not be as comfortably stupid as he would like to think. Hannah Van Evan was rather alert, in fact. She wasn't sophisticated or particularly well educated. She wasn't necessarily brilliantly intelligent—though it dawned on him that even this was not out of the question. She simply wasn't packaged and presented in the same way as all the other smart women he'd known. Nardi worried that this girl was not so much naive and trusting as she was just following along, minding her own business—and biding her time.

He added, "Be sure to hide whatever you bring, and Sébastien won't interfere."

For a moment more she smiled, her expression somehow complicated: gentle and benign, yet aware—though of what

or of how much, Nardi couldn't fathom. Then her ready
high spirits broke through this indecipherable mood. Her
smile lost its ambiguity. She grinned brightly. "So you think
your brother won't make trouble if he finds I like to visit
you?"

"I am sure he won't make trouble." Nardi grasped this
fact from the sea of uncertainty floating around him, like a
drowning man attaching himself to a piece of flotsam. "I
have just extracted a promise from him—he will let you
come if you want to."

"You asked him? I have permission? You actually *want*
me to come?"

"Well, yes." Wasn't this what he'd been saying all along?

"Oh, how sweet of you!" And, damn her anyway, she
brought her gloved hands together in a damper-clap of pure,
guileless ecstasy. She did a little dance standing there. "Oh,
I shall come, then. Soon. That would be unbelievably nice."

"*C'est ça,* that would describe it, mam'zelle. *Incroyable.*"
Unbelievable. Beyond reason. Nardi couldn't get a fix on
Hannah Van Evan. He couldn't classify her, couldn't grasp
who she was, what she was, how she could be like this. And
trying to made him dizzy; she took his breath away.

"Merciful heaven, will you look at this!" Amelia Besom
stood inside Sébastien's office, about to go out the door that
led onto the terrace. Now, however, her hand hovered above
the doorknob as she stared though lace curtains. "It is your
brother and my secretary, Miss Van Evan. And, oh, dear
Lord—" Amelia drew in her breath sharply, disbelieving,
horrified even as she said the words: "Why, the girl is
wearing no petticoat!"

Indeed, Miss Van Evan's skirt fell straight over her hips.
Amelia could faintly see the outline of leg, the round curve
of the girl's backside.

Under her breath, Amelia murmured, "Dear God, please
let her be wearing drawers!"

"Pardon?" The proximity of Sébastien's voice put him much closer than she had realized.

"Get your brother away from her!" Amelia demanded.

"What?"

"I know Bernard. He loves loose women."

"I beg your pardon?"

Flustered, Amelia turned on him, then corrected herself. "I mean, he might make a loose woman *of* her."

Sébastien frowned then raised his eyes, trying to spy round her head through the curtains. After a moment of this he said, "They are only talking." Then his handsome, serious mouth did an unusual thing. It curved into a slight smile as he said, "Well, what do you know."

"'Well, what do you know' indeed!" His tone made Amelia feel defensive. She turned back herself, pulling the curtain up so they could both see better.

The girl was backing toward the door, her tail end swinging, while the drunken scoundrel of the de Saint Vallier family smiled at her.

"Get him away from her," Amelia insisted again.

Sébastien gave his voice a perfectly pompous, superior air. "Get *him* away from *her*? With her behaving so"—he paused before he said—"*enchantingly* toward him?" He made enchantment sound like something negotiated in the dead of night under lampposts.

"Don't be disgusting," Amelia said. "She's innocent. He's slime. He's swamp muck. Is he still drinking ether?"

Sébastien didn't answer.

"Is he?" Amelia demanded.

"At the moment, he's not, *chère madame*."

"Don't 'shair madam' me!" She was about to upbraid him, explaining in no uncertain terms all the very good reasons she had for concern. There was Miami, after all, and Miss Van Evan's odd associations there with fancy, worthless young men—and there she stood making calf eyes at one of the most fancy-pants, worthless young men Amelia had ever known in her life. Then Amelia thought better of explaining anything to Sébastien; she felt in a quandary.

What she would have liked was more information. She asked instead, "You were going to tell me something about Miss Van Evan? Something about an 'unfortunate incident'?"

Sébastien left a pensive pause, then said almost absently, "Never mind. *N'importe*."

Amelia torqued her head around to stare at him. He *never* spoke to her in French. He even thought in English, she was fairly certain. But by the look on his face the stupid frog *connived* in his native tongue.

"What are you thinking, Sébastien?" she asked.

"*Vous dites?* Oh, nothing." Whatever it was, he wasn't going to say. He'd begun to smile again faintly.

Amelia clamped her mouth shut, turned, and stared out again at her adulterated handiwork: Miss Van Evan walking backward, dressed perfectly, all but for the fact that she hadn't much of anything on between her posterior and a skirt of gray summer worsted. Amelia could only whimper to herself. Dear Lord, just look at her. The girl was laughing, her manner natural, so easy. She had the most provocative way about her. . . .

Amelia grimaced as she thought of Miami again. She wished she had remained in Miami long enough to find out the particulars about what had happened there. Oh, references, references, she lamented to herself. How she wished she had a fistful of them now, like warranties, that could assure her that Miss Van Evan was as sweet and bright and resourceful as she appeared—just subject to outrageous lapses in taste—and not what rumors and oddities of behavior were beginning to suggest: an ebulliently unrepentant, scarlet creature of the first order.

Chapter 12

A DAY LATER, when Hannah came upon Monsieur de Saint
Vallier in a dilapidated ballroom, she said directly, "I have
been to see your brother." She wanted answers to what was
becoming the puzzle of Nardi de Saint Vallier.

"So he tells me," Monsieur de Saint Vallier answered. He
was inspecting an ivory-inlaid chestnut-and-silk settee that
sat in the center of the ballroom with the rest of the room's
furnishings. In his hand he held an inventory, a treasure-
trove list of all to be removed from the room in the next day
or so, sold or stored elsewhere, while renovations got under
way.

"What's wrong with him?" Hannah asked.

Monsieur de Saint Vallier glanced at her before saying,
"He's a lush, if you must know. He'll drink almost anything,
so I would appreciate it if you wouldn't bring him any
intoxicants, including ether, which I know he has asked you
for."

"Why?"

"Why?" he said with a snort as he focused on the list in
his hand. "Because he may one day poison himself if we
can't keep—"

"No, why does he drink ether?" Before he could give
another glib answer, Hannah asked, "What happened to
him?"

This won her a quick assessing look over the top of the

inventory page. Then Monsieur de Saint Vallier turned and
sat down into the settee. "He used to be a sculptor, a rather
fine one," he said. "I suppose he's disappointed in himself."

"Why? What happened?" she repeated.

Sébastien de Saint Vallier lay his arm on the armrest, his
pen dangling from his fingers. His face was dark against the
white wing of his high collar, a collar so stiff it seemed
made more of starch than linen. His cravat folded softly
beneath this, a perfect knot. His suit, the dark blue of the
French navy, was immaculately pressed and tailored—a
sartorial splendor as unforgiving as the pensive look he now
fixed upon Hannah. "There is no deep, dark trauma in my
brother's past," he declared, "if that's what your thinking.
Nothing so romantic as that. My brother merely buckled
under the pressure of little things, the sort of minutiae that
plague all our lives."

"Minutiae?"

He drew in an impatient breath. "Normal, daily living. He
met up with some harsh critics. Brutal actually, though any
seasoned artist knows these sorts of people exist—clever,
small-minded critics delighted to display their venomous
wit." He shrugged, as if criticism as vicious as snakebites
were common to all human experience. "Nothing to throw
a promising career away over. Then there was a large statue
that Nardi had worked on for over a year. He tapped the
stone wrong one day, and the piece split in two, neatly right
down the middle." He thought a moment and added, "About
then, also, he developed a touch of rheumatism, something
anyone who works with plaster and wet clay day in and day
out is bound to do. It froze up the joint of one finger."

Monsieur de Saint Vallier shook his head. "I don't mean
to minimize Nardi's suffering, but these things are not death
or trauma. His disintegration involved no dark discoveries,
no deep-burning passion for love lost. Artists with far less
talent than Nardi have struggled through much greater
adversity. As to such mundane matters, well—sculptors buy
new stone. They work in heated rooms. They soak their
hands in warm oil at night and use glycerin by day, instead

of water, to keep the clay wet. And most of all, they ignore the critics and make new work. This is the only mature approach, really. You don't just walk away. Or put yourself to sleep."

With unflappable severity, he added, "It was awful for the family. Our mother nearly went mad the first time he disappeared on a binge. She cried herself into a state of collapse. Our father—who was at one time or another the mayor of Paris, an adviser to a president, and a counselor to a king—never recovered. Public attention, with its attendant gossipy solicitude, was unbearable for him. His pride and dignity required he retire from public life. Besides this, we all had a great deal of time and money invested in Nardi. Building a really fine career in the arts requires more than just talent. There are connections to be made, exhibits, parties, not to mention the fact that stone and bronze castings are enormously expensive. There was not a one of us, not Pater, Mater, our sisters, or myself, who hadn't made sacrifices to help along the career of this 'amazingly talented sculptor' among us. Then he humiliated the whole family, along with himself, by putting himself to sleep like the family dog that got mouth cancer."

Hannah hadn't expected such a long speech, nor such honest bitterness. She didn't know what to say.

Sébastien de Saint Vallier contemplated her as he crossed his legs, one neatly creased and cuffed trouser leg to the other. It was one of those near-prissy movements that only a real gentleman could carry off without looking a fool. This man, this Parisian lawyer, carried it off with panache. He had a kind of steely assurance that went beyond self-confidence, like a man burdened, though managing heroically, thank you, with omnipotence.

He said, "Miss Van Evan, what do you think of this château?"

Hannah was taken aback by the change of subject. "It's, ah, enormous."

He laughed. "An enormous headache." Then his face grew earnest. "But it can be repaired. It can be remade back into its former glory, and I intend to do just that. And so can Nardi." He left a meaningful break. "He's a handsome man, yes?"

Oh yes.

"And witty and amusing?" asked the oh-so-sure-of-himself man in the settee.

Hannah nodded yes.

"Worth saving?"

Of course he was. Yet, even at this moment, Hannah knew the line of reasoning Monsieur de Saint Vallier was offering to be dangerous. People didn't remake other people.

"The right woman can change a man," pronounced Sébastien de Saint Vallier. Hannah knew he was appealing to her vanity. "If I could get your cooperation in remaking Nardi in the same way I have gotten your help in remaking the château, why, there would be no limit to how fine a man he could be. I know him. He could be great again. . . ."

Something he'd said a moment ago sprang suddenly into a concrete idea. Hannah, the pharmacist's daughter, thought of a way she could help.

And, from here, her thinking leaped to presumption: Why, if someone could only get Nardi de Saint Vallier sculpting again, she told herself, he could resume his former proficiency as an artist and flourish as human being. All he needed was someone to give him the proper benevolent shove in the right direction. And Hannah hereby ordained herself as this "someone," accepting this mission as whole-heartedly as a young nun in the first hour of her calling.

Chapter 13

I once inhaled a pretty full dose of ether, with the determination to put on record, at the earliest moment of regaining consciousness, the thought I should find uppermost in my mind. The mighty music of the triumphal march into nothingness reverberated through my brain, and filled me with a sense of infinite possibilities. . . . The one great truth which underlies all human experience flashed upon me. . . . Staggering to my desk, I wrote, in ill-shaped straggling characters, the all-embracing truth still glimmering in my consciousness. The words were these (children may smile; the wise will ponder): "A strong smell of turpentine prevails throughout."

—Oliver Wendell Holmes, *Mechanism in Thought and Morals,* 1892

SULFURIC ETHER WAS sweet and hot, pungent and burning to the palate. It did not smell the least, to Nardi, of turpentine, but rather of large, white, oversweet flowers, fat, fleshy, prehistoric in their size and substance. He thought of these flowers as fringed, mouthed, and pistiled with sticky aroma, with pink-tipped, translucent styles and stigmas that moved in flower throats like beckoning fingers. Lush, languorously

163

heavy, meltingly ephemeral, an indigene to the New World tropics or an Old World greenhouse—something akin to night-blooming cereus. Ether, to him, was the nectar of such flowers, gathered and carried in the mouths of foot-long bumblebees, its aroma as old as Egypt, as modern as white-walled hospitals, as personal and familiar as his own vague, euphoric befuddlement.

This evening, in addition, ether represented something worth celebrating. Nardi possessed Sébastien's defeat in the form of a brown glass bottle that fit snugly into the hollow of his fist.

This triumph over his brother was so sweet and according to plan that Nardi was only mildly put out by the miserliness of the offering itself. The scrubwoman had sent him only a few drams in a bottle necessarily small enough to hide in a bowl of lettuce. With a larger amount, he would have gulped it, perhaps held his nose and mouth to keep the vapor from rising. But only six or seven drams. He stared at the bottle. It contained hardly more than a liquid ounce, just under an ounce by weight, under a half-ounce avoirdupois—when a seasoned etherist such as himself could have pegged two ounces in a swallow, belched, stood up and wobbled off, looking for more. On a long and generous debauch, Nardi had known himself to go through a pint. This was going to be one shot. One rather stingy shot. But enough, he reminded himself, that, had Sébastien known, he would have had a seizure.

Buoyed by this thought, Nardi prepared for the whole ritual, setting glasses out. The second shift of Swiss order-lies was on duty and accounted for: Hans was walking the dinner tray, and the girl who had brought it, back up to the kitchen. Stefan loudly pursued his own passion; he was behind the cottage in the woods shooting squirrels. Nardi drew water from the sink tap, filling two glasses—one rinse of water before to cool his mouth and throat, one after to weigh the ether down in his stomach. Meanwhile he kept his small bottle of contraband on the floor behind the counter, corked, low, and out of sight of the doorway.

Nardi pulled a comfortable chair over to the sink then opened the cabinet beneath the counter. He would operate from inside this, off the top shelf. He sat down into this little corner of privacy he made for himself, a chair wedged between counter and cabinet door. Leaning between his knees, he loosened the cork of the ether bottle then set this inside the cabinet. He had just thrown back the first water and picked up his little bottle, when a voice above him spoke.

"What are you doing?"

Nardi bashed his knee on the cabinet door in his rush to close it, half drowning on the water in his mouth—it went down wrong. He braced his forearm on the counter's edge, coughing like a man with consumption. As he violently cleared his pipes his eyes focused tearily on a blur of red hair.

A small hand patted his back. "Are you all right?" asked Hannah of the copious chignon the color of henna. She lay above him, half on the countertop, bent over it onto her bosom and one forearm, her other hand stretched over to beat his back. Nardi stared at her feet on the far side of the counter visibly kicking up skirt—no petticoats, which at this moment he resented. She was entirely too quiet without her usual tumult of underskirts.

Nardi drew in a clear breath and spewed out, "You idiot! What the fuck are you doing here? You simpleminded, intruding, backwoods foreigner . . ." Happily he fumed away entirely in rapid French, for a moment later he noticed something there at her elbow on the counter. A very interesting something. The sight made him rise from his chair.

It was a brown glass jug containing a clear liquid—about a half gallon of it, God bless this dear, sweet woman.

Meanwhile the dear, sweet woman was greatly ruffled by his angry outburst. Hannah slid backward, coming down onto her feet on the other side of the countertop to stare at Nardi. Well, no, she thought, apparently she wasn't as welcome here as she had supposed from his invitation.

The man before her, risen to his full, stately height, then said, *"Je m'excuse, ma petite chérie.* You startled me." He smiled, suddenly cordial. He reached for the jug. "What do we have here?" he asked.

Hannah distrusted this quick shift of mood. She offered hesitantly, "I brought you a present."

"I can see that." His fingers slid down along the curve of the jug. Then Nardi uncorked the jug and, putting his nose to it as to a bouquet of flowers, took a big whiff. He frowned abruptly. With rude dissatisfaction, he said, "What is it?"

"Glycerin."

"Glycerin?"

Hannah looked around the room. "There's clay here, isn't there?" Slightly more positive, she walked round the counter. If she could find some clay, she would show how fine a gift this was.

When she bent to look in a cabinet door he took her arm and said, "The clay box is over here." He walked her over to a large wood trunk and lifted the lid. "If this is what you want, there is a ton of it."

Indeed, the canvas-lined box contained a small mountain of reddish raw earth. "Oh, perfect," Hannah said. It was: The clay was rock hard in places, dry about the edges, bereft of moisture.

She brought the open jug over, then, mixing with her hands, began to drizzle and pat glycerin into the clay's highest summit. The glycerin mixed readily, the dryness dissolving away, creating a kind of muddiness where she couldn't immediately mix it adequately. "You see," she said with growing enthusiasm, "your brother mentioned that glycerin could help a sculptor with rheumatism, so I went into town and asked the local pharmacist, who was ever so helpful, to supply with me some. . . ." She talked, afraid to stop for fear of what Nardi might say in the interim. If she could just get across to him how good it would be for him to use glycerin, for his art, his life, and his future. "At my father's pharmacy, there were always gallons of glycerin, so I knew. . . ."

Nardi de Saint Vallier was not happy, and Hannah could see this on his handsome face. She spoke faster, pouring and mixing, pouring and patting. "You see, you wet the clay with glycerin," she said, "instead of water. Glycerin doesn't evaporate as quickly and thus makes the clay less cold, much less a problem for aching fingers."

"I don't use clay," he murmured.

"Well, no, but you could." She poured some glycerin in a thick stream.

Nardi bent down, leaning one hand on the rim of the clay box, putting the other under the flow. He rubbed his fingers together a moment, as if testing the viscosity. Then he wiped his fingers on her cheek. "Stop it," he said.

Hannah flinched, blinked, frowning, then explained, "You don't understand. This will make it so you can handle the clay easier."

He reached into the mess. He *was* feeling it.

She smiled up at him. "You see? It's warm!" Then Hannah was startled by something hitting her chest.

"Do not fix me," he said.

She looked down. Square in the middle of her white blouse was a zinnia-burst of muddy, red clay. "You've messed my clothes."

"*Ma chérie,* you want to mess in my life. Do not interfere."

She scowled at him a moment, then grabbed up a wad of clay and threw it back at him. It splattered, hitting his cheek, neck, and collarbone.

Nardi let out a sound of anger, surprise, then leaned across the box, grabbed Hannah by the arm, and pulled her forward. She caught herself in the clay, sinking up to her wrist, ruining a white cuff. The stupid, stubborn— He turned his back on her, walking away toward the sink.

Hannah was suddenly infuriated. "Why won't you even try this?" She wanted to knock him down, force him to see reason. "You pigheaded fool. This could be a boon to you, if you weren't so—"

At the sink he glanced sidelong at her as he washed his

hands. "Why are you doing this? What are you trying to prove?"

"Nothing, you idiot. If you would only—"

"*Ma chérie*," he said, "every person who has ever tried to save me has had some sort of stake. Sébastien. My family. Women or friends who missed my past glory. What is your investment? Look at yourself."

She did. She had her arm cocked, her hand loaded with a glob of solid, slippery mud, ready to plaster him with it. She lowered this arm. "Nothing," she said. "No investment—"

"Then why are you so angry?"

"Because you won't let me help, when this idea is really so good—"

"It is a pointless idea." He bent over the sink and rinsed his neck, splashing as he said, "Here." He offered her a towel from a hook at the side of the counter. "You should sponge your dress."

She took the towel, then, using an empty glass on the counter, poured water over her jacket and shirtfront then down her skirt, where a few red droplets had spattered.

Nardi wiped his own neck and face as he said, "I haven't used plaster castings from clay models since I was twenty."

"So what does the great sculptor use?"

"Now you sound like my brother." When Hannah threw him a look of pucker-mouthed apology, he shrugged then answered, "I work directly in stone. It is not that difficult." He sniffed. "Though Sébastien finds the process pretentious. 'The Michelangelo of tombstones,' he calls me."

"Present tense? You still make things."

"In Paris I was still hammering out the occasional monument"—he panned the room, giving the place a wan regard—"before my family brought me here. I could do a small tombstone in a day, complete with 'Here lies the remains of . . .' in neatly carved letters, Roman or Gothic, your pleasure." He laughed dryly. "Meanwhile"—he jerked his head in the direction of the clay box—"Sébastien brings in a ton of clay. 'All a big mistake,' he tells me. 'If you model in clay first again, like a less grandiose artist, you could produce decent work.'" Nardi ended this with a distasteful face, then looked away with his usual grim expression whenever he spoke of his brother.

Hannah rinsed her sleeve cuff in the sink and said, "Your brother cares about you."

"It is not too late for me to drop you in the clay box, buttocks first, you know."

"What?"

"First glycerin. Now cheap sentiment."

"I'm not trying to fix you again, if that's what you think. I was stating a fact." She picked up the hem of her dress and wrung out a small puddle of water. She glared up at him, repeating unhesitantly, "Your brother cares about you."

He let out a disgusted sound. "Would you like to know how much my brother cares about me?" He laid his towel down and leaned against the counter. "When I was seventeen and throwing up regularly before exhibits—out of sheer terror—my brother found me a little something so I could calm down and perform like the amazing de Saint Vallier that he wanted me to be. Do you know what he brought me?"

"No."

"Ether." When she said nothing, he asked, "Shocked?"

"Yes. At the direction of your anger. You're the one who drank it."

He snorted and turned his back on her. "How neat and tidy your little world must be, that you can say something that self-righteous. Go play with Sébastien, will you?"

"No. He doesn't like me. So why did you drink it?"

Nardi turned around to look at her, a little insolently this time. He ignored her question and asked instead, "You think I like you better than Sébastien does?"

Hannah frowned down into her wet skirts. No, he mustn't like her too much. He wouldn't let her help him. He threw clay at her. Her spirits sulked. Of course, Nardi de Saint Vallier wasn't overly fond of her. How could someone as lovely and worldly, someone as Parisian as he like anyone as gauche as herself? Then she caught a glimpse—a faint smile, unguarded, teasing—of what was coming to be a familiar look on his face. She said, "Actually I don't know. Do you?"

He folded his arms over his chest and tilted his head at her. Again he didn't answer directly. He said, "You really puzzle me. I have just pulled you over into a boxful of wet clay. Are you just a hopeless optimist? Or do you have some sort of second sight?"

Hannah felt a smile begin to grow. "You do, then?" she asked.

"Do what?"

"Like me," she said.

He laughed, a resonant, throaty sound that was both appealing and vaguely worrisome. His laughter seemed somehow more complicated than the simple statement— *you like me*—to which it responded. He leaned toward her enough that she felt compelled to take a step back. He whispered something she couldn't understand.

A little irritated, she said, "I can't hear you. Speak up."

"Sans doute," he said.

"Speak English."

He laughed again and said, "Definitely. I definitely like you, Mademoiselle Van Evan." His laughter this time seemed a true release, an honest bewilderment. "Though I have no idea why. You are not at all what I would conjure up, were I to dream up a female companion for myself out here."

Hannah's timid smile became confident. It broke onto her face with her standing there dripping water and clay all over. "I thought so," she said. Her smile was hopeless, coming out everywhere. This information so pleased her.

It apparently depressed him. He stood there stoicly and said, "Be careful of me."

She was going to argue with him and tell him how perfectly wonderful he was—when he wasn't throwing clay at her—but he gave her such a narrow look as to silence her.

"Je t'aime bien, toi," he said. "I like you, but there's a certain danger in that. There is a side to me that is more

foreign to your sweet, light nature, *chérie,* than anything you have experienced in the whole of France. You don't speak my language, and I don't mean French. To deal with me, you would have to relearn everything you ever knew."

Surely he was telling her to be frightened, but her foolish smile kept coming and coming, irrepressibly fearless. It was so broad it hurt her face. "I might know more than you think," she said.

"You might know less than you can imagine."

Hannah shrugged, still aware of the ridiculous smile she wore as she stood there in her dripping dress. She couldn't seem to stop her own hopeful, confident voice from answering, "I learn quickly."

This finally elicited what she wanted. He laughed, a sincerely delighted sound. "Then see if you can learn this." He kicked the edge of her dress. "You cannot fix me. I am the devil himself when it comes to people trying to. Ask Sébastien. I broke two of his ribs then his nose—that is when he finally let go, with his nose gushing blood and him screaming at me, calling me a crazy, *eh, espèce de con,* a son of a bitch. I rather agreed with him."

"You only threw a little clay at me, Nardi. I can't believe you'd—"

"No, Hannah. That is what you must learn. If you had not let go and were *still* trying to fix me, as Sébastien is tempted to do, I would think of something worse. Don't doubt it. I don't let people make me over. I fight them if they try. And I fight without rules—a little style I picked up by living these last few years in the backstreets of Paris, with the dregs of humanity. They don't give quarter to women there. They don't make allowances for good intentions."

"Have you ever hit a woman?"

He laughed. "No. Though I have plastered and clayed a few. And I did push a woman once into a pile of horse dung on the street."

"I don't think you're one of these people, these dregs—"

"I am, Hannah, in my way. That is what I'm telling you. I was raised a gentleman. I won't bash you in the head, but

I can hurt you. And I can hurt you intentionally, with no compunction, out of nothing more than self-defense. I know because I have hurt enough people, men and women, until I am sick to my stomach from it."

"Nardi, you're being ridiculous—"

"You are being naive." Out of the blue he asked, "Would you like to lose your job, Hannah?"

"No," she said. "Of course not. I love my job—"

He wiped a spot of clay from her shoulder, nudging her. "Would you like me to kiss you?" he asked.

She was so taken aback. "I—ah–don't know, um—"

"Yes, you do," he said. "Do you or don't you?"

"Um." She wet her lips and tried not to look at his sharp-featured face, at his lovely, wet, messy shirt. She tried not to think of the strange, dark business that lay beneath his question. She tried to think of a coherent answer.

After a moment he said, "This will help. I am going to kiss you. If you don't want me to, just push me away."

His mouth touched hers, and she felt such a rush of sensation. Melting knees. Panting, breathless giddiness. Up close, he smelled of the raw earth with which she had pelted him. His hair was damp; it smelled of rustic soap. Against her wrists his sleeves were wet where he'd washed up. He was cool to the touch, all but for his mouth. His lips were hot and a little rough. As they brushed against hers she realized they were slightly chapped. And wholly marvelous. Heaven above, if this was the pain he was talking about, she was a glutton for it. For a second more his mouth was hot and dry against hers. Then not so dry: His tongue wet her lips. And Hannah opened her mouth like a fledgling ready for supper.

He pulled back, smiled at her confusion, was about to speak—and she threw herself at him. Arms, mouth, full body. She pulled his head down to her and kissed him soundly.

He let out a guttural of surprise, a deep, startled, satisfied garble. His hands floundered a moment. For two seconds she held his head and kissed his mouth while the rest of him

tried to pull back from her assault. Then, blissfully, he gave
in. He moved toward her, turning her slightly to flatten her
against the counter. His body pressed her backbone into the
edge, while his tongue came straight into her mouth. He
locked his fingers into hers, stretching her captured hands
out along countertop, bending her back slightly. Hannah
could feel the sinew and muscle of him, arm against arm,
chest against chest; she could feel at her buttocks the outline
of a drawer knob, such was the pressure of his body, the
power of his grip. While his mouth, oh, his mouth, his
tongue made the most heavenly rude intrusions; wet,
forceful, deep.

He kissed her ferociously; lips, teeth, the inside of her
cheeks, gums, tongue, throat, entering her mouth more
thoroughly than she would ever have imagined a man might
want to. It was amazing and delicious. The only thing she
might have liked was a dash more freedom. He held her
pinned there, as if she might leave the moment he let go.

This was hardly the case. In fact, she would have liked to
touch him, feel the hard curvatures of his chest, run her
hands along the thews of his arms. She began to long for this
so much that when he eased back and let go of her wrists,
her hands came up of their own accord, spread-palmed, to
survey his chest.

He started to say something then sucked in his breath. He
took a step back.

Hannah took a step forward. The feel of him was simply,
utterly gorgeous under her fingers. He was a solid as stone,
substantial, contoured. She drew her thumbs down the deep
indention along his breastbone.

He took another step back, muttering, *"Eh, bon Dieu—"*

Hannah followed, her fingers spreading across his belly.
Beneath his ribs, his abdomen was hard, the muscles there
individually delineated. When he moved—he stepped back
again, regaining his balance on the back of a chair as he
tripped over the jug where she'd left it on the floor—his
belly moved by segmented sinew. The front of him was
plated, corrugated in places, smooth and rippling.

She let her hands slide around his ribs and heard him take another deep breath. He grabbed her wrists. But she freed her hands, up and around his, to caress his fingers. His hands were wonderful, almost courtly in their grace, with long, tapered fingertips. He must have backed up another step, because his heel suddenly, soundly hit against the wood end inset of the clay box. Hannah realized a split second too late that her grab to save him only made him evade further. He backed away where there was no room to—and fell backward into the clay, landing with a loud, perfectly obscene squish.

There was a moment of stunned silence, Nardi staring up at Hannah, a man astounded, while Hannah gawked down at him.

"Oh, I'm so very sor—" she began.

He laughed, though it took a moment to realize this was what he was doing. He couldn't quite catch his breath. *"Sacré nom de Dieu,"* he panted. "You are in much more trouble than I ever—" He broke off, laughing deeper. *"We,"* he corrected, "are in much more trouble than I realized."

Dimly, Hannah grasped something. Trouble. There was trouble here. Where was it coming from? She *was* in trouble, but she couldn't remember how.

Then, panting and swallowing between breaths, as he sat there with his elbows on the box rim, he laughed out the direction and scope of her potential for disaster: "You are much more of a *eh, putain, eh,* tramp than I realized."

Hannah felt her throat tighten, her eyes well up. "I am not!"

He cocked his head as he smiled a crooked smile, the smug look of a man sitting in a clay box who had nonetheless made his point. "No, you are not, but she worries you are."

"What?"

He thrust himself up awkwardly, his shoes gooshing with wet clay as his feet found the floor. Clay ran down the sides of his trousers. "Amelia Besom," he clarified. "We both know her well. What do you suppose would happen if she found out I were sleeping with you?" He looked down at his pants, shaking himself.

"I—I didn't sleep with you. I only kissed you. Besides, I—I thought you were immune or something."

He smiled up at her. "Not to you apparently." He gave her his full attention. "So as a hypothetical question, Hannah, what do you suppose she would do?"

"She'd fire me."

"Bravo," he said. "And you still want to fool with me?"

Hannah drew herself up in an imitation of Mrs. Besom's grandeur and dignity. "That seems a rather arrogant leap, to suppose that I would sleep with you just because I liked kissing you."

He laughed. "You are a babe in the woods. I wish I didn't like that so much about you, my sweet, round, fresh little radish." He tilted his head. "So, little Hannah, do you want to sleep with me?"

She lifted her chin, confident in her answer. "No."

"Because I have been a little mean to you?" He laughed. "What if I were nice?" His laugh took on a distinctly wicked edge. "Or only a little bit mean in the right way, like a moment ago, mean in the way you like?" He wiggled his eyebrows and grinned. "Your own special little brand of whips and chains?"

"Whips and chains?" Hannah blinked. "What are you talking about?" She stepped back.

"Ah," he said. "Whips and chains not to your fancy?"

"They're to yours?"

"*Chérie,* anything is to my fancy. Nothing shocks me. I am from Paris, remember?" When she only stood there transfixed, horrified-fascinated, he asked, "How good was that kiss for you just a moment ago? For me it was *abasourdissant*—ah, how you say—astounding. I cannot remember enjoying kissing a woman so much, not in a very long time."

Hannah wanted to shut him up. His honesty shocked her; it made her feel odd, squirming, uncomfortable. No, she didn't like him at all. Not one bit. Then she heard herself say, "Yes, I liked it, so I'll kiss you again if you want me to."

He let out a laugh. "Yes, kissing you is definitely interesting. I want to do it again." Then his face grew serious. He lowered his gravelly voice into something near a whisper, hardly more than a rasp, and said, "I want to kiss you when we are alone, and no one can walk in on us, and you are feeling good and loose and happy. I will wrap my alpaca coat around you and kiss you and tell you all about Paris, yes?"

"Well, n-no, I don't—"

"And slide my stomach against yours and kiss your neck and cheeks and eyes and mouth. Until you lie down with me and I can keep you against me all night, while I lick you like a cat."

Hannah felt her face heat up. "No," she said, "I'd lose my job if I stayed out all night."

"Précisément. That is what I am saying."

"I simply couldn't. If I lost my job, well, France is so foreign to me—"

"Bravo. And Sébastien would not hesitate to throw you out in the street in the bargain."

Hannah drew back from him. She understood. She couldn't kiss him anymore, though—Jesus, Mary, and Joseph—it was nice. She said in a small voice, "You're right. I don't know what I would do if I were suddenly without food or money or a roof. I have no friends or relations here."

"That is not entirely true. You have one friend." His smile became benign. It took a moment for Hannah realize Nardi was speaking of himself. "But he is undependable. I know myself, Hannah. Financially I can't help you. I can't even help myself. Sometimes I can confront Sébastien, sometimes I can't. I lose my temper and become a raving lunatic. Your situation is ripe for chaos—you see, I should tell you something else. Already I make love to you in my sleep."

She looked up. "You do?" she said.

"I do. And after that kiss, I doubt I will think of much else, day or night."

Dear heaven, it was terrible how this knowledge affected her. It made her mouth dry, her heart thump. She *loved* hearing this. She said, "You could deal with Sébastien. You don't need to make him feel so bad all the time, just because he's trying to—"

"You are missing the point. I *want* to make him feel bad."

"But I could help you—"

"I don't want your help. I *enjoy* hurting him. As much or more than kissing you."

"But I could help you so you didn't. I could save you all the hurt and—"

His face tightened. "You cannot. That is what I am telling you. Only *I* can save me, and I don't want to. So stop being such an interfering, backwoods, ignorant, tarting little yokel, will you?"

Hannah's face drained of blood.

Nardi saw this and had to steel himself if he was to go on. He had, just yesterday, heroically rescued this young woman's future with the truth. He'd told Sébastien she was innocent, and she was. Now he meant to spare her further: this time from herself.

"I am wrong for you, Hannah," he said as he strolled over to the cabinet. He bent, opened the door, and pulled out the bottle of ether.

He was going to frighten her—or disgust her, either one would do—out of any hankering for him. She thought him bold and heroic and fine. Well, he could show her otherwise.

He put a hand on the counter and swung himself up and around to sit on it, swinging his legs as he uncorked the ether. The fumes permeated the air in moments.

She looked at the bottle as he raised it, scowled, then said, "You're not supposed to have that."

"No, I am not. So when I finally get some, I like to enjoy it. Now, if you will just trot along, mam'zelle . . ."

She remained glued to the spot. "That's poisonous."

"*Évidemment.*"

"And volatile and inflammable."

He shrugged. "I like that it is a little dangerous."

"A little? If it doesn't poison you, ignite, or explode in your face, its vapor can asphyxiate you." She said tightly, "You can't drink that."

"No, I can't. Not with you *foutrement* lecturing at me as if you were my mother, so if you will frolic off now to bother someone else."

She stayed where she was, her dark eyes staring majestically. "You could be so much better." Her lovely intense eyes were the sort that could make a man long to be what he wasn't. "You could be a prince," she said.

Nardi laughed. "Ah, so now we have it, your stake in my 'improvement.' I am supposed to be a prince for you." He lowered the bottle to rest on his thigh. "I can't be, Hannah. That is what I have been trying to tell you. I am a drunk and a failure. A handsome one"—he laughed again dryly—"and a rather stylish one, I like to think. But nonetheless I am a man who has drunk away all his best possibilities. I am not the prince of your dreams."

She didn't say anything for a moment, but he knew he'd hit close to home: dear God, the look of dismay that came into her face. She murmured finally, "You are self-destructive."

He laughed. "Now where have I heard that before? *Ah, oui.* Everyone tells me this."

"And useless—"

"Useless again?" Nardi arched his spine. This stupid word brought him off the counter and onto his feet. It made him disproportionately angry to hear it again. "Damn your fanciful nonsense! Are you not listening to me?"

"You have talent, intelligence—"

"*Merde.*" He took a breath. "*Écoute,* I have disappointed you, *mais mon Dieu,* a woman who sees life so much *la vie en rose* must live constantly with disappointment. Will you please leave now?"

She stood up to her full, short height. "You are worse than useless," she said. "You have no values, no respect for yourself or others." Her voice broke. "You are rich and wellborn, handsome and clever—you have everything, education, family, leisure, money—"

Laughter burst from him. "Hardly—"

"You have everything I ever wanted. You could do anything that you pleased. And what you please to do is this"—she pointed a reprehending finger at the bottle he held—"to put yourself to sleep like, like—like a dog with mouth cancer. What you do is worse than doing nothing. It's vile."

For a moment more she stood there, her lips tight, the bottom one out. She looked positively juvenile—all but for her eyes. They held a kind of fierceness, a clear, self-reliant intransigence that he just couldn't put with her round, pretty face or her small, curved, soft-looking body. "I will never come here again," she said.

"Good." What an absurd threat. The child. "I don't care where you go." She was gullible to have believed him. Stupid woman. He could never respect anyone who had such poor taste as to like *him*. He didn't *want* to see her again.

Nardi raised the bottle. He was going to drink the ether in front of her, but she preempted him: After one split second of wide-eyed incredulity, Mademoiselle Hannah ran past him, around the counter, then out the door. The sound of her feet tap-tap-tapping down the front porch steps made him so angry that for a moment the room shifted before his eyes; he saw sparks of light in his field of vision.

Damn her, damn her, damn her.

He followed after her, cursing her in French—*"Tu m'emmerdes! Va te faire fiche!"*—his mind went blank in English, or he would have cursed her in her own language. He stood at the doorway, watching her run uphill, slip, grab a jutting stump, recover. She scrambled away from him as fast as her legs and arms and grasping hands would carry her.

"So I am not the man you want me to be," he yelled after her. "Who asked you to wrap me in your silly illusions anyway?" He went to the railing, hanging on to a post,

leaning to call to her as she mounted the embankment. "And
I *like* ether. Which, by the way, is *extrêmement* Parisian and
safer than alcohol——"

At the top of the rise, the edge of the trees, she turned. "It
will take you," she shouted. "It will take you and your
humanity."

He flinched at the sharpness in her voice, narrowed his
eyes, and prepared to yell something profound back at
her—only to discover himself scowling up into a gap in the
trees. There was nothing where she had stood except
swaying branches and leaves that shimmied with anger.

Back inside, as he realized he still held the uncorked
bottle of ether, he pointedly drank its entire contents. What
hadn't spilled or evaporated, however, went down like a
thimble of water. Nothing. It did absolutely nothing for him.

"Merde et sacré merde," he muttered.

He waited an instant longer, then found himself perfectly
capable of cocking his body and throwing the empty bottle.
He flung it with all the force in his arm, in his anger, all the
force of his frustration and self-loathing. The bottle hit the
rough stones just below the mantel of the fireplace, shattering and popping in a small, violent explosion of residual
gases that sent glass back at him—and into the ball of his
hand when he instinctively protected his face.

He pulled the shard of glass from his palm then watched
blood well up to run between his fingers. *"Espèce de con,"*
he murmured to himself. *You stupid bastard.* He tucked his
hand under his arm and pressed, trying to stop the bleeding.
In the end, he tucked both hands under opposite armpits,
leaned his head against the wall, and rocked. *"Espèce de
sacré con,"* he whispered.

He checked his palm again. It was a small cut, just an
ooze. It would be fine. He had not hurt himself, he had not
hurt the girl; he had merely been an ass again. And these
realities brought such relief that Nardi had to force a sob
back down into his chest. He refused to let it come out, and
the effort made his throat convulse from his mandibular

joint down his gullet into his subclavius and pectoral muscles.

It will take you, she'd said.

Well, it could have him, he told himself. And it could have his blessed humanity as well. Then out loud he cursed at the top of his lungs, *"Sacré Dieu au ciel!"* He never used to "tell" himself anything!

She had reawakened this voice, this self, this internal, self-critical narrative of his life. He had successfully lost track of this voice, his attraction to women, to cake, his interest in living—his humanity—and now here it all was again. She had done this horrible thing to him—

No, he was doing it to himself. She was pretty and wholesome and full of sunlight, the antithesis of old dark Nardi, and—stupid bugger that he was—he wanted to touch the sunlit side of himself again. The stupid, ignorant, naive side that had laughed and danced once. The dog with mouth cancer wanted to dance like a man again, to be a human being, and it wanted this with all its poor dumb, benighted soul. . . .

Chapter 14

Aubrignon-sur-Seine, France
5 May 1903

Mrs. Felix Stanton
23 Bay View
Newport, Rhode Island

Dear Mrs. Stanton,

Enclosed you will find a check written to the Ladies' Opera Guild. As I arrived here in Aubrignon, so far from the opera or symphony—or even the pleasure of the lovely choir that you and I share at our own Trinity Episcopal Cathedral in Manhattan—I thought, "Why, I simply must write to Mrs. Stanton, the Guild's endowment chairwoman, and make a donation." In the absence of music and sophisticated culture here in rural France, I have realized how important it is to me that the opera—and of course the Ladies' Opera Guild—continue and flourish. I hope you find this contribution helpful in making the Guild's upcoming season the best it can possibly be.

Since I had need to write to you on the above important matter already, I hope you will not mind that I also include here the request of a small favor. All I need really is a bit of information, if you find it significant enough to relay.

I have recently hired a young woman as my secretary-companion, a Miss Sue-Hannah Van Evan. Since hiring her,

I have discovered that she once kept house for you at your winter home in Miami, Florida. This young woman came to me with the diplomas and good manners that demonstrated her able training, and, since my last secretary had quit on short notice and I needed to leave with haste for Europe, I hired Miss Van Evan. Rumors have come to me, however, of a vague "sordid entanglement" involving the girl while she was in your employ. Straight to the point, if you know such rumors to be false or exaggerations put upon me by gossips, please don't feel compelled to respond to this letter. If, however, you know of genuine reasons why I might have cause to doubt Miss Van Evan's moral fitness to hold the position of secretary-companion to a lady of breeding and society such as myself, I should most appreciate hearing from you on this matter.

I remain grateful for your help—and of course privileged to support the good, dutiful work you and the ladies of the Guild put forth for the benefit of all of us, Episcopalians and non-Episcopalians alike, who love the opera.

Yours very truly,
Mrs. Amelia Besom

II

The Radish Eater

There is no concept, even of the best artist, that is not contained within the mass of a single marble.

—Michelangelo Buonarroti, the Guasti edition, 1863

Just as, milady, with taking away from hard and alpine stone one brings out a living figure, so does grow the more as one cuts away.

—Michelangelo Buonarroti, the Guasti edition, 1863

Chapter 15

Far and away the best prize that life offers is the chance to work hard at work worth doing.
—Teddy Roosevelt

HANNAH HAD BEEN working all day when she lifted the damp pasteboard box from the back of the armoire. The box, a dark, moldy mess, had been stuck to the floorboards out of sight. It wasn't much to look at and would likely be even less exciting to open. Hannah looked around for the razor blade she'd set down a moment ago. She would need it to cut the seal; the box lid was held down with tape.

Mrs. Besom had already been through this room this morning. Over the last few days it had become Hannah's job to come through each room afterward and clean up. Occasionally Hannah got to slit the seal on a box such as this one with the hope that something interesting had been overlooked. So far nothing had, however. Precious objects seemed to call to Amelia Besom from behind closed doors, from within stuck drawers and locked trunks; the woman had a sixth sense that homed in on valuable items like a divining stick to the tiniest trickle of underground water.

Hannah wiped her hands—her fingertips had left a solitary set of prints in the mold—then opened the lid. And her heart sank. Dear, dear, dear, she told herself, for the sinking sensation said she still hadn't learned the lesson.

You are hired help cleaning up, not the blessed woman's partner in exploring and pricing this place. Hannah tried not to be disappointed as she rummaged through papers, all there was in the box. It was bursting with damp sheets and leaflets. Hannah picked up one of the latter. It was an auction catalog. Many of the loose sheets were bills of sale, most of them watermarked but legible—*Une peinture à l'huile,* L'Amour Désarmé, *de William Adolphe Bourguereau, 146,05 x 97,16 cm; signature à gauche audessous, Gallerie de Guerlacque, 19 mai 1882; 880 FF*. After a moment Hannah realized this described an oil painting downstairs in the dining hall. Beneath this were several drawings that seemed to be study sketches for the same painting. There were letters, more sketches, more bills of sale. Well, no, Hannah realized, this box was not entirely a disappointment.

She set it aside feeling a bit better. These *should* be valuable. People might pay extra, she reasoned, for an artwork with a documented history.

It was in this very rational state of mind that she reached back into the dilapidated armoire and felt her hand strike something cold and hard. Just above where the box had been, wedged back behind the armoire's drawer frame, she could feel a piece of stone as thick as her wrist.

Hannah bent down and tried to look underneath but couldn't get a good visual angle, so she reached in as far as she could and rotated the stone blindly. It fell suddenly then surprised her further. Her arm was immediately hit by a second object. Hannah was barely able to catch it in time.

She brought into the open two heavy handfuls: a pair of foot-high statues made of whiter-than-white, very dense, very smooth stone. They had to be marble. She turned the figures, carrying them over to the window for light. They were a small naked man and woman, each carved to such exquisite smoothness and grace that Hannah's throat tightened just looking at them. They were elegant, their marble polished to the sheen of skin. She thought, first, why weren't these figures considered valuable, for her eyes found them to be gorgeous. Then with dawning, mounting glee Hannah realized: Mrs. Besom's divining-stick magic had failed. The woman, purely and simply, had missed what Hannah herself now held.

Hannah's heart did one quick little thud, a knock against her sternum. She had saved something extraordinary, something that would have otherwise been tossed away unnoticed. Her heartbeat became a regular pound that vibrated the walls of her chest. She set the female figure down so she could touch and turn the other in her hands. The weight of the man felt miraculously solid and balanced, the arms, the legs. . . . The posture and musculature seemed so real she half expected the figure to move, a live, beautiful Lilliputian who might scramble away any moment.

"Come on," she said to them as she picked up the woman as well. Clutching both pieces to her, Hannah walked trancelike from the room. She let herself admit it: She had dreamed of making this march, of daring to carry something important down to Amelia Besom.

At the landing Hannah picked up her pace, moving swiftly down the staircase; she hit the ground floor running. She would say, she would tell Mrs. Besom—what? *I want to dig for treasure beside you. I have been too timid to say so, but I am saying it now. I want to share in this uncommon excitement. I want to pull miracles out of the bugs and debris and the mold.* The hard statues poked against her chest, yet Hannah felt only the strangest sense of euphoria, a swell of daring optimism. If *this* could happen, anything could. Good could materialize from the dust, from the dross and dregs of catastrophe. *I want to be in the middle of such a feeling, not outside it watching.*

As Hannah ran through the wide, round social gallery that encircled the ballroom, she was already calling out her excitement. "I have found something you must see, Mrs. Besom! I have found something I must show you!"

The grand dining hall itself slowed Hannah down. This cavernous room, adjoined by the gallery to the ballroom, had been commandeered as the major sorting area from where

items were crated and shipped out or temporarily stored.
Yesterday the furniture from the recital salon and three
upstairs bedchambers had been added to the room's chaos.
Entering it meant entering a kind of corridor of draped
divans stacked with large and small musical instruments.
Hannah zigged and zagged her way through this, then
through a tight maze of crated paintings. Mrs. Besom's gray
head appeared once only to disappear behind a heap of rugs
rolled to go out for reweaving.

"Mrs. Besom!" Hannah called. She at last came into a
cleared area around a long banquet table. She ran down the
length of this to where Amelia Besom was bent over it, her
weight resting on her elbows. "Mrs. Besom!"

"What? What?" The woman frowned over her shoulder
as Hannah all but clamored into her. "What is all this
caterwauling?"

"Look!" Hannah thrust a statue toward her. "It's—I have
found—" She was so breathless from her mad dash, she
couldn't get out a full sentence.

Mrs. Besom raised up from where she'd been hunkered
over a canvas that lay facedown on the tabletop. She put
down a magnifying glass in order to take the statue Hannah
offered her, the female figure.

Hannah set the other statue down onto the table between
some handwritten lists and a small clutter of knickknacks.
The long banquet table had become Mrs. Besom's makeshift
desk from where she directed her project. "Look," Hannah
said again. Once more, her excitement caught in her throat.

Mrs. Besom gazed first at the female figure in her hand
then at the male on the table. After a moment she smiled.
"Well, well," she said, "where did these come from?"

"The armoire—I was cleaning it out—there was a box
full of papers then this, oh I was so excited for you see I
knew right away—"

"Do settle down, Miss Van Evan."

Hannah took a deep breath, determined to give herself
credibility. "Yes. What I mean to say is, I found these statues
in the armoire you told me to clean out then have hauled

away. They would have been lost." She licked her lips then said boldly, "Which would have been such a shame, because they have, I think, originality, wit, and intelligence." Hannah had culled these words from the assortment of descriptive nouns that Mrs. Besom spouted daily. "I have saved something very valuable, something that was about to be thrown out." Hannah added helplessly, "And I am just beside myself with pleasure over it."

Mrs. Besom laughed almost pleasantly. "Indeed, I can see that." She set the small, stone woman beside the statue of the man on the table, picking up her magnifying glass again to examine them. At length she gave another of her ironic little snorts and said, "Well, congratulations. It is a double miracle. First that you should find these. And second, that these are what they are. We have here a de Saint Vallier dug up from none other than the Château d'Aubrignon itself."

"A de-what?" Hannah asked her.

"A de Saint Vallier." With her magnifying glass at her eye, Mrs. Besom bent, leaning around to examine the neck and spine of the male figure. "Bernard de Saint Vallier," she said over her shoulder, "the sculptor. He is Monsieur de Saint Vallier's brother."

Hannah blinked, her agitation spinning around on itself. She tried to focus on the important part of Mrs. Besom's response—*congratulations* and *we*. She tried to discount the rest, saying as forcefully as possible, "Yes. And I think these de Saint Valliers are worth quite a bit." Hannah attempted to imitate Mrs. Besom's confidence. "At least fifteen hundred francs. I think we should put them into the trial auction at the end of the summer." *We, we, we*—oh, if only Mrs. Besom would take up using forever this dear pronoun.

The woman, however, only glanced over her shoulder. She was smiling faintly. "Oh, you do, do you?"

"Yes." Hannah pushed faintheartedness from her. "Yes, I do. And I think I should get a percentage of the commission, since I found them when they would otherwise have been tossed out in the trash bin."

At this the woman turned around toward Hannah, a little huff escaping from her mouth. Then she laughed outright. "You are a nervy girl," she said. "Do you know that?"

Hannah could only agree. "Yes, madam."

Amelia Besom laughed again then turned her attention back toward the figures on the table—she was not angry. Or not too angry. She picked up one of the statues. "And it is not 'these' de Saint Valliers but 'this' de Saint Vallier. It's a single work, cut from a single stone. Watch." She leaned forward, turning the man slightly. "If you face them toward each other, each set of empty arms reaches out to the other set, with what might be disconsolate longing. But when you put them together"—she picked up the woman and, sliding her arms down over the man, locked the two figure together—"they embrace." Legs, arms, necks, torsos entwined, the two statuettes paired perfectly.

How had the artist done this? How could these fit along such a tight line? Hannah wondered. It was as if he could carve from the inside of the stone.

"It's very difficult to do," Mrs. Besom continued, "to control the break so completely, then use it properly, and he did it in Paros marble, a stone particularly susceptible to cracking. It is a small miracle—and one that the smug young creator of these didn't want anyone to miss. Lord, he was so full of himself." She laughed again, not entirely kindly. "He called this work *The Separation,* a title meant to touch on the emotion portrayed as well as call attention to the artist's achievement."

Amelia Besom stood back to look at them a moment, then turned almost the same sort of attention onto Hannah. She looked Hannah up and down, her good humor fading slightly as her brow drew together. Hannah was subjected to what she always felt hovered ominously behind every nice moment she and this woman shared together: an ill-defined ambivalence. The woman liked her; the woman resented that she should like such an unrefined girl from a less than sterling background.

After a few moments Mrs. Besom said gravely, "A young

lady who wanted to be more than a secretary to me would have to wear underclothing."

Hannah wanted to giggle at first. If this was the crucial requirement, well, Hannah already wore loads of underclothing—drawers, a chemise, a health corset that Mrs. Besom had insisted upon for the "proper silhouette" that laced in half Hannah's body, a corset cover, not to mention thick cotton stockings and adjustable garters. Why, Hannah considered herself to be a walking catalog of underclothing—

Hannah realized suddenly that Mrs. Besom was referring to the noisy petticoat she'd taken off, and a laugh did escape in a nervous titter. She said quickly, "Oh, I could wear more underclothing if you want me to." She would have worn a frock coat and top hat if it would have made the woman trust her better.

Mrs. Besom then dumbfounded Hannah: She smiled crookedly and said, "Well, then, yes, my cheeky little creature, we will put these in the auction, and I will give you a piece of the commission, one percent of anything over your price of fifteen hundred francs." She laughed at this bargain; it was some sort of joke. "All provided, of course, that you can get Monsieur de Saint Vallier to agree to sell them in the first place."

Despite herself—and despite all the silly requirements, caveats, and undertones—Hannah's chest expanded. Jubilation. Horror. What had she done? Why fifteen hundred francs? So much. Nevertheless, she felt elation well up inside her. She beamed at the woman. A chance. Here was a chance, an admission, joke or no joke. *We, we* will enter it into the auction; *we, we, oui, oui, oui.*

Mrs. Besom continued. "They were completed when he was not yet twenty-two."

"He?"

"Bernard de Saint Vallier," Mrs. Besom said. "He's here, you know. He's the crazy brother down at the cottage."

Hannah tried to look surprised.

Mrs. Besom regarded her intently a moment, then picked

up a statue again. She turned this in her hands as she talked.
"The pair is actually one of his lesser works, the beginning
of his decline, though no one really saw it then. See how
cool each figure is? They shy away from the emotional heat
of his early youth—he was quite a prodigy, you know.
These, though, are a little overrefined, the sadness too pat
really, a bit predictable in their expressions, their posture.
Of course the angles of the arms are quite nice. And there is
the technical proficiency. We just aren't looking here at the
freshness or insight of his previous work. Still, these are
quite a bit above humdrum, aren't they?"

Hannah looked again at the figures. She couldn't connect
them to the man down at the cottage. They were not the
work of a man who did nothing; they spoke of skill, artistic
vision, even ambition, and certainly enormous talent. They
were—she borrowed another word from Mrs. Besom's
vocabulary again—*exquisite.* Hannah understood with sudden precision why one might need such a word.

Hannah frowned. She could see none of the flaws Mrs.
Besom spoke of, no criticism to name. Moreover, she felt an
odd rush of loyalty to the discovery itself. It was *hers,* and
she did not like to hear it diminished even a little. She
changed the subject. "I should tell you I found a box of
papers as well. Nothing worth so much, but something the
buyers of certain paintings and things might enjoy having
and that you might like to read through also. They're just
tidbits of history really. Bills of sale—"

Mrs. Besom interrupted. "You have found what?" Her
face grew most serious.

"I found a box with some bills of sale in it, some auction
catalogs, sketches—"

The woman craned toward Hannah. "You have found the
provenances to some of the artwork?"

"The provenances?" Hannah was taken aback.

"Yes, the provenances, the written history of past owners,
circumstances, relevant data. Is this what you've found?"

"Yes, I suppose so."

"What room?"

"In the bedchamber where we were working this morning."

Mrs. Besom let out an exasperated sound. "The blasted armoire again?"

"Well, yes. They're sitting beside it now in a box that's falling apart. You see it got wet when—"

Hannah would have explained further, but the woman moved past her so quickly that she gave Hannah almost a rude shove.

"Excuse me," Mrs. Besom muttered. Ten paces beyond, however, she stopped herself and turned around. She cocked her head in a way that made her look strangely undone. Though still frowning, she spoke more politely. "Thank you, my dear," she said. "Now go ask Sébastien about the statues. I hope sincerely he will let us sell them. If he will, you have every right to be excited." She paused, then added, "And even if he won't, you should know that nonetheless you have done nicely."

She had done nicely. How ridiculously pleasing this recognition was. You have done nicely, you have done nicely, Hannah repeated to herself as she pivoted around on one toe. Mrs. Besom's steps diminished, then Hannah followed her. As sedately as possible, she began to retrace her steps back through the warehouselike maze that led out and toward Monsieur de Saint Vallier's office. Around a stack of rugs, she twisted sideways, then she turned down the corridor of divans stacked with a harp, a cello, a double bass, a viola da gamba. . . . Hannah walked along quickly, letting her fingers wipe the dust off a tuba; she ran her thumbnail across the off-key strings of the bass. The sound made her laugh as she veered into a narrow passageway between rows of crated paintings. She negotiated her way breezily through the available space among these objects, her curving, swerving progress so swift and easy, it felt like dancing.

A sense of well-being put a little skip in her step as she came out the end of the labyrinth. Hannah danced across the gallery into the ballroom. With the subsiding sound of Mrs.

Besom's steps indicating the woman was well beyond seeing, Hannah twirled.

"Oh yes, oh yes!" she exclaimed as she did one turn, then two, her arms out. Raised up on her toes, she virtually spun out onto the ballroom dance floor. The room was bare, having been cleaned out completely the day before. Tomorrow workmen would begin on the repair of the walls and ceiling. Hannah found herself in the most glorious open space, not a stick of furniture or crate in the way, save some platform scaffolding in the center of the room. Hannah waltzed a measure or two of Strauss then lifted her skirt up and began to kick to the dum-dum-da-da-da-da of the "Cancan" from *Orpheus in Hades*. What pleasure to be so in control of one's life, to be so filled with hope for one's future—

Hannah tripped a step, her foot hitting something, a bucket of water on the floor by the scaffolding. Beside this, on the white marble tile, there were several other objects she hadn't seen. Her little dance became a kind of hopscotching tarantella for balance as she clattered her way through the bucket, some rags, and a collection of dried plaster chunks.

"Attention, mam'zelle!"

Hannah looked up, way up, cranking her head back.

There was a workman high overhead at the top of the scaffold. From over the edge nearly thirty feet above her, he spoke again. "Why, Mam'zelle Hannah-with-an-H, *bonjour.*"

She leveled down onto the soles of her feet and stared at what she considered impossible: Nardi de Saint Vallier smiling down at her from somewhere near the ceiling, her own surprise being no less than if she'd seen him flap his arms and fly up there.

From over a platform of planks atop a thirty-foot iron framework, Nardi looked down at her. *"Bonjour,"* he said again. In one hand he held a round paintbrush, in the other a small pot, these items having something to do with the ceiling's domed gesso medallion.

The north wing's ballroom stood under one of the wide domes of the château, the ballroom being a large, round interior chamber enclosed by a round wall of windows through which one could look out into a promenade – social gallery that completely encircled the room. The room's huge ceiling medallion above, at which Hannah now stared, had once been a wonder of rococo-baroque swirls and flourishes that arched across more than sixty feet at its widest diameter. Now sections of this decorative plasterwork were missing, broken and fallen, portions chipped, what remained as dull and porous as chalk.

From overhead, Nardi prompted, "It is polite to say *bonjour* back." He shifted to rest his forearm over the top of a bucket.

"I'm not feeling very polite," Hannah replied. " 'Shocked' is more the word. What are you doing here?"

"Fixing the gesso."

When Hannah's dubious look discounted this as a reason, he sighed and disappeared again over the top of the platform.

Hannah had to take a step back in order to see what he was doing. He was on his knees. From this position he dipped his paintbrush into the pot he held, painting whatever was in the pot onto the ceiling. He dipped and painted, dipped and painted, holding both pot and brush close to the process as he worked the brush tip along the gesso's curves, wiggling it down into the recesses. In this somewhat slapdash manner, he was slopping a clear liquid over the pattern — while holding his paintbrush in a kind of prissy grip, his smallest finger held out from the rest.

Hannah watched him, consciously trying to make this man into the sculptor of the statues she'd just left in the dining hall. He had plaster everywhere, in his hair, on his face and shirtsleeves — his one arm, the sleeve rolled back, looked as though he'd been playing in white mud with smears to his elbow. Yet even wearing plaster, Nardi de Saint Vallier did not readily seem to be an artist of any sort. Perhaps it was just that he was too regular of feature, too straight and perfect in proportion and profile, too pretty. He didn't look like a sculptor: He looked more like he should be the statue.

"Are you really here to fix the gesso?" she asked bluntly. "Do you honestly know how?"

He gave her a baleful look over the edge and down thirty feet. *"Oui."*

"So you just took it into your head suddenly to do it?"

"I 'took it into my head' a few days ago. The room was not ready for me till this morning."

Hannah arched her head back, turning slowly to examine the ceiling overhead. If he'd been working all day, his work wasn't very impressive. The medallion looked as bad as it ever had.

He set the pot down at the edge of the plank beside him, throwing the brush into it like a dart into a bull's-eye, then reached across into the bucket beside him. He scooped, bringing three fingers up coated with what had to be plaster—his smallest finger tucked, dry and clean, against the palm of his hand. The gesture had an artificial elegance to it.

"What's wrong with your finger?" Hannah asked. She wanted to hear the rheumatism story from his own lips.

He glanced at his own hand, fingertips poised, full of plaster, then shrugged. "I broke it," he said. With a flick of his wrist, he flung plaster off the backs of his fingertips. Droplets spattered the wet gesso above him.

Hannah came a little closer, moving around, trying to get a better angle of him. "Your brother said you stopped sculpting because of rheumatism."

He glanced down at her. *"Eh bien,* wasn't that nice of him to explain for me. Now I don't have to."

She bit her lip, straightening her back as she rubbed it, looking about the large, empty room. On the floor—what she'd tripped over a minute ago—beside another bucket were dried plaster chunks; castings, she realized.

Nardi's voice overhead said, "Did he also mention that I became, how you say, *rien dans le bide, euh,* nothing-in-the-belly afraid every time the broken finger would ache from rheumatism?" He was dipping and spattering as he spoke. "Do you wish to know how I broke my finger?" Hannah listened. "*Tu vois, toi,* when you quarry marble, to move a large block of it, you keep moving dowels in front of it onto which you roll it. We were on an incline. The marble slid. I didn't get out of the way fast enough. The edge of the block caught my hand. I was lucky. There was a boy helping. It caught his legs. It took ten minutes to roll over him, with all of us trying to hold back or redirect two tons of stone that slid down him anyway, slowly, over his knees then groin then chest, with him screaming the whole time, an animal sound like nothing I have ever heard before."

Hannah was silent. He had her attention again. There above, Nardi was painting with what looked to be a viscous, shiny liquid. She realized he was taking piecemeal impressions of what remained of the medallion's elaborate bas-relief. Deep undercuts in the intricate pattern prevented any large portion from being cast in a single form; it could only be cast in small, strategic pieces that would go together in the end like a giant jigsaw puzzle. If Nardi were actually capable of fixing the medallion by casting new sections from molds of what remained, the repaired whole would be something of an accomplishment—not a very creative one perhaps, but one requiring specialized skill and analytical proficiency.

Overhead, Nardi coated the plaster with the syrupy liquid, his wrist moving with steady twists as he worked the tip of the brush along a deep, swirling indention.

"What is that, that you're putting on the ceiling?" Hannah asked.

He glanced down over the edge of the platform again, a wry look as she came round full circle of the scaffold to stand where she'd started. "Your glycerin," he said. "It is a good releasing agent—and what gave me the idea in the first place. I suddenly had everything necessary to fix the ballroom medallion that Sébastien moans over. *Pourquoi pas?* I thought. Why not?"

He set the brush down then began again at the dipping, spattering game he played with plaster and filliping finger-tips. The droplets impacted with intentional force, building up the face of a mold unmarred by air pockets. He flicked plaster in this manner till it piled up to resemble a mounded stalactite. Then he picked up a spatula, dug into the bucket again to bring out a glob of plaster, and thwacked it onto this mound. He worked quickly, maneuvering and adding plaster with the spatula and a quick turn of his hand. There was no going back over it. The plaster began to set almost as fast as he applied it.

"You really are a sculptor, aren't you?" Hannah said finally. She could almost believe it, at least from the technical aspect.

"Ho, mais oui," he said. "It takes great talent to do this." He reached into the bucket again, this time holding back his sleeve with his left hand to put his right arm into the bucket up to his elbow. He stirred around in the plaster as if trying to find something, then drew out what looked like a piece of plaster-soaked cloth. He spread this over the freshly applied plaster, then changed hands. He let his plastered arm dangle as he held the cloth in place with his other hand, just the tips of three fingers; again he held his smallest finger out. The gesture was so adept it seemed that anyone with any grace should give up the use of a finger for the decorative benefit.

He stood on one knee up there on the plank, his arm dripping, his other raised above him, holding the mold he was making—he couldn't move, Hannah realized, not without ruining the casting.

After a minute or so she said, "I found something of yours."

He shook his head briefly, as if he could not recall losing anything important. Shoe buckles, shirt studs, all cuff buttons accounted for.

"A small sculpture," she said. "Two actually. It's called *The Separation.*"

He glanced at her, a frown under and around his own arm, as his free hand picked up the spatula. He tapped the gesso with this tool as he asked, "Here?" He knew what she referred to.

"Yes."

"What shape is it in?" With the edge of the spatula, he freed the mold. It dropped into his hand.

"Fine. Wonderfully fine."

He tossed the spatula into the bucket with a clatter, set the mold down, and reached for a damp rag on the rung below him. He sat, one leg dangling off the platform, and wiped plaster from his arm, then his fingers one at a time. "How nice," he said. He shrugged again, then changed the subject. "Do you want to walk down to the cottage with me? I need more plaster." He set the rag down, dismissing his little masterpiece as if it were no more than a runaway cat he had thought dead, now found to be alive and living comfortably elsewhere.

"I can't," Hannah said.

She might have said more. She might have told him how extraordinary she found the statues. But she didn't for fear that, in speaking of the statues further, a gushing, raving note would creep into her voice. She liked *The Separation* far better than she felt comfortable telling the man who had made it. She worried that—with an artist's misguided ego—he might think any rhapsodic pleasure she took in the statues might reflect feelings she harbored toward the artist himself.

He turned on his arms and stretched his leg down, beginning to descend through the scaffolding. "Come with me," he said over his shoulder. "I want company."

"No."

"I told you, Sébastien won't stop you."

"It's not that."

Nardi dropped down through the metal framework, as balanced and sure as a circus trapeze artist. Hannah looked away. His physical grace and beauty were developing an edge to them that was mildly irritating; he traveled on them too freely.

There was, however, something in his cocky attitude, in

his dry sense of humor, that spurred something close to respect. He had a kind of noble pigheadedness. The hard-drinking etherist and failed sculptor somehow kept going without either success or inebriation now, refusing anyone's help or pity. Hannah found his stamina, his stubborn resolve to survive, well . . . in a kind of backward, upside-down way . . . admirable.

His shoes—boots actually, round-toed and spattered—clipped down the last bars of the scaffold to step down onto the floor in front of Hannah.

"So that's why you've come up to the château?" she asked again. "To do something useful?" This would be such a healthy thing, she thought.

"No," he said quietly. "I came up here because I was lonely. I kept thinking, Life was so much more interesting when you kept popping up into it." He said again, "Come walk with me. I have to get the plaster."

Hannah kept her eyes focused on the little collection of piece molds at her feet. "No," she said.

"*Sacrebleu,*" he murmured. "I want to be friends again."

"You warned me off that," she said. "You were very convincing."

"I know. I am sorry." He paused, then added, "*Tellement désolé,* so very sorry." She glanced at him, only to find him looking at her, an unbroken, steady regard, while he absently fingered the inside of the mold he'd brought down from the platform. Then he said, "I was at a clinic for a time, where they told me a lot of stupid things. But one of them was this: that I don't believe I deserve a good life, so I chase away every beautiful, wholesome thing that comes in my direction." He left a pause. "Do you think this is possible, that someone could do that?"

Whatever Hannah understood about happiness was intuitive, not something she could analyze or pronounce upon. She shook her head. "I don't know," she told him.

He let out a deep sigh. "*Regarde.* Over there." He pointed—he had a laborer's forearm, corded, sinewy, the hair matted with plaster. "A chaperon. We can always stay within sight of one of them."

Against one of the high windows on a built-in bench, one of the German-speaking men slouched, motionless, one leg drawn up, the other out, his hat down. He was dozing.

"Some chaperon." Hannah laughed but couldn't meet Nardi's eyes.

"He would rally if you screamed, I swear it."

Which was the problem. This strange conversation . . . It gave Hannah the funniest feeling, the odd nervousness again: She was fairly certain she wouldn't scream. "No," she said firmly.

After a moment he said, "*D'accord.* Then I go down alone." He laughed. "But when you pass through here again, you will stop and talk to me, yes? Where anyone can see us, even *la mère* Besom?"

As if by some mad piece of conjury, "Old Lady" Besom's voice suddenly intruded. "Hannah! Where are you?" the woman called from no place that was immediately identifiable. "Oh, there you—"

Hannah saw through the glass, into the shadows of the gallery where Amelia Besom stood stiff-backed, her face sour. Her voice, slightly shrill, bounced off the other side of the window glass up into the dome over the whole area. "Hannah, come here," she said. "I need to speak to you."

"I have to go," Hannah told Nardi. She went immediately.

By the time Hannah crossed the ballroom and rounded into the gallery, Mrs. Besom was already marching away. Hannah had to run to catch up.

"Well, I see you have met the Frog Prince," the woman said crossly.

"The Frog Prince?"

The woman looked at Hannah sidelong. "Bernard. One of the Frenchiest Frogs you will ever meet. And the spoiled Prince of Sensitive Souls. He couldn't live in the real world if he had to—he drinks ether, did you know that?"

"Yes."

"He told you?"

"More or less."

Mrs. Besom stopped. They stood in a part of the wide gallery circle that included a huge statue of a godlike man on a prancing, muscular horse. "And what else has he told you? That you are beautiful, perhaps? That what he really wants to do is use you as a model?"

"Pardon?"

"Which will require that you remove all your clothes, of course."

"No, no, he has never said—" Hannah felt a flush of embarrassment.

"Well, he will. It's not a very original line, but it's worked for him over and over. He's nice looking. You've noticed that, haven't you?"

"Well, ah—"

"Let me instruct you in a few more of the details, Miss Van Evan. When his youthful talent dried up like a case of acne, he let one of the salon society ladies keep him going. A woman supported him. And she wasn't the only one since then. There was a string of women. He's a charmer. People *like* him so easily."

Which explained, Hannah thought, why Amelia Besom would resent him infinitely.

The woman continued. "You have dealt with the sons of rich families before, Miss Van Evan, and I hope you remember the outcome. You are expendable. To the de Saint Valliers you are no better than a milkmaid or shop girl. They could use you then toss you aside and not feel they had done a thing wrong. It's the modern version of droit du seigneur, something like that." Her voice changed. It broke over a faint note of pleading. "*I* am the one—I—I am the *only* one anywhere around offering you a future, Hannah."

Hannah tried to relieve her. "You're treating me very fairly, Mrs. Besom," she said. "Thank you. I am aware of this."

Hannah was also aware that she was going to have to tread gingerly around this woman's fragile, possessive friendship.

* * *

Hannah finally caught up with Sébastien de Saint Vallier in the old courtyard, where he tossed his bags onto the seat of his carriage and climbed in after them.

Over the edge of the open calèche, she asked, "Are you leaving already?" It was his habit to spend weekends at the château, not catching the last train to the city till Sunday evening. Today was Saturday.

"Unfortunately," he said. He opened a satchel and took out some papers. "I have a trial Monday morning and must review some notes at my office in Paris."

He worked very hard here at the château, Hannah knew, from dawn to well past midnight. This morning, in fact, she had come across him unshaven, still dressed in the same clothes he'd worn yesterday, laboring over the day before's consignment contracts. She didn't know where he found the time for this other role, a lawyer who worked weekdays in the capital.

"Do you never rest?" she asked.

His glance told her the question was impertinent. "What do you want?" he said gruffly. "My train won't wait for me."

Hannah was momentarily flustered. It took a moment to muster a rush of words: "Mrs. Besom sent me to inquire after a sculpture we've found. It's called *The Separation*. She says your brother made it." She waited for a reaction while Monsieur de Saint Vallier only stared at her blankly. "It's a small work really that could net you a handsome profit. We"—she grew timid in the face of his hard expression—"that is, Mrs. Besom wants to add it to the list of pieces to be sold at the first auction."

He considered this a moment, impassive, pensive, then settled back into the leather seat of his carriage. "Fine," he said. He tapped the coachman's box in front with the ferrule of his cane.

Hannah stepped forward, taking hold of the carriage's splashboard. "Wait." She couldn't believe she'd heard properly. "Fine?" she repeated.

"Yes, fine."

"We can add it to the contracts?"

"Mademoiselle Van Evan, most people don't continue to pester a person once they've gotten what they've asked for."

"Yes," she said, momentarily at a loss. "Thank you." Her gratitude, however, remained token, marred by a niggling sense of disappointment, annoyance, bewilderment.

The driver looked back at them. "Sir?" he said. The reins were poised in his hands.

Hannah blurted out, "Doesn't your brother's incredibly fine work mean anything to anyone any longer?"

Monsieur de Saint Vallier snorted and paused again to consider her. "Mademoiselle," he said, "*The Separation* is nothing. Bernard did life-size pieces. There are two in Paris, one atop the Fontaine de Blasis. Another inside the Musée d'Art Moderne, with a reproduction outside in the museum's back garden. There is one in Lyons, another in Rouen. There are two in London, one in Milan, and another, if I'm not mistaken, in your very own New York behind your public library. Besides these, there are several dozen noteworthy pieces as well as the entire fresco front of the *École d'Astronomie* at the Sorbonne—for a short time, Nardi was prodigious as well as profoundly talented."

The man's haughty eyes dropped from her face, his attention settling on her in a disconcerting manner, like someone appraising a cow for its milking potential. "But I'm glad to hear your concern. My brother likes you." He smiled perfunctorily. "Be nice to him." Then he made the most unfounded assumption: "If you will be *very* nice to him and would like something for your trouble, I will try to arrange it."

Hannah felt an involuntary surge of anger. The warmth of it flooded her shoulders, her neck, her face as she searched the man's countenance for an innocent meaning.

All she found, however, was obscurity: The Paris lawyer bent his head, adjusting his top hat, its brim quickly casting a ledge of shade over his eyes. He shifted, producing reading glasses from his coat pocket. He hooked these over his ears, then bent his head over the papers again as the carriage lurched out of Hannah's grasp, jangling away from her as she stepped back smartly.

She stood there, lurching and jangling herself in a way that matched the click and snap of the carriage whip, the jingle of harnesses, the grind and clatter of steel wheels and horse hooves on gravel—the vehicle was turning around to get itself headed in the right direction. Hannah tried to do something parallel in herself. She was taking his offer wrong, surely. She was being too sensitive, too aware of her past and what the good people of Miami had been happy to say about her. She was taking offense where no offense was intended.

She thought this as she watched the carriage promenade around in a slow sweep of the courtyard, the man within the carriage looking consummately elegant. In full sun, his stiff collar stood out white against the swartness of his chin and dark mustache; his crisp shirtfront lay snowy in contrast to the silk facings of his frock coat and foulard cravat. Monsieur de Saint Vallier's body moved in response to the carriage, an insouciant wobble, confident, secure, upper-class, as he sat there reading in the shade of his hat brim.

Be nice, the words echoed. Hannah didn't feel nice, but felt rather that something dirty and insulting had transpired. All she could think, as Sébastien de Saint Vallier's vehicle clamored by on its way out the courtyard, was that, had she been a foot taller and a hundred pounds heavier, she would have grabbed him by his natty shirtfront as he passed, jerked him over the door of his jaunty little calèche, and thrown him summarily onto the ground, where she would have pommeled him till he couldn't stand up in his shiny-toed, hand-tooled oxfords.

Chapter 16

*One should either be a work of art or wear a
work of art.*
 —Oscar Wilde
   "Phrases and Philosophies for the Use of the
   Young" *Chameleon*, December, 1894

NARDI DE SAINT VALLIER had an unsuspected appetite for
conversation. Equally surprising, to appease this appetite he
was apparently willing to wander all over the château and
estate to converse with Hannah in particular. Once he found
her, he was a fountain of questions. *Did she miss her home?
Was she ever going back? How did she stand Old Lady
Besom?* He volunteered his own opinions. *He liked the
apples grown in Aubrignon better than any others he'd ever
tasted. No person was as indomitable as Sébastien liked to
think he was. Art and beauty were tangible things that could
change the course of a life.* All this he delivered freely in his
slightly unbelievable French accent from his slightly droll
French perspective.

"Look what I have brought you," he said one morning in
his deep, grainy intonation, all vowels and nasals. *Luke
oo-at Ay av bra'tyoo.*

Hannah was depositing breakfast trays in the kitchen
when Nardi came in behind her, lugging a large, dark wood
box with a funnel-shaped horn atop it—a phonograph at least

a decade or two old. He set this down on the kitchen worktable, telling her, *"Regarde"*—look. He opened a drawer in the wood phonograph case to reveal a collection of fine-grooved record cylinders. The drawer was packed tightly with these standing on end. He lifted one out.

The phonograph was the sort that had a spring motor and hand crank. He loaded a record cylinder onto the shaft, cranked the handle, and set the lever. The needle and horn began to travel along the top of the rotating cylinder, as a wonderfully strong-voiced woman sang out a tinny, hissing tune.

"It's not worth much, *c'est vrai*. It was mine, years ago. Junk now, *mais très amusant,* no? And the records might help with your French—if you sing in a language, your mind works differently. You will be able to pronounce better."

Hannah set her trays down, listening to the timbre and melody as a song rang out with, *"Le gai Pa-ree-zee-an."* She smiled up at Nardi, then tried the next refrain herself.

"Oui, like that," he said, his face pleased. "It's yours, if you like. A peace offering. I already asked Sébastien."

"Really?"

"Vraiment."

Unavoidably happy with the gift, Hannah browsed through the drawer of records, then glanced up at him. "Perhaps there are some English songs." She grinned. "We'll fix your accent, too."

His eyes widened, then he groaned. *"Ah, bon Dieu, mon accent?"* he asked. *"Ah la la."* He seemed to dispute he had one. Then he acquiesced indirectly. "But I don't want to fix my accent."

"Why not?"

He was amused, insulted. "Because," he explained, rolling his eyes at her as if she were stupid for asking, "Englishwomen find it quite charming." He paused a moment then smiled again, his handsome, widemouthed smile. "Don't American women?"

Hannah looked into the drawer again, his question

bringing on what was becoming a familiar, mild, almost pleasurable embarrassment.

When she didn't speak, he continued. "In my day, I was quite the thing in almost every country of Western Europe."

Yes, she could believe that. "'In your day'?" She laughed. "How old are you?"

He lifted himself backward by his arms, scooting his buttocks to sit onto the table. "What year is it?" he asked.

Again she laughed. He was being silly, surely.

He shrugged then filled the year in for himself. "Nineteen oh-three. Let's see, that makes me thirty-two, though I have no clear memory of having passed my last birthday." The gay little song on the phonograph began to slow down. As he reached over to crank the machine again, he said, "I feel as if I were eighty." He moved the handle round and round again, the spring of the motor tick-ticking, then "Le Gai Parisien" picked up its jolly rhythm again.

"So what about American women?" he asked.

"Pardon?"

"Do American women mind the way a Frenchman speaks their language?"

"I can't speak for American women."

"Speak for yourself."

Hannah frowned. Nardi's exaggerated, romantic accent was a perfectly predictable and silly thing for her to take a fancy to. She wished she didn't like it; she tried not to. Then her frown deepened as her eyes focused on his knee. It was in her skirts beside her hip, his leg swinging, brushing in and out, making a *shush-sha-shush* in time to the zippy tin melody playing on the phonograph there beside them. Her embarrassment that had been pleasant a moment ago became something else, something more unsettling and somehow more imperative. Hannah asked, "Why are you doing this? Why are you following me and being nice to me?"

She didn't look at him, but rather heard the longish, puzzled pause this left, as if these questions needed translation. Then Nardi asked, "'I am fascinated by you' is not the proper answer, is it?" After a moment he sighed and said dutifully, "No, of course not. I am bored, that's all, mam'zelle. You are colorful, lively relief from my own ennui, *c'est tout*. I do not flirt"—*fleert*, he said—"with you."

Hannah stared down at his leg. Its movement had stopped, leaving her skirts quiet, his calf nestled into them. There in the kitchen, the little tune on the phonograph slowed once more, the voice from the horn dropping in pitch to a growl. As this faded to silence, Hannah said, "Stupid underskirt. I've had to put the noisy thing back on again."

"I like it," he said immediately. "You sound like a thousand rustling leaves when you walk. It, you, are lovely. That is what I am trying to say by flirting with you."

She glared up. "You said you weren't—"

"I lied. Hannah, I am trying to redeem myself in your eyes. I wish I hadn't yelled all those things at you last week. I wish you weren't now so, *eh, distante, réservée—tu comprends?*"

She continued to frown, refusing to *"comprends."*

He explained further. "I try merely to be mannerly and flattering to you, though what is mannerly and flattering in my scheme of things is clearly not in yours."

"Well, stop trying to be anything and just be honest."

"Oh, honest," he said with an air of feigned insight. "Oh, this always improves things, to be honest. I'm sure, if I speak what is on my mind, we will immediately be on good terms again. You go first."

Hannah had wanted to say, *Don't do this. Don't bring me gifts and ask my favor. Don't wander the château looking for me. And don't, above all else, let these ambiguous little moments accrue. I don't know understand what they mean or what you expect of me.*

But she said nothing and, a day later, he found her again.

Hannah was in the butler's pantry, a large room off the servants' area that amounted to mostly walls and walls of cupboards. Here, she opened and closed, bent and prodded, not really looking for anything, just checking through this room as she had a half-dozen others in this section of the château that Mrs. Besom had given over to her responsibility. Hannah's thorough search so far had yielded no more than mouse droppings. She laughed as she closed the last cabinet, saying to herself, "As empty as Old Mother Hubbard's."

And there he was: "You know Mother Goose?" Nardi said from the doorway. *"Ma Mère l'Oye."*

Hannah jumped, recovering with a giddy laugh, then answered, "Everyone knows Mother Goose."

"She is French."

"Oh, please," she groaned. Nardi was prone to label everything significant or appealing a product of his own culture.

"Mais non, c'est vrai. She is Charles Perrault. He invented Mother Goose. He collected children's country rhymes, country stories; he wrote some. Besides the nursery rhymes, he wrote down 'Cinderella,' 'Sleeping Beauty,' all those stories of French castles." He smiled a baiting smile. "Everything enduring is French. Everything good in life. Food, style, art, poetry"—he raised one brow—"love." He put on a clowning smugness. "We invented love, of course."

She laughed.

"No, no, I do not pull your leg. During the Middle Ages, the French came up with the idea of love as we know it today. I could show you literature. I could prove it." He made a mock-modest face. "But I won't. I won't rub it in: We also invented diplomacy."

Hannah laughed all the harder.

He waited till she had stopped, then said, "I love your laughter. It is so wholehearted, coming from your chest and belly, from deep inside you."

And this indeed seemed to be the problem—he began to perform for her. He was willing to tell jokes, make faces, tease, anything to exert this power he'd discovered he had over her: to make her laugh, to make her happy for a moment.

*   *   *

Perhaps the most surprising thing of all was that Nardi became her good friend, a man who saw and attempted to serve her best interests. This came out clearly the last week of June and had a kind of enlightening effect.

The day before, on her one afternoon off, Hannah had gone to the closest large town, the port of Le Havre, thinking to purchase a modest but quieter petticoat. Once walking down the street of the town, however—while humming "Le Gai Parisien" to herself, the words to which she was getting quite good at—her old petticoat hadn't seemed so terrible. She could suddenly remember how much she had liked the idea of it three months ago when she had ordered it. She could vividly remember her pleasure all at once of first putting the ruffly tulle-and-taffeta thing on. Nardi was right, she decided there on the street; this petticoat was really rather glorious. Not stylish perhaps, but it had something else. . . .

It was in this frame of mind that Hannah spotted a little brooch in a shop window. A round filigree of golden stems and purple flowers, it stopped her progress cold.

Hannah returned home with it, delighted with the little ornament. Amelia Besom's reaction to it, however, was quite different.

"Nardi!" Hannah called. This time she had sought him out, finding him in the back garden, where he was removing animal-hoof glue from his hands. "Nardi," Hannah said again as she came up to him, "what do you think of this pin?" She thrust it out on the flat of her palm, right under his nose, where he squatted over a rag and turpentine.

"Pas mal," he said. *"Qu'est-ce que c'est?"* He looked at it a moment longer, then stood wiping the rag between his fingers.

"It's mine," she said. "I bought it for myself."

He smiled. "Yes, it looks like you. It's pretty."

"Do you like it? Look at it better."

He picked it up, holding it so the light caught one

direction then another. He shrugged. *"C'est très joli.* I told you. Though what I think does not matter so much."

"Do you think I should take it back?"

"If you like it, keep it."

"A person of some taste called it 'pure brummagem' and said it's orma-something-or-other, an alloy of copper and tin made to look like gold, and that the stones are nothing but cheap glass." Hannah hesitated. "I mean, I know it's not real jewelry—"

"I imagine it's exactly the right jewelry for your pocket, Hannah. Who told you such a thing?"

Hannah ignored the question, drawing her palm to her to look at the pin herself again. "I rather liked it," she said truculently. "I was told, however, that a nice bath of gold on a small piece would hardly cost much more, especially if I forgo the bits of cheap glass, and that this person of taste who so criticized my pin would return it with me and then take me over to a dealer she knows in Honfleur where she'd help me pick out something more suitable."

Nardi laughed. "Amelia Besom hates the pin." He tossed the rag then said, "Let me see that gorgeous thing again." He took the small brooch into his fingers and studied it a moment. "Well, to my mind," he said, grinning, "this is a charming piece of adornment. The metal casting is of a lively design, the color placement delighting the eye. *De plus,* this little pin is perfect in that it pretends to be nothing more than what it is—a glittering moment, ephemeral, like Beauty itself. At its essence, this pin is ideal, an abstract notion much grander than its own mere physical *existence"*—he looked at Hannah with teasing seriousness—*"et sans doute,* a hundred times better than any gold-plated imitation jewel that pretends to come from a czar's treasure chest."

He dropped his facetious tone and said, "Hannah, there are as many opinions on anything as there are people to give them. Yours counts as much as Amelia Besom's."

"Not everyone thinks so," Hannah said, "especially when one is talking about art—or old jewelry."

"That's business—Amelia Besom is an expert on *other* people's opinions, how much they will pay for what, whom she can pit against whom to make everyone pay higher. But what *you* buy or wear is none of her business. I think you have unique taste, Hannah, a little bizarre at times"—he reached over and shook her petticoat—"but interesting."

On the way up to the château after this, Hannah pinned the brooch back onto the lapel of her tailor-made. Then a piece of brilliant inspiration: She unbuttoned the bottom six buttons of her gray skirt. And, *voilà,* a small froth of emerald green tulle showed under a large splash of dark purple taffeta—the purple exactly matching the stones of her pin, the whole concoction kicking up with every churning, rustling step as Hannah marched back up into the château.

Chapter 17

WHAT NARDI WOULD later think of as *le fiasco érotique* began as a simple, blue summer day at the beginning of July. He didn't attribute to himself having planned the circumstances exactly. This would have credited too much direction—an actual goal—to his present desultory, moment-by-moment way of living. On the other hand, he was aware even on that sunny afternoon that he had begun to read Hannah's wants and predilections, catering to them much as the old Paris Nardi had done when it had come to women from whom he wanted something. So neither did he count himself innocent. Point in fact, the walk *was* his idea, contrived on the spur of the moment to get Hannah away from the château.

She laughed when he first suggested it. "No, I won't walk with you in the woods." He had found her in the dining-hall-cum-massive-storage-warehouse, no Besom about, busy with what amounted to an inventory, writing entries into a notebook. She smiled and cast her eyes down, looking into a crate of rolled canvases. "Weasels," she said. She seemed to be teasing him.

He shook his head blankly, the explanation, if it was one, inaccessible to him.

She laughed, then explained, "You remember your *belettes*? When we walked up the embankment through the trees that first night? I looked up the word—weasels. That's how you say it in English." She smiled again then put a check beside something on the page of her notebook. "So you see," she said, "the woods are dangerous. The *belettes* are everywhere." At this she bowed her head, putting her pencil to her mouth as if trying to hold her lips closed, then surprisingly descended into laughter again, faintly bubbling with it. Nardi had the distinct feeling that her reference to the skittish *belettes,* when translated into English, spoke of indirect motives.

"No, no," he assured her. "I do not invite you to a mindless, *eh*—how you say?—*méandre* through the woods. *Mais non,"* he insisted with defensive umbrage. The idea came from nowhere. "I want to show you something, something special."

"What?" Only mildly distracted, she kept jotting things down in her silly notebook.

Nardi mentally fumbled around a moment, trying to fish out "something special" from his memory of what existed here at this poor, ramshackle congeries of buildings and grounds. He came up with, "The butterfly garden."

She looked up. "The what?"

"Le jardin des papillons."

Her face didn't believe him for a moment. "There is a garden where someone grows butterflies?"

He nodded. *"Oui, c'est ça. Exactement.* The best place to see it is from the belvedere out on the ridge, from where we can look down on the butterfly garden as well as have a view *panoramique* of the whole of the estate."

She stared an instant longer, during which time he actually saw her pupils dilate slightly. He was treated to one of her open-faced looks, a guileless expression that held both a note of distrust and more than a few notes—a melding arpeggio chord—of growing wonder and curiosity.

Good choice, old Nardi, he thought, you old dog, old devil.

She closed her notebook and set it down. "It's not far, is it?" she asked. "I can only take a few minutes."

*   *   *

Of course, the lively Mademoiselle Hannah wanted to go down *into* a garden of butterflies, not merely look down on it from the belvedere. So, in relative silence, with Nardi's usual retinue of Swiss watchdogs tromping along behind them, Nardi escorted her down toward the garden itself, a place he could only hope existed since he hadn't seen it in almost twenty years. He walked them all down a steep slope along an old path, overgrown in places, so they had to walk around or under limbs, toward where his uncle had once cultivated particular plants in order to attract certain species of insects—butterflies, skippers, and moths—to feed, lay eggs, pupate, then flutter to life and begin the cycle again.

The day was gorgeous, full of the luminous light Hannah so liked, filtered sunlight, a blue sky overhead filled with scudding, wispy clouds. As they made their jagging, awkward way along the path, Nardi watched the woman in front of him. She kept her gaze downward, her full concentration taken up by their tread and skid down the loamy bank of land.

The terrain was broken only by chalk-knob protrusions, white rock that burst through the soil regularly like glaciers that dotted a dark, virid sea. The land was more up and down than Nardi remembered, the ascents and drops steeper, so that he wondered for a time if he had taken them the right way. Then he saw the roof of the old *grenier à pommes,* the apple storehouse. This rose in the distance above rows of scraggly, neglected apple trees. The orchards spread out suddenly in all directions, and he knew it was right.

Then wrong. Wrong in a way that was surprisingly affecting. Nardi stood there, staring across the little clearing in the center of the orchards. "It used to be here," he said, shoving his hands into his trouser pockets. He brought his shoulders up, his arms in.

Like nearly everything else in life, when viewed from sobriety, the garden was much duller than imagined, more a muddle, a disappointment. Butterflies lived off weeds; weeds and dung and carrion. This place was the one thing he'd allowed himself to think that time and nature couldn't destroy. What existed here now, however, was just a field of overgrown nettles. He couldn't understand it. It was summer. There should have been butterflies, many of them, but there weren't. There was not a miserable flying insect in sight.

Nardi slid a glimpse at Hannah, then turned his head fully to look at her profile. Even in a field of nettles, she was comfortable, happy.

More amazing, she wasn't disappointed. "What a fine idea," she said as she stared wistfully about. "I'll bet this place was fabulous to look at when the butterflies used to come."

They ended up talking about the various plants required to attract butterflies — some of which Nardi remembered by name and could see in the field, still visibly present though overgrown by nameless interlopers. There were stinging nettles for the blackish caterpillars of the peacock, gorse and broom for the hairstreaks, horseshoe vetch for the chalkhill blues. All this talk of flora and fauna somehow got her started again on some of the strange things her father had planted in his backyard pharmaceutical garden.

She talked with her hands. More so than Nardi, despite the stereotype of the gesticulating Frenchman. She was fond of wiggling her fingers in the air when a word wouldn't come to her, while saying, "You know," which Nardi usually didn't.

She took the lead, heading back toward the château, then suddenly veering at a tangent toward a higher ridge. She'd seen, high above over a jutting ledge, the belvedere's *épi de faîtage* — its ceramic roof-ridge ornament, a monkey that sat on the crest of the building's slate roof. She climbed toward this, meanwhile elaborating on her father's botanical talents as well as his on-and-off penchant for larceny. He had been very successful at growing cannabis apparently, which he had sold over-the-counter of his pharmacy in the form of a miracle energy tonic until half the town of Miami was walking around drunk on it. Monsieur Van Evan had been quite a character and something of a charlatan. Nardi was entertained. More than entertained. He recognized something as he took Hannah Van Evan by the waist to give her a little push up a particularly steep incline.

With her red hair and dark eyes and pale skin with its rising color, all this bouncing along with a jiggling bosom atop hips that swayed from a waist like a fulcrum . . . well, Hannah Van Evan was more than pretty, more than voluptuous: She was brightly, petitely, curvaceously gorgeous. Against the blue day, her image lit upon his eye, as splendidly colorful as butterflies. It pleased Nardi to think of her in this way—her energy as swift and sailing as swallowtails', as erratic and hypnotic as the flit-and-flutter of skippers. She was both as ordinary as orange tips and as exotically impossible as the monarchs that made their way here every year across the Atlantic. This was her spirit, a thousand butterflies of every category and variety, crossbred into one magnificent specimen. *Lepidoptera Hannaeus.*

The rush of the river grew louder as they climbed toward its clifftop. Then up the last few yards, Nardi happened to glance over his shoulder. It was a self-conscious gesture, given the turn of his mind, to see how far back the guards were.

Nardi couldn't believe it at first when he saw: They weren't there. He leaned backward slightly, torquing his head and shoulders around to look down the fifty yards to the next level landing. His two Swiss nursemaids weren't below either. They seemed to have disappeared entirely. Nardi smiled to himself. He and Hannah—probably due to her delightfully unpredictable progress up and down the uneven landscape—had somehow lost or outdistanced them. A wonderful surge of freedom expanded in his chest. He took Hannah's elbow to help her up the last little shingle of steps, all but lifting her off the ground in his eagerness to go higher, farther, all the way to the top perhaps to fly out over.

On the last step, however, the woman in front of him faltered. Her foot slipped. Hannah turned in his arms then knocked the breath out of him as he caught her right up against him. He saved them both by grabbing an overhead tree branch.

And there he was again in the midst of one of his clinical reactions: ripples and ripples of horripilation. The involuntary response of a man fresh off ether, fresh onto something else. . . . Gooseflesh ran up his back, his neck, down his arms, standing the hair on end, making him shudder.

Then hair was not the only thing that wanted to stand on end. Low, in the nether reaches of his abdomen, there was a lift, a faint stir, a distinct pulse and rush of blood. Standing there, hanging by one arm from a tree branch, while in his other arm he held a small, wiggling woman, Nardi discovered six inches of himself to be just plain thrilled to be here in the country sticks of France, alive and sober.

Hannah squirmed around. "Oh, dear, I, ah, I'm so sorry—if you'll just let me—then I could just—" She was the damnedest woman to hold on to. She couldn't find her feet; she wasn't tall enough to grab the branch overhead. Nardi braced his stance solidly. He balanced, while she became more and more agitated over the fact that he was the only thing solid within reach—and she reached pretty freely.

Her small hands fluttered all over the front of him, trying to push back and reestablish her footing, while refusing to do the one thing that would have allowed this: grab hold of him solidly. This left her more or less maneuvering against his chest, a victim of gravity—and other natural attractions. For several seconds they remained thus, both of them breathing in a slightly labored manner from the climb. Nardi's chest up against Hannah's soft, sliding breasts, her hands at his shoulders, then about his neck, then shoving him in the pectorals, then poking him in the abdomen. Here he and she were, Nardi thought, at the top of the world, free as birds, no one watching.

This was a renewingly pleasant feeling one moment, then—like a man suddenly dizzy from heights—Nardi felt the jab of fear from an old problem. He worried what might be expected of him in this new context. Women at one time had increasingly seemed to expect so much of him that there had been room for nothing but disappointment. How long had it been? Two and half years? Three? Nardi couldn't remember when he had last had sexual relations, though he could recall with regrettable clarity when he had last failed to.

Hesitation cost him the moment. Hannah Van Evan expected only that he wouldn't drop her when she lost her balance on shingled terrain. She found his knee then used it to lever herself up the last step into the belvedere. Nardi followed after her, shoving his hand through his hair. His mouth was dry, his head slightly light, his groin roiling with all he wanted to do—and damnably bursting with the capability to do it.

To call the building on the highest ridge of the estate a belvedere was a little grandiose. It was a kind of open-walled room actually, hardly more than a series of stone arches sitting under a Norman slate roof that overhung an iron-rail perimeter. Hannah ran straight across this outdoor structure to the far side, where she stood with her back to him. Even from thirty feet away he could see her alarm: the rapid rise and fall of her breathing, the way her hands grasped the railing, sliding out along it, letting go, grabbing it again.

The beautiful, redheaded Hannah stood poised at the railing, jewellike, sweet-odored, a creature of the sun. God help her, he thought. And him. For it was more than just wanting her. All mixed into the lust was something else.

When had this happened? Nardi asked himself. When had it become important to him that he see her mouth smile again? When had he begun to be enchanted by the nervous movement of her hands, by the wide swing of her pendulous hips as she walked or danced or stumbled—or sidestepped down a railing away from him as he approached her? Crazy, rattle-brained woman. He wanted to still all her nervous movements with the weight of his own body, weigh her down, settle on her, shifting till he found the right fit that calmed her into soft, crooning compliance. He wanted wet, slow, deep kisses . . . pressed pelvises . . . groaning contact. He wanted to slide between the folds of all her delicate, fibrillating energy, to bury himself deeply in all the life that pulsed and quivered in her. . . .

At her shoulder, Nardi said finally, "Hannah, I want to touch you."

She looked around sharply. "Don't say that."

"I want to." He reached out.

She moved away from him, taking another side step down the railing as she turned to face him.

"I know I frightened you," he said, "by telling you all the unwholesome motives I might have for wanting to make love to you." He talked quickly before she could speak the obvious objections. "*Chérie,* I know no insightful person can ignore these completely; they are there. But I also know I am equally clear-sighted when I tell you my wanting to touch you at this instant does not have a thing to do with Sébastien or Amelia Besom or anything else mean or secondary to simply liking you enormously and finding you utterly lovely."

She stared at him, her back to the railing, her hands wrapped around it so her elbows stuck out over the river, a sheer drop straight down two hundred feet into milky-green water. The width of the Seine stretched behind her, its opaque surface alive with a froth of current. "Stay where you are," she said so seriously she might have been threatening to turn and jump if Nardi didn't halt.

He stopped two feet short of her.

"Don't start with this, Nardi," she said. She took a quick inhalation of salt air. "The ulterior reasons you outlined that afternoon over the clay box are most certainly still valid. You and Mrs. Besom despise each other. And your snobby brother makes me feel—"

"You are wrong. Sébastien thinks you would be—"

She finished huffily, "Yes, I know what he thinks. And what Mrs. Besom would think. She's jealous of any attention I pay you. I can't imagine what she'd do if she found—I'd—well—" She said quickly, "Here, if she found me here." Her shoulders tightened, her hands rotating on the iron bar, so that her elbows wobbled. "Besides, I've been the summer's entertainment for rich, idle men before, and I don't like the result."

Nardi had heard this reference now on several occasions, though this was the first time it worried him. What result? What men? From things she'd said, he'd pieced together that there had been a rich young man in Miami who'd offered her marriage, then retracted the offer. Nardi understood, more from all Hannah hadn't said, that something sexual had taken place with this young man that had left her uncomfortable with her own part in the ensuing scandal.

Then Hannah effectively distracted him by saying, "No, Nardi, I don't want you to touch me: I'm not even tempted." She backed away from him, one hand on the railing.

Nardi followed her with his eyes, surprised by the strength of her resolve—and the injury of these words. He laughed then told her, "Couldn't you at least be tempted, then refuse? This would be ever so much less insulting." If this was a joke, it fell flat, while a place low in his groin—a small warm dragon's egg of lust—thumped and growled blackly.

The really pathetic thing was that, from the terrific vantage point of the belvedere, he could not only watch her turn and run down the far steps, but see her descend all the way down the opposite slope they'd come up, run across a field, over a footbridge and around to race up into the avenue between the canals, then scramble her way up into the back garden, through which she climbed at a mad dash to vanish into the château completely.

Then to the side of all this activity, Nardi noticed something else. From the top of the overlook, he saw where the guards had gotten off to. They sat in the distance, hardly more than pinpoints on the porch of a little storybook cottage. Their absence was no accident, but rather a granting of privacy—a permission, Nardi was almost certain, that had nothing to do with the twisting, turning terrain or good fortune. The two Swiss orderlies on the porch loitered in a

way that was open and official: Almost surely, his sweet,
little moment alone with the lovely Mademoiselle Hannah
was courtesy of Sébastien the Magnificent, Ruler of the
Planet.

Nardi felt a wave of annoyance. This feeling brought back
the old days vividly: Sébastien in control of everything—
now even to the point of his claiming dominion over where
Nardi might put his penis. The stupid, pandering son of a
bitch. Nardi folded his arms and braced his hip on the rail.

So it wasn't meant to be, he thought, he and Hannah.
Perhaps this was the best, for Hannah at least. There were
things he couldn't change. The way Sébastien was. His own
circumstances. He reminded himself that the world—his
family and Georges Du Gard—had plans for him.

Then the world reminded him again more forcefully,
when that evening before dinner Sébastien came down to
see him.

Nardi's brother entered the cottage in unusual disarray, at
least for Sébastien. He needed a haircut. His collar wasn't
buttoned in properly at the back of his shirt. It stood out a
bit at the top. For any other man, these things would have
been minor. For Sébastien, such lapses were akin to nervous
collapse.

Nardi greeted him with, "You look awful."

Sébastien looked harried, exhausted. "I feel awful," he
said as he pulled a chair out at the table. "I feel awful, I look
awful, I'm tired. And I'm ill—mainly because of the
estimates I received two days ago for the repairs to the
hydraulic system." He sat, dropping a document of some
sort in front of him. "It is going to cost almost ten times
what I expected just to get the fountains and reflection pools
working again. To do it, the seawall on the east canal has to
be torn up then put back together again. I don't know where
all this money will come from, unless Amelia outdoes
herself. Meanwhile the woman keeps harping at me to sell
the damn Rembrandt—"

"So do it." Nardi sat down opposite him, at the bare wood table where he and Hannah had once translated telegrams.

Sébastien scowled as he swiped a palm back through his longish hair. "God, that's what Du Gard keeps saying. He says we'll get someone to make a nice copy." He groaned. "A fucking copy. Can you imagine? The Château d'Aubrignon with copies hanging on its walls." He heaved a huge sigh and sat back, looking at Nardi who could only stare at his brother. He knew the profanity to be fairly strong in English; Sébastien rarely expressed himself in a like manner in French, let alone a foreign language.

Sébastien cleared his throat and said, "I've brought something down we all want you to see." On the table he squared in front of him what looked to be two or three legal pages, then he glanced up slyly. "By the way, how is the lovely Mademoiselle Van Evan?"

"None of your business."

"I think she might be loose," Sébastien said encouragingly.

"I wish that were the case."

His brother frowned. "If she isn't, you're doing something wrong. Judging by Amelia Besom's anxiety for the girl's history, our Mademoiselle Van Evan has a past as black as a dockside whore's."

Nardi felt himself blanch. Nothing could be further from the truth of Hannah as he knew her—or even of Hannah as he didn't know her. Whatever it was that she wasn't talking about, it wasn't anything like this.

In response to Nardi's face apparently, Sébastien held up his hand. "Sorry. No offense. She's a lovely young woman. Enjoy her company. It's good for you."

Nardi sniffed.

His brother's face took on the sage look of an older brother giving advice. "Nardi, she's a more worldly creature than she appears. She knows what's what."

"What does she know of my reasons for being here, Sébastien? Does she know about the marriage?"

Sébastien frowned. "She has to know something of it,

doesn't she? I mean, she's been here for months now and, as you like to say, she'd not stupid."

"Have you told her? I have not."

Nardi's brother looked at him a moment, then said, "Yes, I've implied enough that I'm sure she understands. She knows of the marriage"—he bent back over the papers—"which brings us to the reason I've come." He turned the several pages around to put them in front of Nardi.

"What is this?"

"An insurance policy."

Paging through it, Nardi scowled. It was insurance on him. He was worth a million francs dead.

He looked up at Sébastien. "So are you going to blow a hole in me? What *is* this?"

"Don't be melodramatic. It is a policy against a man's life whose existence in recent years has been just a little precarious. If you die, you're covered, that's all. Du Gard wants it. I brought it so you could see specifically that the coverage does not include suicide."

"How comforting." Nardi looked down at it again. "A million francs. Will that fix your hydraulic system, Sébastien?"

"It's your château, not mine. And, no, it would barely repair the canal and seawall. Look at it here." Sébastien reached across the table, pointing to a clause. "It says," he told Nardi, "that in the event of your death, other than at your own hand, this policy will additionally pay in full any debts the de Saint Vallier family might owe the Du Gards. This is a significant clause, Nardi. It means if you decide to do yourself in, could you please arrange to fall face forward in the ether so we can claim it was an accident?"

Nardi scowled at the damn thing. "Do I need to sign it?" he asked. He held out his hand for Sébastien's pen.

Sébastien shook his head. "No. Your permission isn't required. We all have an insurable interest. That is sufficient. I just wanted you to know the policy has been taken out. Don't do anything to void it, please."

Nardi glanced over the pages. Not only did his death pay

off all debts, it left the million francs, he realized, to Marie Nicole Du Gard, soon-to-be de Saint Vallier.

He handed the paper back, not certain which was more annoying: to realize people expected him to give up, to "accidentally" fall face over into his ether, or to understand his true value—the sum of debts, plus a million francs— was less than the renovation of the outside water system. He asked, "When?"

"When what?"

"When is the wedding? I assume you still want me to come."

"It isn't firm yet." Sébastien heaved a deep sigh again. "Du Gard wanted July fourteenth"—he laughed—"which of course would be in a week. It couldn't be organized that quickly. Thank God. He was thinking Bastille Day, fire- works. Your future father-in-law, for the record, loves fireworks. I am having a devil of a time discouraging him from following the final 'I do' with a rocket display out over the river."

Surprised, Nardi asked, "You mean the wedding is going to be here?"

"In the chapel." Sébastien laughed dryly. "With five hundred and twenty-four of your closest friends."

Nardi stared at him. "I don't know five hundred people. Does Du Gard?"

"No. He thinks we do. He's sending invitations to everyone, including the president of the republic."

Nardi was taken aback. Trying to explain this to himself, he said, "Pater, I suppose, knows him."

Sébastien laughed again. "And that is the point of the wedding precisely."

Chapter 18

There is nothing as strong as the libido.
—Sigmund Freud

IT STARTED WITH a mouth, that incredible mouth. Then a face, satisfying lines, and *tout à coup*, Hannah appeared at the end of Nardi's pencil: her petite jaw, her pointy chin, her large eyes, her tiny nose turned up at the end. Her face had an infant's proportion. Hannah's countenance was that of an overserious child, like Hannah herself, a contradiction. Nardi was pleased when he managed to capture this, which he could do in a few pencil strokes with some regularity. Then . . .

Well, then the whole thing pretty much degenerated into bare breasts, belly buttons, large naked buttocks, and open thighs complete with shadowy vulvas sketched around dark, mysterious almond-slit entrances. After a day or two, Nardi had a dozen extremely sexual drawings tacked to the wall over his downstairs table, though none of them looked exactly right to him. They seemed generic. He would study them, frowning, wondering what was wrong and why he wasn't able to undress Hannah more successfully on paper.

When he went up to the château, he found himself missing whole portions of conversation with her. His eye studied her body. The line; the movement; the fit of her jacket ("Here, let me help you take this off. You're going to

get it dirty. . . ."); the way her blouse cleaved to the high
curve of her breasts or floated over her spine as it clung to
her trapezius when she raised, rotated, or drew back her
shoulders. Her muscles tended to be short, compact, well
toned without bunching. The day Nardi noticed her rib cage
hung at a more forward angle than usual—giving structural
reason for her unusually small back—he got so excited, he
abandoned her in midsentence, leaving her puzzled as he
galloped back toward the cottage.

July passed in this way, with Nardi's dozen drawings
becoming an entire wallful. These drawings gained a
skeletal force, a muscular tension. When Nardi looked at the
later ones, he could feel the weight of limbs, the spacial
roundness of torso. And one could—Nardi smiled at
himself—almost feel one's way into the dark unknown
between Hannah's legs that led into the mystifying, mes-
merizing center of her body.

Of course, the drawings were good, Nardi reasoned. He'd
drawn them with his penis. He was inclined to dismiss them
as art, though; they amounted to little more, he thought, than
extraordinarily nice pornography.

By the time August arrived, however, every square inch
of wall was covered by libidinous doodles. At least a dozen
pictures were from more modest angles. Nardi had begun to
experiment with Hannah's movement, the energy in her
posture. He had found the lines for this in among the round
extremes of her femininity, then laid out the mass and
weight of these on paper.

It never once occurred to him to hide these drawings.
Sébastien saw them—and turned away from them like the
nit he was, referring to them occasionally thereafter with a
nervous, ribald wit as predictable and unoriginal as human
beings ever were on such matters. It never once occurred to
Nardi that the woman who had refused ever again to come
to the cottage, or to go anywhere else with him alone for that
matter, would one day run breathlessly down the slopes,
beat on his door violently, then burst in huffing and puffing
to say, "Butterflies! Butterflies!"—then go sheet white, her

eyes becoming moons of shock as she stared at her multiple selves *au naturel* from one end of the room to the other.

Nardi stood up immediately. "*Bonjour,* Hannah," he said as normally as possible, his pencil still in his hand. "How nice to see you."

"Oh, Nardi"—she took a step back from him—"what have you—" She broke off, her mouth open in an O of astonishment as round as her eyes. She couldn't speak for a full minute.

It took Nardi himself the minute to figure out what to say. "Go on," he told her finally, and stepped back. "Look closer. You are truly, *vraiment belle, extraordinaire*-ily beautiful."

She hesitated another moment, then, blushing and wetting her lips as if they were dry as parchment, she came forward. "Oh God, Nardi," she said. "They're horrible." She glanced at him. "They're wonderful." She studied the wall again, staring from one drawing to the next, putting her hands to her cheeks. "They are so blessed—Jesus-Mary-and-Joseph—" She swallowed then tried again. "So blessed—" She seemed to be trying to find a modest word. After a pause, she whispered, "Physical."

"*Oui,* they are that."

"They're beautiful. Lord God, they make me feel—" She halted again, then finished with, "They're gorgeous." Her words rose through her laughter, as if her next observation were a big discovery: "They're obscene"—she laughed with profuse, nervous delight—"but brilliant, absolutely brilliant."

Nardi smiled. "They are not that good, Hannah."

Her round, dark eyes swung up to his face. "No, they're better: Nardi, these are the drawings of a sculptor."

"No, Hannah, these are the drawings of man who wants to sleep with you *jusqu'à la folie,* to the point of madness." He added another home truth for good measure: "They are obsessive."

"Yes," she said quickly, "all really absorbing work is." She cocked her head toward him then leaped in conversation to, "When you made statues, you only worked in marble?"

"Preferably marble. I work in stone—"

"Let's ask Sébastien to get you some marble."

Nardi burst out laughing this time. "Oh, by all means. We will just ask him to order up a piece of really nice Carrara marble. That should only cost him the east salon or the carriageway repaving or the herd of white deer he wants to bring in again to roam the front meadow and forestlands."

Hannah frowned. She glanced at the drawings again, tapping her finger to her chin, then she turned toward him brightly. "I know where there's a piece of marble," she said.

"What?"

Her smile became crazily optimistic, the sort only Hannah could produce, a wide, toothsome display of impossibly high expectation. "And to get to it, we will have to go through the butterfly garden. Just wait till you see, Nardi! I saw it from a rampart window about half an hour ago, then got down here as quickly as I could. I don't know why—the timing, the sun, the moon, the stars, whatever—but your garden has come alive with flying flowers."

The sun was high. The sky was azure blue, virtually cloudless. And the little clearing of nettles in the center of the orchard was a paean to this summer brightness: It leaped and flitted with winged color, filled with butterflies. There were red admirals, swallowtails, silver-spotted skippers, orange tips, and blue Adonis. These swooped and fluttered in the air. There were even two large monarchs darting at the milkweed. All told, there had to be a hundred butterflies that had at last found their way to the old butterfly garden, where they now danced around each other, as if playing a kind of crazy tag or leapfrog over the scraggly shrubs.

"Isn't it wonderful?" Hannah asked. "But why? Why now and not before?"

Nardi, standing beside her, laughing, was equally astonished. *"Eh bien,"* he said, "the skippers over there only come out in August and September, but I cannot make excuses for the rest. I don't know where they've been." He pointed. "Look." Two clouded yellows were spinning spirals round each other. "Mating," he said. He shrugged again. "Perhaps this explains it. Mating is a pursuit *vertigineux, eh*—dizzy, I think, is the word in English. They were too dizzy to find their way here."

She laughed at his little joke, then said, "Come on. We can come back this way if we want to. I want to show you the marble."

Nardi wasn't keen to look at her marble and wouldn't have followed—till she grabbed his hand and tugged at it.

He allowed himself to be pulled along. Her grasp, small, firm, warm, felt splendid in his. As they went into the orchard between a row of apple trees gone wild, he pressed his thumb to her palm, running his fingers over the backs of hers, then slid one finger up and down in between. As they walked along he examined her knuckles and bones from tapered fingertip down to the crux, the pad, the palm. She seemed a little discomposed, though not displeased, for him to play with her hand like this.

She led him toward the apple storehouse, where he pushed one barnlike door open for her, hooking it open on its post. When he turned round again, she was standing in the sunlight at the edge of the storehouse, her fingers clutched into a fist, her hand drawn against her chest, her eyes fixed on him. She stared a moment, as an owl inside hooted then flapped up into the rafters.

Nardi followed when she stepped inside. The storehouse smelled strongly organic, cidery: the residual, musty-winy odor of old wood that had held the fruit of a hundred of apple harvests.

"There," Hannah said. She pointed across the dirt flooring toward a huge, hulking shadow across the dim interior. Nardi walked forward as she turned and went back to open the second of the double doors, admitting more light. "Well, what do you think?" she asked from behind him.

In the diffuse light stood a mammoth white stone that

climbed nearly eight feet to a harsh, shadowed stone face which smiled down malignantly.

Nardi groaned and turned back toward Hannah.

She stood in the doorway's wide beam of daylight, propping the one door open with her back. The beam of light around her was alive with dust particles. It threw her into dazzling, ghostly silhouette, cloaking her in a nimbus, and setting her hair aglow like fire.

This beautiful, otherworldly creature of light said, "I found this statue about two weeks ago. I didn't tell you. I didn't think you'd want to see it. Amelia says it was one of the last pieces you did before you, um"—she gently chose a euphemism—"disappeared." Amelia had said more than this about the statue itself, because Hannah added, "I don't think it's that bad, though, not really."

Nardi laughed and groaned, both. "Yes, it is. Trust me."

"Amelia says it isn't worth anything."

"The stone itself is worth more."

Nardi dared to turn around again. It was his old *Rising Venus*. Facing it was like looking at all his old grievances with his art made manifest, eight feet high, solid as marble, and scowling down at him in angry imperfection. The figure sat stiffly, its hands slightly too large for a woman's, its facial features a mask of exaggerated, half-serious, half-caricature umbrage. It was the work of an angry sculptor, an artist who was not quite sure what in the world he was up to. Even looking at it now, all Nardi could see was a massive failure of focus, an overconfidence that had combined oddly with a gross failure of imagination.

"If you agree that it would not be a bad thing to destroy," Hannah said tentatively, "you could devise something out of it, something much smaller, of course, but there are thick sections, large chunks of marble here. I don't think anyone would mind."

Nardi laughed, a derisive snort. No, no one would mind. Everyone had hated this piece. He walked partway around it, then leaned forward and lay his hands on it. The marble was nice, from the Bettogli quarry. It was first-quality stone.

From behind him the woman said, "There! You see!"

Light closed off. One of the doors shut, and Hannah's footfalls came toward him. She walked up beside him, turned around shoulder to shoulder, and leaned back on the statue, looking him in the face. In the dimmer light, her features were muted. The stone stood out white behind her.

"You see?" She repeated, "You are a sculptor." She explained this conclusion. "When I first came upon this piece I walked round and round it for almost ten minutes. Within thirty seconds of seeing it, you put your hands on it."

"I like to put my hands on things," he said, "but I am not sure that makes me a sculptor." Frowning slightly, he turned to lean his shoulder on a stone thigh, inches from Hannah.

She didn't move away. Though he could feel a disquiet in her, a kind of turmoil coming off her like heat. Out loud she tried to keep him to the role she'd assigned him, that of recovering sculptor. "This isn't like the glycerin," she said. "I'm not trying to fix you. I'm only trying to give you what you already wish you had."

"I know what I wish I had, and it is not a piece of cold stone, however fine, from whatever quarry."

She opened her mouth to answer this, then couldn't. She dropped her head.

Nardi attempted to change the subject to the one he was actually thinking about. "So you like my dirty drawings, do you?" he asked.

"I liked the beautiful ones." She shook her head slowly, a denial. "And even they were a little embarrassing. I didn't have any clothes on."

"I think you would be very beautiful without any clothes on, Hannah." An idea occurred to him. "You will pose for me, yes?"

She looked up, her mouth a grimace of dissatisfaction. She said, "Mrs. Besom told me you would one day ask me this."

"Did she tell you what to answer?"

"I can answer for myself: no. You have more imagination than is good for you; you don't need for me to pose." She turned around and spread both her palms on the stone, then lay her cheek against it. "It is smooth, isn't it? And cool."

Nardi wanted to reach his arm across her back and simply lean, till the front of him was up against her. He would bend his knees and tilt his pelvis as he brought his body up, curving himself against her buttocks while he reached his hands around to cup her breasts and bent his mouth into the crook of her neck so as to lick his way up the length of her sternocleidomastoid. He stared at the muscles of her neck.

If only licking them were welcome. Perhaps he *should* attack this statue, he thought. With a hammer he could probably pulverize it by fall. That would at least give him an outlet. Otherwise he was going to drive himself crazy with this sort of thinking and her maddening mixed messages. He felt sure at moments that she wanted him to touch her; and equally sure that if he did, she would box his ears for him.

Hannah lifted her cheek off the stone, her fervid gaze upon him. "So how can we get this up to the cottage?"

"This?" He thumped the stone.

"Yes."

"*Pas possible.* Too heavy."

"But you know how to move marble."

"*Oui,* with pulleys and lifts. Or with dowels, ropes, and men to help control it, none of which we have. You don't just move a block of marble this large." He heaved a sigh, then tried to explain something. "Hannah," he told her, "I know this old statue is supposed to, how you say, *déclencher, eh,* set off, set in motion a whole number of positive responses in me." He shrugged. "It does not. I feel nothing for this statue, except perhaps the pity one feels for a huge, ugly monstrosity."

"And *The Separation*?" she asked.

"What about it?"

"Do you like it?"

"I used to." He amended, "No, I used to *love* it. I was very proud of that piece at one time."

"Then you should come to the dining hall where it's

stored. There's an auction at the end of the month. It's going to be sold. You should visit it before it goes."

He shook his head no. "I would prefer not to." He held his hands out, a gesture that offered what he knew to be poor explanation. "Hannah, the private part—creation and how I feel about what I made—and the public part—showing it, selling it—well, I have never been able to put these comfortably together. In my rational moments I have always known selling and showing my work was business, nothing more, nothing less. In my irrational moments, though, this commerce makes of my nerves, *eh, en pelote, eh, comme,* like a ball of wool, all tangled, tight, for fear prices, attention, these external things mean something, that people like me—or don't. My art, even old things I have done, I am afraid would still seem too much a part of me. For my own safety, I don't let any of it matter any longer."

She blinked at him through the dimness.

They both grew quiet. Nardi drew in air audibly, glad just to breath after this little spate of honesty—spoken at such close range to a woman for whom he would have given another broken finger or two, just to screw her right here and now.

So he just stood there in an apple storehouse that smelled familiar, the potent aroma of Calvados casks against one wall, the pervasive odor of the apple loft above. The floors and rafters of this place were permeated by the scent of fruit come and gone, piled high, then carted off or turned to brandy. This history penetrated the wood and stirred the air.

Nardi could remember the smell of the fall harvest, the undulating hillocks of fruit everywhere, in piles at the edges of the orchards, in the loft, in barrels up in the kitchen at the château. He said aloud, "I used to climb up in this loft when I was young, especially in August just before the harvest. It was hot. This was the best time to smell the apple ghosts, the strong smell of things that were."

Nardi pushed off the statue to walk around it, trailing his fingers over it, around Hannah then down, till he faced the open doorway. Outside, it was bright as blazes, cool where

he was. He turned and leaned back, each arm on a stone
knee, his back resting into the stone lap of Venus. He tried
to make himself comfortable, content. After a pause he
asked, "Did you ever have a favorite place as a child?"

The woman around the edge of the statue said nothing for
a moment, then her voice echoed up into the rafters. She
called, "Yes, an inlet. My father and I used to fish there."

"You never speak of your mother."

There was another hesitation before she said, "She ran
off. With another man. I wasn't even two, so I don't
remember. But even years later Papa used to get drunk and
lament this—then lecture me a little incoherently about
what he called 'the wildness in a woman's blood.'" She
broke off. The other side of the statue grew inordinately
quiet and still.

"So what did you fish for in your inlet?"

"Barracuda."

"Barracuda? *Ah là là*, you are daring."

She became herself again, letting out a single giggle. "We
fished with spoons," she said. "A barracuda will bite on
anything that sparkles in the water. We would catch them,
then slice them open to retrieve the spoon—they were my
mother's, the spoons, that is. We had four sterling silver
teaspoons she'd left behind." There was another awkward
hiatus, though it was a different kind of awkwardness,
which she relieved by saying, "You must think, 'What a
peasant.' I've seen more sterling silver on your breakfast
tray than I knew in all my growing up." She laughed. "And
we didn't eat with it, we fished with it. What boors, yes?"

"No," he said. When he turned his head in her direction,
he could only see her hand. It lay on a thick stone arm. So
Nardi reached over and took Hannah's hand again.

It was small and thin, slender enough that one could see
the tendons. He smiled to remember how these moved
across the tops of her hands as she spoke, gesturing in
typical animated manner. He ringed her wrist with his
fingers, then ran his hand up her arm. Her forearm was
slender as well. She would have thin legs, that's how he'd

drawn them. She was thin everywhere in fact, except for her hips and bosom and the apple-cheeked wholesomeness of her face.

As he got to her elbow she pulled her arm away. She came into view in front of him. "I have to go," she said. "There's a lot to do. This auction is going to take a lot of my time. I'm not sure if I'll see very much of you."

Then she walked into the beam of light, her silhouette ablaze, her hair aflame, the dust particles spiraling in her wake like a million tiny living things attracted to her, wanting to follow. She walked into this beam of daylight, disappearing into its white blare almost as if it burned her to ash and blew her into the wind.

At least it seemed so to Nardi, who wouldn't be able to find her, except distantly in the midst of her work, for almost two weeks after this.

During this time Hannah herself went back to the apple storehouse on three occasions to see the statue. It was always there, always untouched. Disappointed, she gave up. She didn't exactly avoid Nardi beyond this afternoon in the apple storehouse. She only let herself be consumed by her work life, which grew busier—and by an employer who was only too happy to have her undivided attention.

As the auction approached, Hannah and Amelia Besom worked more and more shoulder to shoulder. The auction at the end of August was to be a kind of trial run for the coming fall season at the big auction houses. Mrs. Besom was still in negotiations with Sotheby's, London. Christie's in New York had taken seventeen lots for two of their major fall auctions, eighteenth-century paintings and antiques from the Orient. In October, *La Compagnie des Commissaires-Priseurs de Paris* would be auctioning off twenty-eight lots of period furniture at the Hôtel Drouot.

So Hannah had plenty to do. She helped with the local auction preparations while also working on the auction-house consignment contracts. It became her job also to keep everything generally organized in what was becoming a whole series of notebooks. During this August, she likewise learned how to arrange for crating, insuring, and shipping, as well as becoming more conversant than any sane person might want to be with the ins and outs of French export laws, taxes, and surcharges.

Hannah saw Nardi several times in the midst of all this activity, but never for more than hello and good-bye: Amelia Besom's near-constant presence deterred him as effectively as bitter quinine did malaria. The only conversation of any substance that Hannah had with Nardi was, in fact, within earshot of both Amelia Besom and Nardi's brother. Several days before the local auction, Nardi fell in step with Hannah just as she was walking out under the main carriage portico, carting out a delicate collection of lapis lazuli figures. Outside under the portico, Hannah handed the box of wrapped figurines to Mrs. Besom as Sébastien de Saint Vallier opened the carriage door for the two women.

Hannah turned toward Nardi before she got into the vehicle. He had stopped behind her under the wide arch of the entry doorway. She said to him, "We're going into town, to the inspection hall." The portable lots for sale were being transported to a hotel in Aubrignon-sur-Seine, where close examination would be offered to potential buyers. The auction itself would take place in the picturesque little village, the château having been judged too noisy and torn apart to accommodate gracefully the rich collectors they hoped would arrive. "*The Separation* is already there," Hannah told Nardi. "Why don't you come with us?"

He shook his head no, but did ask after a moment, "What piece has first position?"

"The Monet painting with the château in the background."

He glared, casting his displeasure over all three of them for a moment. "*The Separation* is better and worth more."

"Come to the auction and see if it is."

He only expelled a disgusted snort, then turned around and left.

"He's a coward," Sébastien said as the carriage pulled out from under the overhang and around the grand driveway. He continued coolly, "In the early days, putting his work on display scared Nardi so badly that he couldn't hold food down before an exhibit. And that was when every exhibit pretty much ended with unanimous public acclaim. When he started to have to face a little criticism, he would lose ten pounds just before an exhibit, then arrive the night of it trying to suppress the dry heaves. He couldn't cope with the public aspect of his art. We got him a doctor, who recommended a small amount of cocaine. But that made him bounce off the walls, especially if he drank coffee. It made his hands shake; he couldn't work. Morphine put him to sleep. Someone suggested ether to me, so I brought him some. It made him pleasantly drunk and wore off quickly. It was also the rage at the time. There was a little recipe floating around at all the parties, *Coupe Jacques à l'éther*, strawberries soaked in it then popped into the mouth."

Hannah leaned back. Counterbalancing as they began the wind down the cliffside, she looked across the open carriage at Sébastien. "He told me you brought him ether."

"I was fairly certain he had. He likes to blame me for it." Sébastien tilted his head down, the brim of his hat hiding his expression all the way to his dark moustache pulled in a tight line over his mouth. "Well, no one expected him to take up drinking it as if it were his life's vocation. And you must understand—we were all busy. Mater organized the grand sculptor's social events, you see. His salon dinners, the formal parties. Pater traveled, wining and dining the possible big commissions. Louise and her husband got Nardi's work or castings of it into more than a hundred galleries. Claire was the resident psychiater-masseuse; she was the only one he'd talk to. I myself handled the finances."

"It sounds as if Nardi was quite an enterprise."

"He was. His future was worth a fortune." He added

honestly, "And what few years we all did enjoy were
damned lucrative. We would, none of us, be in bad shape
now if Nardi had only kept at it."

Hannah didn't see Nardi again till the day of the auction,
though she couldn't for the life of her get him completely
out of her mind. She found herself at the end of each day
exhausted and vaguely irritable, with a sense of something
left undone. This something, whatever it was, in some way
was attached to a series of visits she began to make to the
ballroom at night. She would wake suddenly, listening to the
château and the French countryside beyond, all still and
quiet. Then she would get up. The first time, she told herself
she was hungry; she had not had much dinner. But by the
second time, she didn't even bother with this lie. She
wandered straight down to the ballroom where, by day,
Nardi was repairing the ceiling, and stood there in her
nightgown.

In this manner, visit by visit, she watched the gesso
medallion burst onto the clean, newly painted ceiling,
spreading out in a sunburst of rococo, lamplit shadows.

The buyers began to arrive the next day, by boat, by
carriage, by train, by coach: seven men from France and
England, three Americans traveling abroad, an Irishman, an
Austrian, two Germans, and a very pompous Spanish
gentleman with a pointed goatee and a monocle. The buyers
were all male to a one—Hannah was beginning to understand how truly exceptional Mrs. Besom's position was.
Virtually all "important" art that Hannah had seen or heard
of was the work of men; virtually all buyers and collectors
were male. Men as well dominated the handling, appraising,
and auctions.

To even a greater degree than outside the arts, the male
half of the species—its creative output, tastes, and sensi-
bilities—dominated Hannah's chosen line of interest, something she acknowledged that week and decided to make the
best of. Hannah figured she knew what men liked, espe-

cially upper-class men, and she could serve it up to them as well as any male art-and-antique dealer. No, better. That evening she opened her skirt a few more buttons, put her "piratical" earrings back on, and smiled her way into dinner, where she thoroughly enjoyed herself as she wined and dined the buyers over an elaborate meal beside Mrs. Besom.

Chapter 19

Yet, forgive me, God,
That I do brag thus! This your air of France
Hath blown that vice in me.
            —William Shakespeare, *Henry V*, III: vi

AUBRIGNON-SUR-SEINE WAS NESTLED at the edge of the Seine River, between grassy marsh and climbing bluff. To get down to it, one descended through trees, over roads cut into chalk cliffs, the carriageway often seeming to be cantilevered out into thin air. Eventually one's carriage trundled along over flatter, lower land, traveling through a cluster of houses that ended just before the town's center, the village square. This small public plaza was little more than the intersection of three country roads, a greensward traversed by two cobbled walks that bisected each other at a central fountain-well, the whole surrounded by a dozen storefronts. Monsieur de Saint Vallier and Mrs. Besom had lobbied the town's council for the use of this public square, on which today, at its center and to the side of its fountain, stood a dark, damson blue canopy. Under this, Hannah Van Evan stood while rolling then unrolling an auction catalog.

The "catalog" was actually only a single, fine-printed sheet folded in half, listing a modest forty-seven items. Somewhat immodestly, this page heralded the gathering before Hannah as *The de Saint Vallier Collection: A Summer*

Preview. And indeed "The de Saint Vallier Collection" would be "previewed" in an artfully summery milieu: The canopy overhead sheltered a raised platform that looked out over an audience of folding chairs, each chair caparisoned in a white tailored slipcover that tied in back at a bow. These crisp-white chairs were arranged in neat rows, at the ends of which, under gently flapping scallops of blue-black canvas, stood pedestals topped off by potfuls of white tulips. To Hannah, as the buyers in their top hats and frock coats milled in to take their seats, they looked more like the arriving guests to an English garden party than the big spenders, whom she hoped they were, willing to travel the backwoods of France in order to buy art and antiques.

She sat down in the last row, one in from the aisle. The rest of the row was empty. There were more seats than necessary, as Aubrignon's town council had been invited to sit under the canopy, an invitation of goodwill that so far had gone unanswered. In the plaza beyond the canopy, locals hung about, obviously fascinated but wary. They, too, felt the sense of something significant taking place here. The scallops of canvas, with their trim of heavy gold fringe, had been blowing all morning in a way that seemed to announce this, a flapping, glinting flutter of sunlight and that beat, *tat-a-tat,* in the wind like a relentless drumroll.

Hannah curled her auction catalog into a tube and held it in her fists as she stared straight into the heart of her own excitement and apprehension: The lovely, entwining statues carved by the seemingly mythic sculptor, Bernard de Saint Vallier, stood in clear view on the dais in front. Her find. Her future. And with, please, a little luck, her commission. She prayed for a bid near the fifteen hundred francs she'd promised, wanting, even more than the money, the credibility and opportunities this might bring her.

From this distance, over top hats and the shoulders of murmuring gentlemen as they were being seated, the two statues that formed *The Separation* looked to Hannah to be more delicate and graceful than she remembered, but also

much, much smaller. They seemed easy to overlook amidst
the sparkle of crystal sailing ships, silver candelabra, and
rich paintings framed in elaborate gold. Up there on the
display table, "her" poor little statues seemed overwhelmed
by all the priceless things around them.

No, no, they were impossibly beautiful, better than
anything, Hannah told herself, like small diamonds among
chunks of rock salt; only a fool would ignore them.

The buyers grew alert. Each man had been given a
numbered paddle, which each now moved into a downward
position as the auctioneer mounted the dais. At the same
moment, the wind off the water kicked up, making the
canvas overhead whoop slightly, a deep sound accompanied
by the gentle whir of the blowing fringe.

Her anxiety was so high, Hannah couldn't even say when
the auctioneer had begun to call numbers. She only knew he
was calling them first in English then in French, his voice
rising sharply then falling in a kind of stylized enthusiasm.
Hannah found this ricochet of syllables, back and forth in
two languages, difficult to follow. Without being able to
penetrate the full process, she recognized that a painting, a
carved trunk, and a set of jade Foo dogs had been sold.
Paddles moved. A bearded Englishman in the front row and
across signaled with a lift of his wrist. A stout man behind
him rotated his hand out of the bend of his folded arms.
Hannah watched, intent, trying to attune herself.

There were only three bids on the crystal sailing ship, but
the price rose geometrically as preemptive bids were called
out from the floor. Mrs. Besom all but came out of her chair
as the hammer banged down on a selling price of forty-three
hundred francs, close to eight hundred dollars; the most
optimism she had ever had the courage to voice was five.
Mrs. Besom was sitting across and up a row from Hannah
beside a stoic Sébastien de Saint Vallier, who kept crossing
and recrossing his legs, first one direction then the other. His
folded arms were wound together so tightly across his chest
that the back of his frock coat bowed between his shoulder
blades. As the crystal ship was taken away Mrs. Besom

murmured something to him then leaned back to glimpse around at Hannah. This was followed by a surprisingly satisfied moment, two colleagues sharing a triumph, as Hannah congratulated the woman with a smile. This sale was the first inkling that both Mrs. Besom and her client were going to make far more money here than anyone had dared dream.

Not that the auction was without its disappointments: A seventeenth-century giltwood-and-marble side table, one of the more noteworthy pieces being offered, did not meet its reserve and was thus taken unsold off the bidding floor. The featured Monet went for exactly its reserve, that is, the lowest acceptable price or about two-thirds of its low estimate. Hannah herself felt the anguish of letting the picture go at this price; it was a beautiful painting full of light and water, with a lovely distant castle in the background. Most items, however, were selling at or above their predicted value. Everything was disappearing—except *The Separation,* which stood out lonelier and lonelier on the display table.

Meanwhile, at the periphery of her vision, a group of curious locals had crowded forward, a man, saliently taller than the rest, among them. She wasn't expecting to see Nardi, so it didn't register at first that he was here, that he had come despite refusals, fears, and philosophical biases. At that moment she only knew that a tall man stood just off to the side, somehow more interested than the other men around him, somehow self-conscious, shifting on his feet, shyly wanting to see.

Hannah wasn't certain when exactly this man became Nardi to her, but she saw that he straightened slightly and walked under the canopy, where he gripped the back of the far chair across the aisle from her. He didn't see her. His attention was riveted toward the front: for simultaneously *The Separation* had been brought forward.

The auctioneer announced a bidding floor of fifteen thousand francs. This amount registered—the error of it—but before Hannah could get her heart out of her throat over the misplaced zero (she had only blustered a price of fifteen *hundred* to Mrs. Besom!) a paddle came up. The Frenchman who'd spoken with a slight lisp over dinner last night had made some sort of mistake; he'd meant to scratch his nose or something, but the auctioneer had taken him up on a bid.

The auctioneer continued rattling. *"Vingt?* Do I hear twenty? *Entendons vingt mille francs. . . ."*

Hannah leaned, stiff-armed, onto the seat of the empty chair beside her, inclining toward the aisle. She should get up, say something, put an end to the auctioneer's mistake that could do nothing but breed confusion. Then, ridiculously, the stout gentleman in the front row abetted the man on the dais by raising his paddle. The auctioneer nodded at him, repeated the new bid, twenty thousand francs, then asked for twenty-five.

The man sitting in front of Hannah shifted in his chair—she couldn't see exactly what he did—but his movement was taken for a bid. Hannah's palms grew wet suddenly, her underarms clammy: He was one of the six attending private collectors, the buyers who were generally the most knowledgeable as well as those most likely to spend the high-rolling money. This was no joke, she realized, no mistake.

"Twenty-five thousand," the auctioneer announced. Then, "Thirty . . . thirty-five . . . forty," as the paddles of these three men took turns moving into upright positions. It looked for a moment as if *The Separation* was going to go for this deliciously outrageous amount, when a fourth paddle came into play.

"Fifty," a man at the side called. The second of the private collectors had jumped into the bidding.

Hannah put her hand over her mouth. Fifty thousand French francs. Almost ten thousand dollars. For two statues, clever though they were, that stood, neither one, much beyond a foot high. Lord, oh lordy.

"Fifty-five."

"Sixty."

Hannah stood up, catching her balance on the back of a chair. She scooted into the aisle and around, pacing to the edge of the canopied area, hearing as she did so, "Sixty-five. *Soixante-cinq. Soixante-dix.* Seventy." She stood just under the fluttering, vibrating fringe of the canvas, her arms across herself, her hands gripping her own elbows. Out of the corner of her eye she saw Nardi rise up to full height, letting go of the chair back he'd been gripping. His hands at his sides spread to a full-fingered stretch then contracted into fists. And by this, for the first time, there seemed a true, tangible connection between him and the works of art on the bidding platform. His body was rigid, poised, as if he might at any moment leap over the rows of men and chairs in front of him to rush toward the dais.

The bidding continued—seventy-five, eighty, eighty-five—until it was no more than a blur of sound. When the hammer finally came down, Hannah was purely stunned to hear the selling price: The two pieces of interlocking marble had gone for one hundred three thousand French francs.

Across the aisle from her, Nardi stood stock-still, a statue himself of stone disbelief, incomprehension. Then Hannah lost track of him. Caught up in the drama of her own moment, she was red-faced and hyperventilating—and madly doing mental arithmetic. One hundred three thousand francs. Almost nineteen thousand dollars! Mrs. Besom had promised one percent of anything over fifteen hundred: Nineteen thousand minus the fifteen hundred left seventeen thousand five hundred, times one percent—dear Lord, Hannah had one hundred seventy-five dollars coming. More than a year's wages!

The auction resumed. Mrs. Besom had turned in her seat to look back. She caught Hannah's attention. The woman smiled her oblique, superior smile at Hannah—she had known that fifteen hundred francs was low!—then nodded a smug congratulations.

Hallelujah! Hannah thought. She turned around, pacing away from the group around the fountain, then paced back.

She heard the next item go for sixty-eight thousand francs. Oh Lord, oh Lord, she thought!

Hannah decided then and there that she liked money. It was so straightforward, so effective, so simple. It was a grand commodity for exchange, bringing with it freedom, respect, and glory. Whatever else she might want in life, she most certainly wanted this: money, more money, lots and lots of money.

And she wanted to earn it finding and selling treasure. She loved hunting through the château. She wanted to hunt in it endlessly, all over, without restriction, the way kings of old had hunted private, reserved forests. She wanted to hunt it, haunt it and places just like it, for the rest of her life. And these prices were validation of her own taste and discrimination. They made her part of an inner sanctum, part of the coterie of the Few, the Knowledgeable and Informed. These prices meant it was true: that in uncovering the amazing booty of the Château d'Aubrignon, she was touching, seeing, and roaming among the finest, most beautiful things life had to offer, wonders, the best humans ever witnessed. She was wandering Olympus, in contact with gifts from the gods. This was what she'd been missing, she thought; here was that vaguely irritating "something" that had made her wander the château late at night, looking at gorgeous ceilings, yet somehow feeling less than whole. . . .

No, she would think later. *This* was the deceptive moment. The euphoric auction left her walking in the ether of glittering objects, swimming among the silver spoons like her barracuda. Her head was absorbed with sparkling images, her senses and emotions weaving strange, rich, misty filaments around her intellect, obscuring like smoke the truth of the situation—and the truth of her own desires.

For four hours Hannah and Mrs. Besom sat at a table at *Le Gaulois*, a café designated as their temporary office which fronted onto the village square. Here the two women took payments and tidied up transactions. They did sums, adding on buyer premiums, taxes, and shipping costs. They took

bank drafts, deposits; they extended credit. They produced
certificates, provenances, and sales receipts. Hannah worked
beside Mrs. Besom until the last grand carriage had pulled
round the square then up onto the main road, the lowering
sun gleaming off its polished leather, its brass fittings
jingling in the distance.

After this, Mrs. Besom and Monsieur de Saint Vallier had
only to settle up with the auctioneer. So Hannah left them to
it, stretching, gathering up her notebooks and souvenir
catalog, then stepping out into the twilight—to stare straight
into an unexplainable development: Some locals had moved
in under the canopy.

Several woman were dragging chairs into an arrangement
that lined seats up in clusters under the perimeter of fringe.
The slipcovers were gone. The pleated skirt around the dais
had been removed. Meanwhile, across from this, a half-
dozen farmers were setting Mrs. Besom's flowers and
pedestals into a haphazard collection behind the fountain.
Over this came a sudden disharmony of music, the caterwauling of tuning instruments.

Hannah began to walk across the grass toward this,
bending as she went so as to see up under the canopy where
the caterwauling noise was coming from. She saw six legs
that became three men on the bare dais platform, each man
holding an instrument: a fiddle, guitar, and accordion. Other
locals stood about. Farmers and their wives and sons and
daughters. She recognized the woman who ran the café
across the street, the man from the post office, and one of
the tellers from the little bank she frequented.

One by one, lanterns began to glow. At least a dozen lit
up, each hung over the top of a pitched pole of the canopy.
As the last one began to burn brightly, the discordant music
became a run of accordion notes. The guitar and fiddle
joined him. Night seemed to fall abruptly into a swell of
music, with crickets and night frogs chirping between the
bars of a country tune.

Almost immediately Mrs. Besom came scurrying up,
complaining irately, but it was too late. She tried to make

Sébastien get these "crude, horrible people" away from her
things. All attempts to get the locals to leave, however, were
met with gracious hostility: Please stay. Please join us. Or
get out of our way. The people of Aubrignon were fascinated by the rich canopy, their proprietary interest in it
seeming to stem from a moral imperative to get as much use
from it as possible before it had to come down. Sébastien
tried to explain this in cultural terms to Mrs. Besom,
something about French rurals viewing waste in the same
vein as Mortal Sin, but Mrs. Besom could not be brought to
understand. In the end Sébastien managed to convince her
that it was impolitic to do otherwise than allow these people
their "despicably presumptive and boorish" fun.

He further persuaded her to sit down. After all, he
reminded her, she might want to hold another auction here,
since this one had been so successful; be nice, burned
bridges, et cetera, he told her. So Amelia Besom joined
Sébastien at a corner cluster of chairs. But her annoyance
only grew as she watched "yokels" dance under her fine,
gold-fringed canopy.

Hannah sat down beside her disgruntled employer, she
herself rather enjoying the sight of people bouncing in pairs
at a kind of gallop to music.

After perhaps five minutes Amelia Besom stood up.
"Well, I have had enough of this," she announced.

It was at this moment that Hannah caught sight of Nardi
again. He came toward them, dancing through the locals,
jubilant, even dancing for a moment with a man who
grabbed on to him, a man with a wooden leg who couldn't
seem to find a partner. The Nardi who turned this man once
around then set him into a chair was no longer shy or
uncertain. The Nardi who wove his way through the
townspeople was bold and happy—and none-too-secretly
pleased with himself.

He laughed outright at something someone said in passing, his laughter a deep, bass vibration that echoed beneath
the bright music, distinct and rich—a sound that was to
Hannah akin to that of a dozen heavy gold doubloons being

dropped into a deep Ming jar. Gold, yes. That was what Nardi looked like as he came toward her. The lanterns that swayed at the edges of the canopy shed a yellowish glow, making his white shirt a soft, golden ivory. This same lamplight cast streaks of gilt in his hair. His very cheeks glinted, the planes of them flecked with a day's growth of fair beard that shone like bits of mica in stone. He wore an amber-brown vest with a pale, fine stripe in it, the stripe becoming aureate in the warm light, like traceable veins of ore along the earthen wall of a mine.

He was a sight. Richly handsome, polished, brilliant upon the eye. And more relaxed than she had ever seen him. "What a wonderful day," he said as he came up.

Mrs. Besom threw him a glare as she bent to gather her sales receipts from the chair beside her. "Are you still going on about the sale of your silly statues?" she asked.

He smiled. "*Oui, vraiment,* I am. They went for almost as much as they are worth." Like the smile that cut deep creases into his cheeks, his tone was gleefully prideful. "My piece was the star of this auction," he pronounced.

Mrs. Besom gave him a pasty smile. "Well, yes, Bernard. But we can always get a lot more for the work of a dead artist."

He only laughed at her, saying something in French. It must have been rude, because Sébastien's head whipped around to him. "You didn't do anything here today, Nardi. You could be a little less arrogant."

Nardi ignored them both, turning toward Hannah, still smiling. He asked, "You will dance with me, yes?"

Mrs. Besom answered for her. "She can't. We're leaving."

Sébastien adjusted his hat as he stood. "Madame," he said, "my brother knows how to get back to the château. He can get himself and the young lady a ride with any one of half a dozen people here."

Mrs. Besom resisted. She looked from Nardi to Hannah, accusing Hannah with a narrow look of unspoken—

unspeakable—imprudence in simply considering to remain here. "You should come with us, Hannah," she said.

Hannah bristled at the judgment in her voice. "I'll be fine. I'll come along soon."

"She'll be fine," Sébastien confirmed. Then he took Amelia Besom by the elbow.

And, *voilà,* Hannah found herself being pulled by the hand into the crush of dancers, following in a path cut by Nardi's twisting, jostling shoulders.

Hannah felt something let go inside her. Pure joy. Celebration. She let her head fall back, laughing as Nardi called to her over the music. The man with the wooden leg had climbed up on the platform with the musicians. He thumped his peg on the floorboards as he sang of how he'd lost his leg. Nardi translated: The man claimed he'd cut it off himself while lost in the wild. Gangrene. He broke it in the same fall that broke his horse's neck. He ate the horse. What an appetite, Hannah said in French— *"Quel appétit"*— which was the extent of her ability to comment. Though she was pleased to realize she understood Nardi's answer: Yes, an appetite for fabrication, he told her. They both laughed.

She felt good and smart and successful as Nardi pulled her around and put his hand on her waist. He was in such a fine mood. "You still love those statues, don't you?" she asked.

He looked down at her in a way that recognized her march into conversational territory that had only ever brought them to disagreement. *"Oui,"* he said. "Though in a manner I cannot explain."

He wanted to join in with the fun that jigged and bounded around them; she could feel the tension in his body. Yet he remained motionless for her, willing to be questioned. Hannah brought her face close to his so as to be heard in the midst of the fray, her bosom brushing him. She asked, "And Mrs. Besom was one of the people who criticized them a dozen years ago?"

"Oh, yes."

"Was *The Separation* the first piece she criticized?"

He smiled. "Mam'zelle, you want to rummage through me like an old château."

Yes. And she was feeling oh so close to him, so insightful. Hannah said, "Tell me. Was it *The Separation* and her criticism of it that made her no friend of yours?"

He laughed, his head falling back. Then he pulled her to him and murmured in her ear, "Oh, I hated her long before that." And from here he leaped into the dance, carrying Hannah with him.

The songs all banged along pretty much to the same repetitive rhythm. The little band stayed with what it did well, keeping time and making exuberant noise.

Nardi danced Hannah around to this, so full of himself that part of her wanted to chase and clap and send the stupid, strutting rooster into a flap. She could have. His pleasure in the sale was too personal, making him impossibly vulnerable — anyone who enjoyed public approval this much was still likely to be crushed by public condemnation. She could have said, *An artist can't care what other people think, or he will begin to play it safe — and end by drawing portraits for the tourists on the Pont Neuf. Who knows what people really pay for when they buy art?* She could have told him, *A sunset is beautiful, yet no one pays a hundred and three thousand francs for it.* She could have humbled him easily with even some of his own defensive philosophy, and he might have seen the danger of his present inflated high spirits. But she didn't. Instead her silly self, there in his arms, just kept smiling and smiling at his strutting antics. Her face hurt from smiling, yet she couldn't stop.

"Art," he said suddenly as they turned to a slide of the fiddle, "with the possible exception of our part in bringing forth new babies, is the only thing we do worthy of heaven. Everything else is drudgery. In every other regard, we are no different from the ants."

Just to be contrary, Hannah said, "Love is what separates us from the ants."

He rolled his eyes at her, his beautiful fair eyes. They sparkled, catching the light of the lanterns, then he leaned forward. "Whatever that is," he said. "I am not even sure love exists." He stepped back to turn her under his outstretched arm.

"And a Frenchman, too," she teased as she came round to set her hand on his shoulder again.

"The French are romancers and seducers. By the time a Frenchman is sixteen he has usually 'loved' so many women the word has no more meaning than 'potatoes': 'I think I am madly in potatoes with that beautiful woman down the street.' "

Hannah laughed. "Have you ever been 'in potatoes' yourself?"

"Countless times. You?"

She shrugged. "Once. Maybe twice."

"*Eh bien,* then it is not potatoes yet. You get credit for being in love."

"No." She shook her head, knowing as she looked at him that she had never been in love. She kept dancing, raised up a little on her toes because of his height, moving her feet in time to the music of a farmer's accordion, a glazer's fiddle, a guitar, and to the tap of a wooden leg; beautiful music that made this man move in synchrony with her. She tried not to be aware of the grip of his hand around hers, of the firm pressure of his palm on her back, of his legs brushing between hers as they spun in turns. She tried not to notice the squeeze of her chest that seemed to tighten and loosen in time to the jolly movement of accordion bellows, to the reedy polka of notes.

"I think you are in potatoes with your statues," she said. "I think that these, art in general perhaps, somewhere along the way disappointed you. I think you are angry with art and have turned your back on it out of a wounded lover's pique."

He only shook his head, confident that she was wrong, and looked at her. Then stunned her: "No, I think I am more in potatoes with you," he said.

He drew her up against the front of him, wrapping his one arm tight round her back, dancing her other hand straight out into the air. Then in time to the music, as if it were part of it, he kissed her full on the mouth.

It was a warm, dry kiss, full of confidence and innocent energy, something done for the simple adult pleasure of it, like dancing—though Hannah herself couldn't quite manage both. She stumbled, unable to coordinate her feet and mouth gracefully, while his lips brushed against hers, just enough pressure that she could feel their round, firm shape. Then he lifted his face, letting his lips trail up her cheek, and pulled his head back, smiling.

Up near the front, a woman with a voice as dry as a husk joined in the song, rasping out loud lyrics. Others joined in, with Hannah understanding little but the exaggerated syllables of the refrain. "Le Gai *Paree-zee-an*," the song from the phonograph. She mouthed the words as people began to clap and encourage the singer up front. "*Allez, allez,*" they called.

The music changed slightly, and Nardi drew Hannah alongside him, till they danced hipbone to hipbone, his arm stretched across her chest. People all around began to *la-la-la* along with the refrain, Nardi included. He knew the song, the movements. As he crossed her over to the other side of him, he brushed his mouth across her temple, then he pushed her backward into a turn and kissed her again.

Oh, how well he danced. How well he kissed. How well he did them both, Hannah thought. Here was a man who had danced and kissed in Paris.

And here was a woman who hadn't: This time he opened his mouth slightly, letting his lower lip catch against hers. He let his tongue trace along her lips. Again Hannah missed a step, then couldn't refind the rhythm for being all feet and fluster and sighs and pleasure. He kissed her again two steps later, leaning her back into the end refrain of the dance. As he did so, she more felt than heard the sound he made, a soft groan in his chest that counterpointed the *oompah* of the music as he pressed her lips apart.

Hannah's heart rose right up into her kissed mouth. She opened her jaw further, as if she might let his tongue touch

her throat, her pulsing heart. There was no part of her, inside
or out, she didn't want him to touch. *Slice me open, Nardi,
if you like. Run your fingers through my kidneys. Kiss my
liver. Lick my lungs. Knead my entrails.* Heavens, yes, was
she ever in potatoes; was she ever in hot water. Hannah felt
peeled, boiled, baked, puréed in love.

Half a minute later he was rubbing his lips lightly in the
hair of her temple then down her cheek to the corner of her
mouth as he drew in a long breath. He inhaled her,
whispering something in French that she didn't understand,
then he pressed her, turning her into the dance as he found
her mouth again. And again and again and again. No one
seemed to think anything of it as Nardi danced himself and
Hannah in and out of the shadows of swaying gas lamps.
People all about them continued to laugh, to roar at times.
Some had drunk quite a bit. Still, it all felt so harmless, so
safe here in public. Safe and marvelous and deliciously
wicked.

He kissed her an uncounted number of times, till her lips
felt slightly puffed and swollen from this activity, though
she wouldn't have stopped him for a minute. Hannah
reveled in it, in both the surprise yet the sureness that she
would be kissed again, delicious little touches like a box of
creamy-smooth chocolates, each one different inside, never
quite knowing, only certain that she intended to eat up every
last one of them. He might bend slightly and his lips would
touch her jawbone and she would turn her mouth to his. Or
he would turn her in a waltz and waltz her right up against
him and into his mouth. He never suggested anything more
than this. He just danced and kissed her till she was ready to
die from the pleasure of it and they were both dry in the
throat.

"Do you want some cider?" he asked. "I will bring you
some. It is *très normand*. You should try it."

It turned out that he himself didn't like it. To Hannah the
cider tasted like sour, bubbly wine, so devoid of sweetness
it was almost salty; it smelled of overripe apples. The cider
made her head light almost immediately. She didn't finish it

but ended up quenching her thirst at the public fountain.
They both did, all but dipping their heads into the water.

Hannah was bent over the fountain—her face dripping,
the lantern light from behind shifting on the surface of the
water—when Nardi asked, "You truly liked my statues?"

"Yes."

He seemed to think about this answer as his silhouette sat
there on the edge of the fountain splashing his face with
water. "My uncle Pascal bought *The Separation*. That is
why it is here. Before he died, he tried to buy up my sagging
reputation. He bought four or five things, including that
monstrosity in the apple storehouse." He shrugged, wiping
his face with his hand, then looked over at her. "I just
thought you might like to know. There might be a few more
pieces here, but *The Separation* was by far the best. I am
glad you found it."

Hannah stood, shaking her wet hands, then drying them
on her skirt. "Me too," she said.

He dried his hands on his trousers. "I was brilliant once,
you know," he told her.

"Yes, I know."

This answer took him aback for a moment. Then he went
on. "I cannot tell you what it was like, the triumph of a piece
that was really good . . . a statue that you look at and your
heart swells with wonder at yourself, at the process, at
mankind and all that imagination can accomplish. You
wonder where it comes from. It feels godlike." He broke off,
laughing briefly and a little artificially. Then he quickly
became quiet. And circumspect: "I bore you with my
vanity?"

Hannah released a euphoric breath. "No, to the contrary. You are quite entertaining swelled up with self-
congratulations."

"Ah, mon Dieu." He made a low mock growl of French
indignity. "I am so insulted. You were supposed to say it
was not vanity, only due pride." He asked again, once more
very earnest, "You really liked them, yes?"

"The Separation?"

His shadow nodded.

He didn't seem to tire of hearing this, so she told him again, "Oh yes. They're stunning."

This brought forth a low peal of laughter, a dark rumble of smug satisfaction. He came toward her, a man in pursuit.

Hannah backed toward the light, watching his silhouette— his erect posture, his broad square shoulders, the long-legged lankiness that made up the rest of his height. He was elegantly proportioned. He carried himself regally, like a prince, like the aristocracy his family was. When he came into the penumbra of swaying lanterns, he was gilded in lamplight again. And something low in Hannah's abdomen grew warm just looking at him. She turned, calling over her shoulder, "I want to dance."

Nardi caught her just under the canopy, at the edge of the light and music, where he swooped her back into the clanking, squeeze-box rhythms, without question, without remonstrance.

It registered perhaps five minutes back into the dancing that she had stopped nothing. Not the momentum of Nardi's relentless brand of courtship. And not the yearning in herself. All summer with Nardi seemed to add up tonight to a kind of a devastating patience that Hannah had simply never encountered before. She had wrestled at least half a dozen young men in brief encounters, the conspicuously common feature of these matches being each young man's haste, which she had interpreted at the time as a flattering eagerness. The whole tempo of these earlier situations, however, collapsed now in hindsight to plain old randy selfishness. Nardi was ten years older than Edward Stanton and his friends from Harvard and New York, and ten times as poised—or perhaps just ten times as purposive. Tonight, with Nardi, there seemed to be a nerve-thrilling premeditation.

He hadn't given up. He was just waiting.

Let him wait, Hannah thought. She leaned back in his arms, enjoying his suddenly fierce grip as he countered the centrifugal force of a spin, a quick pivot of steps that danced his legs between hers. She closed her eyes and let herself feel the dizzy bang and thrum of music, taking enormous pleasure in herself and Nardi moving in perfect, opposed rhythm. Hannah lost track of everything around her. She spun and bounded and turned in Nardi's arms until she was near feverish from heat and sweat, until she was moving on pure adrenaline: until the little makeshift band was packing up their instruments and dragging their music cases behind them.

This seemed to happen suddenly. Hannah was surprised to find herself standing all at once in relative silence, nothing but the murmurs of receding voices, the fading clatter of wheels on cobbles. The lanterns had become no more than little buds of light moving off, townspeople walking home. She stood there, sobered by the night air as it blew cool and brisk across her face.

Nardi's hand provided a solid contrast: warm and sure where his palm and fingers wrapped snugly around her own. *"Zut,"* he muttered as he looked around them. He seemed as dazed as she. "I meant to ask LeBec for a ride." There was nothing, no one, except the wee-hour faces of shuttered buildings standing in quiet witness to a town drifting off to sleep. He let out a long sigh. "I am sorry," he said, "but there is no help for it. We have a three-mile walk and all of it uphill."

They made it across thirty level feet. At the end of a narrow street beside a darkened house in the shadows of its eaves, Nardi kissed her again, this time his hand cupping her breast.

Hannah was going to protest; she must have put up some sort of resistance, surely, for in her mind she was saying, No one would think well of a woman who did this. Her father would roll in his grave. Worse, Amelia Besom, who was very much alive, would fire her. Meanwhile Nardi stood belly to belly with her, his face at her cheek. Hannah could hear his intake of breath, then feel the warm release of each exhalation at her mouth. She opened her lips. Her resolve to turn him away became something else. She took his face in

her hands, his dear, wonderful face, holding his angular jaw
in her palms while she followed the line of his cheekbones
with her thumbs. Then she pulled this face to her, just to
touch his mouth again, saying to herself, I'm going to kiss
him again, just once in private. After all the dancing and
kissing tonight, once more could hardly matter.

But this kiss was nothing like those that had preceded it.
Nardi pressed himself against her. There was no dancing, no
playfulness. He twisted his head and took the kiss openmouthed, deep, and thorough as he pushed her straight back
under the eaves and against the wall of the house. Hannah
shuddered from the sheer satisfaction of feeling the pressure
of him. She heard a rush of air through his nose, an
unvoiced groan, and he began to rub himself against her till
she felt the rhythmic press of rough mortar across her
buttocks.

She expected flurry and frenzy from here, a commotion
of possession. Nardi gasped, his muscles shook, but he
delayed. When Hannah ran her hands along his shoulders—
the broad, muscular shoulders that had worked in casting
facilities and stone quarries, shoulders that had hefted
blocks of marble—he grabbed her hands, lifting them up
and over her head. He slid his palms down the outside of her
arm, into the hollows of her armpits, over her breasts, along
her ribs, fitting his hands into the curves of her waist, then
over her belly. *"Je veux te regarder."* He had to draw a deep
breath and reach for the English. *"Je veux"*—he stopped—"I
want—I want to look at you. I want to feel you, all of you,
rub my imagination over you, inside you." He ran his hands
down her blouse and skirt front, feeling the stiff concoction
of hooks and laces beneath, then a moment later his fingers,
uninhibited and unapologetic, were opening buttons as if
flipping the caps off tubes of paints.

He undid the neckline of her corset cover, and suddenly
there she was, half-bare breasts pushed up and forward, out
over the top of a straight, steel-busked corset. He rubbed his
open mouth over the available curve of breast, and Hannah
let out a stifled sound, a vocal frisson of pleasure as his

hands went down her back and tried to press her pelvis to
him—the steel busks of her corset prevented this.

They ran down the front of her, from sternum to hipbone,
as intractable as the wall behind her; they wouldn't let her
hips bend forward. Nardi backed off, lifting skirts and
petticoats with a mutter of French surprise and exasperation,
only to find the whole contraption battened down by elastic
suspenders affixed to each stocking in three places by garter
trolleys. He let out a growl of complaint, longing, as he
reached under skirts and petticoats, loading them onto his
arms. Hannah felt midcorset hooks loosen, which yielded
some play in the bottom lacings. He released stockings from
garters. Then her steel busks folded up like opened lids from
tin cans.

He undid her hair. It came down heavily into his hands as
he pressed his face into it. Her drawers were just another
drawstring. She was coming undone. A moment of panic
followed this realization. She wanted to be proper and good,
not "wild" like the people in Miami said she was. *Her
mother was wild, too, you know.* She wanted to be what Mrs.
Besom wanted her to be. Yet, oh, how she wanted this, too.

Nardi caught her leg just under the knee, lifting it as he
put his finger into the back seam of her stocking and slid it
down the back of her thigh to behind her knee, down her
calf, along the tendon of her ankle.

"Mon Dieu, que tu es belle," he crooned. He drew her
foot round his waist and half lifted her onto him.

Not a single item of Hannah's clothing was off exactly,
but Nardi had produced in fairly short order enough gaps as
to allow the night air to ripple into the warmest, most private
crooks of her body. "Ah—" Hannah took in one quick
breath then another. "Ah—heaven above! Ah—"

His fingers grazed her once, twice, as he unbuttoned his
trousers. Hannah's mouth went dry. She could barely suck
in enough breath. A moment later his fingertips touched her,
separating folds, delicately delineating the most private
parts of her, as if exploring shape, line, curve, as if even here
he was possessed of a creative curiosity. He muttered

something, incantations, paeans of praise to Eros, though by this time he was incoherent and certainly not speaking English. He pulled back. There was a brief moment wherein she was empty, lacking, hungry for invasion with nothing but the night air playing at her. Then she felt him briefly, hot and heavy against her belly, and the next moment he drove himself into her so deeply that the length of him moved something inside at the core of her body. He was thick and solid, a weighty presence that worried for one agonizingly slow thrust about her sexual experience—a politeness that was not required since there was no intact hymen. Then Hannah arched, taking him. He began to move inside her, a strong, sure rhythm. There were a few moments of blissful purpose, when it seemed that Hannah could make this delirious satisfaction go on and on, but he gripped her buttocks and in that gesture brought them both to instinctive spasm.

Nardi's body jerked. He expelled a guttural outcry, while Hannah's body convulsed with sharp, physical raptus. These convulsions repeated and repeated as she gripped Nardi's back by the shoulder blades, and at her ear in murmurs he stifled a string of mounting invocations. Or blasphemies; it was hard to tell—there were multiple references to God and the sacred blood of saints. Then he collapsed forward, catching his weight on one arm. Hannah's back hit solidly against the wall. Her raised leg was tangled somehow in his trousers then fettered by her own downed drawers. And there was no finding her balance. She clung a moment, suspended as Nardi tried to save her; he caught her then followed her down. He could only break their fall.

This was when they first heard the distant clackety-clack of a cart, as they lay there panting on the dry, gritty ground, trying to untangle clothing while hunting buttons and corset hooks in the dark.

Chapter 20

NARDI MADE HIMSELF be still, trying to separate the warm private space there in the dark that contained only him and Hannah from the outside world that contained everything else. A bouncing, grinding creak was coming toward them at a pretty good clop: a single animal pulling a cart with steel-rimmed wheels over the gravel roadbed at the end of the street.

"LeBec," he murmured. It occurred to him: "If he had to take Moreau home, he is doubling back. We can still get a ride."

Nardi leaped up, the hero who would get them into the back of an applecart, if he could only button his fly fast enough. "I will delay him," he said as he managed the top two buttons. "You get yourself together." He pulled his shirttail out to cover the rest, then still had to run a dozen yards up the road in order to hail the farmer in his wagon. For perhaps five minutes the two men waited for Hannah before, in response to LeBec's growing impatience, Nardi finally went back to see what had become of her.

He found her still in the shadows sitting on the ground under the eaves of the house. *"Viens,"* Nardi said. "LeBec will not wait forever."

She seemed to be trying to do up her blouse, but her hands were shaking so badly the task would not be accomplished tonight if she didn't get help. Nardi bent, pushing one button then another through its hole. "Are you all right?" he asked.

She nodded yes, brushed his hands away, and said, "I have it, I have it." Her tone was testy, and there was something more in her voice, an emotion he couldn't identify, harshly restrained.

"Hannah?"

"Damned blouse," she said. She gave it up, then attacked her corset. Her fingers yanked at the ties—small, shadowy jerks of consternation that proved just as ineffectual as her efforts with her blouse. She threw her hands up after a few seconds. "I can't—" she said. She let out a small, chagrined breath. "I can't put anything aright. I'm a mess—"

"Here, let me." Nardi squatted beside her to pull the edges of her corset straight. He didn't bother to thread or hook anything, but just tightened and tied what lacings hadn't been rent asunder in the throes of lovemaking. He straightened her blouse and did another button, then said, "Come on. Our ride is going to leave us here if we don't hurry."

When he drew her to her feet, however, her drawers fell. She hadn't secured them either. Nardi couldn't figure this out. In the time he'd left her here, she'd done absolutely nothing to put herself in order. Baffled, Nardi tied up her drawers, gave a shake to her skirts, then trundled her down the street toward the road and into the cart.

LeBec clicked his tongue to his donkey, and the cart lurched forward. Meantime, Nardi's mind lurched backward into visions of Hannah only minutes ago: the sudden spectacle of her small rib cage, round little shoulders, thin arms, all her diminutive grace contrasted dramatically by the hugest swells of bare breasts he'd ever seen in his life. Hannah's breasts were so large that when he pressed his palm firmly against one, he couldn't span its width with the stretch of his fingers. Hannah's palmed breasts ran from the center of her rib cage to collarbone to under her arms. Her breasts were purely amazing. Firm, full, ridiculously, lushly female. And perfectly suited to the rest of her: extravagant, luscious Hannah . . . Hannah of the sweet, petite face and large, wary-wise eyes . . . Hannah of the luxurious hair that uncoiled down past her minuscule waist to flop and curl about her gorgeously round derrière . . . splendorous Hannah, bared in the shadowy moonlight, floundering and squirming among flailing stays and loose corset strings . . . These impressions were all so quintessentially the woman he'd wanted all summer that Nardi was hardly aware of the somber, silent woman beside him.

The racket of steel rims on the rocky, potholed road, meanwhile, was hardly conducive to conversation. Likewise, when Nardi tried to draw Hannah closer to him, the wagon's movement knocked the crown of her head solidly against his cheekbone, after which he held his distance. A fond kiss or caress was out of the question, at least if he valued tongue, limbs, or other body parts. Eventually the effort of simply trying to counter the bump and wobble of the wagon became so tedious that Nardi lay back, taking Hannah by the hand and dragging her with him. She let him.

He retained her hand, clenching it as they clamored along, up roads that shook their kidneys and bumped their backbones on the struts of the wagon bed. At one point Nardi looked over and smiled—only to meet the dark shadows of trees passing over her somber profile. His own smile waned.

Surely nothing was wrong, he thought. What could be wrong on a night like this? He let his head roll back, looking up into the jiggling stars as his mind slipped forward into libidinous fancies: Hannah, upstairs in bed at the cottage. Interior walls. Privacy. Hannah, downstairs on the rug by the hearth, naked, all that steel-reinforced underclothing out of the way. Naked Hannah on the chassis, with Nardi running his hands over her curves and into her crevices, knowing her, flirting with the idea of sculpting her, all the while penetrating her to the gentle clack-clack of the chassis's ball bearings. . . .

When LeBec let them out at the entrance to the estate, however, Hannah's round torso was in Nardi's hands one

moment as he helped her out of the cart, then with a wiggle
and shove gone. His hands were empty.

She turned to face him from three feet away, crossing her
arms, holding herself like that, by her elbows, as if her own
unwilling prisoner to a reluctant new mood. "Nardi—" she
said. "Oh, I'm sorry—" She cast her face down and finished
ominously. "I can't—it's just—" She turned and walked
briskly away, into the tunnel of trees that lined the estate's
carriage drive.

Nardi trotted up and around her silhouette, walking
backward, having to sidestep one way then another to stop
her from circumventing him. "And may I ask, mam'zelle,
what it is exactly that you cannot do?"

She tried to push him aside. "Oh, don't make me
explain—"

The cart clattered distantly around and down a hillside
turn, and the night became quiet, save the swoop of a bird
somewhere in the trees. It was near pitch-black, the moonlight faint where he and Hannah stood chest to chest under
a dark canopy of tall, branching wych-elms.

"What is wrong?" he asked. He wasn't feeling too suave.
He thought he might deserve a dash of overwrought pique
from a female he had just screwed against an outside public
wall. Yet her reaction here still seemed de trop. *"Qu'est-ce
que tu as?"* he asked. Again, *what's wrong?*

There was a moment wherein she choked back what
might have been a more rational response. She ended by
only shaking her head. "Oh, Nardi, please," she said again.
"Just get out of my way—"

Nardi stepped aside as a gentlemanly gesture of cooperation. "Hannah, if it is that I—"

The damned woman bolted. Hannah shot around him like
a phantom sliding into the bowery darkness of the woods
along the driveway.

For some moments he couldn't locate her. "Hannah?"

She didn't answer, but the sound of her darted among the
tree trunks and branches. Nardi could only follow with
deliberation, listening then trailing after her movement.

"Hannah!" he called. He pursued the crunch of leaves and the snap of twigs. "Why are you doing this?"

"I'm sorry," she said again. "Go back to the cottage." Her voice spoke from the trees near the front of the château. "I'll see you in the morning."

"Tu es folle!" he called. Crazy woman. He caught sight of her in silhouette as she broke across the carriage drive that led round to the servants' courtyard.

Even with her dark figure identified, it still took Nardi almost thirty yards on the dead run to catch her. "Hannah—" Just inside the courtyard walls, he swung her around by the arm and asked, "What kind of game is this?" The question came out angrier than he would have liked.

"It's not a game." She pulled away again, her face suddenly in open moonlight. She looked wildly frightened, determined, alarmed.

Nardi was incensed by the look, by its separateness from him. As if he weren't her friend any longer, her lover, but rather her enemy, a monster from whom she must run. "What have I done?" he asked.

Pulling her arm free, she ran straight for the château's service entrance. If he hadn't outraced her, she would have gone in: She yanked on the door handle once, then saw her problem. His arm, stretched over her head, held the door closed. She backed herself around, up against the wood planks, then stood there in the shadows of the château, in the shadow of his arm, panting.

Nardi repeated, "What have I done? I have a right to know."

"Nothing. It's me. Let me go in."

"What have *you* done?"

She lifted forward slightly, and moonlight broke over her features again, casting the light and dark angles of a defiant expression. Her sweet voice, as it echoed off the courtyard walls, was soft, as clear as the night, and positively resolute. "Mrs. Besom was right," she said. "I'm just—" She stopped. "We can't—you mustn't—"

This mention of the old she-goat did not exactly soothe

Nardi. He said, "You are telling me that I cannot touch you because Amelia Besom says so?"

She shook her head no. "You don't understand. I'm trying not to do here what I did before once, in Miami."

"Which would be?"

"Oh, it's so hard to explain—" She shook her head again, then said, "You see, I have a weakness for beautiful things"—she choked on the next—"and men—"

He laughed, a spontaneous, bleak burst.

Angrily she rebuked him for this, saying again, "You don't understand. I'm weak and wicked. I—I—I like your vest, your hair, your shoulders, your coat. I am so superficial—"

"My dear," Nardi said, "I am an expert on vice and weakness and I will tell you: I consider to be among my best qualities the fact that I am attracted to women and that I can appreciate and know life's beauty. I think you are mad to question these things in yourself. To enjoy beauty in all its many forms is merely to be human. To enjoy men, well, that is to be female, no?"

"Lord," she groaned, "you almost make sexuality sound moral."

"It is moral."

She sniffed at this. "I can think of a whole townful of people in Florida who would disagree with you."

Nardi felt some of his anger dissipate. If this was the problem—that age-old piece of nonsense, her womanly virtue—he knew of effective remedies against social consequence. She could do what the ladies of Paris did: sleep with whom she chose by night while, by day, she and he both pretended she hadn't. Nardi got only two words into this remarkably simple solution, however— *"Écoute, chérie"*—before Hannah's small body rose off the door planks.

She said crossly, "I'm not your 'shair-ee.'" She took a militant breath then burst out with, "Edward Stanton used to call me 'sweetie pie.' His friend Michael, whom I only knew a week, called me 'cupcake' from the start. I hated it."

She poked him in the chest rhythmically: "You—every—last—one of you—can keep your stupid—belittling—nick-names—to yourself—"

Nardi frowned as he removed himself half a step back from her poking, reprehending finger. "I am not this fellow, Eduard Machin—whoever. And *chérie* is a fond word, an endearment—" He thought he could cut through all her anxiety and resentment, or whatever it was that had her in its grip, by saying, "Hannah, I don't think less of you for sleeping with that fellow who wanted to marry you. I expected this was part of the scandal—"

She shook her head, a single, brisk, vehement no, then said flatly: "I didn't sleep with Edward Stanton."

"All right." He would go along with this assertion, though it seemed a little silly. The woman with whom he'd just had sexual relations had slept with someone before him, and this Edward fellow was the most likely candidate. "Whomever." He didn't know why he added, "One of your local suitors—"

"And I wouldn't sleep with some stupid farmer who expects me to tie on an apron, have twenty children, and grow tomatoes with him forever."

"Fine." Only it wasn't fine. Who the hell was he supposed to think she had slept with then? Nardi released a breath and brought himself back to the issue. *"Quoi que tu dis,* I care only that you sleep with me. Come down to where it is private."

"No, no, no," she said, groaning. "Oh, Nardi, look at you. You are handsome, cultured, clever, and so well-off you needn't lift a finger—"

"Tu dis?" he said, startled. "Hannah, surely you don't think all the money you see at the château—"

"Oh, I know," she said quickly. "It's family money—"

He let out a laugh of rebuttal. "Hannah, I am—" *Not rich,* he was going to say. Nardi stopped cold.

The fact that he should need to say these words made the blood thud in his stomach. If Hannah didn't understand that he himself was just a shade above poor, then exactly how ignorant was she of the matrimonial obligations that were supposed to correct his near poverty?

She continued, "And you're enormously talented. So here you are—finally feeling like yourself after a long, unhealthy binge and bored out of your mind. This isn't love. This is convenience on your part and a most unfair coincidence of fate on mine. I'm sorry I was so weak as to encourage things tonight. Now let me go in. I'm trying to be good—"

"*Sacredieu, you are* good!" Nardi proclaimed the one thing he was sure of in the midst of this disconcerting muddle: "*Tu es douce et bonne jusqu'au fond de*—that is, *euh,* you are sweet and good to the center of your soul, Hannah, and I adore this about you. But I like, too, that you are, how you say, *provocative et, ah*—" Emotion, earnestness itself was robbing him of English words. "You are, ah, *érotiquement . . . eh, charnelle*"—he corrected—"carnal, *tu sais,* you understand *carnal?*"

Her head lay back against the door with a soft thud, her face seeming to fix on him.

He continued, "These qualities, *qualités extraordinaires,* do not prevent that you are also pure and good. The one does not contradict the other."

Her small silhouette stared up at him.

He said, "You must understand. There are times when it is good to be wanton. With me, *par example,*" he said. "Now."

This long, emotional speech was followed by a brief silence filled with the sound of cicadas, a tree frog, a bird out over the river. Then she laughed weakly. "Well, you certainly are, as Mrs. Besom says, very French about all this."

"It is not French. It is mature."

She laughed again. "Well, she'd fire me for being this mature."

Nardi wouldn't leave it at that. He said seriously, "Hannah, Amelia Besom is very, how you say, *comme il faut.* She not only subscribes to the social order, her kind invented it." He left a pause, then finished ardently, "Whatever you did before, I'm sure you had your reasons. And whatever it was, it doesn't matter. What is between you and me is separate; it is good. It is as good as life gets."

There was a long, quiet moment in which Nardi thought he had convinced her. She seemed poised between Amelia Besom's—society's—unswerving, compassionless rules and his own faith in whatever choices she'd made in the past. But she said finally, "I would like for you to be right, Nardi. I don't know—I feel so confused."

When he pushed close to her again, about to unconfuse her with a kiss, her hand came up. It held him back.

Nardi set his jaw as he stared down at this hand on his chest. "I wait all summer for you. Now you want to think about making me wait some more."

There was a click. Nardi realized that she had reached behind her and unlatched the door. "Good night," she said. She was perfectly composed. It was even possible that she smiled as her head bobbed toward him. She gave him a light peck on the mouth that landed at a dry angle across his lips. Then she disappeared round the door.

Nardi felt charmed, angry, chagrined. He caught the door before it closed.

She jumped when she looked back over her shoulder just inside the corridor. "You can't come in here," she said. She laughed. It was a surprised sound, light, breathless. She whispered further, "Mrs. Besom is upstairs asleep. Your brother sleeps just down this hallway. You have to go now."

In the narrow passageway, it was easy to block her progress. Nardi simply caught up at a corner bend and extended his arm across the turn. He felt her brace of alarm when he took her waist in his other hand. This time he managed to kiss her. He felt her weaken, allow it, even enjoy it for a moment. Then she pushed him back again with another small nervous laugh. "They'll hear. Go back."

He didn't move except to run his palm over her shoulder and down her arm and, by this, pull her to him. He pressed his mouth to the crook of her neck as he whispered, "If you are going to your room, then I am going, too."

More nervous laughter erupted from her. She gave a small, ineffective shove. Since she seemed to want to, he let her duck under his arm. She wasn't precisely in flight this time. There was something tantalizing, a hesitation, a too-long moment, as her breasts slid round his chest. As she rotated in the narrow space to get by, her loose hair swept his shoulder.

It became a kind of game. Nardi followed, letting her lead the way, set the pace. She turned twice, three times, and looked back at him through the dark, but she ceased asking him to go back, seeming more interested in merely checking to see if he was still following. She went silently into the kitchen, through the scullery, into the wet laundry, out and across the main gallery, and up the wide staircase. While he pursued her quiet, swaying shadow up one landing then two, always about a half-dozen feet behind her.

He wasn't sure what she was thinking, what she was admitting to herself. But she leaped in startlement when her bedroom door wouldn't close: Nardi stopped it by grasping its edge. He came round it, inside, and closed it behind them both.

He leaned back against the door and let his eyes adjust. The room was small, most of its space taken up by a single bed, a narrow wardrobe, and washstand that doubled as a night table. The only capacious aspect of the room was its ceiling that rose fifteen feet up, the window being actually a long, thin French door that gave out onto an ornamental balcony overlooking dark treetops and stars at the back of the estate.

Hannah stood at the center of this room, both her hands wrapped round the top bar of her bed's metal footrail. The little bed looked lumpy, but pristine, the coverlet smooth. There were books about, one open on the bed, a small pile on the floor, several more balanced on the edge of the washstand.

Whether a sincere plea or an intentional goad, Hannah whispered, "Nardi, she's asleep just on the other side of the wall. She'll know."

With a snort, Nardi crossed and, taking hold of the footrail to the outside of her own grip, pressed himself against her.

"She'll hear," Hannah insisted an inch from his face. "I swear, she has the ears of a bat."

"Shh. She won't. Not unless she can hear through three feet of stone."

Hannah licked her lips as he put his mouth against hers; she licked both their mouths wet. Nardi's head swam in quick erotic cresendo. He slid his face, cheeks, mouth down her body, taking her hands and stretching her arms taut, straight out along the railing as he sank to his knees, breathing his way down nipples, tracing corset stays with his teeth. In the dark . . . alone . . . at last . . . dear God, he was going to devour her. . . .

She let out a small yelp of shock, surprise, pleasure when he kissed her through her skirt. She began to quiver, her muscles shaking. From there, on his knees, he undressed her where she stood, till she was naked, her legs parted beneath the breath of his mouth.

At one time Nardi had done things to please women, performing while never once questioning whether these things pleased himself. Now, what he did shocked Hannah. And—entirely selfish—he talked her through it anyway, with her so mesmerized by new sensation she kept forgetting to inhale or exhale, breathing only sporadically in rushes of recalled respiration. In these starts and faltering stops, she followed his lead, hesitantly making her way over to him along the bridge of growing trust between them.

Nardi wanted to touch her in every conceivable way, and new ways kept occurring to him. He made love to her everywhere with his fingers and tongue and lips, then took her onto the bed and made love to her with a part of himself that—like the whole of him—he realized was becoming reliable.

On the bed, Hannah gave herself up completely, her face turning from side to side, her body moving—she was actually becoming hard to hold on to, and Nardi reveled in this. The strength of his own passion was a match for it. He thrust hard, each deep, severe stroke releasing a slightly vocal breath from her. "Ah—ah—" the sound was wonderful, a soft emphatic sound that rose in intensity as he plunged himself into her. He kissed her, his own groan escaping into her throat, her warm, moist expulsions of air blowing rhythmically into his mouth, at which point the spasms began to overtake him. Warm, lubricous, instinctive surges, welcomely familiar. He felt her shiver in his arms as something released inside her, a hot flood of quivering, pulling contractions that wrung him out as efficiently as fists wringing a rag. He let out a sound, an agonized rasp that erupted up from out of his chest as a cry of grief for the end of what he wanted to endure for just—he murmured, *"Seigneur Dieu, s'il te plaît"*—one more minute. He pummeled the last of himself into this blissful torture, even as the spasms slackened, as long as anatomical capability allowed him. He held her, gripped her, while Hannah stirred and wiggled and struggled with her own biology there in his arms. When he let go of her mouth momentarily, her face twisted away, impossible to catch again, while her sweet, soft voice strained in a crescendo of "Oh-oh-oh. O-o-o-o-ooooh."

They made love all night, until Hannah whispered, laughing, "No, I can't anymore. I'm sore."

Her demur gave Nardi a chance at last to admit that he himself was chafed to the point of wanting to sleep naked with his legs apart. What an idiot. What a gluttonous, greedy, thoroughly-satisfied-with-himself idiot. Nardi settled down, contenting himself with the feel of Hannah's hair under his stroking hand and the warmth of her crown under the press of his lips. Her hair smelled of a mingle of things: jasmine soap, sweat from dancing, stone walls, and him.

Lying there with her, he remembered he had to tell her about Du Gard, the marriage, the whole story of why he was here. It wasn't so bad, really, for the arrangement would leave them both secure for the rest of their lives. He should explain in these languid moments of postcoital affection.

Hannah yawned and curled toward him, her skin as pale and soft as a baby's. Then she spoke of something else. "Were you very famous?"

"Pardon?"

"The young sculptor, Bernard de Saint Vallier. Was he very famous?"

"Mmm," he said. "*Oui.* Paris, London, even New York knew him. Everyone loved him."

"Ahhh," she said. She liked the idea. "It must have been wonderful."

Yes, wonderful. His old celebrity had even seemed a little wonderful again tonight. Nardi sighed. "It was not real," he said. "People told me I was a god, and I believed them. I got caught up in the myth of me. When I fell to earth, to reality, it was a very long fall." He paused, amazed by the simplicity of his decline when put this way.

He heard—felt—Hannah sigh, her warm breath stirring the hair on his chest. "How very seductive awe must be," she whispered. "I can barely imagine what it would be like to have the whole world admire me. I think it would be delicious."

Nardi thought a moment then said, "It made me arrogant." He admitted quietly, "Which—you are right—is a feeling I still sometimes miss."

She let the conversation go here.

Or more accurately, consciousness let *her* go. Nardi felt her body grow slack, her limbs relax against him. The rise and fall of her breathing settled into something soft and regular. Lying there, Nardi relished this new knowledge of her: Hannah's style of falling asleep was akin to the way one might drop off a cliff, instant and complete. She didn't stir. She made no noise. Her small body simply collapsed as she plunged into sleep as sweetly unconscious as a child's.

Nardi, of course, knew only the exact opposite experience. It still took him hours to get to sleep, if he slept at all. So he lay there awake beside her, his mind alive with the evening, this night, alive with the last bits of what he'd just told her.

It was easy enough for Nardi to say he was arrogant. He knew he had been and remained somewhat arrogant at times still, though nothing like before. The thing he had never admitted aloud was that he missed his old, obnoxious arrogance. He remembered the attention, the sense of self-importance; he missed a life lived in the spotlight, to the sound of trumpets. His old arrogance had been lofty and righteous—humanly uninformed. It had been a powerful feeling, immensely enjoyable—a vainglory that to this day a part of him wished he could have back.

Now? Nardi saw the fallacies in this line of thought, but was out of practice with coping with life. He lost patience with others and himself too quickly. He was used to the quick remedy of ether. He was not accustomed to the calm, steady relative uneventfulness of personal satisfaction. He did not feel prepared for the knocks and blows of daily life. Cold sober, it all seemed like such a long, hard road to hoe for comparably paltry reward.

Though, come to think of it, that had not held true tonight. Tonight, the reward didn't seem so paltry. There was dancing and sweating and laughing. There was hot, sticky sex against a rough wall in the breathless dark. Nardi laughed to himself to remember: and sex that tugged him through a château, as if it had hold of him by the end of his penis, up a staircase, down a dark corridor, and, finally, into a bed with a woman he wanted like no woman he could remember wanting before. Now there was this warm, laughing creature beside him, who could be silly and wise by turns. There was Hannah, and suddenly a lifetime of sober evenings did not seem so distressing.

Then the words—"a lifetime"—stood out saliently in his mind. Nardi had to make certain she understood about Du Gard, about the limits and rewards of their future together. He would speak to her about this tomorrow.

Nardi was awakened by a solid shove, a knee in the kidneys. *"Aie?"* he hissed out. *"Qu'est-ce qui se passe?"* It was daylight.

"Shhh." The whisper of Hannah's warm breath came over his shoulder as her hair touched the skin on his back. "I can't believe you're still here! Get out!"

"En voilà du joli" — a fine state of affairs — Nardi muttered as he sat up. He couldn't find his pants.

Hannah had already hopped from bed, a pretty, naked sprite with wobbling breasts as she leaped and stooped about the room, half-fretful, half-angry. She picked up his trousers and shirt and waistcoat. "Get out! Get out!" she kept whispering as she threw each at him. When she brought his shoes and socks over to him, he didn't take them but grasped her arms instead. He drew her between his legs. He kissed her belly while — her hands full of shoes — she tried to prevent him with elbows and blocking forearms and whispers. He kissed the inside curve of her breast, there being so much breast everywhere, it was impossible for her to protect every square inch. She groaned as much from pleasure as in frustration.

"I adore you," he murmured. "You are the sweetest, most earnest, most angelically good — "

Hannah stiffened and put her finger over his lip, as a voice beyond the bedroom door said, "Hannah?"

It was the old cow. Amelis Besom rapped on the door from the other side of it out in the hall.

There in Nardi's arms, Hannah clutched his shoes to her pubis like absurd fig leaves. "Yes?" she called back.

Nardi watched her posture straighten, her mien become anxious. She was genuinely frightened. Reality set in. Hannah needed this job; she had no family monies or rich marriage to lend her security. Moreover, through some impenetrable line of reasoning, she liked the work she was doing with Old Besom. No, Hannah loved what she was doing.

Nardi stood, gently guiding Hannah backward and onto the bed in his place. He stepped into his trousers then, looked about — he and Hannah both looked about — for someplace to hide him. Buttoning his trousers, he mouthed

the word, *Where?* In such a small room, where did one put
a six-foot-plus Frenchman?

Hannah shrugged, seeming more anxious by the moment.

The two of them mouthed a pantomime. *Will the old
battle-ax come in? Is the door locked?* he asked.

Did you lock it?

No.

Besom's voice in the hallway asked, "Are you muttering
to yourself in there, Hannah?"

"Yes," she called back.

"Well, stop it. Are you ready? Why are you banging
around? What are you doing in there?"

Hannah had lifted the sheet and pulled it around her, as if
she might draw it right over her head. Sitting there like this,
she looked peculiarly lost, undone.

Nardi frowned, grabbing his shirt.

Mrs. Besom's voice said, "I thought we would have a
look in the general area where you found that de Saint
Vallier. It went for a pretty price, didn't it?" She knocked on
the door again. "Are you dressed? May I come in?"

Hannah just sat there like a prisoner awaiting her walk up
the steps to the guillotine.

When the door opened, Nardi had his shoes against his
chest, his fists round his socks, suspenders, and waistcoat.
He shot out onto the little ornamental balcony, pressing
against the wall. He stood on a ledge that was about a foot
wide. Three stories. Three tall stories. The ground below
was at least fifty feet straight down, without a vine or tree
branch or any of the things that were supposed to be
conveniently to hand in order to aid lovers in such circumstances. Nardi was stuck on the balcony, unless he wanted
to break his bones, then crawl off quietly.

"Why, Hannah," he heard old Besom say. "You're—
you're only wearing a sheet. Where is your nightgown?"

Poor Hannah sounded dazed. "I—ah—I don't know."

"You don't know?" There was a huffy little pause,
presumably the old dragon surveying Hannah's room, the

one place that should have been Hannah's inviolably. "And your clothes! They're everywhere!"

The old trout, old sour wine sack. She had no right to do this. Nardi wanted to charge in there and tell her so. He waited for Hannah to come fiercely to her own defense.

She didn't. "I—ah—was very tired last night," she said.

There was another uncomfortably long silence that left Nardi furious. He could only imagine Hannah sitting there naked beneath the sheet, defenseless against her all-important, overjudgmental employer. Nardi sputtered mentally. The old cow-dragon-vulture, chimera of his nightmares! How dare she breathe down the neck of the plucky young woman of his dreams!

In the end, Old Besom retreated into the hallway again while Hannah dressed, and Nardi stepped back into the room. He tried to pantomime a solution to her. *Tell her to go the devil. You can live with me at the cottage. You can find another job. Meanwhile I won't let anyone harm you. Sébastien will cooperate.* This was, however, much too much to try to convey without voice. Worse, Nardi had to deliver it in pieces, since Hannah wouldn't stop lacing her corset long enough more than to glance up at him momentarily.

She pulled her blouse on, buttoning it with a proficiency far beyond any she had had last night. Just before she left, she held out one hand and looked at him: helpless, busy, work, work, work. . . .

As the door closed behind her Nardi felt a stab of jealousy. He resented the attention Hannah paid to Besom, resented the devotion Hannah showed toward her daily occupation—and was sick to death of himself for competing with these things. A little ether might shoo away these petty emotions, he thought. Then, no, the ridiculousness of this—that ether could somehow make him into a better man—struck him. The truth was that Hannah loved him, and he knew it. He tried to talk himself out of his less than worthy feelings. Never mind Old Besom. He should be glad that Hannah enjoyed a life beyond him, a full life. His problem was that he didn't have much of a life himself beyond Hannah—

Then the next instants revealed to him how perfectly untrue this notion was. Nardi was sitting on the edge of the bed, mumbling to himself as he pulled on his socks, when the bedroom door swung open again. Nardi jumped half a foot as his brother came in.

"Ah, there you are," Sébastien said. "I thought so." He paused, looking entirely too pleased with himself. "Yesterday's auction went brilliantly, didn't it?"

Nardi assented with a mutter.

Sébastien continued. "And you, Bernard"—he looked around the room—"you're doing well yourself, too, aren't you?" Sébastien didn't wait for an answer this time, but only clapped his brother on the back as he sat down on the bed beside him. "In fact," he said, "as I was watching you dance last night I was struck with how very well you've been doing lately. I said to myself, 'You know, it is time for a visit to Paris.' So I wired Du Gard this morning, and we're off. He can't wait to present you to friends and family. And to his daughter, of course. She is most eager to meet the fine, handsome, pedigreed fellow her father has found for her."

Chapter 21

LATE THAT AFTERNOON Nardi stepped off a train down onto a platform at the Gare d'Orsay in Paris, his brother stepping down not two feet behind him. Outside, a motorcar waited for them, sent by Georges Du Gard. The ride to the house was brief. Like this whole trip, it left Nardi feeling ill prepared: a man trying to live by his promises, yet lost in their speedy reality. What logic had led him here? he kept asking himself. Why exactly was he preparing to marry a rich stranger? Nardi was sure he could refind the reasons, the old reference points in his life, that had once made marrying Du Gard's daughter into a good idea. For the moment, however, trying to find them was like trying to find the horizon while doing somersaults in midair.

A butler admitted them, the same butler, if Nardi remembered correctly, whom he had shouldered to the floor when the man wouldn't let him in five months ago. This time the man politely took Nardi's hat and overnight bag, murmuring, "This way, messieurs." Nardi fell in behind the other two men, taken by the strangeness, the sober sense of déjà vu that accompanied walking once more down the hallway of the Du Gards' home in the faubourg Saint-Germain.

Georges Du Gard himself was waiting for them in the music salon, directing servants as they rolled up rugs and moved chairs against the walls. The room appeared to be in the process of conversion, from recital salon to dancing floor. Du Gard stopped the moment Sébastien and Nardi entered, greeting them cordially, even effusively—willing even to part himself from his ubiquitous cigar, setting it into a dish on the piano, so he could embrace each man by turn as if he were beloved family.

Over Du Gard's shoulder, Nardi stared at the piano. "Is that the one?" he asked Sébastien. What had remained of Nardi's own very small bank account had been wiped out to buy the Du Gards a new instrument. Their former piano had been irreparable, having had its strings, pads, and sound-board dowsed liberally in stomach acid.

Du Gard answered for Sébastien. "This is indeed the pianoforte you bought for my daughter, and she couldn't be more pleased. You hit upon a most generous and perfect engagement present." He segued immediately into explanations of the room's disorder. There would be "a little dancing after dinner tonight, just intimate friends and immediate family, to meet the groom, you know."

From here, the game became obvious: They were all going to pretend that Nardi had never been in this house before, which was easy enough for him since he hadn't ever been in it fully conscious and coherent.

The rude truth entered to create only one touchy moment. When Nardi refused some sherry, Du Gard insisted, "But you *must* have some. It's excellent." He winked. "And very hard to come by—you know, expensive but worth it."

"No, thank you." When this was met with puzzled offense, Nardi explained, "At the clinic. They told me I am better off not having anything, neither stimulant, nor depressant—no alcohol."

These words were followed by dumb, staring silence. For Sébastien's part, the silence seemed to be one of pure incredulity. Nardi had amazed himself. He hadn't been aware that anything the doctors had said at the clinic had made so much as a chink in his thinking.

Du Gard's silence, however, was not as selfless. He puffed a furious cloud of black smoke then asked through it,

"You're not going to say anything like that tonight, are you? About the clinic, I mean."

Nardi replied, "No, not so long as you don't tell me what to drink."

Du Gard frowned at this suspiciously intractable answer, then leaned forward to put his cigar out, scowling as he ground the tobacco stump into the dish. He said, glaring over this, "Maybe you *should* have a drink of *something*. It might make you less edgy."

He meant, It might make you more manageable.

Sébastien rescued the conversation by interjecting some nonsense or other about the château, arrangements for the wedding, how impressive it was all going to be.

Marie Du Gard and her mother came in shortly thereafter, entering in a swirl of pleated, ruffled chiffon. The mother was quite a bundle of it. She stood no more than five feet and was as broad as she was tall. The daughter towered over her, not at all thin herself, though considerably less chunky.

Nardi knew immediately that he wanted to speak to his finally-there-in-the-very-solid-flesh bride-to-be. He wanted to make some sort of human contact. This was not going to be easy, however. The ladies brought with them not only a notebook full of nuptial and prenuptial plans, they brought also in person two caterers, a florist, a decorator, and a gentleman's tailor. Nardi's opinions were solicited (then rejected, if they didn't coincide to plans already well under way), while he stood with his legs open, his arms out, being measured for a suit of clothing about which he knew not so much as the fabric (though formal velvet court breeches were rather horrifyingly mentioned).

The magnitude of the forthcoming event, as Nardi took in the details, was no less than shocking. It had grown to six hundred twelve guests. A bishop was coming to perform the ceremony. The reception included fifty cases of vintage champagne and a thirty-two-piece orchestra. An elaborate wedding was less than a month away, though no one had thought to mention the date to the groom till this very moment.

In fact, Nardi's position in this house, over the course of the afternoon, seemed to him to be less like that of a groom and more like that of a vague acquaintance, somehow puzzlingly in possession of an invitation, whom the Du Gards, though they had racked their brains, could think of no polite way of uninviting.

A "few intimate friends and immediate family" proved to be more than three dozen people for dinner and dancing. Nardi's own family had sent regrets. Sébastien was required to pacify this slight by staying for dinner as representative.

During aperitifs, Nardi talked to Marie Du Gard for about two seconds before her father pressed her into playing the piano. She complied with trilling waltzes and busy fugues, playing both with extraordinary proficiency, though without the involvement of someone who loved what she did. Her parents were nonetheless deeply pleased by her performance. They asked her to play Mozart, then jubilantly expressed their wonder as they chatted from person to person: "You realize she is playing the full sonata from memory." Proud was not the word, Nardi realized, for how the Du Gards viewed their only offspring. They exalted her. She was the showpiece they prized above all other possessions.

At dinner Nardi sat directly beside this obedient, revered daughter, making polite overtures to conversation through soup, a fish course, then entrée. Marie Du Gard responded consistently with terse nods and monosyllables, though Nardi decided her curtness was due more to her attire than from any reticence or antagonism. Up close, her wrist and rib cage had the compacted look of heavy corsetry. Her dress had the drape and fold of clever camouflage. She sat stiffly beside him, looking breathlessly uncomfortable on the edge of her chair all the way through dessert, which she refused—to the unfortunate and beaming pleasure of her parents. Her mother even went so far as to say, "Marie, dearest, you look so very slender tonight," "slender" being a synonym for "beautiful."

It was hard to say if Marie Du Gard were beautiful. She

was, as the euphemism went, "well fed," with the indignant, slightly surly demeanor of a hungry woman combating an unfashionable corpulence. She was substantial, a real presence, perhaps even formidable. Beyond this, Nardi couldn't see or decide what to make of her.

Nardi was unable to build any substantive conversation between himself and Marie Du Gard at dinner. He didn't actually know what he might want to say to her, though he continued to be plagued by a sense of there being something terribly important to communicate. In any event, the issue became moot. The gathering moved from the dining room into the music-salon-cum-dance-parlor. The bride-to-be danced with Nardi four times, then, while Nardi was dutifully dancing with the second of her female relatives, she retired early. "She's a little overwrought, the excitement, bridal jitters, all that," her father explained solicitously.

"If only I had known it was that easy," Nardi told his brother as he walked Sébastien to the door of the music salon. Sébastien was also leaving early. "I think I'll make similar excuses in another ten minutes."

Behind them, a piano/string quartet leaped into a piece of café concert music, complete with someone twittering birdcalls—nightingales—at the strategic rests and *ritenutoes*.

From the doorway, quietly over this, Sébastien reverted to English. "Don't leave early," he said. "Du Gard expects every last measure of courtesy from you. Remember the sherry. He took your refusal as a complaint against it."

Nardi grunted, a noncommittal reply, as he stared beyond people into the Du Gards' material world he was expected soon to inhabit. The walls of the music salon were dark wood with crystal-beaded wall lamps mounted at intervals on the carved panels. The room's copious draperies matched its chairs, burgundy velvet tied in untold yards of ropy gold tassels. At the far end of the room, middling paintings hung in elaborate gilt frames worth more than the canvases. The room looked to Nardi like a cross between the reading room of a posh English gentlemen's club and the dance parlor of an expensive French bordello.

He was not particularly uncomfortable in either of these places, though this was not where he would have expected to marry. He must have laughed at fate, fortune, whatever, for Sébastien asked him, "What's so amusing?"

Quite suddenly Nardi realized: "Hannah," he said. "She would love this soirée. This is her idea of a fancy gathering."

Sébastien's eyes panned the room, then he said blandly, "Yes, the Du Gards have the taste of gypsies."

Nardi laughed again. This meant, of course, that Hannah did, too. And it was true; she did. Though, if he weren't mistaken, Sébastien meant this as criticism. "Why is it that you don't like her?" Nardi asked.

"Who?"

"Hannah."

"I like her fine." Sébastien shrugged. "There's just something rather, mm"—he looked for a word—"crude," he said, "about her."

Nardi was taken aback. "Crude?"

Sébastien waved his hand. "I don't know." Then he made it worse. He said, "Animal." When Nardi scowled, his brother amended, "I mean no offense. It's just that she's not, well, very sophisticated or even bright. She's too"—again he settled on this disconcerting word—"animal," he repeated.

"Hannah's *very* bright—"

Sébastien interrupted, smiling sagely as he tapped his hat against his leg. "You needn't defend her. I understand that lewdness might not be a bad thing in a mistress."

Now Hannah was lewd. Under different circumstances—without the trilling stretches of a cappella bird-warbling in the background to keep this whole conversation in ludicrous perspective—Nardi would have enjoyed running Sébastien's face into the doorjamb. Nardi only said irritably, *"Ah, oui. Et toi, qui baise tant de femmes, t'es expert en sexualité"*—accusing his brother, backhandedly, of being anything but an authority on sexual matters.

Sébastien, an expert on everything in his own mind at least, said with the tried patience of a saint, "I have five children, you know."

"Ah, yes. With the Virgin Mary." Marguerite, Sébastien's wife, was the only person Nardi knew whose demeanor suggested more strongly than Sébastien's a sense of virtue and purity. Nardi looked at his brother and said, "So how many women have you fucked, Sébastien, for the pure, carnal pleasure of it? I'm asking you—do you even know what it is like to want to ravish a woman? To be an animal yourself?"

Sébastien glanced at him with a nervous frown. "I don't speak of such things," he said. "I'm more private than you are."

"More prudish," Nardi corrected. *"Comme une vieille fille."* Like an old girl, an old maid.

Sébastien's mouth tightened. "Well, since you seem to need to know: besides my wife, I have had exactly eight women."

Nardi laughed. "How nice for you. And you keep perfect count."

"You couldn't if you wanted to. You can't count into triple digits."

Nardi threw his brother a snide look. *"Et combien d'orgasmes, 'Bastien?* How many, eh?"

Sébastien snorted and looked away, but not before a sheepish look had passed across his face.

Nardi chuckled, this time a true release. Poor Sébastien had some sort of statistic on this as well. In some way, he kept track. How funny. How sad. Sébastien counted his orgasms, presumably to measure his total against some standard. Even his private life had to measure up.

There seemed little point in trying to explain the virtues of Hannah to a man who thought this way. Nardi added only, "Hannah is more than you give her credit for. She has the intelligence and innate integrity of nature itself, while being blissfully, blatantly—naturally—erotic, *sexuelle avec exubérance.* Hannah *is* animal," he said. "Which is won-

derful. Because the act is both animal and magical, Sébastien, and Hannah is capable of both—an *animalité* that
overturns itself into the magical, *le—le mythique*, shooting
stars, bursts of light. She transports me."

As Nardi reentered the Du Gards' music salon he reveled
in a momentary sense of ruthless superiority—for the
simple fact that he enjoyed a freer, simpler, less solemn sex
life than his brother. This lasted till he had danced once
around the sumptuous room, a room that Hannah would
love but would never enter. Nardi immediately felt less
pleased with himself. The rhythmical gaiety of strings,
percussion, and bird noises—music to which Hannah would
have laughed and danced—told him that any triumph he
felt over Sébastien was false and petty. Nardi spent the next
twenty minutes using Marie Du Gard's excuse to make his
ever-so-gracious good-nights. Then, disappointed in himself
and generally frustrated, he fled across the house toward the
staircase that led to the guest room.

Halfway up this staircase, however, he noticed something
unusual. Over the banister, beyond the dining room, light
from the main kitchen shone under the servants' door. The
cook, no doubt, Nardi thought, and climbed another step.
Then, no, he stepped back down and looked over the
banister again. The cook, he remembered from some conversation or other, was day help; she'd gone home. The
main kitchen had been closed an hour ago. Nardi stood there
staring and asking himself, Now where would an "overwrought" and probably hungry bride go if she were no more
tired and excited than he was?

Nardi turned around, bounded down the stairs, and
crossed the dining room.

Marie Du Gard started when he came in, then quite
sanguinely dug a long-handled spoon into a deep, frosty
can. She was having the dessert she'd missed at dinner, ice
cream flavored with whiskey and served with shards of
burnt sugar. After a moment's hesitation she threw him a
wry look then returned to what she was doing. Without
either of them saying a word, Nardi pulled out a stool. It

scraped along the rough wood floor. As he sat down opposite her he watched her scoop herself a second helping—or maybe a third or fourth, who knew?—into an empty bowl already coated in golden cream and crumbs of sugar crisp.

She was still dressed in her frothy yellow dinner dress, though she had loosened the neck flounce and top buttons. She had a slight double chin.

For the first few minutes he chatted aimlessly, as if they'd just happened to meet by chance here in the kitchen. He tried to be pleasant, still not sure why he had sought her out, stalling while trying to figure himself out and simultaneously, to take her measure.

Marie Du Gard herself was not particularly pleasant. She had a chip on her shoulder, giving the impression of a slightly bossy woman, superior in the way an only child could be sometimes—like one of those ten-year-old girls one knew growing up who were always herding everyone about, a seeming expert in the mysteries and management of rules. Of course, this girl, this only child, was a grown woman, not young just not very mature. Nardi stared at her corpulence, at the ice cream going into her mouth by the heaping spoonful.

All at once she met his stare and said, "Yes, I'm fat. Does this bother you?"

Nardi only looked at her. Rubenesque—and, in truth, she was a bit more than Rubenesque—was not exactly his idea of beauty. Though it was not Marie Du Gard's bulk, he realized, that would hamper him in embracing her as a woman, a partner, a wife. He didn't like her. Some aspect about her, something in her character, took her rich life too much for granted: that is, she reminded him too much of her father.

"No," he answered truthfully. Her "fatness" was a long way from the heart of the problem.

"Let's get some things straight," she said, taking a bite of ice cream then pointing her spoon at him. "I am almost your age. Twenty-nine. I am not married for two reasons. One, my father never thought anyone good enough to bother wooing until you—for the record, you are *his* choice, not mine. And two, no man on his own ever came forward; I am not an attractive woman."

She continued, "You are much better looking than I am. As one of my gaga friends so ridiculously puts it, when you walk down the street, ladies stumble, drop packages—and they drop their jaws. You turn heads. Besides this, you are better born than I, a gentleman by birth. It is in your bones, your manners, the way you stand, dress, speak. It shows. I am not particularly impressed by all this. I am not a romantic. But I listen to my parents, who value these sorts of things—and, in doing so, are apparently, as usual, right again: Everyone else seems to value them, too. My friend," she explained, "the friend I was telling you about, says I am the luckiest girl in the world. She is jealous of me. Five feet two and a hundred pounds, and *she* is jealous of *me*. And I like it. In her mind I am marrying the handsomest man in the world, a talented artist with a dark, romantic past—"

Nardi laughed abruptly. He couldn't help it, remembering that this "romance" consisted of binges, lost nights, lost weeks, all of it sprinkled liberally with indigestion and emesis. His reaction stopped Marie Du Gard's little diatribe.

With a clang she dropped the spoon in the empty bowl. "Don't laugh," she said. She cocked her head at him suspiciously. "Unless you have ether upstairs in your bag."

He said nothing. He was sick to death of people sticking their nose into what was ultimately his responsibility.

She reiterated, "There had better never *be* any. My wants are simple. You behave well. No ether. Though you can have a little wine now and then if you like." She made a distasteful face. "And no other women. I won't tolerate it."

"Wait one moment." Nardi shifted forward on the stool to settle on his forearms, leaning slightly across the table. He leveled his eyes at her. There *was* another woman, and this, he realized, was what he had come to tell her.

Marie Du Gard opened her plump little mouth, then closed it. Something very sad came into her expression as she faced his changed attitude and its implications. Disappointment. What on God's earth had she expected? Nardi wondered. Then resignation. She grasped the meaning of his simple, three-word, voiced objection. Wait one moment—

She waited for him to tell her that he intended to take mistresses.

He murmured only, "I will always be discreet. I will never embarrass you." He tried to humor her ego, as if this were all her idea anyway. "Which is what you are asking for really. Publicly I will be a good husband." He wasn't very happy with the sound of these words as he uttered them. It was Sébastien's arrangement: the public husband, the private scoundrel. His brother saw his wife only at Christmas and rites of passage: baptisms, communions, weddings, and funerals. It was the role of husband reduced to an escort service, like those louche enterprises in Paris where a woman could hire a man to take her places and, for a fee, negotiate stud privileges.

Marie Du Gard's face became vague, the lost look of a woman who knew she had no acceptable recourse. She made one last attempt. "If you see other women, I will tell Papa—"

"I'm seeing another woman. Tell him what you like. I won't stop seeing her." He let her know by his expression that this part of the agreement was nonnegotiable.

She tightened her mouth into a resentful look.

He tried to normalize their highly abnormal situation: "Your father has a mistress, and your mother knows." If this were new information, he attempted to soften it. "My father has had several, most with my mother's knowledge and consent. It's not unusual—"

"It's unusual to announce this to your fiancée, to bring a mistress into a marriage. A gentleman breaks off before his wedding—"

He said quietly, "Marie—" The use of her familiar name momentarily disarmed her. He pushed ahead, not daring to relent. "I don't mean for this to be painful for you. I will handle it as kindly as I can. But you must understand that I will not cut myself off from her. I will see her frequently. I will be gone occasionally all night."

He hadn't meant to, but he seemed to have explained to her that he was in love with this woman, with Hannah. How surprising to find out this was true—and that he was explaining it to the woman, a woman other than the one he loved, whom he intended to marry.

Marie Du Gard looked down. Her hand went to her mouth, covering her lips. She sat perhaps a minute like this. Then she took her hand away, sat up straight, and let her eyes settle on him again. These eyes were wide and watery, but in perfect control. They were pretty, he realized, a liquid brown. She was one of those women people spoke of sadly, in terms that were patronizingly trite: She had "beautiful features if only she'd lose weight"—an event unlikely to occur in light of her habits and family. Meanwhile her pretty eyes said the wound he'd delivered was sharper and deeper than he'd anticipated. He still couldn't fathom what she had expected of this arranged marriage, but he felt guilty, unhappy with his own stance, and unable to think of anything to remedy their situation.

She looked at him for a long moment, her fine, brown eyes filled oddly with things he hadn't expected to find there: anguish, intelligence, and acceptance. Perhaps he *could* live with this woman, he thought. He hoped he could. He was going to try.

When she spoke, her voice wasn't quite as brave as her direct look or dignified posture. "All right," she said. After a moment she added a bit defiantly, "And I will take lovers, too, if it pleases me."

He nodded. "Certainly."

She seemed almost dismayed. She looked down again. The awkwardness stretched out. Finally she asked, "Where do you see us in ten years' time?" She added in the smallest voice, "What are we doing?"

Nardi had no doubt about what they were doing. "We are marrying the way our forefathers and mothers married, for society, procreation, for the union of families and the stability of money and status."

She whispered, "Will we have children?"

"If you want them. If you bring any home to me by someone else, I will acknowledge them. I will make your life as happy as I am capable of making it." He reached across the table and touched her hand, the right hand, the hand that would wear the ring. "We have honesty at least, which I was most keen to establish and will do my utmost to maintain between us. What I hope for is that, ten years from now, we are the best of friends, kind to each other, realistic and compassionate partners, with a domestic—"

He would have continued, but surprisingly she broke down then. She covered her face and began to sob into her childlike hands—they were sweet hands, pink, fleshy, tiny, proportioned like a baby's. He sat there, reaching across the table, nudging her elbow, crooning to his disillusioned bride-to-be that it wasn't so bad, it wasn't so bad. . . .

But she was right. It was ghastly.

Across the river near the Bois de Boulogne, Sébastien de Saint Vallier stepped out of his carriage down onto a dark, tree-lined street in the sixteenth arrondissement. He retrieved a cumbersome package from the boot then went up the walk, turned his key in the lock of an impressively fashionable town house, and stepped through its doorway. He set the package down into a small, dimly lit entry hall. Beyond, in the dining room, he could hear a young girl's voice—it sounded like his eldest daughter, Germaine, pleading earnestly to be allowed to go somewhere.

Sébastien rounded the corner just as his wife, Marguerite, pronounced a serene and final "no." She looked up as he came into the doorway. All conversation stopped.

Sébastien stared a moment. The dining room was tasteful, elegant, perfect. Overhead, a thousand-piece chandelier hung, immaculate, each crystal clean enough to give off light like a diamond. This shone down on a mahogany table set with white lace linens. Across the table, the glass of a

large window captured the table's surface in duplicate. In
reflection, it reiterated candles, a huge bouquet of white
orchids, an orderly progression of crystal and gold-rimmed
china, this surrounded by a dark scallop of scrolled chair
backs through the lattices of which showed the small,
shining heads that were his children.

In the window glass Sébastien watched himself step into
this room as if he stepped into another life from out there
beyond himself in the dark. He felt oddly distant as he said,
"Which one is Michelle?"

This was a game. He knew perfectly well which of his
children was which. But Michelle, the youngest, had once
accused him of not being able to tell her from Jeannette, a
year older. For some reason, tonight no one laughed, not
even Sébastien.

Marguerite stood immediately, saying, "We didn't hear
you." She smiled. His lovely wife had a smile straight from
the canvases of old Italian paintings, Madonna-like. When
she moved, it was as if, beneath her dress, there were swan
feathers and water, not legs and flooring. Marguerite glided
toward him. She was thin, even after five children, lovely, as
everyone said, an ethereal beauty.

Sébastien found himself pronouncing silently what he
had said a thousand times. Marguerite was an ideal wife.
Why didn't he live here? This house, this woman were an
oasis. When she touched his shoulder, using it for balance as
she raised up to kiss his cheek, both the touch of her hand
and her mouth were as light as a phantom's; they left no
impression.

Sébastien spoke across her head. "There is a present for
you, Michelle, by the front door. You may get it when you
are dismissed from the table. Happy birthday."

"Thank you, Papa." His daughter grinned shyly. "Do you
know how old I am?"

His back straightened. "Of course I do." He calculated
quickly. "You are six," he said a little more severely than
he'd meant to. He glanced at Marguerite. "I ate on the
train," he said. "I'll wait for you in the bedroom."

An hour later Sébastien was atop Marguerite, having raised her nightgown only as far as need be in a gentlemanly effort to guard her modesty. He touched her considerately, being ever so respectful, and relieved himself quickly.

Afterward, as he stared up into the dark, he found himself pondering whether or not this lovely woman "transported" him.

Transport. He considered the idea for a time, then decided the whole notion was dangerous. It was for people with wild, unrealistic imaginations. For people who could drink ether or who, like his brother, could trade one ridiculous intoxication for another.

Chapter 22

ALL THE WAY back to Aubrignon, Nardi stewed over his predicament. He could think of no graceful way to tell Hannah he was about to marry someone else; he could think of no practical approach to telling Sébastien he wanted to back out.

"How much money do we owe Georges Du Gard?" he asked Sébastien as they climbed down onto the gravel of the château courtyard.

"Why?"

"I just wanted to know our debt, our liability."

Sébastien pulled a skeptical face as he yanked his overnight bag from the carriage boot. "Nardi," he said as he hefted then handed out Nardi's bag too, "you *have* to marry her."

"I know. I'm going to." Nardi studied his own shoes as he and Sébastien walked toward the side entrance.

Sébastien added for good measure, "Our finances are hopelessly mixed into theirs—"

"That is what I want to know. How hopelessly? I would like specifics."

Sébastien shook his head as he opened the door and led the way in. "Well, off the top of my head: The treatment at the clinic ran about fifteen thousand francs. The fire cost an additional forty, not counting the replacement of assorted lost items of your wardrobe. Then there is the train fare

every time the doctor has to come here now"—he glanced
back at Nardi with a long-suffering look—"and of course
his fees, plus the four orderlies who live round the clock on
the premises. Then there is the setup of the cottage, clay,
plaster of paris—"

"I didn't ask for that." Nardi hadn't asked for any of this.
Nonetheless, he had the hollow feeling that asking or not
was irrelevant.

His brother snorted. "Shall I continue, or are you cowed
yet?"

Distantly, across the château, Monday-morning noises
could be heard, voices calling, echoing through the cavernous stone rooms across the length of the main building. On
Friday, workmen in the ballroom, Nardi knew, had begun to
replace broken tile in the flooring.

"What is the total?"

"A lot. And Du Gard has sunk hundreds of thousands of
francs into the château—"

"Which is his property and not our responsibility—"

"Actually the hectares north of the stream belong to Pater
now, for hunting. Louise has claimed her paintings. Du
Gard's promises to the family have all more or less been
dispersed."

Nardi stopped in the kitchen. "And why exactly would
Du Gard do that? Why give anyone anything before the
wedding?"

"'Goodwill,' he called it, which it was. Everyone was
more than pleased to have their reward. Moreover, Du Gard
is not a fool. Each 'gift' is guaranteed by family monies.
Should the marriage not take place for reasons attributable
to our side, all property is forfeit with sizable financial
penalties. It would economically cripple every de Saint
Vallier involved."

Nardi stood there, frowning. "And if I die tomorrow?
Why would any of you put yourself in this position?"

"The insurance policy covers that eventuality." Sébastien
paused, then continued coolly. "Nardi," he explained, "this
is business, and Georges Du Gard is an astute player. Before

he was willing to invest what is amounting to a great deal of money, he wanted certain assurances. The early exchange of property and guarantees was a way to ensure that he gets the son-in-law he wants. You are as good as married to his daughter. You *can't* back out, so stop torturing yourself with all your noble misgivings—which come, I am sure, from your involvement with your little American *donzelle*. Honestly, Mademoiselle Van Evan is not worth it. Point in fact, I think you will find her perfectly willing to live as your mistress. It's not something she hasn't at least contemplated before."

Having summed both Nardi and Hannah up so conveniently, Sébastien proceeded into his office. Nardi followed him, stopping at the doorway to lean his shoulder onto the doorjamb. Inside the office, his brother threw his travel satchel into a corner, then opened a ledger, sat, and picked up a pen. Nardi said, "You told me Hannah knew about this marriage. She doesn't, Sébastien."

Sébastien began to write, denying Hannah's ignorance with a single, impatient shake of his head. "She *has* to. *Everyone* who works at the château knows why you're here."

"And 'everyone' who works here, with the exception of Hannah and Besom, speaks French not English. Hannah does not talk to 'everyone,' Sébastien. Does Besom know?"

"Certainly." Sébastien stopped long enough to contemplate this answer, then amended, "I believe so." Going back to his books, and without a moment's concern, he recanted further. "Actually, I'm not sure Amelia has taken the trouble to understand fully, but she has the general idea."

"Hannah thinks I am rich."

"You *will* be rich."

"She speaks of the château as ours—"

"It *is* ours for all practical purposes."

"And of the money going to repair it as family money."

Sébastien glared up over the top of his bifocals. "It *will* be family money," he asserted. "Miss Van Evan merely speaks with the wisdom of a woman who has already accepted the inevitable."

The noises—raised voices—from across the building pierced the air again. The intonations were English not French, Nardi realized. He looked toward the sound. Someone was screaming his damned head off.

Her damned head off: A shrill screech echoed then diminished. It was Besom in a fit over something. Her voice rose to a loud, distressed peak.

Sébastien stood. "What in the world—" He set his glasses down and came around the desk.

Sébastien may have followed or may have not. Nardi didn't take the time to find out. He headed at a trot in the direction of the commotion.

It was not the ballroom from which Besom's screeching was emanating, but rather from the grand dining hall just beyond the ballroom. Nardi arrived at the edge of this storehouse of furniture and boxes, having to work his way through before finding Hannah and Besom faced off over an open crate.

Besom, her back to him, was flapping a piece of paper in the air as she said with draconian severity, "What am I supposed to do? Just what am I supposed to do? Ignore this?"

"Yes. If you're my friend." Hannah's face was sheet white, her expression like that of a woman who had just witnessed a grisly accident. She said, "That letter is malicious. Anyone can read in its tone that Mildred Stanton hates me."

Amelia Besom leaned toward Hannah, bracing her knuckles on the crate edge as she shook the paper in Hannah's face. "Then you deny what she says here?"

Hannah's expression remained closed, neither denying nor admitting anything. Neither did she seem relieved, when she caught sight of Nardi as he came forward.

"What is going on here?" he asked.

Besom glanced at him over her shoulder, then raised the paper in the air again. "This . . . this . . . young woman . . . well, I have a letter here arrived in the day's post that . . . well—" She leaned violently toward Hannah again. "If you have nothing to say for yourself, then you know what I must do."

"You will do what you think is right," Hannah told her. But Nardi could hear in her voice that something terrible was happening here. He came round beside her, touching her arm.

Amelia Besom paused, swallowed, then looked away. Her face twisted with emotion—fury and frustration caught in a kind of bereavement. She said, "This would not have been a difficult choice once, Hannah. I would have fired any other young woman without a thought." Her voice broke. "If you denied this . . . this horrible accusation, I would believe you. I have come to trust you that much."

Hannah said softly, "It's my private business, Amelia."

Amelia Besom looked away for a moment, murmuring almost to herself. "Hannah, you must understand. My place in society—" She repeated this like a mantra: "My place in society . . ." Her voice trailed off. She frowned, glancing around as if looking for another way out. When she brought her eyes back to Hannah, Nardi would have thought their positions reversed, as if *she* were the recipient of her own harsh decision. "Hannah," she said, "I have no choice—"

Nardi expected Hannah to break, to weep at the implication. But she only raised her eyes to look around the large room, filled as it was with all the treasures she had wanted to handle—log, price, sell, and ship. Nardi took her hand and squeezed it.

Amelia Besom's eyes fixed on their clutched hands; then, surprisingly, someone did begin to crumble. Besom's voice quavered into a stammer as she said, "P-put the n-n-note-b-book here." She indicated the crate as a tearless sob broke from her chest.

Hannah dropped her notebook into the box, then added the pencil from her hair. "You'll want these, too," she said. From a pocket she withdrew identification tags, shipping papers, and a loose collection of odd coins and franc notes.

She held these out. "The change is from the post office this morning." When Besom made no move to accept this, Hannah dropped these, too, into the wood crate that stood between the two women.

Amelia Besom exhaled an involuntary shudder, then a hiccup, before she admitted her emotion far enough to put her hand to her mouth. She spoke through her fingers. "I will write you a check for your wages to date. Now go upstairs and pack your things, and get out."

"Fine." To Nardi, Hannah said, "Will you come help me?"

"Hannah," the old woman called. "Deny it," she pleaded. "You are good at this. I like you." More softly she murmured, "And no one has liked me as you have, not in such a very long time."

Over her shoulder, Hannah surveyed the woman for a long moment, the sort of look reserved for hopeless sights, lost causes, last chances used up and gone. Then she said to Nardi again, "Please help me."

From behind as they left, Old Besom's voice rose angrily. "You've slept with him, too, haven't you?" she called. "Oh, you horrible girl. You horrible, horrible girl. You horrible . . ."

This repetitive diatribe continued as Nardi escorted Hannah into the narrow corridor of stacked objects which, as they walked through them, seemed to look down with a valedictory sadness. All the while, Besom's words followed, echoing in the high-domed ceiling. *You horrible, horrible* . . . Until the wretched human being behind them, having just dismissed the only person who might have felt something akin to love for her, fell into loud, baleful crying.

A day later Sébastien would show Nardi the letter itself, retrieved from the scene when he stayed back to assist Amelia Besom into a chair. By then Hannah herself would already have thrown more details at Nardi than anyone else knew. Still, even a day late and in full knowledge, Mildred Stanton's letter would go down in Nardi's memory as an amazing piece of spite. It read:

Dear Mrs. Besom,

You asked me the nature of what keeps me from writing a reference for my former housekeeper, your employee, Miss Sue-Hannah Van Evan. I will tell you specifically. Miss Van Evan used her sweet face and innocent ways to lure my son toward the altar. We were all very lucky, however. Before my son could act on his naive affection and sense of gentlemanly responsibility for having indulged in physical liberties with Miss Van Evan, another rich young man appeared. It is common knowledge that Miss Van Evan gave herself to this other young man, Mr. Michael O'Hare, who happened also to be my son's best friend, for Miss Van Evan herself admitted she did so in front of myself, my husband, my son, and half the neighborhood who had gathered by the time my son had beat his friend half to death in our front garden for "slandering" his "beloved." It was no slander as it turned out, only the unbearable truth that my poor son had to learn to live with. In Miami, Miss Van Evan is known as she deserves to be: Polite people call her Miss Seven-Minutes-of-Heaven, or some call her "a rich boy's good time." I myself prefer not to mince words. The young woman in your employ is a fortune hunter at best, looking for a wealthy, gullible man. At worst, she is a vulgar little whore. If you value your own reputation in society, you should undoubtedly dismiss her. I did and am happy to have done so. I would do it again in a moment.

> Yours most truly,
> Mildred Stanton

III

Disintoxication

Then there is Adulation, full of trouble,
Young, adept, and beautiful to look upon,
Covered with more colors in more raiments
Than Heaven in springtime gives to flowers
Getting what she wants with sweet deceptions,
    Saying only what pleases others,
She has both tears and smiles with a single
    volition,
Adoring with her eyes, while with her hands she
    steals.

—Michelangelo Buonarroti
    Poem 163, DuJauc edition, 1901

Chapter 23

As MATTER-OF-FACTLY AS possible, Hannah told Nardi the contents of the letter, while upstairs they threw her things together. He seemed to accept the information then move on to the logistics of their new situation. Of course, she would not go to a hotel. She would stay with him at the cottage. Hannah accepted the offer. Nardi seemed pleased as he tossed her hairbrush, pins, and nightgown into her trunk himself. Shouldering the small steamer trunk, he all but jogged down to the gingerbread house at the edge of the estate.

Just in sight of the little house, the trouble began. "So it was this Edward fellow's friend you liked," he said.

"No," she answered, "I didn't like him. I barely knew him."

Nardi tripped a step, then had to set the trunk down in the clearing. He glanced at her over it.

She found herself explaining, "I slept with him because Edward was crazy."

"I don't follow."

"Nardi, can we just get the trunk inside and give this whole thing a rest for a while? I really don't want to talk about it."

He made a grunt of acquiescence as he heaved the trunk up again.

Inside, he dropped it on the wood floor with a loud *clonk*, then went around the central counter, took out a glass, and ran the tap. "Water?" he asked. His brow was furrowed, his jaw set as if he willfully held inappropriate questions locked behind his teeth. He said finally, "Dinner should be down soon. Are you hungry?"

"No."

He drank a full glass of water, then came back around, picked up the trunk, and said, "Come on. We will get this upstairs and make some room for your things."

His bedroom upstairs was, like the downstairs, one large room. It gave the impression of being a bit smaller than the room below for the fact of its ceiling sloping down at the exact angle of the steep cottage rooftop. At the center the ceiling was perhaps twenty feet high, while being no more than six feet at the two shorter walls—low enough that Nardi himself could not stand upright when he looked through his chest of drawers. The room contained a lot of furniture in addition to the chest, all of it brand-new chic or old-money antique: a feather bed with red-marble-topped nightstands that matched the chest of drawers, two mirrored wardrobes, a torchère lamp beside a Biedermeier writing table, an overstuffed chair with matching ottoman, plus a painted Chinese screen behind which were presumably hygienic facilities.

Nardi stomped around this beautiful room, sorting through his chest so as to leave its top drawer empty, then moving clothes back and forth between the two wardrobes till there was hanging room for Hannah's dresses. Inside the wardrobes were an astonishing number of trousers, shirts, coats, shoes. On the door of one hung more than a half-dozen sets of suspenders beside an avalanche of colorful, silken unused neckties. Nardi threw these things around carelessly, all the while saying nothing, his forehead creased with muzzled queries.

Hannah plonked into the chair and sighed. "All right, Nardi. Maybe I owe you an explanation." She took a deep breath and tried to sum up quickly this miserable little piece of her history. "Edward was making a mess of things. He wanted to marry me and wouldn't take no for an answer. The house was in chaos. At the rate he was going, I was going to lose my job anyway. I *had* to do something, to bring order to the situation, you see. To show Edward how impossible it was that we would ever marry."

"Why was it impossible?"

"His parents would never allow it."

"But you told me once before that he was willing to flout them."

She shook her head no as she said, "Oh, he was just being brave and romantic. Any marriage would have left his family hating us, his friends puzzled. Worse, Edward would have had to bear up under poverty in a way he simply could not imagine—his parents promised to cut him off without a dime if he married me, which meant that for a year and a half till he came into his grandparents' trust for him, we would have been living hand-to-mouth, with neither of us immediately employed. So he introduced me to his best friend who came to visit and who also happened to be a braggart; I slept with him, and that settled that."

"Oh, yes, I am sure that made everything much clearer."

Hannah gave him her full, glaring attention. "It did for me."

"Hannah," Nardi said, "could you not have taken Edward aside, had a long talk with him, just told him 'no thank you'?"

She stood up, pushing past him. "Oh, Nardi, you weren't there. It was much too complicated."

"In what way?"

"You're beginning to sound like everyone else: What an immoral woman."

"I am not passing judgment. I am just saying that sleeping with your near-fiancé's best friend was a . . . an alarming choice, to say the least."

Hannah expelled a breath. *Hmff.* "Well, if that's not judgment, I don't know what is." She went to the staircase. "I am hungry after all. Can I go downstairs and look around to see what you have? I think I saw an apple."

Nardi followed her downstairs, like a damned hound sniffing on the trail of something peculiar.

As she picked up the apple he said, "Don't walk away from me. Tell me why. I am asking you something serious."

"With your mind already made up as to the answer."

"Change my mind, then."

"You're angry."

"A little. You would not sleep with *me* for the longest time. Then I find you have leaped into bed with a passing stranger."

"It wasn't like that."

"What was it like then?"

She felt a little flurry of panic. She looked around her, not sure what she was looking for. She accused him: "I thought you were on my side."

"I *am* on your side. I don't believe you would have done such a thing without reason."

Irritated, she said, "But I didn't have any more reason than I've told you. It was reason enough that Edward had gone to his parents, said he was going to flout them and marry me anyway. I had to stop him. That was the reason: I slept with Michael to stop such bravado. It worked."

"While nearly drowning you in shame in the process. Why, Hannah? Why would you do something so stupid?"

"I don't know. Believe what you want." She put her back to him and walked away, biting into the apple.

Behind her, he said, "I believe you are a fine, capable, intelligent woman—"

She laughed. "Then you don't know me very well."

"—who has done something that so puzzles me I don't know what to think."

She turned on him and said defiantly, "I told you, think what you like. My way of handling things in Miami pleased me. You've seen how I am with you. Michael was very handsome. He took me dancing at a marvelous hotel. Afterward I went up to his room with him. He touched me. It felt very good. I *liked* it."

"Hannah—"

When he reached out, she hit his hand away. "Maybe I did it for the exact reason everyone says: Maybe I'm just bad."

He said nothing. A tension inside her seemed to make her quaver. Her knees began to tremble. Before her eyes, Nardi's image took on a liquid glitter. A watery halo appeared around him. While his pensive, intractable expression watched her with an unwavering demand; he wanted answers she didn't have. The halos spread. They ringed a chair behind him, the staircase. They blurred the wall of drawings. Hannah focused all of her energy on keeping her eyes from blinking, trying to see through this blur of hateful potential tears. She would not cry over this again. She had acted with intention and purpose.

"You are not bad," he murmured.

"Well, then, stupid and cruel."

"Yes, it was a cruel thing you did to Edward and his family. But it was crueler to yourself."

With a knuckle she dashed at her eyes and looked away. "Leave me alone. I have to go—" Go where? She remembered she had nowhere else.

He caught her by the elbow. "I won't leave you alone. You are done being alone, Hannah. And you're done tormenting yourself, and me, with this. You're going to explain."

"I can't explain, damn you! I *have* explained! I am cruel and stupid and cowardly—"

"Cowardly?" He frowned over the use of this word, as if it demonstrated yet more stupidity.

Stupid, stupid. No, of course, it didn't make sense, but she tried to explain anyway. "I was frightened, don't you understand?"

"Afraid? Of O'Hare?"

"No, no, no." Her patience fled, all rationality ending. "The Stantons. They were so powerful—"

"It was a matter of power?" His brow furrowed deeper in a confused frown, a squint of disbelieving. "Are you talking about some sort of political scandal? Was something going on with Stanton?"

"No, you have it all wrong. Mr. Stanton was perfect. They were all rich and clever and well traveled. Edward was handsome. He dressed with sophistication. He had a smooth Harvard accent. He, his parents, were everything I admired."

"Then why did you not—"

"Damn it, don't you see? I was frightened I would trade for all that."

"Trade what?"

It only reached her conscious mind as she laid it out for him: "I was scared to death I was going to marry a man I didn't love. A rich, stylish"—she borrowed a phrase from Amelia Besom—"nincompoop with a nice house and a good background."

She wobbled a minute as she lost her orientation. Tears had filled her eyes right up over the irises and pupils. The apple dropped from her fingers as she tipped her head back. If she could hold off gravity for a minute, the tears would evaporate. "I wanted to marry for love," she said.

Even through the blur of tears, she saw the effect of these words on Nardi's face just above her: His handsome features pulled into a deeply pained expression. *"Tu es courageuse,"* he said finally. She was brave.

"I love you," she answered.

He nodded; he knew. Then he drew her up against his chest till she could hear his heart thump—but could no longer see his face. And this is when the tears silently overflowed the rims of her eyes and ran down onto her cheeks: as Hannah stood there pressed against Nardi, feeling a sudden presentiment, like a shudder, for their future together. She was genuinely fearful for several long seconds.

He could have relieved this by rushing in with words of love and commitment. He did find the words finally, but not before five or six dreadful seconds, the amount of time that made the difference between the right words said at the right moment and the right words delayed in an untimely manner.

He said at last, *"Mon amour,* I never imagined, before I knew you, that a man could feel for a woman what I feel for you." There was another long, indecipherable—terrible— pause, before he continued. "I love you like I love breathing. *Je t'adore. Je t'aime. Je te chéris."* His words came like an avalanche after this. "I want you beside me forever. I want to brush up against you every morning, every evening, and every moment in between and after. *J'ai besoin de toi, chérie, à tout jamais. . . ."* In English and French he whispered words of love, speaking in terms of undying affection and eternity, saying all and more that just seconds before would have reassured her.

But a voice inside Hannah's head began to ask, *So if he loves me so much and wants to be with me forever, why aren't we speaking of marriage?* And, for the first time, she had to admit consciously: Nardi was avoiding this subject. Something was wrong. He didn't love her perfectly. And she couldn't trust him entirely.

Chapter 24

SEABIRDS SET UP a squawk and took to the air—herons and bitterns, petrels and shearwaters, a duck or two, a small flock of swans. Out the cottage's west window, a collection of flapping, calling waterfowl exploded into view as if blown up out of the water, the sky suddenly alive with their numbers. This commotion was followed immediately by a distant roar coming from below the trees down the cliffside.

"Do you hear it?" Nardi asked Hannah that evening just before dinner. He could not recall her ever having been here before at this time of day.

She was sitting on the sofa. She looked over its back at him, to where Nardi sat drawing at the table. Her eyes were introspective, almost vacant; her mind seemed elsewhere. After a moment she said, "What?"

"The *mascaret*." No, in English it was something else. "The bore," he corrected.

"The what?"

"The tidal bore. This close to the Channel, high tide comes in with a, *eh, fanfare*." Nardi put his pencil down. "Do you want to go see it?"

"No." She turned her attention back toward her lap, presumably returning it to the book she held there.

"You should let me show you sometime. *C'est spectaculaire*." Nardi tried to interest her in the noise outside the window by barraging her with everything he knew about it.

"The Seine's estuary onto the Channel is narrow, shaped like a, *euh,* how you call, funnel. The tide changes are huge and abrupt. At the mouth there is a sandbar. When high tide breaks over it, the tide rushes upriver as a nine-foot wall of water, bank to bank, traveling more than ten miles per hour. Ships, boats, barges, everything stops."

Any possible conversation was drowned out by the roar of water below that grew like the surge of a large crowd hurraying and applauding Nardi's little travelogue of river phenomena.

As this din subsided Nardi said, "We can go see it tomorrow."

"Or the next day," Hannah said without looking up. She was not interested.

Nothing interested her the next day, either. She hardly touched her breakfast. Instead of eating—or talking or doing much of anything—she spent the morning either gazing at him with this new, peculiarly deliberating regard or else gazing out one window or another up toward the domes of her beloved château.

These long contemplations of the château at least were not mysterious: Nardi knew about unfinished projects and unmet aspirations, and he accepted that her blue funk would last awhile.

This new and unusual mood of Hannah's didn't make her into the most lively company, but it produced a side result. When, in an attempt to cheer her, Nardi suggested he and she press-gang the whole Swiss crew—Hans, Werner, Stefan, and Emil—into helping move Nardi's old *Rising Venus* from the apple storehouse out into the light where he might look at it better, she became briefly involved. She directed the activity as the five men, with a lot of strain and sweat and ropes thrown over the storehouse rafters, managed to inch the half-ton of marble out the door of the storehouse and into the sunlit orchard. Once this was done, however, Hannah sat right down again and did what she could suddenly do so very well these days: She stared off into space without moving so much as an eyelash.

She became a near-perfect model.

The orchard was bright. Nardi knew that the cottage contained an assortment of chisels, a splitting tool, and a stone-carving hammer. Cutting into this stone seemed inevitable at this point. So he walked back, retrieved the tools, and with them began to chip his way into his old statue, trying to find within it the vision of Hannah his mind could see there.

Three more bores, unnoticed by Hannah so far as Nardi could discern, roared by below them. At the end of which time he was looking at a new face, neck, and shoulders coming up out of the hulking stone. It was an amazing face, full and pretty and vibrant, turned upward, eyes closed, cheeks prominent, full-mouthed: Hannah's face, though no colorless stone could do her full justice. Nonetheless, the work was surprisingly effortless. The statue seemed all but to be recutting itself—which gave Nardi the idea of putting a chisel and hammer into the hands of the figure. By the end of the week, he had roughed out a woman, a beautiful, round, healthy human being, chipping and climbing her way out of her old, gray stone self.

It took exactly this long, one week, for Hannah to leap up off the blanket in the orchard, clap her lovely small hands together, and announce, standing there in only her petticoat, chemise, corset, and corset cover, that she was going to Paris.

"You're what?"

"I'm going to look for work in Paris. There's a big auction house there—I typed and sent all Mrs. Besom's contracts for their fall sale. And there is a slew of smaller dealers and appraisers with whom I have also corresponded personally. They know me. I'll go to Paris, and one of them will hire me."

Nardi was alarmed by the naïveté of this plan. "You don't speak French, Hannah."

But she climbed up onto the old knee of the statue to stand right beside him and reply buoyantly, "But I read and write it fairly well, especially the business vocabulary that has to do with art and antiques." She added, teasing, "And I can sing it—my pronunciation is improving."

"You can't just go to Paris. Where will you live? You know no one."

"I have my commission from *The Separation* sale, almost a year's salary—"

"In Paris this money won't go as far as you think."

She saw through him, to his deepest worry. "Nardi," she said, "Sébastien works in Paris yet spends a great deal of time here. I can, too. I'm not leaving you. I just need to proceed with my life, fix what I can of it, accept what I can't." With this, she threw her arms around his neck, hugged him, then scooted backward off the stone lap of a thickset Venus and went tripping up to the cottage where she began to write a feverish battery of letters.

One fact stood out saliently in Nardi's mind: She'd never asked that he come with her.

He couldn't, of course—not without having Sébastien, Du Gard, and a whole parade of people coming after him.

And then there was the word "accept"; this sounded extremely good.

She knew, he thought. He'd said nothing of his looming nuptials. When Hannah had been depressed, to mention the Du Gard marriage had seemed a ridiculous bit of cruel timing. If she didn't know by now, what could a few more days matter? With her happiness possibly restored, however, Nardi now simply didn't *want* to mention it. She knew, he told himself. That's why she didn't suggest he leave the château or embark on this new adventure with her. As Sébastien kept insisting, Hannah was aware of the limitations of her future with Nardi.

Overall, Nardi told himself, the present was better than he could ever have anticipated. Hannah was content with her new prospects. Moreover, she loved him; he knew it. Meanwhile, the marble flew off his new statue within the statue, as he scattered chips and chunks of marble all over the orchard.

For another eight or ten days Nardi climbed up and down

his statue. He teased Hannah about things French. He read over her letters to Paris for errors, of which there were hardly any, at least so far as he could see. He made love to Hannah in the orchard, in the cottage, and up in the loft of the apple storehouse. Early one evening, he even climbed with her up to the belvedere from where they watched the bore come in over the orchards and butterfly garden.

Nardi felt like a man coming out of a coma.

His emotional existence, like his awakened sexuality, both long thought anesthetized into a permanent numbness, proved to have been merely quiescent, unused, uncalled upon, until now. It wasn't just a matter of feeling alive. Nardi was happy. Nardi could hardly remember what had driven him into exile from himself, into the swamp, the land of ether and forgetfulness. It was there, he knew. A place he didn't want to go. A miasma of unsorted feelings, half-forgotten events, resentments, unresolved umbrages and offense. But he wouldn't think about it now.

Nardi was too content with Hannah and the pleasure of refound productivity. His days were filled with satisfying work. His senses were filled with the woman beside him, with whom he settled in, forever so far as he was concerned, to live as happily ever after as possible—which certainly seemed forever in the limbo reality of a nursery-rhyme cottage at the edge of a fairy-tale castle.

Her letters to Paris began to receive answers. The first three were from small art appraisers who were not interested in hiring an American. But the fourth response was the heartbreaker: The big auction house La Compagnie des Commissaires-Priseurs de Paris was most interested in an affiliate who might deal readily with New York and London. In florid, formal French they wrote to Hannah saying they were most impressed with her listed skills and experience. As soon as they received her references, they would most eagerly schedule an interview, sending until then, *Madame* [sic], their most distinguished sentiments.

"References!" Hannah screamed out. She shredded the letter and threw it into the canal—after which she pronounced that this missive from Paris was actually encouraging. Someone was going to want her abilities, one of the smaller art dealers perhaps, someone more trusting and less stuffy. She would simply keep trying till someone would accept her as she was: "Without references," she lamented, "perpetually without references."

Nardi was somewhat relieved that she didn't ask him to find her some references. Sébastien might have written an impressive letter for her. Sébastien or Pater or one of Pater's or Mater's artsy friends. But had Hannah asked Nardi to do this for her, he would have been put in a bind again. Sébastien had taken him aside: Du Gard's daughter had complained to Papa. Hannah had become That Woman who was suddenly starting to make everyone, even Sébastien, a bit nervous. "All mistresses," Sébastien advised his younger brother, "have their tenure of usefulness. Hers is almost at an end. Get rid of her. We don't want you marching down the aisle with her clinging to your ankle."

Nardi intended neither to get rid of Hannah nor for her to become a problem when it came to the business of family marriages.

Because she knew. She knew. She accepted. There was no problem here at all.

Nardi had convinced himself of this so thoroughly that he responded with utter innocence and honesty when Hannah rose up naked off his chest, looked him in his face, and said, "I would marry you if you asked me."

He smiled and answered, "And I would ask you if I could."

Her face went brutally still.

Only then did his mind allow him to see it: her surprise as the riverbed of her ignorance was flooded suddenly with the high tide of her horror. He felt himself groping, tumbling backward on explanations he hadn't made, hadn't offered, like a man being pitched and carried, sobbing and choking on the volume of all he hadn't said, a regular tidal bore of self-deception and silence.

"You're married," she said flatly.

"No." The relief on her face was short-lived. He added, "Not yet."

Then, staring straight up into her dark, round eyes above him, he explained as best and succinctly as possible. He told her about Du Gard, the families, the château, the expenses, the clinic, and ultimately of the marriage that was supposed to bring all this into a harmonious whole, ending with, *"Dieu au ciel,* I thought you knew"—he changed his words more honestly to—"no, I hoped you knew. Sébastien said you did."

She shoved him in the chest. "And since when did you start believing Sébastien?"

A good point.

She got up. "I *did* know. I knew there was something. It just never occurred to me that it was this insulting." She snatched up her knickers from the floor.

"Mais non, Hannah—"

"Mais oui, you—you—" She shook her underwear at him, berating him as she stood there naked. "What did you imagine, Nardi? That I would live down here at this cottage while you kept house with this, this—your new bride up at the château?"

Nardi frowned. He must have thought something like this. But he thought it best to put on an innocent face, blank, as if nothing like such an arrangement had ever occurred to him and say, "No, Hannah—"

"Mais oui," she said again, "that's what you thought." She thrust her legs into her knickers and yanked them up. "You stupid—" She was still looking for a name contemptuous enough. She found one: "Frenchman." She grabbed up her skirt and blouse.

"Where are you going?"

"To the train station."

"Are you coming back?"

"I don't know."

"What do you expect me to do?" he asked. "I cannot undo what was done before I met you."

She glared down at herself—she was so angry she had put her knickers on backward. Irately she shoved them down, stepped out, then started over. "You could tell her no," she suggested.

He pulled a face and took a cheap shot. "Or find her best friend and sleep with her."

Phew, would he have loved to have taken that one back! Hannah charged him, tripping over her own half-down knickers, then making the most of her fall by clearing the entire surface of the nightstand over onto him—coins, drawing pencils, packaged condoms, her dictionary, as well as a solid brass reading lamp. This was followed by her own small body propelled by the force of her fury. She knocked him backward and landed on top of him. "You lied!" She clipped him soundly in the ear before he could get a firm hold on her.

"I never lied. I just did not say." He narrowly blocked a knee to the groin then rolled over onto her.

"The same thing."

If Nardi had ever thought holding a woman a foot shorter and sixty pounds lighter than he would be easy, Hannah beneath him altered this opinion forever. He tussled with small but highly energetic elbows, fists, and flailing knees, while catching several blows of heel bone in his backside, a particularly sharp one striking him on his coccyx. *"Arrête! Hannah, stop."* Nardi gave up, standing on his knees, containing her limbs as best he could long enough to pull away from her tantrum.

She sat on her shins to throw a pillow at him. "You piece of *merde*!" Through her fierce anger, however, he could see something else: a profound disillusion. "How could you?" she murmured. "You let me love you when I have no future." Her lower lip came out, then pulled up tightly to her upper one.

"You have a future," he said.

"Yes, the future every mean person ever predicted for me—a strumpet's future. No marriage, no home, no children. No mate of my own. You have treated me abominably."

His chest tightened. He shook his head. "No—"

"Yes. You could not have done anything to have injured me more." Her lower lip, secure against her teeth, nonetheless began to tremble slightly. "I thought you wanted me," she murmured.

"I do." This sounded hollow. "I don't want to hurt you, Hannah." Stupid, callous, contrived; how many times had he said this to a woman? This was all sounding like the end of a dozen affairs in Paris, and the notion *end* petrified him. "I love you," he said. More words. His head buzzed with them, English ones, French ones, but not a one that seemed to say appropriately how he felt.

Then suddenly words occurred to him that would mean something "*Oui,* you're right. I want you forever, Hannah, for my own. I won't marry her. I will tell them."

It was that easy. So easy. Too easy to say this, another thing of course to follow through with such a promise. But he meant it.

He continued, "It won't be neat, but I will get out of it somehow and marry you—that is what you want, is it not?"

Now she was speechless. She clutched the sheets to her for an instant, then nodded vigorously. "Oh, yes." She scrambled off the bed and flung herself at him, hugging him. And with her there against him, his arms around her, the mess he'd just opened up before him didn't matter. He would brave it for her. He would indeed find a way. Because he loved this woman so much he could not imagine life without her.

Hannah spent that day in a state of euphoria. Almost twenty-four hours passed in a bright blur—through which she watched Nardi chew on his pencils. He would find a way to unravel everyone else's plans for him. He was brave and clever and handsome and funny and kind and wonderful. She adored him. Oh yes, Nardi de Saint Vallier was just about everything that thrilled her. Except for one tiny little thing that had occurred to her by the following morning.

Over the breakfast tray, she said, "If you don't marry this woman from Paris, you'll be poor, won't you?"

Nardi stopped in midmotion, his coffee cup halfway to his mouth. "So you are saying you *want* me to marry her?"

"I want you to marry me and be *rich*."

He laughed, took a swallow of coffee, and set the cup down. "Then you will have to earn, inherit, or steal a fortune. Because without this marriage, neither I nor my family have enough money even to meet next month's bills." He shrugged. "That is little problem, though. I can go back to tombstones for a while. I can make enough money to make ends meet with that, at least for us. We won't starve."

He continued, "I have an atelier in Paris. I own it. We can live there. I have a friend who owes me money. We will buy a larger bed. I can earn food money with a little left over for other expenses. The problem, though, is I seem to owe Georges Du Gard a lot of money, as does my family. I don't know how he will accept payment or what he will want. . . ." Nardi went on, but Hannah didn't hear him precisely.

Their financial situation struck her with all the force of, well, a comeuppance. She had not exactly envisioned a rich life with Nardi, but she had foreseen perhaps an easy one. A life lived with fancy alpaca coats, armloads of pastries, pretty petticoats, and both of them doing pretty much what they wanted, not simply what was required to eke out an existence.

Of course, work had never bothered her. She could work; they could both work. They would do fine. It was just, she told herself, that this new perspective on life with Nardi required some adjustment on her part. Nonetheless, at that moment some nasty, materialistic little part of her sat there, up in arms like a child at Christmas who, having seen a terrific display the night before, had awoken to find every present, every luxury, with someone else's name on it.

Nardi continued, "Financially we will do the best we can. Du Gard may try to ruin us—and may succeed to some extent." He laughed. "But then, for a while at least, there won't be much to ruin. And we shall be together no matter what."

Yes, Hannah thought. Together. This was a wonderful thought. Though the previous concept—ruin—was not one that appealed to her very much. Together in ruin.

Ruin. Wasn't this something she'd been trying to avoid all her life?

Chapter 25

NARDI HAD NO trouble in getting to see Du Gard. Sébastien was only too happy to put him on the train again, this time with only one single admonishment to guard him through his journey: "Don't aggravate Du Gard, Nardi," Sébastien warned. "Not a word about how you'd like to keep your little American *donzelle*. And no words of reluctance about the marriage itself. You know what you have to do, so do it with grace, will you?"

Ho, mais oui, Nardi could do that all right. In Paris, he sat through a noonday meal with the Du Gard family, after which he asked Georges Du Gard if he could speak to him privately. The two men retired to a large library lined with books, floor to ceiling, wall-to-wall, every spine of every book gleaming of new, embossed leather—not a book visible that looked to have been held in the hand for longer than it took to shelve it. In a cozy corner of these well-furnished shelves, Nardi sat down into a brass-nailed Cordovan wing chair across from Du Gard, resting his anklebone to his knee, and began with, "I can't marry Marie. Our marrying was a terrible idea from the start."

He explained that he wanted to breach his promise, that he knew there were legalities involved, that he was willing to make restitution, take full responsibility, do whatever was necessary.

Du Gard's reaction was livid and to the point. "I don't

wish to renegotiate a bargain for something I have already bought and paid for." The man was speaking of *him*, Nardi realized. From within a cloud of black cigar smoke, Du Gard declared, "I cleaned you up for my daughter, not for some interloping stranger. You will marry my Marie or spend the rest of your life regretting you haven't."

Nardi had hoped for a more reasonable discussion, but left feeling he had done his best. The disentanglement had begun, and he knew it was going to get rougher.

Late that evening Hannah was bent over the table at the cottage, scratching out more letters that requested employment in Paris. She still daydreamed about this city she'd never seen. The beauty of it. The possibilities. Paris was where great thinkers could rouse public conscience with boldness; *j'accuse*. It was a place where a woman could discover radium. Or write great novels while living unmarried with a great composer. Or where monocled gentlemen tipped their hats in stylish manner, even toward women who laughed and danced the cancan. There had to be a position in the French capital. This city, she was sure, would accept her.

Hannah's mind ran to these thoughts as she wrote and la-di-da'ed to the phonograph playing in the background. She wrote her letters between sips of fresh warm milk that she drank directly from the farm jug, while she picked at a dinner of late strawberries, fresh black currants, and a small heart-shaped cheese that lay on a straw mat. She was content enough, writing, nibbling, humming, while listening with one ear, as she had been for hours, waiting for Nardi's return. She sat in her nightgown, wrapped in his coat that smelled faintly of bay from the shaving soap he used.

She knew him by the sound coming down through the woods, his walk, his way of moving. She knew, without looking up, when he came in. He lifted the needle off the phonograph cylinder, and the cottage become quiet, just the chirp of cicadas at hand and the distant, low rush of the river current.

She asked, "How did it go?" as she wrote out the last sentence.

Nardi came over, took a drink of her milk, then his fingers took her pen away. He leaned onto his hands over the tabletop, kissed her forehead as she looked up at him, and asked, "How daring are you, Hannah?"

Hannah blinked, shrugged, and stared blankly. "How daring for what?"

He told her, "If you are willing, we can be married tomorrow morning."

She rose partway out of her chair. "What? How—"

"We have to leave tonight." When she glanced out apprehensively into the dark, he reached over, returning her face toward him. "*Ne t'en fais pas.* We go up through the woods, around the château, and down into the village. There is a train for Paris at nine-fifteen. We get on it, leave no word, nothing, tell no one, just disappear. In Paris we go directly to a magistrate. We can send word to whomever tomorrow or the next day, after the fact. Sébastien, the rest, of course, will be in an uproar over what we do, but one thing at least will be *irréversible:* We will be man and wife. And this will put an end *définitivement* to everyone else's designs for us."

"You are suggesting an e-elopement?" Hannah asked hesitantly. Yes, of course he was! The idea dawned with simple brilliance. "To Paris no less," she said. What a perfect, crazy—and incredibly romantic—solution!

"*Oui,* would you like that?" Nardi laughed as he came round the table.

Would she *like* this? Would she like running off to marry the man she adored? In the city of her dreams? Hannah rose up onto her toes and embraced Nardi while he slid his palms down either side of her spine to the small of her back and pressed. A moment later he was kissing her mouth, holding the back of her head with one hand as with his other arm he pushed a clatter of milk jug, berry bowl, and cheese mat down the table, laying her backward onto her letters.

Nardi took his own coat from her shoulders, lifting her slightly as he slid her nightgown up over her hips. And the blood in Hannah's veins lit. Her brain quieted in a wonderful, strange way; unthinking, unblinking. She wrapped her legs around him, her hands round the backs of his arms. Taking him down on top of her was always akin to coming in at winter to a fire: not knowing how cold she'd been till she felt the sudden warmth, staring into the source of this warmth till her mind ceased to function. Lord, how she loved this man. When he lay his hand on her bare belly, it was like rolling over to press her abdomen onto the hot bricks inside the hollow of a fireplace. Home. Or like a cinder log dropping onto her—Nardi opened his trousers. He covered her, pulling his weight up onto his elbows. In the process, above Hannah's head, something clanged over the edge of the table to thud then roll, a liquid gurgle of milk pouring out onto the floor. Nardi must have put his hand in the cheese at the same time, because he licked three fingers, and in the next instant his mouth tasted bloomy of moussy cheese and soft mold.

Hannah clung to him as he entered her, the little table wobbling under them. She arched but kept her eyes open narrowly, watching Nardi as he rose straight-armed above her to an exquisite elevation of angle, then from here, eyes open or not, she saw nothing more, heard nothing. There was only pure, abstract longing, dancing light, licking, leaping . . . no self, no remedy but to burn . . . only heat in her brain that hissed, that whispered, Oh how she longed to be close to this man, how much she wanted him for her mate, her equal. . . .

An hour later, as Hannah boarded the night express with Nardi, then shot toward Paris, she felt stunned by the speed of events. Her senses of reality and romanticism mingled, interchangeable. Everything seemed to be happening so fast, she couldn't sort it all out. She was left in the throes of something faintly dreamlike, an ecstatic state. Thus, it was that in a blur of bliss—real, romantic, or otherwise— Hannah became Madame Bernard de Saint Vallier in a French magistrate's office on the rue Rivoli in the year 1903, August 26, at eleven-thirty in the morning.

* * *

Nardi's apartment sat at the top of a steep, narrow street in a block of row houses in a north section of Paris called Montmartre. As he stuck his key into the front door, he told Hannah, "It's not elegant." Yet, as pleased with himself as she had ever seen him, he said, *"Et voilà,"* and he opened the door. "Comfortable, no? And very, *euh, spacieux?*"

"Spacious," she confirmed, and stepped inside.

This was an understatement. Nardi's Paris apartment would have been spacious for a barn. It consisted of a large ground-floor room with a railed sleeping loft above, the main floor area looking like what it was, a larger than usual artist's studio, rawly furnished. Simple. Ascetic. The two or three chairs appeared to be used more as shelving for chisels and gouges. There were two more chassis. One wall had a series of framed sketches on it; not Nardi's—thick lines of more abstract images than he rendered. Beyond this, it was impossible to tell if the walls were painted, papered, or just plastered: They were covered with tacked-up sketches that were indisputably the work of Nardi's pencils and pens. On the floor, stone bits were everywhere, mixed liberally with dirt and dust balls. The place seemed to be missing a kitchen. There was only a cookstove on a wood table in the corner.

When Hannah had to use the toilet facilities, she found her new home to be also lacking something else she considered vital. "This isn't the toilet," she said when she opened the basement door that Nardi had indicated to her.

"Si, si, it is."

"It's a hole in the ground, Nardi." With the doorknob still in her hand, Hannah faced into what seemed to be about a three-foot-square pitch-black little closet, in the floor of which was a small, foul-smelling pit dug in the dirt beneath the building's foundation.

"Oui, c'est—euh—it is a—ah—Turkish toilet. Just aim over it."

Hannah shuddered and did what was necessary, leaving the door open for light and fresh air. When she came out again, she asked hesitantly, "And a bath? Where do you bathe?"

Nardi smiled and announced triumphantly, "This is one of the reasons I bought this apartment." She stared dumbfounded at his good cheer when he said, "The public bathhouse is only three doors down. It is very convenient."

Hannah tried to be positive. "You own this apartment?"

"*Oui*, I bought it about ten years ago." He made a face. "It was one of the things on which Sébastien felt I had 'squandered' my money. But, Hannah, it is worth something." He cocked his head, smiling ruefully this time. "If you don't like it, we can sell it and buy something else." His smile became fond. "Or we can put in a toilet chair and sewage plumbing, once we get a little more money."

Hannah nodded, returning his smile faintly. "Now, there's something to look forward to."

He laughed. "It is not that bad really." He took her hand. "*Viens*. I want to show you something."

She followed, trying to hide her unease over the drastic difference between this place and . . . well, whatever it was that she had imagined as Nardi's life in Paris. Whatever it was, it had not been this, not this variety of . . . genteel squalor.

He led her up the spiral stairway to the loft then cleared off the single bedside table, moving it out, then stood on it. He reached overhead to open the attic door that turned out to fold down into a hinged ladder. "Up you go," he said as he stepped down himself and held out his hand.

As Hannah ascended into the dark, musty overhead space, she vaguely discerned shapes beneath sloping rafters. She could hear pigeons cooing under the eaves outside as she came partway into the attic, her feet to the top of the ladder. Her eyes adjusted. Then what came into view amazed her.

A moment later Nardi was standing on the step below her feet. As he put his arms around her he brought a gas lamp across her shoulder to set it at her elbow just inside the attic. The room lit.

"This, I think," Nardi murmured at her ear, "is the way we are going to manage."

The room was filled with statues, a regular salon gathering of marble people, horses, gladiators, lions, and centaurs.

"It was the last exhibit," he said. "The one everyone hated, minus of course the *Rising Venus*. My uncle bought that—because it was the worst, I think." He laughed. "Of course, some of the rest here are still *terrible*. But some of it is not bad either. I was always very sorry that, because some of it was ghastly, all of it was rejected in general. And now of course I am almost happy there are some really bad pieces—it gives me marble I could not otherwise afford." He kissed the nape of her neck. "With which I can now make more Hannahs. *On va regarder?*" Do we go up and look?

They both crawled up, then passed the lantern between them to better see a stone face or the stone lateral muscles atop bestial stone hindquarters. Some were truly fabulous, so far as Hannah could see. She murmured, "Well, Amelia Besom doesn't know everything, does she?" Stopped at the near-divine face of a Diana in repose, she said with wonder, "How could she have missed this?"

Nardi clicked his tongue smugly. *"Précisément,"* he said. "Which is why I want you to manage the showing and selling for me."

"What?" Hannah bent under a stone arm to come up against Nardi in the crowded quarters.

Nardi explained, "I would be terrible at organizing it or arranging for galleries or selling it or doing anything with it." He shrugged. "I just don't have the interest or possibly even the ability. You do it, Hannah. It won't be selling old art or antiques, but it has to be similar. Even some of the contacts and buyers must be the same, plus I know some places you can go." He added, "And if you are successful, I have friends who would probably like you to sell their work as well. You can charge a commission." He laughed into her ear as he whispered, "I would be happy to give you a good reference."

He continued, "We can take a good bit of abuse financially from Du Gard with the profits from this. We can live off the rest if we are frugal. I have few material wants beyond what you see here. When this all settles, I would love dearly if there were enough to buy you diamonds." He murmured to her, "I know you want a rich life, Hannah. I would have been able to give it to you once—if I had found you sooner or if I had been less foolish or if fate had spared me and given me enemies less ambitious or shrewd than Georges Du Gard and my brother."

In the musty dark of the attic, Hannah felt heartened at last. And so very impressed with the real Nardi de Saint Vallier. He might not be a prince, but he was heroic: a man ready to face his nemesis, all that had worn him down before. Better than the fancy trousers and pretty coats that had once impressed her, this man had a magnificent fortitude.

When they stepped down into the bed loft again, they noticed some less aesthetic works by Bernard de Saint Vallier propped against the loft railing: rough but complete tombstones. Nardi was annoyed to discover these. Someone was supposed to have picked them up then paid him for them ages ago. But of course: His life had been interrupted so thoroughly that such details had fallen down into the huge cracks. He took them over that night to the fellow who had wanted them—and was paid enough money to buy dinner and groceries.

The next morning, however, he had more on his mind than mere daily survival. "Time for more daring," he said. The gentlest way to begin the battle that lay before them, he felt, was to take it on directly. "I want to introduce my new wife to my mother and father."

Nardi's father was "napping." His mother met them in the grand salon of a fabulously elegant home in an area of Paris considerably more homogeneous than Montmartre.

Nardi introduced Hannah then set her into a sofa that seemed to breathe out puffs of comfort. Hannah sank into cushions that were lighter than feathers.

Meanwhile Madame de Saint Vallier, the elder, never for a moment flinched or seemed the least bit discomposed, though she was by no means pleased with her new daughter-in-law. She said, "We thought you had done something like this, Nardi," as she touched his cheek then sat opposite them.

Nardi took Hannah's hand into his as his mother began in French. He interrupted, "Hannah does not understand French perfectly. I wish to speak to you in English."

His mother smile patronizingly, then began in the perfect, slightly accented English of a woman who had married a statesman. "Nardi," she said, "you have always been my most beautiful, most talented child—and perhaps the least practical man on the face of the earth. You cannot marry this young woman."

"I already have."

"Don't be infantile."

He smiled politely. "I have never felt more adult."

"Then insane."

"Nor more sane." He added, "Or more happy."

She scowled briefly. "Well, now I *know* you are mad. You yourself set this other very suitable marriage into motion. Everyone, as you fully realize, has money—nearly everything—invested in the outcome. Enormous amounts. And, well, if we were only talking about money, anything might be possible, you see, dear"—she smiled again, again condescending—"but, well, we are talking about principle. Monsieur Du Gard has invested his pride, inviting more than six hundred witnesses to what he considers the social coup of the century. It is pure, rash insanity for you to tell me you are throwing all this over to—to marry some foreign shop girl." She glanced at Hannah, as if Hannah were a green sofa cushion. "I mean, she is a pretty little thing, Nardi, but really, darling—"

Nardi's hand tightened about Hannah's fingers, while Hannah herself felt a sense of angry disillusion that was beginning to feel familiar. Another myth destroyed: another snob who again, in a stunningly thorough way, right in Hannah's own ears, was willing to reduce her to nothing.

This was not supposed to happen in Paris.

The brief interview apparently over, Madame de Saint Vallier rose. "I'm going to call Sébastien," she said. "You sit right here. Sébastien can straighten all this out. Don't you worry."

Nardi and Hannah left while hearing her in a nearby room turn the crank of a telephone, then ask the operator for the Aubrignon post office telephone exchange.

"You mustn't fret," Nardi told Hannah. "Mater is flustered. And she is always nasty. This has gone almost as expected. Sébastien will be on the next train from Aubrignon or the one after."

Chapter 26

When the gods wish to punish us, they answer our prayers.

—Oscar Wilde

SURPRISINGLY, SEBASTIEN DID not arrive for two weeks.

In the meantime the rightness of taking Hannah for his wife settled on Nardi with all the certainty of a ballast. He knew what he wanted from life and felt he had it: a companion he adored, whom he enjoyed championing, both emotionally and as best he could financially, and who championed him in his own enterprises that were becoming increasingly more absorbing and meaningful.

As to Hannah, she adored him right back, though less and less for the reasons she had once thought she would. In fact, her love for Nardi became something of a puzzle to her. His hands were often filthy from work. Unlike the poet or revolutionary or prince of her dreams, he more often than not smelled of sweat and dust and polishing oil. He argued with her over who had the time to go out and buy a much-needed broom—when her neat, clean dreams never needed a broom, and her prince never disputed anything but always met her every expressed desire. In her dreams Hannah had drunk champagne—without worrying that her prince, if he took a sip, ran the risk of getting and staying mindlessly inebriated. She had dream-dined in fancy res-

343

taurants on dream-dinners of pleasant and roasted new potatoes while wearing feathered hats and flouncy dresses. In dreams she'd never sat on the floor in her underclothes eating black sausage and bread for dinner while discussing with her beloved how they would pay for breakfast tomorrow.

Hannah and Nardi's finances were a disaster. Nardi sold two more tombstones, though he wasn't paid for them or even for one from the last batch. It was normal, apparently, that the man who commissioned them only paid Nardi as the stones were sold. So Nardi and Hannah more or less lived off her money, which dwindled at an alarming rate: Everything—from food to brooms to ointment for a cut on the sole of Hannah's foot acquired by stepping on a splinter of marble—cost *beaucoup* francs in the French capital.

Moreover, Paris itself was not exactly as Hannah had imagined. Oh, it had wide boulevards all right and squares abloom with flowers. But Paris also had beggars, dirty women with babies in one arm, their other hand held out, unshaven men who leaned at street corners eyeing greedily the baguette of bread one carried. The sanitation of some areas was odorously abominable. And of course there seemed as much human intolerance here as anywhere, right down to Hannah's new mother-in-law being the haughtiest woman Hannah had ever laid eyes on. Moreover, the city was quieter than Hannah had imagined. Shop after shop kept their awnings down.

"It is August," Nardi explained. "Most Parisians are on holiday during this month of the year. They close up and leave the city. The place will come alive again in September."

Hannah found Paris to be, like love itself perhaps, teeming with contradictions, beautiful yet more gritty than anticipated, with easier, gayer times postponed.

It was normal, she told herself, that she should occasionally miss her old dreams, even as she knew herself to be slowly replacing them with new, more realistic, more splendidly vivid expectations: She reveled in the growing intimacy between herself and her new husband, the sexual being metaphorical for the emotional. She was aware that she laughed with Nardi a great deal. Small achievements—finding a fresh chicken, for instance, in a shop only a ten-minute walk away—became a double triumph when she shared them with him. Worries—when she voiced them—seemed cut in half, shared out between two, instead of hoarded by one. And of course plans, devised together, made for new prospects, new dreams.

There is an apartment available on rue Levec.

One with a toilet chair?

Oui, and a bath and a closet off the bedroom that could be tortured into a nursery if necessary. I would have to rent a studio elsewhere, but the kitchen is large; I could work there till I find one. You could work off the table in the dining alcove. We could eat sitting on the floor for a while longer.

Of course, there were anxieties Hannah didn't dare name, not even to herself. There were moments when she felt turned around by all the upheaval in her life. She was, at these moments, at the mercy of the most flighty, dithery aspects of own personality. Hannah was coming to understand that not only was Nardi not exactly as she had imagined, love itself was different from what she'd thought. The emotion she felt for him was almost frightening; it felt tenuous, not at all solid, not even precisely definable. There were times when she wished for her old dreams back, when material accomplishment seemed so certain, so graspable. Living with, and loving, her dear, funny, talented, handsome husband was like living perpetually three feet off the ground, while looking down endlessly, fretting over the loss of gravity.

It was a time of flux for Hannah, a time when she knew herself to be caught in the unsettling hiatus between an old life and a new one.

It was on the Friday of the second week of this confused wedded bliss that a loud noise awakened her and Nardi;

both she and he ended up bent over the loft railing looking down: And there was Sébastien.

"The door was unlocked," he said, already in their apartment—standing in its ecstatic, unstable atmosphere so well represented in reality by the mess and commotion of the downstairs itself.

Nardi's studio, which necessarily doubled as their parlor, dining room, and kitchen, was impossible to keep neat, for no sooner did Hannah (dragooning Nardi into being help-mate) have the mess swept up than Nardi was suddenly slinging chunks of rock all over it again while she herself was piling up letters, dictionaries, and lists of potential temporary employers.

As Hannah and Nardi came down the stairs, Sébastien, in high hat and sporting an attaché case, took note of their disordered lives with one quick perusal of high-browed disgust.

He himself, in fact, did not look so very fine. Once he removed his hat, Hannah could see dark circles beneath his eyes. If anything, his mien was too tidy, his collar starched to the stiffness of pasteboard, his hair slicked back with enough pomade to subjugate locks considerably less unruly than his own—Hannah realized for the first time that Sébastien's hair was slightly curly. His eyes had a glassy shine, as if from a slight fever. His movement itself was abrupt. He marched through the debris, around a tomb monument, to their little table, which he rid of the cookstove and a letter of Hannah's, moving these to the floor, then set his case on the empty surface.

He had to clear his throat twice then cough into his rolled hand before speaking. "The two of you will want to see these," he said as he unfastened the latch of the case. He pulled out a half-inch stack of what looked like legal documents, organizing these for a moment before pulling a ladder-back chair around. Sébastien the lawyer sat on this as he put on his glasses.

"Nardi," he began, "these are dated in April." He handed the first few sheets off his stack across the table.

Nardi took them, standing, while offering Hannah the only other chair.

His brother continued. "They are certificates from three doctors, two outside physicians plus the admitting doctor from the clinic in Zurich, stating that the confused mind of one Bernard de Saint Vallier rendered impossible his own consent to hospitalization, that said treatment included constant surveillance and was immediately imperative for the mental well-being of the patient to the extent that it warranted physical force and incarceration." He handed over another wad of papers. "These are the admission documents that put you in the hands of the clinic, *sur demande d'un tiers,* that is, on request of a third interested party, your family. Pater signed them. We have here" —more papers—"the necessary renewals." Sébastien looked up over the tops of his reading glasses, first at Hannah then back to Nardi. "The loss of personal liberty is a serious matter and is by law reviewed periodically. You will notice the last renewal, dated three weeks ago, pronounced you still mentally unstable.

"Mental incompetence was really just a formality." He brought forth another paper. "It wasn't difficult to convince the panel of judges, considering I had a doctor whose clinic you'd set afire, an orderly whose hand you'd slammed in a door, and a barber who swore you'd tried to slit his throat. So here you are"—he handed over another sheet of paper— "*inhabile,* that is to say, mentally incompetent. You realize, of course, this renders you incapable of entering into any legally binding contract, including that of marriage."

He stopped here for a moment to let what he had just said sink in. Then he dealt out two more pages off the top of the pile, launching these individually, one toward Nardi, one toward Hannah, with the maddening sang-froid of a casino dealer who played this game, all stakes, all comers, and won often. "This writ, in the name of your family, Nardi, declares you to be a single man, never married, denying all claims that Mademoiselle Van Evan might make. The two of you are not man and wife. You never were, since your difficulties predate your marriage."

Hannah's world seemed to drift for a moment. Behind her, Nardi swore softly. From several minutes hereafter, she could only piece together threads of conversation. Nardi cursed additionally, saying emphatic things to his brother in French. This was accompanied by a flurry of papers. It rained papers—over Hannah, over Sébastien, papers scattering, fluttering—Nardi must have thrown them.

As the last of this storm floated down, a gentle zigzag float of papers, Nardi asked in English, "How can you do this, Sébastien?"

His brother answered, "I can do it because I believe, in the long run, it is the best for everyone, even for you, Nardi—" Sébastien broke off, flinching as if preparing for a blow.

Nardi, however, had only leaned forward, his palms onto the tabletop. "You presumptuous, controlling son of—"

"Don't be childish." Sébastien smiled slightly. He was goading his brother.

For a split second the muscles of Nardi's arms, in steep profile, tightened, the clench of his jaw worked into a knot, and Hannah thought Sébastien might get the blow he was expecting. Or worse. Nardi was taller than his brother, nearly as heavy—and truly furious. Also, Sébastien was not his usual self. He coughed again, turning away from his brother's nose-to-nose anger to cover his mouth with the top of his fist.

During which time, surprisingly, Nardi drew back, letting out a long loud sigh. Both Sébastien and Hannah looked at him when he said in a perfectly rational voice, "What am I to do with you? I'm not going to let you run my life again, yet I can't seem to get completely free of you either."

Sébastien blinked over his raised fist, coughed again, then blustered inappropriately, "Now, see here, you must calm yourself. Your anger—"

"I am not angry," Nardi said, "just frustrated." He sighed again, adding, "I am not twelve any longer, Sébastien. I

simply don't need for you to do or decide what is 'best' for
me."

Sébastien seemed more puzzled than anything else, a man
prepared fully for a violent argument that was not going to
take place.

"So," Nardi said, "can you tell me, as my lawyer and
brother, just how I am supposed to reclaim my mental
competence?"

Sébastien sat back, appraising the situation. He offered,
"Well, you could try to get the doctor who knows your
circumstances best to sign the necessary papers and appear
in court on your behalf."

"The doctor from Switzerland."

"Yes."

"Whose clinic I half burned down?"

"Any other qualified physician would want to observe
you for a time before claiming to be familiar enough with
your problems to state that they are resolved."

"They would want to put me in another clinic?"

"Without Du Gard's money, it would be a public asylum."

Nardi let out a breath, then looked at Hannah, biting his
lips together for a moment. He asked her, "Well, *chérie*,
what do you think I should do?"

She didn't know. "How would you feel about being
locked away again?"

Nardi told her, "I would hate it. But it would be better
than being locked for a lifetime into a marriage I did not
choose. And when I came out, I could marry you again. You
should know, Hannah, that I would marry you over and
over, as many times as it takes to make the world see I love
you."

This should have brought a kind of peace, a calm to
Hannah, but it was here that the real devastation began.

Sébastien sat back in his chair, dabbing his forehead with
his handkerchief. He had begun to perspire slightly. There
was a look on his face, a strategy, that assessed them both
for a moment, then he said, "May I make a suggestion?"
When neither Hannah nor Nardi objected, he continued.

"Come to the wedding as planned. We will have the doctor sign the papers there just before the marriage. Then, when you get to the significant question, if you still do not wish to marry Marie Du Gard, simply answer no." He shrugged. "What could be easier?"

When Nardi and Hannah both cast a dubious look at what was too easy a solution, he smiled. "I'm betting you will say yes," he said. "For, you see, I have a further offer." He folded his arms over his chest. "Mademoiselle Van Evan, Sotheby's, London, is looking for someone to manage their dealings with an estate in Brussels. I have taken the liberty of securing you a few letters." He dealt the last several sheets off his pile of papers.

Hannah stared down at three letters in English, all written to one of the most prestigious auction houses in Europe. The first was from Sébastien himself. He explained her function and triumphs at the Château d'Aubrignon, extolling her abilities in florid language. Another effusive letter was from one of the buyers at the auction, the buyer of *The Separation,* if Hannah wasn't mistaken. The third letter was actually a certificate from the president of the Republic of France saying that Hannah had been instrumental in preserving rare French heritage and culture. Hannah looked at this one twice. The president of France "applauded" her "unstinting devotion to the resurrection and maintenance, through private means, of irreplaceable French history."

References. Hannah was holding in her hand the most glowing references a person could ever hope to possess.

Sébastien continued, "I assure you, mademoiselle, you have the job in London, if you want it. Or you can choose not to work at all for the rest of your life. I have been authorized to set up an account for you that will yield eight hundred American dollars a year interest. I am also to see you outfitted with new clothes and accessories suitable to this income, as well as to buy you a vehicle—a carriage or motorcar—of your choice. Can you drive a motorcar, Mademoiselle Van Evan?"

"A motorcar," Hannah repeated blankly. She shook her head no.

"Well, I can leave the one outside for you as well as Monsieur Du Gard's chauffeur, who will teach you to drive, if you'd like. Of course, all this comes with a string attached—though not so bad a string as you might think, so don't nobly reject all this outright."

Sébastien turned toward Nardi. "Which brings me to you. We have found something of your doing, I believe, out in the apple orchard at the château. It is most impressive, Nardi. Amelia Besom went quite mad over it." He glanced at Hannah again. "Are you familiar with Michelangelo's *concetto* theory, Mademoiselle Van Evan?"

Hannah shook her head again no. She wasn't thinking too clearly. She didn't know what she knew at this point.

"Well, the good signor Buonarroti believed that the idea for a sculpture was alive inside the stone, put there by God or whomever, already extant before the sculptor ever picked up his chisel. The good sculptor is only a clear-sighted one, he claimed, who can see inside the stone to the living concept, which he frees by chipping away what doesn't belong to it." Sébastien smiled at his brother. "It was a brilliant idea, Nardi," he continued, "your stone Hannah chiseling her way out of the old stiff figure." He nodded to Hannah. "And she is lovely. Active, living, with incredible muscular tension and energy. We are going to call her The Concetto: *The True Venus Rising*. Amelia expects it to bring a fortune. Oh, and I should mention that Du Gard is not making a fuss over your destroying the original piece, which of course belonged to the estate. You hammered away on his statue, you know. But all is forgiven—we are merely reclaiming the new statue as the old in a new form.

"You will be happy to know that we will give you full credit for doing it, Nardi. Du Gard, in fact, is so thrilled that, if the wedding goes well, he wants to finance some exhibits. Nardi, all your former glory lies before you. You can have back what you miss most—acclaim and a measure of unqualified praise."

Nardi laughed. "Minus the Muse who allowed it to happen."

Hannah sat up straight as she realized what he might think. "Nardi," she said, "my timing may be terrible, but I must tell you: I did nothing. You saved yourself, as you said you would. Whatever has appeared in the stone came from inside you. It materialized because *you* opened your eyes, because of how *you* look at the world."

Nardi held her regard a moment, then let his gaze fall.

There in a shabby, barnlike apartment smelling faintly of Turkish hygiene, Sébastien began to enumerate his "strings," as he called them. "And for all this great good, all the two of you need do is to try it all on for the two weeks before the wedding, see how it all fits for size. You can ask for changes, other things you might desire that we didn't think of. Then, if either one of you chooses to accept, all you need promise is that each of you will never go within five miles of the other for the rest of your life. Beyond this five-mile radius, the world will be your oyster. We can work out the details later." He held out his hands, satisfied with himself, smiling.

Nardi looked at Hannah and said, "I think you should try it, Hannah. I know you have been disappointed about the money, the apartment, with Paris itself." He added, "Perhaps even with me, *chérie*. You should try it, learn to drive the motorcar at least. I can see you doing that. It is the sort of thing you would like."

Hannah didn't know what Nardi meant by telling her this. She knew there were aspects of his own life that he might have wished otherwise. She knew she was imperfect, that she sent him out for brooms, made him sweep up stone chips when he didn't want to, that she made him look for new apartments when he was happy with his old. She wished for his earlier attitude, that he would swear again that he loved her and would marry her over and over, even if she didn't have a father who wanted to bring all of France to its knees in front of his statue.

But Nardi only sat there, silently staring down at his own

hand, a hand that ever so delicately, one finger out, pressed a crease into the trousers Hannah hadn't had—and probably never would have—the time or inclination to iron.

For a dozen more days Hannah remained with Nardi while box after box of dresses, hankies, rings, and reticules arrived at their apartment. At the end of the first week of this, Nardi watched Hannah sink behind a growing mound of material wonders. She sat in the midst of opened boxes on a wad of satin, holding in her hand a kid shoe with glass buttons, seemingly distraught, bewildered. "What do they expect of me?" she asked.

Nardi would have liked to have launched into a harangue from here, lecturing on the evils of lucre and crass materialism and on the wickedness of people who attempted by these means to manipulate others. But he could not bring himself into the properly self-righteous frame of mind, since he liked nice things, too, and it was simply a matter of him not liking to compete with them. He didn't want to manipulate Hannah in any way at all.

What he wanted was for her to freely choose him.

So he pretended, as Hannah seemed to want him to, that all the finery meant nothing to her, all the while knowing the battle going on inside this small-town girl with big dreams of success. Hannah sent everything back—then turned out the lights and went to sleep beside a man whom she wasn't married to, whose future remained uncertain.

The degree of Hannah's turmoil over what she was doing evidenced itself most at night. She thrashed around in the throes of nightmares. One in particular terrorized her. In it, a woman was falling from the sky, falling from nowhere. Just before the woman hit the ground, Hannah recognized the woman as herself, this other self shattering like a pumpkin. In her dream Hannah stood on the street outside their apartment and watched this happen. Then, in the impossible way of dreams, she began to clean her pumpkin-self up. At first she couldn't grasp the pieces for all the slippery seeds and pulp. But this was her job; she knew it, so she had to continue. When she did finally grasp a chunk, it became in her hand warm flesh and sharp-splintered bone. Hannah always awoke from this dream shivering and having to control the urge to wretch.

Meanwhile Nardi found himself sleeping easily, awakened by her nightmares but able to drop off again as he soothed Hannah in his arms. He slept better than he had in a decade. For Nardi, the choices presented to him by Sébastien represented no dilemma at all. Nardi prepared to go to Aubrignon, stand before a crowd of people, and simple say *non* when the appropriate moment arrived. He felt unusually calm in this decision—and this calm, he suspected, became his crime.

Hannah grew irritable, partly from lack of sleep, partly from worry—in the twelve days nothing eased in their financial situation. Her money left by sous and centimes as they needed to eat. The last night that she slept in the apartment, after a delivery of a cashmere motoring coat and felt motoring hat bedecked with silk flowers tied down with bobbinet veiling, she said suddenly and crossly to Nardi, "Your whole snotty-cool family hates me."

"*Oui, c'est vrai,*" he answered. It was true.

"And it doesn't even bother you that they do."

He shrugged. "Let them. I don't care."

"Edward was glad that his family hated me. That was the point."

"I am not Edward."

"But you have to admit that you are not entirely unhappy to find yourself with a woman who puts your family up in arms."

"They are not up in arms."

"So tell me, then," she said, "that I am not a little bit sweet revenge in your war against them. Tell me you wish I were someone they approved of, a fine lady perhaps from a good French background."

Nardi was not so stupid as to tell her such a thing. He did not wish Hannah to be other than she was, least of all some sort of upper-class priss the likes of which his family might choose. He said merely, "I love you as you are."

"What you love is that I make everyone irate. Look how they want to be rid of me"—she lifted the hat from the box, raising it above her head like a flag, a banner to her point of view—"and at what extravagant cost!"

It was worthless telling her that her insecurities made her think this way; he had already tried. Nardi pulled a face. "*Oui.* I am delighted."

She threw the hatbox at him. "Damn you," she whimpered, "and your whole cold-blooded, high-toned kinfolk."

The next morning, a motorcar was delivered. Hannah walked round and round it for a very long time, then got in it for a driving lesson.

That night, when she still hadn't returned, Nardi went out and bought himself a bottle of ether. It wasn't to drink. He simply brought it home, naming it his Untouched Quart, and stared at it till he fell asleep. He wished Hannah didn't hate herself so much for being tempted. He wished he could tell her: He was tempted himself by unwholesome things; everyone had their ether, one way or another. Temptation was not something a person could eliminate; he or she could only resist it.

Chapter 27

And in this wretched moment it is your face
That lends me light and shadow like the sun.
    —Michelangelo Buonarroti, fragment of a lost
    madrigal, DuJauc edition, 1901

THE MORNING OF the wedding, the clouds that usually hung
so delicately on the dome finials of the château puffed up
into billowing black thunderheads, then opened up with a
deluge. Rain poured down, lightning turning the countryside
into livid flashes of stark, unshadowed landscape.

Nardi arrived in this with the rest of the wedding
entourage, whom he had joined in Paris at the train station:
It had taken three private train cars to carry the families and
wedding attendants, while servants, seamstresses, tailors,
and a caterer's assistant filled several second-class passen-
ger cars; more than forty people in all. The caterers
themselves, along with a battalion of florists, were already
in residence at the château. An orchestra for the evening as
well as a string quartet for this afternoon and the ceremony
itself were traveling separately by the slower train omnibus.
Besides this, eleven carriages with coachmen, plus thirty-
one horses, had been trained in yesterday, there to meet
everyone at the Aubrignon train station—Nardi got all these
figures from Du Gard, who sat beside him all the way from

Paris. The man was so wrought up and excited over the coming day, he might as well have been the bride himself.

The château, as the line of carriages sloshed out of the avenue of trees toward it, looked surprisingly elegant from behind a curtain of rain. And there was more water: Faulty hydraulics or not, Sébastien had apparently gotten the front fountain working. Like a massive symphony of highs and lows and varying melodies, the front fountain played its old rhythms through the rain, making the front facade of Château d'Aubrignon a soft, moving blur of rose-colored bricks and cream-colored limestone set off by the green, manicured geometry of a topiary Sun King garden.

Nardi watched this at length since his carriage ended up in line for a time, waiting to get up into the main carriage portico. Unloading everyone and everything out of their vehicles was a slow process. Only three vehicles would fit at a time under the shelter. Then Nardi, part of the second batch of passengers to unload, stepped down to see there was an additional obstruction: Right by the front door, under the portico, the château's little calèche, its top up and windows closed for the rain, was in the process of being decorated by a florist in white roses, streamers, and bows. Mildly appalled, Nardi walked once around the calèche anyway as an excuse to look in all directions for any sign of a little motorcar with a short, redheaded woman driving.

He had not seen Hannah since the day she had driven away in the automobile almost a week ago. But she knew when and where the wedding was; he expected to see her here. Long ago it seemed now, on the first night after Sébastien had left them in this predicament, she had said she would come. Nardi believed she would: She would not make him go through this ordeal alone.

For the present, however, there was no sign of either Hannah or the automobile she'd driven off in, so Nardi entered the château through the formal front entry room then through a circuitous setup of stanchions and thick velvet ropes, as one might see in a museum, that funneled him along with everyone else into the grand-dining-hall-cum-storage-warehouse.

Nardi was surprised to find himself walking down a straight path cleared through the giant storage area's glittering treasures. Then he wasn't so surprised. How clever, in fact. No guest would see much of the château on this visit, but what better way to impress than parade everyone through the room that housed the château's most glorious possessions? Along the cleared pathway, rare paintings were turned outward so people could see them. A wood statue of St. Joan from the sixteenth century stood casually on a crate top beside an Egyptian canopic vase. Other crates, harboring furniture, tapestries, and statues, faced open. It was a soul-stirring walk if one knew anything about art or French history.

The wedding party was routed from here into the round gallery that surrounded the ballroom, the ballroom itself being dark, all its windows drawn in curtains. At the end of this gallery, Nardi found his family making slow progress through the old castle. Except for Sébastien, it was the first time any of them had been in the old place in almost twenty years.

As he moved into their midst his mother and sister Louise were already picking apart the "Du Gard" aspects of "their" château. Sébastien agreed. Pater nodded sagely. Claire, saucer-eyed, followed everyone's opinion save that Nardi looked tired; Claire claimed he looked marvelously handsome. How funny and typical they all were, he thought as they walked toward the rooms assigned them for dressing. He felt an odd sense of affection for each member of his family—and not a tremor of conscience for what he was about to do to them.

He had been a fool last April to imagine that owning the château again would make any of them happy. They were happiest like this: berating the rest of the world for not measuring up to their own superior standards. He couldn't help them, and thankfully, somewhere along the line Nardi seemed to have stopped trying. For months now he had realized he had been controlling the one person he could, himself, acting on his own, taking satisfaction in doing what was good for him, taking responsibility for what he needed to watch or change in himself—while learning how to read and touch and respond to Hannah. He felt a world away from his old self today.

When, two hours later, the curtains of the ballroom drew back and the lights went on, they revealed a sumptuously renovated room, at the center of which stood Nardi's statue, his *Concetto: The True Venus Rising*. It seemed an appropriate name. And, more than Nardi realized or remembered, it seemed an astounding statue. He had only polished parts of it. Hannah's face, her cheeks and lips, her shoulders, her round arms and fingers. Her hair was rough yet. The chipped stone immediately around her was craggy. But, my, she was a beautiful sight. Nardi was overjoyed to see her, even if it was just in stone as she cut and climbed her way out of rigid confinement.

By early afternoon, people—arriving guests, half a dozen art critics, several society columnists—were milling about this statue with plates of paté and *amuse-bouche* in their hands, while Nardi stood in near proximity, discussing his work with whomever asked, taking credit, acknowledging an "incredible model." He thanked those who praised him. He smiled when Amelia Besom reminded a group that this was only one piece that followed a string of lesser results.

It had never been Old Besom's criticism, he realized, that rankled, but rather her objectivity. Nardi saw the statue behind him through a blur, through the unobjectifiable morass of untempered affection, the emotional embrace of a creator. Hannah was right. He identified with his work, the best of it having to do with the affection he had for the best parts of *himself,* delivered like a miracle into the world from the womb of his imagination. Seeing this—and having others connect with it, one way or another—was a kind of communion that made him higher than any ether he might drink. He felt a little nervous but was essentially pleased to be here.

All that was needed to make the moment complete was that the stone Hannah become real. Nardi continued to watch for her.

"How are you doing?" asked Sébastien, coming up to Nardi.

"Fine."

"A grand display, no?" asked Sébastien. These, the opening festivities, were part of Sébastien's none-too-subtle seduction. Nardi's brother had orchestrated what he had been so good at so many years ago: a social gathering centered around an art exhibit. "They love you," Sébastien added.

No, "they" didn't, Nardi thought. Hannah loved him. These people didn't even know him.

"Come this way, Nardi," Sébastien said. "A photographer wants to take your picture."

Nardi resisted for a moment. "Where is the doctor, Sébastien? I don't see him."

"Oh, he's here. He'll be signing those papers as you are walking down the aisle. Now, stop worrying and enjoy what is happening to you."

Nardi indeed was the center of attention. People pulled back, surrounding the camera, himself. Flashes popped, the area filling with wisps of smoke and the smell of sulfur. A woman was pushed forward to join him, and the room broke into applause.

"Put your arm around the bride, please," someone said.

Nardi did, though it took him one crazy second to figure out who she was. This Marie Du Gard was not the same woman he had last seen in Paris. In a straight, simple dress that hung from her shoulders on pearl straps, she looked, well, almost lithe. And pretty. Her hair was a shiny brown, her eyes the color of coffee. Something about her—her mettlesome presence in a somehow taller, more stately body—made an affecting difference. The whole was quite striking.

"You look stunning," he told her honestly. It seemed the

least he could say to a woman whom, in five hours, he intended to jilt.

She glanced up, a woman unused to such compliments. As if the credit belonged elsewhere, she murmured, "I lost nineteen more pounds. My parents said to. For all the important guests that are here, you understand." Another flash went off. She put her hand to her face.

Nardi looked at her with faint disbelief. "You lost weight for your parents?" he said.

Perhaps he smirked, because she took offense immediately, telling him in a harsh whisper, "Well, obviously I did it for myself as well. But I owe my parents everything. They've made sacrifices—"

He interrupted. "Well, don't let them make too many." He thought he was speaking for her sake. "Be leery of those who would invest themselves in you without limits. They will expect limitless return. The trade can even become, Do as I say, as I want. Live your life for me, since I live my life for you." Nardi, of course, was speaking for himself, thinking of his mother especially and Sébastien.

Marie Du Gard's attention remained fixed on Nardi, as if nonetheless he had given voice to a concern of her own. Then the photographer interrupted, teasing her about staring at the groom when she was supposed to be looking at the camera.

Her father called out, "Marie, look here. Smile, my little darling."

And her face became vacant, staring at Nardi as if he were speaking in tongues. She smiled at the camera, then threw Nardi a last puzzled look before she disappeared into the gathering.

Nardi was left to his own ends, which more and more became scouting the crowd for Hannah. She will come, he thought. Then this sounded to him like a piece of overromantic, misplaced faith. There was really no reason for her to show up suddenly except that he wanted her to. Where had she gone? Why hadn't she let him know where she was?

Why had she left him in the first place? What was she doing?

What Hannah was doing was driving the bejesus out of the little motorcar that had already been from Paris to Le Havre, across the Channel by ferry, to London, and back to France again. She had had a busy few days that put her now about a half a mile away from Nardi, having arrived at Le Havre just under an hour ago with every intention of finding him, then standing where he could see her faithful presence while he wreaked the necessary havoc with the necessary *non*.

Shame had sent her away from him. The shameful agony of watching his patience with her greed, when she herself had had no patience with it whatsoever. She had hated herself for wanting precisely all the things that Sébastien was offering. She had hated herself for whining inwardly, *I don't deserve this awful dilemma. I deserve* all *my dreams come true, not just one part exclusive of the other.* And this word—*deserve*—had set her aright again. There was only one thing, when she came right down to it, that she genuinely deserved. She had damned well *earned* those references that Sébastien de Saint Vallier had left her.

So she had taken them to London and secured a job through which she could begin to buy for herself the rest of what she wanted. Now she was coming back to claim the last of what she deserved: the undivided affection of a good man whom she adored. She wanted Nardi to move with her to London. Or, if he wouldn't, she would work at Sotheby's long enough to get a good reference and hire herself back across the Channel to Paris. There were ways to do this. . . .

"There are ways to do this," she muttered as she put the car in reverse and rocked backward in the mud that had gripped a front wheel of the little vehicle, while rain beat down on the motorcar roof like the coming of the Flood. She sloshed the little car back and forth, eventually cutting the wheel enough to take the car back onto more solid roadbed. Then, as she rounded the bend that rose toward the château's entry drive, she was stymied completely: The road all the way up and into the drive itself was packed with vehicles. There was no room to get through.

"Jesus, Mary, and Joseph," she said with disgust. A moment later she unlatched the door, got out in the downpour, and began the trek up to the château through the mud.

Nardi was ready well before the ceremony, so he wandered the château, from window view to window view, hoping to see a little motorcar or one of the hansoms from the train station or anything besides the endless array of posh parked coaches and occasional motored sedan that, through the rain, lined the château carriageways.

"She's not coming," Sébastien said as he joined Nardi at the château's front windows.

"She has been delayed," Nardi explained to him. It was a fairly silly thing to say, since he knew no such thing. But this faith, this stupid faith had taken hold inside him.

"She's in London, Nardi," Sébastien asserted. "She took the job at Sotheby's yesterday afternoon. My friend there wired me this morning."

Nardi threw a scowl over his shoulder. "You are lying."

"I'm not. And I hope you won't destroy all the great good left to you over some sort of romantic misconception. She's in London. Thomas Landon at Sotheby's hired her. She's not coming back, Nardi. She's made her choice. So please, as you make yours, think it through carefully."

Nardi went up alone after this to the small dressing room they had assigned him, where he madly rummaged through his bag for his talisman: his Untouched Quart, his bottle of ether. Finding it was a relief. He ran his hands up and down the glass bottle, then held it to the light, watching the liquid move. He knew just what it would taste like and just how quickly it would render him oblivious. He knew what it smelled like, the heavy, sweet odor—which was all perfectly resistible, of course.

He was going to confirm this, just run the smell of it

under his nose, he thought. But when he uncorked the bottle, he heard footfalls suddenly outside the room. There was a knock. Nardi spilled the ether, a splash on his lapel, and the door opened.

It was only a servant, the boy come to take the baggage. "Shall I come back later?" he asked, wide-eyed. The room had become quickly ripe with the surgicallike odor.

"No," Nardi answered. "Everything is ready."

He recorked the bottle and put it into his suitcase, latching the case closed again, then shoved that and another bag toward him.

As the last of the guests were being seated in the chapel, Sébastien spotted Nardi and Du Gard under the line of canopies that had been set up between château and chapel to protect people from the elements. There seemed to be some sort of altercation taking place between the two men, for down that tunnel of dryness, the rain beating all around them, Du Gard turned nose to nose to Nardi then grabbed him suddenly by the shirtfront. Nardi shoved the man's hands emphatically from him, leaning over Du Gard—and Sébastien tore out under the canopy toward them.

"What's wrong?" he yelled over a whoosh of rain as he came up on the two idiots. "Everyone's waiting."

"Just smell the son of a bitch," Du Gard shouted.

It wasn't something he had to ask Sébastien to do twice: The smell of ether was a strong one. "For the love of God, Nardi—"

"Don't 'for the love of God' me. I spilled some, that is all."

"What are you doing with it?" Du Gard yelled. "If you bollix this up—" His rage was punctuated by a clap of thunder.

Sébastien put himself between Nardi and the father of the bride as a sudden blast of wind doused the bottoms of all three men's trousers as if with a bucket of water. "Go on, Nardi," Sébastien yelled over the downpour. "I can hear the music," he lied. "They're waiting for you." After a recalci-

trant moment, Nardi turned then stalked off in the direction
of the chapel.

Du Gard glared angrily after him, calling to Sébastien, "I
won't put my daughter into a carriage with him passed out
onto the floor of it. I want that son of a bitch's ether. Where
the hell did he get it?"

"We'll find it," Sébastien called. "Now come inside."

Sébastien might have gotten Du Gard calmed down at
this point, but over the rain a voice—as hair-raising as a
risen ghost—called suddenly across the lawn. "Sébastien!
Sébastien!" it said. "Is he in the chapel already? Has the
ceremony begun?" The voice was speaking English.

In disbelief Sébastien turned, and there she was: Mademoiselle Hannah of Sotheby's, on leave apparently in
Aubrignon, France. She was running toward him, drenched,
slopping through the mud at her own crazy, wobbling gait.

Du Gard stared at her as she burst through the curtain of
torrenting elements into the drier canopied walkway. Glancing at Sébastien, he said in French, "It's her, isn't it? She's
the one in the statue." He took the young woman's arm and
began to pull her in the opposite direction from the way
Sébastien wanted to usher the man, with Miss Van Evan
wiggling and resisting, her alarm rising.

Sébastien yelled in French to Du Gard, "Don't hurt her.
What are you doing?"

As Du Gard scooted and shoved her he called back, "I'm
not going to hurt her, though I am damn well going to lock
her in the first room I find in the château that has a key in
the doorknob. Now, go."

Sébastien hesitated as Miss Van Evan stared at him
around the Frenchman, floundering first around one shoulder, then lurching to look round an elbow. Her skirts were
soaked and heavy with water, her hair dark and matted to
her head. Her vivid eyes stood out, large and beseeching,
uncertain as to what exactly was happening. These eyes
asked him to translate the situation, this man's actions; they
asked for help.

Poor, simple creature. He called out to her, "It's all right,

Miss Van Evan. Go with Monsieur. He will take you to Nardi." Then Sébastien didn't wait further, but turned and strode back to the chapel as quickly as his legs would carry him.

Hannah followed with growing suspicion, wondering if this short, overdressed Frenchman could possibly produce Nardi. Just inside the château, she halted, wiping the water from her face and shaking out her skirts from where they clung to her legs—at which point she was impatiently scooped up by the elbow. Propelled along, she tried to ask the man where exactly Nardi was, but the Frenchman only dashed through the château, opening doors, looking into rooms, as if Nardi might be in any of a dozen rooms, all the while dragging her along in this slapdash search.

"Listen," she stammered. "Let me go, and I can check some of the rooms if you don't know exactly—"

The brusque fellow put her in front of him and shoved her while maintaining hold of the back of her skirt.

"Now see here—"

He yanked her toward the main staircase, offering no explanation or apology, only muttering obscurely in French something about the rooms on the first floor having *"trop de fenêtres"*—too many windows. At the top of the stairs, he paused long enough to light a cigar, which seemed to calm him. He let out a billow of smoke, then with a leap they were off again down a hallway.

"You haven't a clue, have you?" Hannah muttered. He had no better idea than she where Nardi was. "We would be better off going to the chapel and waiting for him there—" but the deranged fool with a firm grip of her forearm was not to be appeased or distracted. He dragged her pell-mell through another tour of room after room, opening doors, poking his head in, leaving little puffs of smoke in each room before slamming its door noisily.

"Aha!" he said finally and tried to push her into a crowded, windowless storage room.

"You wait one moment," Hannah said as she resisted. "I can find him myself better than—"

He grabbed her by both arms and lifted her off her feet, intending to put her in the room as if she were no more animate than the stone deer she suddenly found at her back. She braced herself against a granite antler.

Into the midst of their grunting little struggle, a voice spoke in English. "Just what do you think you are doing?" it said.

Hannah elbowed the Frenchman in the neck, half crawling over his shoulder toward a most welcome sight. The only person who would have not a speck of interest in weddings or marching around in rainstorms had stepped out of a nearby parlor. Amelia Besom, her fists on her hips, her body drawn up to a tall, indignant posture, asked further, "And what gives you the right to make all this infernal noise"—she sniffed the air—"and make this odious cigar stink—" She broke off. "Why, Miss Van Evan—"

For one instant her face melted into an almost joyous, pleased expression.

Then she frowned quickly and looked at the French fellow. "Monsieur Du Gard," she said, "you will miss your daughter's wedding." She came forward.

Monsieur Du Gard. Hannah and Amelia Besom seemed to understand what was happening in one and the same instant. Mrs. Besom latched a big, bony hand onto the arm of a Frenchman no bigger than herself. Unprying his fingers off Hannah, she said, "Run, my dear."

Hannah did. She turned and fled as fast as she could, hearing a diatribe fade behind her: "No, sir, you aren't going anywhere, not unless you want to go there dragging me behind you. And take that nasty cigar out of your—here, give it to me. Oh, stop babbling. You know English. All you French people do. You just pretend when it's convenient. . . ."

"Let me through," Hannah said.

No one did. All the doors of the chapel were blocked by locals who had crowded the doorways to see the spectacle inside. No one understood Hannah's plea, or else no one was willing to answer it. She was stuck out in the rain again, hopping, jostling, trying to peer over heads and shoulders.

The force of the rain had weakened into a steady patter. Hannah could hear the clergyman speaking over it, yet she was unable to discern exactly what beyond this might be happening inside the chapel. Over the people in front of her, she could make out a bishop's miter nodding, moving. Hannah wiggled forward, jumping from one toe to the other, trying to see—until over a woman's shoulder, between two heads, she caught a glimpse, just the back of Nardi's head. He stood at the altar beside a woman with a headpiece made up of yards of elaborate white lace veiling.

"Nardi!" Hannah called out as the sky cracked with thunder, drowning her out. She succeeded only in making the people around her shush and elbow her quiet.

Inside, the wedding ceremony could be heard, the drone of the bishop. In a panic, she called out from behind everyone, "Say no!" With all her voice, she bellowed, "Say no!"

Beside her, someone laughed.

It was intuitive: Hannah cried out loudly in the simple French she knew. *"Dis non, chéri!"* she said.

A few of the locals turned. It seemed one or two of them possibly even recognized her from the dance after the auction and that they disapproved of the man in the chapel marrying any other than his dancing-kissing partner. Someone off to the side laughed and murmured, *"Dis non."*

Someone else picked it up. *"Dis non."* The mischief grew like a chant. *"Dis non, dis non, dis non."* Until the bishop's miter rose then leveled back, presumably so the bishop could direct a lofty ecclesiastical scowl toward the crowd. The mischief makers—or else matchmakers, it was hard to tell—hushed, and the ceremony continued.

He will say no, Hannah thought. He understands. He will say no.

But he didn't: Instead, the bishop asked, *"Mademoiselle, voulez-vous prendre pour époux Monsieur Bernard Guy Henri de Saint Vallier ici présent?"*

There was a rainy pause, a patter of water on stones and stained glass. Then a woman's voice inside rose strongly above this, as clear as the crack of nearby thunder: *"Non! Non pas! Non! Je ne le veux pas!"*

This was followed by a startled stir among the guests inside, a manifold gasp, then the echo of a woman's high-heeled shoes on the stone flooring of a cavernous-ceilinged chapel. The crowd of locals opened like the Red Sea for Moses, crushing Hannah back in its wake, as a bride, with her wedding gown wadded up in her fists, her veil still over her face, dashed through the middle of the people right by Hannah.

A moment later Nardi's face appeared on the far side of the surging crowd. He was pushing his way through.

"Hannah!" He saw her! Short as she was, behind twenty farmers, he saw her! "Hannah!" he called again. It was only moments later that Hannah felt Nardi, dry and warm against her cold, wet chest, his strong arms gathering her up against him.

And it was only seconds beyond this when they heard the explosion. It quaked the ground, sending everyone screaming and scurrying as if the earth's crust were splitting open.

Chapter 28

Dearest,

I have found us a lovely little apartment. It has a sunroom that I think we can make into a studio for you. I look forward to showing it to you next week when you come. Oh, please, sell your apartment quickly and get some of your stone shipped here. I miss you so very much.

Meanwhile my new job is hectic, but at least very interesting. Sotheby's is so much grander and more specific an enterprise than Amelia Besom's, but I like it. Oh, and Amelia as she headed off today for New York specifically asked that I send you her love—really! She is so grateful to have been able to stay with me while she recovered—and she really, truly, is most grateful to you. If you hadn't dragged her out and held her back, she admits she would have probably burned herself up going back and back into the château, trying to save everything. How sad that so many fabulous things were all in one place—and that the dining-storage area should be directly in the path of a rampant fire!

What a horror! Imagine Monsieur Du Gard deciding to search your bags for ether! And finding it—while holding a lit cigar in his mouth in a tiny, closed-up carriage! What an

371

insane thing to do! And what a horrible chain of coincidences! I am glad to hear from you that he regains consciousness from time to time now, though a little sad for him since the pain must be terrible. If I burn my finger, I weep like a child. I can't imagine burning half the skin on my body. I don't agree with you incidentally: I don't think it was pure controlling ego that made him look for your ether. I think the man was genuinely trying to protect his daughter, or at least this was partly his motive.

I am pleased to hear that your family is out from under any legal obligations or reprisals. I think Marie Du Gard did a very brave thing, all things considered, and a very good thing for herself. Meanwhile has anyone spoken to Sébastien since that night? (And does anyone know why it took him and Marie Du Gard, wherever they were, so long to realize there was a fire?) Like you, I worry. I still see his face sometimes, the terrible devastation in his expression as he watches the conflagration, the red of the fire reflecting off his skin. Even Amelia agrees that he was the real casualty of the fire. Never mind the château. In a strange way the Château d'Aubrignon *was* Sébastien, or a part of him (not the best part of him, I don't think). Seeing it, or seeing all its best art and furnishings at least, go up in smoke had to be excruciatingly painful for him. He put so much store in being able to repair everything. I just hope he is able to "repair" himself now. If you see him, give him my love.

I love you and miss you and can't wait to show you the place where I think we shall be quite happy until I can get sufficient experience and references to work my way back to the city we both love. Give Paris a big kiss for me. I study my French daily. Never fear, my darling, we shall get back to the City of Light. I can't imagine making my permanent home anywhere else.

With great love and affection,
Hannah

Epilogue

11 March 1905

Well, the press in Rome has blasted me, but I have made a discovery that I think might pass for wisdom: <u>Unjust criticism is not nearly the problem that unjust praise is.</u> I underline this, for, you see, though the critics disliked the show, the Vatican loved the statue of St. Joan and has asked me, in language that exudes wonder and admiration, to do the monument at the Duomo in Florence. I can't, of course (I am away too much already; the baby will think she has no father), but I blush at how flattered I was. I couldn't eat my breakfast once I'd opened the letter. I only wanted to read the words over and over. I wonder if I shall ever understand this about myself, why I am so needy. I am like a beggar on the street—throw me anything—when it comes to the good opinion of strangers.

> —From a letter to his wife in Paris,
>   Bernard de Saint Vallier, sculptor, in Rome,
>   from the Sébastien de Saint Vallier translation,
>   *The Collected Papers,* Bouvier: Paris, 1933